NEW FRONTIER OF LOVE

BOOK TWO
AMERICAN WILDERNESS SERIES ROMANCE

DOROTHY WILEY

NEW FRONTIER OF LOVE

Dorothy Wiley

Copyright © 2014 Dorothy Wiley

All rights reserved, including the right to reproduce this book, or portions thereof, in any form.

To obtain permission to excerpt portions of the text, please contact the author.

First Edition: 2014

ISBN: 1497438640

ISBN-13: 978-1497438644

Cover design by Erin Dameron-Hill

Author website www.dorothywiley.com

New Frontier of Love is a fictional novel inspired by history, rather than a precise account of history. Except for historically prominent personages, the characters are fictional and names, places, and incidents either are the product of the author's imagination or are used fictitiously. Any resemblance to actual persons, living or dead, events or locales is entirely coincidental. Each book in the series can be read independently.

For the sake of understanding, the author used language for her characters for the modern reader rather than strictly reflecting the far more formal speech and writing patterns of the 18th century.

Dedication

To my son Robert, whose courageous ancestors inspired this novel. Thanks for being the wonderful son and person you are.

CHAPTER 1
Kentucky, Summer 1797

Captain Sam Wyllie looked ahead, anxious to catch his first glimpse of the remote Fort. His back and his legs ached from months on the trail. Ignoring his fatigue, he kept a keen eye on the surrounding rugged forest and made himself sit up straighter in the saddle. As if complaining, the saddle leather creaked beneath his weight even more than normal. Even the saddle had had enough. It wouldn't be long now. They were nearly there.

Maybe here, at the edge of a vast wilderness, he could forget. He wanted a new life in a new place, away from the pain of his violent past. Surely, he could find it here—a thousand miles from his New Hampshire home. A place on the edge of the future—Kentucky.

A new world for the brave.

Their small group had been fortunate, at least for the last few days. Boone's Trace, a branch of the Wilderness Road, leading to the Kentucky River, brought them, at long last, close to Fort Boonesborough. As they passed lush blue-green meadows, rising and falling hills, and ancient verdant forests, they saw no signs of native Indians on the last leg of their long journey. And lately, the weather chose to be mercifully mild. Perhaps God knew they had all endured enough. He and his brothers William, John, and adopted brother Bear, accompanied his youngest brother Stephen and his wife Jane, and their daughters, on the trip here. Along the way, misfortune brought first the widow Catherine and later the young woman Kelly into their group as well.

Sometimes tragedy gives birth to new beginnings.

He pressed his legs against Alex's flanks, urging the big horse forward. The gelding picked up his trot and Sam led them all to the edge of the settlement.

About a hundred yards from the Fort, he spotted a sizable tent set up under an old oak very close to the road. Six horses stood tied nearby. Parked in the tall weeds was a good-sized wagon holding numerous skins. Probably buffalo hides Sam thought. As they drew closer, he could see that they were indeed fresh buffalo skins. An enormous swarm of flies hovered over the reeking pile. Empty whiskey casks lay strewn about in the mud along with corn cobs, discarded rags, and other trash. He'd seen pig sties that looked neater and smelled less foul.

"Whoever they are, they're messy fellows," Sam told Stephen.

"If cleanliness is next to Godliness, then I'd say these fellows are closer to the devil," Stephen agreed.

A man, untying his leather breeches, emerged from the tent. The man looked up and saw Sam and his brothers. Then the hunter shifted bloodshot eyes to Catherine and Jane, each driving one of their two wagon teams. Shockingly, he left his filthy pants untied.

"Ah, what do we have here? Lovely womenfolk arriving in

Boonesborough," he said in a lecherous tone. He gave Catherine, whose wagon was closer to the man, a greasy smile.

The obnoxious man's grating voice had an edge to it that put Sam's warrior instinct instantly on alert. He sensed dirt on this man's soul. And plenty on his body too.

Sam stopped his horse and gave the lewd man a censuring stare through squinted eyes. "Did you wake up ill-mannered this morning or were you born insolent?"

The bulky boorish man, with a very large rounded nose, dark eyes set deep in a puffy face, and tangled black hair, ignored him and the other men. But he continued to eye the women, a mix of lust and envy exposed on his face.

"Keep your ugly eyes off my wife," Stephen yelled, positioning his horse next to Jane's wagon.

"You're the one parading them right in front of my grand home," the man called back. "And they are a sight to awaken a man's cock for damn sure."

Stephen reached for his whip and Bear pulled out his hatchet.

"Stephen don't!" Sam ordered in a voice of authority. "Bear, put it away."

The man's head swung lazily back toward the tent. "Men, come out and take a gander at these two beauties."

Five other rough-looking men emerged from the tent, one after the other.

Stephen's hand remained on the whip, but he didn't move his horse toward the man and Bear said, "Are ye sure Captain? It would give me great pleasure to take the man's head off."

"I understand, but let's not begin our time in Kentucky with a killing," Sam said. "Unless we have no choice," he amended, looking directly at the foul-mouthed man.

Sam watched warily as the man's five cronies, all well-armed, casually took seats on whiskey casks, seeming to wait for the show.

"Aren't those two sweet looking?" the man asked his men. "I like that black-haired one. She'll be the best-looking woman in Boonesborough."

"I'm partial to the red-haired one. Look at those fiery green eyes," another man said.

Although he couldn't see Jane from his vantage point, Sam could well imagine the scorching glare she was probably leveling on these men.

"Bloody buggers!" Bear hissed the words out between his teeth. "Let me cut the impudent man's tongue out of his filthy mouth."

"And look, there's a young blonde just now poking her head out of that first wagon. I'd sure like to give her a poke," the biggest man crowed.

Sam wanted to throttle the man. He saw Kelly pale and start to shake. Terror, stark and vivid, flashed in the young woman's big eyes. Kelly had been about to climb out the front of Catherine's wagon to join her on the bench, but now stopped frozen with fear.

William bristled and side-stepped his horse next to Kelly. Every muscle of his face spoke defiance. "Bastard," William hissed at the man. "One more insult to these women and we'll find some rope to hang the lot of you."

The leader didn't move, but his five men all pulled weapons, brandishing pistols and knives.

Kelly gasped, panting in fear.

"Kelly, get back inside the wagon," Sam instructed. "Don't worry, we won't let them hurt you."

Catherine put her hand on Kelly's shoulder, urging her back in the wagon. "Get back inside the wagon now, Kelly."

After Kelly got under cover again, Sam pulled his horse closer to Catherine's wagon and looked over at his brothers, all four were lined up next to the wagons and facing the six hunters. "Let this bunch of snakes crawl back into their den," Sam urged, his voice taut with suppressed anger, all the while eyeing the coarse bunch of men. "The best way to not get snake bit is to move away from the snake."

Sam's brother John immediately turned his mount toward Boonesborough, his young son Little John riding beside him. His other brothers remained where they were.

"Ignore them, they're just ill-bred ruffians," Catherine told them. Then she fixed her gaze straight ahead and composed her features, although Sam could see the suppressed anger in the firm set of her jaw.

Sam agreed with Catherine. When crossed his temper could be almost uncontrollable. But he had trained himself to carefully control his anger, unleashing it only when it served his purpose, usually at the height of battle.

"I'm sorry you had to hear all that," Sam told Catherine, loud enough for the brutes to hear.

"I didn't hear anything. There's nothing that man could say that I would lower myself to hear," Catherine said, glaring over her shoulder at the vulgar man.

"She doesn't sound sweet on you just yet Frank," one of the hunters taunted.

The raucous sounds of the men's laughter filled the foul-smelling air between them.

Sam gave each one of the men a withering stare, not taking his eyes off them until their laughter stopped. Then he said, "I am patient with stupidity but not when it is combined with poor manners. That just turns men into jackasses." He turned back to Catherine. "My apologies."

"No need to apologize. They deserve worse," Catherine said.

With murky eyes, submerged in a face heavily lined more by alcohol than age, the menacing hunter, who seemed to be the leader of the disagreeable bunch, curled his lip and gave first Sam and then Catherine a look of utter disdain.

The man took a few steps closer to her.

Sam took a firm grip on his long knife.

"Welcome to Boonesborough." The hunter threw the words at her like rocks.

Sam longed to unleash his blade, but his well-trained heart throttled his anger. He turned his mount and kept the horse at a steady walk leaving the buffalo hunters behind. But with each step his horse took away from the bullies, his fists clenched tighter. He glanced back. Keeping wary eyes on the hunters, his other brothers followed on their horses, flanking the two wagons carrying the women and girls.

Their first encounter in Boonesborough nearly ended in disaster. But they had traveled far to get here and he wasn't going to let the incident ruin their arrival. For now, he'd forget the crude men.

He trotted his horse out in front of their group.

His heartbeat quickened, as he took in his first glimpses of the Fort and the roughhewn town. The fortress' blemished walls and bulwarks, blackened by fires and pitted by lead and arrows, called to the warrior in him. Sam knew that the blood of scores of pioneers wounded or killed by the British or Shawnee stained the Fort's ramparts. Despite its battle scars, like an old soldier, the Fort seemed to stand proudly, having succeeded in keeping Boonesborough's first settlers alive.

Now, against the fortress' sturdy fifteen-foot palisade, dozens of settlers completed daily chores or passed the time near lean-tos or crude tents made of hides or oiled cloth, trying to make do in a wilderness highly intolerant of the ill prepared or underprivileged.

He watched dirty squealing children chase one another in the sunshine between the tents, finding joy among the somber adults. But the blank looks on many of their parents' faces made him wonder how many wanted to return to where they had come from.

He vowed that would never happen to him.

From the Fort's walls, Boonesborough expanded to the west on either side of a wide muddy main road.

"It's even bigger than I thought," Stephen said, joining him. "I read that over the last ten years Boonesborough grew briskly. It now boasts more than a hundred and twenty houses and stores."

"It looks like even more to me," Sam observed.

"Agreed," Stephen said as he settled his tricorne hat more snugly on his head. "That man back there is lucky to be alive. If it hadn't been you asking, I would not have held myself back."

"The snake certainly tested my self-control. But we can't let men like him drag us down. This town holds great potential for both fortune and trouble. Many of the men here, like that bunch, will have little regard for either divine or human authority."

"Some of them look like oversized coyotes," Stephen said, looking around. He turned his horse. "I'm going back to Jane."

Sam thought that was a good idea. Protectively, he again positioned his horse closer to Catherine's wagon, something he did only rarely because it caused her to smile at him. And before her smile, as warm as the summer sun, his defenses always seemed to melt away. It was a peculiar feeling and he still wasn't sure why it happened. Or how to deal with it.

Since the beautiful widow joined their group a few weeks back, he had often became ill-tempered as he tried to convince himself to stop thinking about her. He never wanted to have feelings for a woman again. But why did he have to keep telling himself that over and over?

The worst part was that he didn't know what he felt. So he brooded to himself, making every effort to avoid her. At least most of the time.

Just talking couldn't hurt, he told himself, and perhaps it would help calm his still prickling anger. He snugged Alex up close to Catherine's wagon bench. "Kelly, are you okay?" he called into the wagon.

"I'm all...right, Captain," Kelly called out to him without sticking her head out of the wagon cover. "But I'll stay in here for...a little while longer."

Sam could hear the smothered sobs in Kelly's voice and it broke his heart. Those bastards had reawakened the misery that still haunted her. "It will take her a while to recover," Sam said in a low voice.

"It's understandable, of course," Catherine said.

"And you, Catherine? Those were some nasty fellows back there."

When she lifted her eyes toward him, anger still flickered there. "As you know it's not the first time I've encountered men of their sort. And I'm sure it won't be the last."

Sam chuckled, admiring her pluck. He looked ahead and decided to change the subject to something more positive. "Well, at last, we are here Catherine. A new place to make your own destiny."

Catherine glanced over at him, keeping a tight grip on the reins and firm control of the horses pulling her wagon. The streets of Boonesborough were crowded with people, horses, and other wagons and she could only proceed slowly.

"Yes, Captain. I remember what you told me about destiny. About the west being a place where people can make their own future. I never had a choice in the future my father and late husband created for me, as though I were a helpless child."

She was far from being either helpless or a child. He remembered when they first found her on the trail, shortly after she courageously killed one of the three thieves who murdered her husband and tried to attack her. The Wilderness Trail was the last place he expected to find a fine lady like Catherine. The woman's breathtaking beauty had immediately stunned him. Her classically sculpted features and pearl-white skin made her blue eyes and dark brows dominate her face. Her high cheekbones, strong jaw line, and the strength in her voice gave her a proud, almost noble quality. That day, she had worn a stunning blue lace-trimmed gown that seemed incongruous on a woman driving a wagon in the wilderness. Even more unusual for a woman, she carried an impressive dagger attached to a belt around her narrow waist.

Now, she wore a more practical black and tan striped cotton gown suitable for the hard trip they just completed. Yet the garment managed to show off the curves of her firm young body, which always smelt of flowers. A waft of her fragrance caught on the breeze and reached him. The alluring scent stirred his blood.

Catherine's hair, black as a moonless night, hung down her back to her waist in a thick braid and several windblown strands framed her face, now no longer as pale. Today, her skin nearly glowed with a healthy reddish pink from exposure to the sun these past weeks.

He couldn't remember ever seeing a more striking woman.

The fact that he took notice of her beauty surprised him. For years, ever since that catastrophic day, he remained indifferent to all woman, no matter how beautiful. For some unexplainable reason, Catherine affected him differently. Perhaps it was the strength and stamina she exhibited or maybe it was the extraordinary dagger she always carried. Where did a woman get a blade like that and why did she always have it attached to her person? Perhaps for the same reason he carried his own unique knife.

Nevertheless, it didn't matter because he had no interest in her or any other woman. He studied the establishments and people of the busy frontier town with interest. But they didn't hold his attention for long.

He would talk to her just to be polite.

"I hope you know I meant no disrespect to your father or departed husband, when I said you could determine your own destiny," he said. "I wasn't trying to dissuade you from asking for your father's guidance. I just believe women should have the same opportunities as men to make their own choices and to make of their life whatever they will."

A tired look of sadness passed over her face. "I understood your meaning. They *did* take my life away from me. I could only do their bidding with absolutely no say in what I would do with my life. And if I had gone back to Boston after my husband's murder, it would have happened all over again. My father would have made sure of that."

Her bearing was stiff and proud, but he sensed a spirit in chaos.

"I know you expected to arrive here with your husband, not all of us. What now? What are your plans?" He wondered if she was ready to begin thinking about her future. Even now as she handled her horse team expertly, she looked out of place. An elegant woman caught in an inelegant place. He hoped the young widow had made the right decision to continue on to Kentucky.

"Let me think about that question for a moment, Captain," she said, a pensive shadow in her eyes.

He waited, but caught himself repeatedly glancing over his shoulder at her. Since meeting her, he consistently made an effort to keep his distance. He tried to remain cordial, but detached. Pleasant, but not over friendly. He was definitely not interested in pursuing a relationship with her and he hoped she didn't presume that he was.

But she was so damn pleasing to look at.

She couldn't possibly be attracted to him. He was a tough and scarred warrior without wealth. He owned nothing but what he carried on the horse he rode. A gentlewoman like Catherine would need what someone of the landed gentry could provide. Not him.

He turned his attention back to the town, keeping a leisurely pace for the tired animals.

Even if he were acceptable to her, it would never work. He could face any enemy, but when it came to thoughts of love, he possessed absolutely no courage. Over time, he had vigilantly built a formidable wall around his heart. And, he wanted it to stay that way. She was the last thing he needed or wanted in his life and he was hell-bent on keeping her at arm's length.

Catherine finally answered his question, and seemed to choose her words carefully. "I honestly don't know yet what I will do—whether I will stay here in Kentucky or go back to Boston. But I'm very glad *I* will be the one deciding it. I do know I want a future that includes love," she said with regal certainty. "Having known the lack of it, I know how important it is to one's happiness."

Sam hesitated, measuring her for a moment. Unprepared for the directness of her answer, his back stiffened. He recently learned from Stephen's wife Jane that Catherine's first marriage had been arranged and loveless, but her frank admission astounded him. He hoped she hadn't noticed his reaction. He cleared his throat and willed his voice to remain even, but she spoke first.

"Love is the most important part of anyone's future, don't you think Captain?"

He quickly decided against agreeing with her. "I think I should catch up to Stephen and see what his plans are for making camp." He sheathed his inner feelings, then nudged his horse and hurried away, bewildered by his own reaction to her simple question.

Catherine watched him ride off, toward his brothers. Oh dear. Perhaps she had been too forward or said the wrong thing.

Not so, her heart whispered.

After spending all these weeks with him and his family, she assumed she could be frank with him. She wanted him to understand her. To share her hopes with him. But even the mention of love seemed off limits. Why? When she had asked the question, she saw his square jaw tense and a sadness pass quickly through his eyes. She sensed a heavy weight on his heart. And, she suspected, a secret pain he kept very close.

On the trail here, she repeatedly debated with herself over whether she should return to Boston. She was being beyond foolish. Raised a well-bred gentlewoman from a wealthy Boston family, she and her parents were prominent members of the city's gentry. Beyond any doubt, staying on this journey without her husband was not the proper thing to do. In fact, her parents would think it scandalous. She should return to her family home. Several times, she decided to do just that, but at the last second, would always change her mind. While traveling with them for her protection, she had grown fond of the Wyllies and their adopted Scots brother Bear. It had been too long since she felt this sense of family and belonging. Moreover, without reluctance, they had accepted her into their family's group.

But, if she were honest, the main reason she hesitated to return to her home was Sam. She found herself disconcertingly drawn to the man. His sun-bronzed face, tall muscled form, broad chest, and harsh masculinity made her wonder what it would feel like if he encircled her in his arms. Even his scarred strong jaw charmed her. The feeling was unsettling, yet pleasing. Like nothing else she had ever experienced.

She found herself, on those rare occasions when he would hold her gaze, getting lost in his indigo blue eyes. They were the eyes of a man with steel in his character and a dark, almost mysterious, intensity. And the bright sparkle in them reflected a keen intelligence. She was certain the Captain was both well-educated and a deep thinker. And behind his rugged warrior facade, she saw a pleasing civility and a kind heart.

That uncommon mixture of ruggedness and refinement made him truly unique. It was another reason she found Sam so intriguing. And, immensely appealing.

Although, as yet, the feeling did not seem mutual. Pointedly ignoring her, the Captain went out of his way to avoid being near her. In fact, there was an air of deliberate isolation about him. When his lackluster attitude toward her finally annoyed her enough, she deliberately tried to entice him into paying more attention to her. She believed it had worked, but then he turned cold, barely able to say more than good morning to her.

She couldn't understand it.

Catherine shifted her body on her wagon's seat and straightened her back. Well, if that's how it is going to be, so be it. She didn't want a man who didn't want her, who didn't find her attractive. And she would never love a man who didn't love her in return. Never. She knew what a loveless marriage was like. It was tedious, unexciting, and boring. The absence of desire and passion made for a mind and absolutely body-numbing experience in the marriage bed. No, that certainly wasn't going to happen again.

She would forget the Captain. She lifted her chin and made herself focus on the various establishments and shops lining Boonesborough's busy main road instead of Sam's broad back.

"Can I come out now?" Kelly called timidly from inside the wagon.

"Yes, of course. Come look at the new town with me," Catherine called over her shoulder into the wagon. "Are you feeling better now?"

"Yes, I'm not afraid anymore," Kelly said, as she climbed out and took a seat on the wagon bench next to her. But Catherine could tell the young woman was trying to be brave.

"Look at all the stores here," Catherine said. The town was far larger than she expected. Her eyes opened wide. Ah, a seamstress. Delighted to see some sign of civilization, she would definitely visit the dressmaker's establishment and soon. The trip had not been kind to her wardrobe. "I'll be shopping at that store soon," she told Kelly. "Every dress I own is suffering from either rips or stains." She always took great pride in her appearance. She did not intend to stop now.

Then she let out a long sigh. Why was she even thinking about buying new gowns? She should go back to Boston where she belonged, enjoy the kind of life she was accustomed to, and find a husband who would love her. There were plenty of eligible bachelors in Boston. There must be one there that she could consider marrying. But why couldn't she name even one? They all seemed pompous and vain, as though polite society had bred away their manhood. When she compared them to the Captain, they all came up short.

She slowed to let another wagon filled with fresh-smelling lumber turn in front of her. Then she gave the reins in her gloved hands a snap, urging her horse team along. She followed closely behind Sam, the oldest of the brothers, and the other four horseback men in his family.

She thought a lot of all of them—brave, good men, who would do anything for one another. Despite her best efforts to stop thinking about Sam, an odd longing filled her. He now rode next to Stephen. He sat his horse ramrod straight and shoulders squared, his deerhide shirt stretched across the large muscles of his back. The slight breeze ruffled his shoulder length dark hair. Unlike his brothers, who all wore the traditional tricorne three-cornered hat, Sam wore no head covering at all unless it was bad weather. Knee-high rugged moccasins covered his feet instead of customary leather boots and reached up to his dark leather breeches.

But it was his huge knife that contributed the most to his daunting appearance. Although attached to a beautifully carved deer horn handle, the blade left no question as to its purpose—to kill and kill swiftly.

Sam looked to her as if he belonged here on the frontier, at the edge of civilization. He was a man as powerful as the intimidating long knife he carried. If anyone belonged here, he did.

But did she?

"It's hard to believe we're really here," Kelly marveled. "You, all the way from Boston, and me from the woods of Virginia. Do you suppose we both wound up here with the Wyllies, for a reason?"

"Maybe so. Fate has a way of choosing our path," she said.

Kelly inclined her blonde head toward her and said, "No, I believe God has a way of pointing us toward our future."

Maybe her destiny was in Kentucky, Catherine mused. Was she pointed here for a reason? If so, what was it? She wanted more in life than society balls and practicing fancy needlework. She wanted to do something meaningful. Something important. But what?

She knew only one thing for sure. She would decide her future.

CHAPTER 2

After they rode past the Fort and well into the town itself, Sam studied the faces of Bear and his younger brothers, Stephen, John, and William. The four now rode next to him, side by side, nearly connected as one. Despite their obvious excitement at having finally reached their destination, the faces of all four appeared weathered and drawn. The journey had taken its toll. Even the faces of the three children looked haggard. Hell, even the faces of the ox and horse wagon-teams looked weary. He couldn't blame them.

With a single-minded obsession, he'd pushed them relentlessly, traveling sunrise to sunset for months, steadily southward, passing big cities, and small towns, further and further apart. He desperately wanted to arrive in time to secure their land and get homes built before winter.

He had led them due west, on an old trading path that colonists improved into a road following the Revolution. They replenished their supplies in Lancaster, Pennsylvania, the last major town and the edge of the frontier.

By July, they travelled southwesterly, through Virginia's

Shenandoah Valley, between the Appalachian and Blue Ridge mountain ranges, before turning north and passing into Kentucky through the Cumberland Gap.

"We left New Hampshire in late April," Stephen said. "It took us a hundred and twenty three days. We would not have made it without you, Sam. Even back there with those hunters, you kept it from turning into a blood bath."

"The frontier is no place for the hot-headed," Sam said.

"You were the rock we all leaned on," John agreed.

"He is hard headed," William added with a chuckle. "But in all seriousness, you did teach us how to be ever alert and cautious. I learned that the hard way."

"The wilderness is also no place for the careless," Sam said.

"And na place for amateurs," Bear said.

Sadly, the wilderness was full of them. Sometimes on the Wilderness Trail, they saw the camps of other travelers, but wary of strangers Sam urged that they keep to themselves. Some of those travelers experienced an even more trying trip. They rode draft horses or mules or walked and most were unkempt and ill clad in homespun. Several times, they saw entire families on foot with all their meager belongings tied to their bent backs. Sam pitied them. They journeyed west with little more than an abundance of hope.

With his brothers and Little John well mounted and the women and girls riding in the relative comforts of the wagons, their large group was more prepared than most. Before they left, he had carefully compiled a long supplies list, knowing that adequate provisions could mean the difference between success and failure—and life and death.

They did not fail.

"At last, we are here!" Stephen declared, his voice choked with emotion.

They wouldn't fail here either. He was not about to let that happen.

"Indeed we are. Let the future begin," Sam said. Although every fiber in his body warned him against it, he turned his horse back toward Catherine's wagon.

༄

As they made their way through Boonesborough, several people shouted their greetings or waved.

"Seems like it might be a friendly place after all," Catherine said.

"Indeed," Sam agreed, relieved the town wasn't full of people like the six slovenly hunters. The people of Boonesborough would understand all too well what their journey from the east had meant, having made the passage over the Wilderness Trail themselves not so long ago.

A trek like that changed people. Sometimes for the better, but often not.

He saw changes in his own family. William and John each came through their journey differently. William left the impulsive and footloose ladies' man behind. In his place, was a responsible brother he could now respect.

John, on the other hand, still struggled with the harsh brutality of the frontier and the courage it required. The architect's gentle intellectual nature would undoubtedly clash with the realities of the rough-edged world they just entered.

But of his three brothers, the trip affected his youngest brother the most. Stephen now knew the high cost a man must pay for his dreams. Sometimes those dreams can only be bought with what is most precious to us—life. And Stephen learned that it takes courage to defend life, not just weapons. For Stephen, courage had been the difference between living and dying.

Bear had proven his courage many times. Oddly, he thought Bear was more like him than any of his brothers. An experienced fighter, with admirable skills as a hunter and an exceptional knowledge of weapons, he greatly admired Bear. During their journey, Bear grew closer to all of them.

But all these changes were just the beginning. Kentucky would compel each of them to find new destinies and new lives. Just what he wanted.

It would start now.

He motioned for Catherine and Jane to steer their wagons toward a magnificent elm near the center of town where a group of townspeople congregated. Some sat at old weathered wooden tables and some stood talking in small clusters.

Jane yelled to slow the oxen, tugging their guide ropes to steer the wagon underneath the immense tree. Catherine pulled her team up close as well. Sam, Stephen, and the other horseback men all assembled close to the two wagons. The tree's far-reaching branches shaded them all from the sun.

William dismounted, dusting off his clothing as he approached the townsfolk gathered at the shady spot.

"Welcome to Boonesborough. You fine folk have ventured a far piece to be sure. Where you folks from?" asked one of the men. The other townspeople gathered around the newcomers.

"New Hampshire," William answered, enthusiastically shaking

the man's hand, "except for Mrs. Adams in that wagon, who met with misfortune and was widowed on the way here, she's from Boston, and Miss McGuffin sitting next to her, who is from a remote place in Virginia near Cat Springs. They both decided to travel to Kentucky with us for their protection."

"New Hampshire is indeed a far piece—about as far as you can get from here," another man said.

William made all the other introductions and they met several of the townspeople, including a balding stout man named Thomas Wolf, the man that greeted them first.

"It's my pleasure, Sirs, to make your acquaintances. I know you have endured a long and no doubt difficult trip. We'll assist you in getting settled as much as we can," Mr. Wolf offered graciously. "There are no accommodations available at our one inn, but you may camp by the Fort as so many others have, or on the other side of Boonesborough along the river. It is considerably quieter there and we have no problems with the natives at present. May I have the pleasure of showing you around the town?"

"Kind of you Sir to offer, but we'll be moving on shortly," Sam replied. He realized he sounded curt, and the man's offer probably came from just being hospitable, but he didn't know this man. He hadn't made it this far taking offers from strangers.

"Well, I could sure use help with my thirst," William said, smiling broadly. "I've been looking forward to having an ale here for about a thousand miles. What direction is your tavern, Sir?"

Mr. Wolf pointed down the street and led the way.

"Join me as soon as you've made camp," William yelled back, strolling swiftly away with his horse, Mr. Wolf, and several of the town's other men in tow.

Stephen scowled. "We're here five minutes and he disappears to a tavern."

"William has his own way of doing things," Sam said. "By the time we get to that tavern, he'll know more about this town and who's who than we'd learn in a week."

Sam led them through the noisy town, a way station for settlers going elsewhere. They made their way through the street crowded with wagons of all types—farm wagons, lumber wagons, freight wagons, and carts loaded with the fly-covered furs of trappers. Horses from all the wagons littered the streets liberally with fresh manure making walking only possible in a zigzag fashion.

"What do you think, Sam?" Stephen asked.

"It's exactly as I had imagined," Sam answered.

Thirteen years earlier, *Adventures*, Daniel Boone's book, had inspired him and he had remained captivated by the idea of Kentucky. He wasn't alone. Proof of the power of the written word to shape a nation, the book called tens of thousands to this virgin wilderness.

He rode past many of those daring souls now. Rough looking men and women stood everywhere, talking, making deals, telling stories. Some were the epitome of the free spirit of the wilderness. Backcountry long-hunters, self-schooled doctors, blacksmiths, farriers, gunsmiths, and merchants. Others were the embodiment of those motivated only by greed—fortune seekers who came only for a chance to profit at the expense of others.

Unlike his brother Stephen, for Sam going to Kentucky was about adventure, and a new beginning, not land. The journey allowed him to draw upon his courage and experience freedom—

the freedom for which he, as a Captain in the Continental Army, had fought so hard and for which so many others died. They won more than a war. They won a country. And the freshest part of that new country was Kentucky—that's what drew his family here.

Now that they were here, would he find a new beginning? Or would his past cling to him like a cold wet blanket? Even as his mind asked the question, he fought against disturbing reflections of long-ago. The sight of the Fort had triggered memories of his own battles. His shoulders grew tight with tension and his forearms hardened beneath his sleeves. He grimaced, remembering the comrades he lost, many under his own command, during the Revolution. Some of those he'd ordered to fight were little more than boys. He saw their faces most often in his nightmares.

He should have died with those young men. And, several times, his injuries were so severe he nearly did. But for some reason, against all odds, he still lived. He rubbed his jaw, now covered in several months of whiskers, wondering why the Almighty had spared him.

Perhaps because his brothers and the others needed him.

As they made their way further into the busy town, his edgy nerves put him on high alert. Sometimes when that happened, it merely made him more cautious. But at other times, it was a warning. He studied Boonesborough through the eyes of the warrior he had become, his mind a strange mixture of both hope and caution.

Catherine didn't know what to think of Boonesborough. It was unlike any place she had ever seen, and she had traveled extensively, even to Europe with her parents and their servants.

Jane steered her wagon alongside hers and they both shifted closer to each other on their benches. "This is nothing like New Hampshire," Jane said.

"It's a far cry from Boston too," Catherine called back. She remembered hearing stories of frontier lawlessness, drunkenness, gambling, and white men taking Indian wives, usually without the sanctity of marriage vows. From the looks of this town and some of its people, she decided the stories were all truthful.

Boonesborough seemed to affect Kelly, who sat on the wagon bench beside Catherine, quite differently. Having never seen the places Catherine and Jane remembered, the bustling town and the sights before them seemed to astound the young woman. "Have you ever seen so many bodies in one place? It's a wonder they don't run into each other," Kelly said, "and it's so noisy." Kelly covered her ears with her hands, trying to shut out the din of horses' hooves, wagon axles, people yelling, dogs barking, and the myriad of other loud noises in the town.

Kelly was used to the solitude and peace of the deep woods, where her abusive trapper father often left her on her own for months at a time. A motherless, pretty, young woman, Kelly was forced to grow up much too fast. Her rape by the men who had killed Catherine's husband, had left Kelly emotionally scarred.

Catherine was relieved that Stephen and William killed the two vile murderers and that William had suggested Kelly join their group on their journey. She smiled, remembering the squawking chickens, milk cow, and old mule, Kelly insisted on bringing with her—all still a part of their entourage. The animals had become like a family to Kelly and her only means to fight the severe loneliness of complete isolation.

Catherine returned her attention to the town. Long ragged

beards covered the faces of a good many men and unkempt hair hung to their shoulders. She wondered if there was a shortage of barbers, scissors, and soap in Boonesborough. Many wore heavily stained buckskin-hunting shirts that reached their knees. She was sure the sour smell she caught from time to time came from their unwashed bodies.

She also noticed a few smartly attired men accompanied by fashionably dressed women. They would look fitting on the streets of Boston. The frontier town seemed to hold a bizarre mixture of all kinds of people, some of whom appeared to live here, while others looked to be passing through.

Catherine and Jane pulled their wagons to a halt side-by-side to let a woman, heavy with child, waddle slowly across the muddy street. She glanced over at Jane. Stephen's beautiful red-haired wife was with child and her belly would soon look much like this woman's, but she was sure Jane would still be just as lovely as she was now.

Jane's young daughters, Martha and Polly, leaned out of the front of the wagon, staring wide-eyed from behind their mother's back. The girls both had birthdays on their long trek from New Hampshire, but she suspected the two, along with John's son Little John, matured in other ways too, having gone through experiences well beyond the normal realm of childhood. Stephen and Jane were desperate to find a new safe home for their girls, where they could once again return to the trouble-free world of children.

"Is this Kentucky?" Catherine heard Polly ask loudly.

Polly, age six, looked much like her father, with dark hair that flowed from a center part, pointing to bright blue eyes. But Polly's eight-year-old sister Martha was a redheaded green-eyed miniature of her mother. Martha's braided hair was unable to restrain the small curls twisting across the girl's freckled forehead and cheeks.

She'd already grown very fond of both girls on their way here.

"No silly," Martha said, "this is a town with Kentucky people."

"Momma, Kentucky people are mean and dirty looking," Polly said.

"These are frontier people Polly. They have a hard life out here in the wilderness and it shows on some folks more than others," Jane said.

"I hope it won't show on us like that," Martha declared.

Catherine grinned, silently agreeing. She wondered how her life would change if she stayed in Kentucky.

Would she find love in the wilderness?

Or loneliness?

CHAPTER 3

Off to Sam's right, the waters of the Kentucky River, painted by the afternoon sun, flowed by like molten gold. Bouncing sparkles reflected off the water's surface and reminded Sam of the way his knife glistened in the sun.

As they entered Boonesborough and passed through the busy town, he had felt uneasy. But now, as they searched for a good site to set up camp on the other side of the settlement, he watched the peaceful river flow beside him, surprised to feel his heart beating faster, his mouth curling in a half-grin.

For months on the trail, he could hardly stand the wait. He often wanted to push the clock ahead. Forward to that moment in time when he would step out of the stirrup and put his feet down on Boonesborough's soil. And now, the time had come.

He spotted a secluded spot by the river, shaded by immense sycamores, with nearly white trunks, polished by generations of elk, buffalo, and deer rubbing against them on their way to water. The ancient river ran deep, flanked by rocks and limestone cliffs on its rugged southern side and on the north by dense woods that covered hills near and far beyond.

"Let's camp over there," he yelled to the others, pointing to the spot.

Near the river, he threw his leg over the saddle, stepped out of the stirrup, and felt at home for the first time in his adult life.

&

Sam took charge with quiet assurance, his back to her.

Catherine stared at his broad shoulders, wondering if they would ever tire of the secret burden he carried. And if he could open up, would he be as passionate about love as he was about fighting for his freedom and his family?

She had a feeling he would be an ardent lover, taking passion as seriously as he did everything else. This perplexing, handsome man, unlike any she had ever known, awakened parts of her for the first time. Was one of those parts her heart?

Sam turned around and she saw that his face radiated a vitality she hadn't seen before. It was a though he'd suddenly come alive, sure of himself and his rightful place.

Was reaching Kentucky that important to him?

Then he looked over at her and there seemed to be a deeper significance to the look he gave her.

She tried to figure out what it meant, but only grew more confused.

Besides, it was time to get settled in. She wrenched herself away from this ridiculous preoccupation with the man.

&

As they set up camp, Sam situated the two wagons and livestock to allow good visibility of the immediate area.

Then he helped Catherine unhitch her team of two stout horses. Wearing sturdy gloves to protect her delicate hands, she moved with remarkable speed and skill, and exhibited a strength at odds with her slender body. The widow continued to surprise him. This was not the same woman he first met on the trail. She was adapting to the wilderness, confronting it head on, picking up the skills she would need here on the frontier. He had to admire that.

As he grabbed a halter for one of the horses, she reached out and placed her hand on his forearm. Even through her gloves, the warmth of her personal contact made his heart clench.

"Thanks for your help, Captain." Then she smiled at him again and hastily drew her hand away, but continued to eye him with a calculating expression.

Sam felt a warm shudder pulsate up his spine. Why did her smiles affect him so?

He nodded to her and then quickly turned to go help Stephen, at work unhitching Jane's team of oxen. Now that Stephen had learned Jane was with child, his brother would want to get her settled as soon as possible. Jane badly needed rest. They all did.

It had been a long week traveling the difficult final stretch of the Wilderness Road. They had passed a half dozen shallow creeks as they neared Boonesborough, most filled with muddy and often stagnant water. Twice this morning, they stuck a wheel. He scrunched his nose, smelling the foul mud dappled on his leather breeches. He needed a bath and a chance to give his clothing a good scrubbing.

They made camp in a subdued mood; the arduous trip hard on

all of them. Tired of sleeping outdoors, dirty clothes, ticks, mosquitos, infrequent baths, and severe storms, for the last few weeks they started dreading each day rather than eagerly anticipating it. Despite making the journey on fine horses and well-equipped wagons, it required an effort now for each to keep their spirits up.

Normally, his brothers spent their days joking and trading jests and tales. But lately, fatigue and the monotony of the journey had sombered even the jovial William. It didn't surprise him when William went in search of an ale and companionship at the local tavern as soon as they arrived. The last few days, he had seemed quieter than normal. Frustrated at the slow pace the wagons forced them to travel, lately William had acted preoccupied and kept to himself reading or cleaning his weapons. Sam suspected his most handsome brother missed the comforts of their old local tavern, including female companionship, and sorely missed his job as town Sheriff. On their journey, William had wanted to spend some time in Philadelphia and Virginia, visiting with some of the lawyers and statesmen there, but Sam had refused, knowing how important it was to reach Kentucky and get homes built before winter.

A keen observer of human behavior, Sam sighed a breath of relief when they had finally neared their destination, because tempers were growing shorter and little annoyances were becoming bigger irritants.

Stephen unsuccessfully tried to comfort Jane, whose pregnancy sapped her energy and made her more irritable by the day. She lost her temper fully twice that week, and Stephen swore it was for no good reason at all.

Now, Sam heard her threatening to brain Stephen with her

stew pot when he suggested that she looked worn-out.

"How could that have made her mad?" Stephen asked, looking baffled.

Sam shook his head from side to side. He had no idea. He was as bewildered as Stephen was.

He saw Bear walking over to help Catherine unload her trunk. Bear had tried several times to engage her in conversation but Sam noticed that so far she had not warmed up to his adopted brother. He had to admit, that pleased him.

The children, however, had grown fonder of their giant friend by the day. Bear's nickname reflected both his personality and his daunting appearance. A giant, hair-covered man, originally from Scotland, he was orphaned on his journey to the American colonies. Sam's parents had graciously adopted the young man into their family.

Sam helped Stephen remove the oxbow and tie and secure the oxen, then Stephen told his daughters they could get out of their wagon. Sam watched the two excitedly pop out and squeal as they jumped to the ground. At least the gleeful girls still had energy. The two ran off.

"Stay close girls," he and Stephen both yelled at once.

He looked over at John who was just finishing unsaddling the horses. John had spent most of his free time on this trip fishing and continuing to miss his deceased wife. Lately, the architect had had no luck fishing and had broken his best pole. John had spent the previous evening repairing it, and then tried fishing again, only to bring back dozens of mosquito bites. Sam grinned as he noticed John scratching himself in several places as he led several of their horses, including Sam's, to the river to water. Walking beside his father, six-year old Little John, John's only child, led his beloved horse Dan. Before long, the boy would carry a real weapon not his toy rifle. Kentucky would likely force the child to become a man before his time. When that time came, he would be sure Little John was prepared. John had already asked Sam to teach his son how to use a knife. Soon, the boy would begin lessons on shooting as well.

As she was now, Kelly was often quiet, no doubt spending her private thoughts sorting through turbulent feelings. Jane told Sam that after the rape, feelings of guilt and anger, and often nightmares, still plagued the eighteen-year-old. Jane said Kelly wanted nothing to do with men for the rest of her life. Maybe if his family showed her enough kindness, she could learn to trust men again. He decided to try to serve as a brother to the young woman. Here, she would need a big brother to look out for her.

He strode over to help Kelly unload her chicken crates from her pack mule.

"Is this one Genesis, Exodus, or Leviticus?" he asked. She'd cleverly named the chickens after the first few books of the Old Testament.

"No, that one's Deuteronomy," Kelly said, bringing a hand up to stifle a giggle.

Good, at least he'd managed to make the young woman chuckle.

"Now that we're here in Boonesborough, I need to acquire a rooster," she explained, letting several chickens loose.

"My guess is he'll either be named Joshua or Samuel," he offered.

"I think I just might name him Sam," Kelly said, tilting her head at him as she smiled.

Barely able to keep the laughter from his voice, he said, "Then he'll be a mighty fine warrior, protecting all your hens."

Surprising her, and himself, he promptly did his best rooster imitation, which wasn't all that good, but it sent Kelly into hysterics. Soon everyone gathered around them and joined in sharing the young woman's amusement. Then Bear tried to imitate the crow of a rooster. Martha and Polly liked Bear's animated version the best and begged him to do it a second time. Good naturedly, Bear complied, while chasing one of the chickens around in a circle. Catherine burst out laughing. Her laugh was marvelous, catching, and a ripple of mirth flickered through Sam. He suddenly felt ten-years younger than his thirty-nine years.

Sam guessed it was fatigue and relief making them all so silly, but whatever the reason, it felt good. They needed a few moments of merriment after the rigors of their journey.

After the amusing diversion, he felt more elated than tired. Light-hearted, he took a deep breath, enjoying the feel of the fresh air expanding his lungs. Even dead tired and stinking dirty, he was exactly where he wanted to be. Before they left New Hampshire, he had come to realize that the war had extinguished the fire within him just as surely as blowing out a candle snuffed out its light. After he had left the Continental Army and returned to his home in New Hampshire, life held little meaning or purpose. As a mapmaker and sometimes guide through the wilderness, he managed to make a decent living. But, it was just work. It made him feel unfulfilled, empty, and oftentimes lonely. Like a shadow of his former prewar self.

But now his life would change. Although he felt the physical burdens of constant travel and little rest, his mind and heart had grown stronger with each passing mile. Every day seemed to have more meaning. Every hour his spirit felt more alive and filled with cautious hope. He had savored every minute that brought him further into the wilderness and this new frontier.

A place where, with a bit of luck, he could experience life once again.

He watched Catherine out of the corner of his eye as she clapped her hands following Bear's last performance. Joy bubbled in her gentle laugh and life shone in her eyes.

CHAPTER 4

After setting up camp, Sam, Stephen, and Bear prepared to ride back toward Boonesborough to join William. John agreed to stay behind saying he would help the women and children settle in. Before he left, Stephen made sure John and Jane kept their rifles loaded and nearby while they went to town and Sam asked Catherine and Kelly to do the same with their weapons.

"How do you suppose William is doing?" Stephen asked, pointing his beloved horse George toward town.

"My guess is William has either gotten himself elected mayor or thrown in jail. Hard to tell which," Sam said.

"Aye. He is unpredictable," Bear confirmed. "At least William makes more friends than enemies."

They tied their horses in front of the Bear Trap Tavern next to William's horse and pushed through the rough door. The noisy place smelled of a mixture of the clean scent of the pine log walls and the musky dirty men who sat at the tables. By the time their eyes adjusted to the dim indoor light, every eye in the place focused on them, including two from a woman at the top of the stairs.

William sat with a man at a table near a large stone hearth, unlit due to the summer heat. His brother spotted them and waved them over. "Sit down and have a drink. You boys have some catching up to do," William called to them with his usual wide smile.

Sam blatantly studied every face in the place before he made a move.

The woman at the top of the stairs flashed a saucy smile and swayed her enormous breasts and ample hips suggestively. Sam took in her shapely form and, despite himself, found himself smiling back.

"You can't start a fire if you keep the flint in the box," she told him, winking.

He chuckled, along with several other men who heard the ribald remark. But he wasn't ready for a fire—he wasn't even ready for a spark.

He quickly turned toward the others. Right away, he appreciated the Bear Trap's atmosphere and mood. Unlike the taverns in New Hampshire, he saw no billiard tables, or fancy drinks sitting in front of men wearing fine fashionable clothing. Here, weathered men in soiled clothing and dirty boots filled the tavern, their faces and bodies hardened by the near daily life and death challenges of the wilderness. These men were part of a new breed of Americans. Like him, this breed thrived on the lack of civilization, not the presence of it.

Nevertheless, as men do everywhere, they occasionally shared the need for a soothing drink and the companionship of others who face the same hard challenges of life.

As he ambled toward William, Sam heard conversations about current crop prices, two men negotiating a trade, a man reading a newspaper aloud to his companion, and several men discussing odds on an upcoming horse race. The tavern windows, all open, allowed a slight breeze to float through, cooling the large room.

William motioned the tavern owner over. "Three more of those good ales if you don't mind Sir," William said grinning.

"Certainly, and their first round is on the house. I understand you gentlemen just arrived in Boonesborough. An accomplishment like that deserves more than ale at its end, but that's all I have to offer," said the genial owner of the Bear Trap. "I've been expecting a load of Marcus' good whiskey, but it hasn't arrived just yet. Will a tasty ale suit you?" The portly owner with a large red nose looked to Sam for an answer to his question.

"Ale suits us fine." He inclined his head in a gesture of thanks. "We appreciate your generosity, Sir," Sam said and then introduced himself and the others. The tavern keeper's name was Charles O'Hara.

"I'll be back, Sirs, with the best ales you've ever tasted," O'Hara said, walking away.

William nodded his blonde head vigorously. "He's right, this ale is the best I've ever tasted, maybe because I was so thirsty and it's been far too long since I've enjoyed one."

"Nope, it's the water around these parts," the man at the table said. "Nothing better than Kentucky water. Makes good whiskey too."

"Glad to hear it," William said. "I want you three to meet my new acquaintance, Lucky McGintey. Lucky, these handsome fellows are my family—my two brothers, Captain Sam, and

Stephen, and our adopted brother Bear McKee."

The man stood to shake their hands. Dressed much like Sam, Lucky wore a hunting shirt dyed black, buckskin leggings, and moccasins. He carried a pistol, tomahawk, and long knife in his leather belt and a well-used long rifle leaned against the table next to him. His powder horn appeared similar to theirs except that intricate and artistic carvings decorated it. A coonskin cap covered his long grey hair tied at the back of his neck in a queue pigtail. His sun-darkened skin bore the seasoned look of someone who had coped with the frontier for some time. Sam soon learned that the man had.

William explained that Lucky was one of the first stouthearted men to come to the Kentucky frontier with Daniel Boone and that the man called himself a backcountry long-hunter, because of the far-reaching distances he covered in pursuit of wild game. Lucky supplied food for the settlement including wild bear, white-tailed deer, buffalo, elk, and wild turkey.

"I truly fancy hunting," Lucky said, patting his long rifle with fingers beginning to look gnarled with age. "It gives me a chance to get away from all this noise and commotion here in town."

Sam understood that for men like Lucky, the wild woods made them feel free and offered a chance for adventure. The rich forests held everything he needed to live—game and wild vegetables, fruit, nuts, and berries for food, natural brine salt licks, and hides for clothes. What few items nature didn't provide, mostly tobacco and powder and ball for his rifle, could be bartered for here in Boonesborough or in one of Kentucky's three other larger settlements centered around a fort—Lexington, Harrodsburgh, and Louisville.

William patted his new friend on the back. "Lucky's been a

hunter and wagon driver for Daniel Boone and been captured by Indians three times. Escaped twice and released once. That's why they call him Lucky," William explained.

"Aye. A man captured by natives three times and still alive to tell a yarn about it is indeed a mighty lucky fellow," Bear declared.

"Or exceedingly clever," Sam said.

Lucky winked a twinkling eye at Sam, acknowledging the compliment.

William continued, "He was just telling me all about Boonesborough. Says the town now boasts a large tobacco warehouse for storage and inspection of tobacco crops, a post office, a newspaper, a fur trade operation, several busy stores, three taverns like this one, and a ferry operated by the Callaway family."

Lucky took a quick sip of his ale and then said, "That's right, the town's growing as fast as spring weeds. But Kentucky's still the right place to be if you like the wilderness. Once you get away from Boonesborough, the place is a hunter's paradise. There are so many buffalo, it looks as if the meadows will sink beneath their weight and there are so many turkeys, they can't all fly at the same time."

The men all laughed. Even Sam managed a small chuckle.

"Sir, why did you say 'once you get away from Boonesborough'?" Bear asked.

"Improvident woodsmen have driven away what used to be multitudes of big game. Now you have to hunt fifteen, twenty or even thirty miles from here for large game," Lucky explained. "You carry a mighty long blade there, Captain. I've seen men shorter than that blade."

"It serves me well," he said. "Makes it easy to hurt a man's feelings."

"If you use that on a man, I doubt he'd be feeling much of anything," Lucky said.

"That's what I mean," Sam said.

Lucky cackled until tears ran down his leathery face, covered with so many deep wrinkles going in every direction it rather resembled a map. "I don't know about the rest of these gentlemen, but you'll do just fine in Kentucky Captain."

Sam had a feeling Lucky was right. There was something about this new state that made him feel hopeful for the first time in a long while.

"Is Daniel Boone in town?" Sam asked, remembering that Little John wanted to meet the man. He had to admit, he'd like to meet the legend too. Not because he was famous, but because he admired him.

"No Sir. He's facing some trouble with lawyers. The bastards are taking his land. Boone claimed one-hundred-thousand acres more or less, but failed to get legal title to it."

"I'm certain he was too busy fighting natives and protecting settlers," Sam said. He remembered their stories well. The town's first fighting force of thirty men and twenty boys, aided by the courage and marksmanship of the women, though far outnumbered, fought nobly for a place in the vast wilderness. Blackfish's Shawnee, wanting to rid their hunting ground of the strange invaders, attacked the Fort repeatedly, butchered cattle and burned cornfields. The settlers became virtual captives trapped within the Fort's walls. By the time Blackfish finally withdrew, the starving settlers barely clung to life. Nevertheless, the Fort, to its credit, and the surviving settlers, to their glory, did endure. Almost none who came afterward, though, would recall their names. Sam swore he would never forget their sacrifices and their dauntless courage, including Colonel Boone's.

Lucky nodded in agreement with Sam. "Sadly, the Colonel's footsteps have too often been through blood. And his nights were often dark and sleepless. Boone lost two of his own sons and a brother to savage hands. Almost lost his daughter Jemima too when she and two Callaway girls got stole away down by the river by a Cherokee-Shawnee raiding party. But we gave chase and finally got the young women back after two days."

"Were the girls hurt?" Stephen asked.

"No, Jemima said the Indians were kind to them."

"So why are they taking Boone's land?" Sam asked.

"Lawyers are suing for his claims and it looks like the greedy weasels will succeed in defrauding him. Boone was so disgusted he transported himself and his wife to the mouth of the Little Sandy River in northeastern Kentucky. He has a nice cabin near here, but I don't know if he'll ever be back."

Little John would be sorely disappointed. Sam was himself. He had a lot of respect for Daniel Boone and the treatment of him that Lucky just described made him angry. He slapped his hand against the tabletop. "Fine way to repay the man for all he's done settling this frontier. They ought to let those lawyers fight some Indians. Run them through the gauntlet."

"What's a gauntlet?" William asked him.

Sam turned to William. "From what I've read, Shawnees forced Boone to run the gauntlet. Native young men form two long rows and force their prisoner to run between them, beating their captive viciously with heavy sticks. Most men don't survive, but Daniel escaped serious injury by surprising them and running in a zigzag pattern and butting the last warrior with his head, knocking him over," Sam explained.

"That's what happened all right," Lucky agreed. He cleared his throat and added, "After that, Chief Blackfish was so impressed he adopted Boone into the tribe, taking him to the river for a ceremony to 'wash away' his white blood. Daniel was so badly beaten up it washed away a lot of red blood too."

Sam bent his head and studied his hands as he thought about the irony of that bizarre bathing ritual. "Red or white, a man's blood runs the same way in a river." Then he took a long drink of his ale.

"I'd like to see a lawyer run the gauntlet," Lucky said.

William lifted his blond head and sat up straighter. "Courts of law are gauntlets of the mind. It takes more skill to maneuver through them than most can imagine."

"I suppose you might be right about that," Lucky admitted.

"You said Kentucky was a hunter's paradise," Stephen said. "Looks to me like a cattleman would find it to his liking."

"What's not mountains, or covered in forest so solid you can't see daylight, is good land for grazing cattle. In fact, the Cherokee call Kentucky the Great Meadow. But most of the grass here gets turned into buffalo meat, not beef. Ain't many here yet who have tried to raise up a herd. But the soil is fertile and I believe it will amply reward a man's toil," Lucky said. "The taste of a juicy beef steak is indeed a rare treat around here."

Just how many names did the natives have for Kentucky? 'Land of Tomorrow', 'The Dark and Bloody Ground', and now the 'Great

Meadow'. It seemed to Sam like even the Indians had a hard time figuring out this extraordinary place.

Lucky took a long swallow of his ale, wiped his mouth with the back of his hand and said, "Pasture land's already gettin' scarce. Speculators buy it—run the price up. And a hell of a lot has gone out to veterans of the Revolution as compensation for service. I never found much use for land myself. At the end of my life, I'll just have an old worn out saddle and about a thousand good stories."

"Indeed," Sam said, chuckling. He admired Lucky and his way of life. But he was here to help his brothers. "Where do you suggest we try to settle?"

"You'll find some land that will suit you," Lucky said, "but getting it won't be easy, and you've got to be willing to go off quite a ways from this settlement and, if needed, fight for it."

Unprepared for what Lucky just said, Sam saw Stephen's face cloud with uneasiness. Stephen was probably worried that he had brought Jane and his girls to even more danger, and he may have. They would certainly need to take great care when they selected and claimed their land.

He gave Stephen a look telling him to calm down. Stephen rolled his eyes and then leaned back in his chair.

Sam turned back to Lucky. "Are there any speculators that are honest, ones a man could trust?"

"An honest speculator? Now that's something to make a man scratch his head." Lucky sniggered as he thought for a moment before continuing. "That man that brought William in here—Tom Wolf. He just left before you three came in. He has a reputation for honesty, despite his name. Don't have any idea how much he's selling land for though."

"I'll be talking to the gentleman at the Land Office tomorrow," Sam said, "about a Bounty Grant for my service in the Revolution." He turned toward Stephen. "We'll find some good cattle land near my land grant."

"The Land Office won't open until the first of the month, but you should receive a larger and better grant because of your rank Captain. At least that's what I've heard," Lucky said.

"Hope you're right," Sam said, lighting his pipe. He inhaled deeply, savoring the sweet and pungent smell.

"I'm certainly disappointed that we have to wait several days," Stephen grumbled.

"Nothin' to be done about that," Bear said. "It'll give you a chance to rest up some."

"I'm not interested in rest, I'm interested in land," Stephen said, his expression darkening with worry.

"I would advise you men to be more than a little careful about the land you choose. Men fight each other here over land about as often as they fight the Indians or fight over women. Maybe more," Lucky said. "And don't set your homes up too close to the river. Come a big rain here one night. That water really got to running. Washed out a number of folks."

Sam and Stephen exchanged glances. They would have thought of that, but it was a good reminder. He had read that the rivers here could crest far above their normal levels and their banks often spread beyond what people would expect.

"There's good land out yonder, but you have to go get it, it ain't coming to you," Lucky said.

"Tell me, how far is yonder?" Sam asked, smiling at the man's term.

"Can't tell you. It's just where you need a horse to get to it," the older man replied.

On their way back to camp, Sam thought about Lucky and chuckled as he said, "That Lucky McGintey is a tough old fellow. He's got a lot of bark on him." He hoped they would meet again, maybe even become friends in the weeks ahead.

"I didn't like what he had to say. It would be a hell of a note to have come this far and not be able to get the land we need," Stephen said, nearly growling.

"It's too soon to worry. Don't borrow trouble," William said. "In a few days we'll find Mr. Wolf and seek his help. He told me where his office is, but said he would be gone for a few days visiting his son."

After that, the men hardly spoke at all until they reached their camp.

Deep in thought, Sam let Stephen and William tell the others about their conversation with Lucky McGintey. For some reason, he couldn't keep his eyes off Catherine as she listened intently to what his brothers said. What was she thinking? Was she considering finding her own land? Or was she going back to Boston? And why, for heaven's sake, did the woman have to look so beautiful just sitting there? Her figure was curving and regal and her fiery eyes gleamed, full of life and warmth.

"If Daniel Boone's having trouble keeping his land, it makes me wonder how we'll fare," John said, sounding worried.

Sam reluctantly forced himself to refocus his attention on the conversation.

"It is difficult to comprehend," Stephen agreed. "The man is a legend."

"Even legends sometimes struggle with life, and the law," William said.

"We'll get our land," Sam pronounced, recognizing it sounded, even to him, more like a threat than a promise.

Catherine glanced over at him, her eyes sharp and assessing. She remained motionless for a moment, then hugged her arms to her.

As his eyes met hers, he saw a spark of some hidden emotion.

If he wasn't mistaken, it was longing.

CHAPTER 5

Sam carefully wiped the long maple stock of his Kentucky rifle. Keeping the rifle clean helped the weapon to perform well, and that could mean the difference between life and death.

Like Sam, Stephen and William immediately fell in love with the weapon and both brothers sat next to him, cleaning their rifles as well. Before they left, he'd used most of his savings to purchase new Kentucky rifles, made by Pennsylvania gunsmiths, for each of the men and one for Jane as well. He taught them all to use the newly designed lighter rifles, and the exceedingly accurate weapons enabled them to protect themselves and to acquire a steady supply of food.

"What makes these weapons so accurate?" Stephen asked.

"First and foremost, the skill of the German gunsmiths in Pennsylvania. And, the long narrow barrel gives powder more time to burn, increasing the muzzle's velocity and accuracy."

"I know you can shoot the wings off a bee a hundred yards away, but I need more practice with this rifle," Stephen told him.

"Preferably on four-legged creatures," he said. "How about a hunt tomorrow?"

"It might do us all good to just rest for a day or two. If Bear, William, and John will stay with the women and children, you and I can stretch our legs some. I feel like I've developed bow legs from sitting on George for so long," Stephen said. "I never thought I could grow weary of being in the saddle, but I am beginning to think I am."

"Indeed," William agreed, "my ass feels like it's turned to rock. Of course, I'll stay with them. Where else am I going to go?"

Sam knew better than to ask William to come along. William only enjoyed hunting outlaws.

"You're a pretty fair shot already Stephen, but do you think you'll ever be as good as Sam?" William asked.

"If I could be half the shot Sam is, I'd be happy," Stephen said. "I saw him win a shooting contest once. They pounded nails into boards, and set them off a fair distance. The shooter who could hit the nail on the head would win. Our brother was the only shooter there who hit the nail on the head."

"That sounds like our big brother," William said, smiling at Sam.

Bear and the children were relaxing, stretched out underneath a massive Sycamore closer to the river.

"Bear, can you join us a minute?" Stephen yelled down to him.

Bear ambled back to the wagons and Stephen asked, "Sam and I are going hunting in the morning—stretch our legs some—will you stay with the ladies and children? I'm sure they're safe here, but I'd feel better if you remained here to be certain they are."

"Aye," Bear answered, "I'll be their guardian angel."

Sam took in all six and a half feet of Bear from head to toe. "You don't look much like a guardian angel to me." Bear wasn't just tall, he was big and broad. He had hands the size of a frying pan and with legs the size of tree trunks, his booted feet made a sound resembling thunder when he walked.

"Nae, I'm no Gabriel," Bear said, shaking his big head and grinning.

"I know one pretty lady that may need protection *from* you," William teased, looking at Bear with amusement in his eyes.

Sam realized he was obviously not the only one who had noticed Bear's attempts to gain Catherine's friendship. Quickly annoyed, he rubbed the back of his neck and pressed his lips together as he struggled to keep his feelings to himself.

His mood light, William continued to jest. "I think there just might be a wolf lurking around here." He ambled over to the wagon, put up his cleaning materials, and retrieved a law book.

"Wolves," Bear said, clearly choosing to ignore William's implication, "are beasts to take seriously, as Stephen knows all too well. Did you know wolves have forty-two teeth, each strong enough to crush bone?"

Stephen unconsciously rubbed the scar on his neck. If not for his brother's unfaltering courage, Stephen would be dead. He was lucky to be alive.

Bear was an expert wolf hunter, having slain many wolves that roamed too close to their New Hampshire town and mounting their heads on posts, the customary way to collect the bounty offered by landowners for their killing. "And they always hunt in packs of at least two," Bear added, looking directly at Sam.

Sam boldly meet Bear's gaze straight on. He found a perverse pleasure in the subtle challenge.

"Wolves or not, while we're gone," Stephen said, "I would feel better with you here and standing watch. Will you keep your eyes open?"

"I'll keep a careful watch over *all* of them, even wee William here," Bear teased, patting William's shoulder.

"There's nothing wee about me where it counts," William retorted.

Bear threw back his head and let out a great peal of laughter. Sam and Stephen both chuckled, while William raised a blonde brow and winked at Bear.

"I'll be going back to the little ones now. Their spirits have been lifted some by our checkers game," Bear said. "And Martha's beat me twice. I need to even the score."

"You might as well give up now," Stephen said, "I can never beat her at that game."

Sam found himself wondering whether leaving for a long hunt was such a good idea. His mind raced trying to determine if Bear was just taunting him. Or, would Bear use Sam's absence as a chance to spend time with Catherine? And why was he even thinking about this? He couldn't afford to be distracted by romantic notions or get caught up in some competition for a woman's attention. It was foolish schoolboy jealousy and nothing more.

Besides, how could he be jealous? He had no interest in the woman. Well, maybe some interest if truth be told. But not now, not yet.

He slowly exhaled a deep breath, trying to force his thoughts back to their hunt—one of his favorite pastimes. He and Stephen had hunted together since they were boys.

"Remember when Father used to take us out to hunt?" he asked Stephen. "You and I used to beg him to take us every time he went. You'd even tell him you knew where the deer grazed and, if he took you, you'd show him. He'd laugh, pat you on the back and bring you along."

"But John and I only went when he forced us to. We didn't enjoy it much. John was more content to study mathematics and architecture and I just wanted to practice on my fiddle or jest with mother and sister," William confessed.

Sam looked over at John. As usual, he was absorbed in some thick book on architecture.

"That's the truth. Father probably had all he could handle anyway taking the two of us. Sam tried to kill anything that moved, and I never wanted to get out of father's shadow. I swear that man could walk fast, and he was Indian quiet," Stephen recalled.

"He could track like one too. I think he could have trailed a butterfly flying over solid rock," Sam said.

"And once he started a track, he kept after it till he found what he was looking for," Stephen added.

"Wasn't much give up in that old man was there," William said.

"No there wasn't," Stephen agreed.

"Never knew him to give up on anything," Sam added.

"Much like you," Stephen said.

"We've many fond memories of that mountain," Sam reminisced. "Strange, the mountain he loved so much killed him."

"Don't think it did. It was the heavy rain that caused the

mudslide," Stephen said.

Stephen could never blame the land for their father's death. "Maybe so," Sam mused. "I know he loved his land. You learned that from him. He was the land and the land was him. He was aware of every tree, every high spot and low spot, everything there was to know about his place."

"Do you think he'd have come with us to Kentucky if he were still alive?" Stephen asked.

"Don't know. But I think it would have been his idea for us to go," Sam said. "He would have wanted you to get the land you need."

Stephen smiled at that.

Would their father have wanted the same for him? Sam suddenly wondered.

CHAPTER 6

Catherine awoke feeling good about the decision she finally made during the night. She'd been restless and unable to sleep for much of the night, and it gave her time to think. After bathing with a wet cloth, dressing, and then putting her hair in a thick braid, all the while trying not to wake Kelly who also slept in her wagon, she climbed out to a stunningly beautiful morning.

When they had arrived yesterday, she was too tired to notice much of anything. But this morning, the splendor of their surroundings made her gasp in wonder. The warm early morning light poked through a rich tapestry of trees, vines, and brush to reveal the vivid colors of flowers and lush grass. The soft pure air held no hint of the heavy mugginess they'd endured the last few days. In its place, a light wind of cooler air lifted her spirits as well as the leaves of the hardwoods. She raised her chin, relishing the soothing sound and feel of the gentle breeze brushing against her face and through her hair. The soft fragrance of a variety of Aster, Foxglove, and other wildflowers made her expand her lungs and inhale deeply.

Finally, she would have a day without feeling the rocky

movement of wagon wheels beneath her. The wagons wobbled so much so that ever since Kelly arrived with her milk cow, Jane tied a wooden butter churn filled with fresh milk to the side of the wagon every morning. By the evening meal, they all enjoyed creamy butter on their hot biscuits.

She hated to admit it, but she needed some rest. They all needed a quiet day. She strolled up to the cook fire as Jane, yawning, poured water into the coffee pot and hung it to brew.

"Good morning," Jane greeted. "Looks like it will be a quiet one for a change. Stephen and Sam went hunting. They've spent so many days with their legs stretched across a horse's back, they're starting to waddle when they walk," she said, with a grin. "They decided they wanted to stretch their legs and we needed some time to rest."

"I was just thinking something similar. I've spent so much time on that bloody wagon, walking feels strange because the ground isn't moving."

"I agree. Maybe that's how sailors feel when they're on land again," Jane said.

"Where are the others?"

"William's feeding and brushing down the horses and John and Bear took the children to the river to fish for breakfast."

"Good, I'm famished," Catherine said.

"Polly's discovered that she loves to fish. I hope they'll have better luck than John did yesterday evening. I'd enjoy trout or catfish for breakfast. Although, I'm so hungry, I think I could eat a whale all by myself," Jane said chuckling, and rubbing her bulging stomach. "This baby has an exceptionally healthy appetite."

"Yes, he seems to have grown overnight. Rest sounds

marvelous to me. It will be nice to just be in one place for a change, if only for a few days," she said. "What do you plan to do on this gorgeous day?"

"More than anything, while we're here at the river, I want to bathe, and wash my hair and clothes. I need to mend Martha's shoes if I can, maybe make some baby clothes. I brought fabric I can use," Jane answered.

"Doesn't sound like you'll be getting much rest. At least you can do the mending and sewing sitting down. Remember, you don't have to do it all in one day. I'll help you with what I can. I've never sewn much though. We used dressmakers in Boston," she said. "I noticed there's one in town. I can't wait to visit that establishment. And I'm sure we could find new shoes in town for Martha."

"Catherine, why did you and your husband leave Boston alone?" Jane asked.

"He wanted to get to Kentucky quickly to claim a prime site of land. That's why he was in such a hurry. He didn't want traveling with others to slow us down and he was egotistical enough to think he could defend us himself. He figured we'd meet up with other travelers once we got further along into dangerous territory anyway."

"What kind of land would justify the hazard of traveling alone?"

"He never told me much. He possessed some papers about it. He hid the documents in my wagon, but I've never read them. Your question reminds me that I need to. Maybe I'll do that later today. How could I have been married to a man and know so little about him?"

"From what you've told me, it wasn't much of a marriage. That's how," Jane said.

"Maybe you're right; he never discussed his affairs with me. I never knew if he was worried about something or if anything good had happened. He considered business affairs 'too burdensome for a woman's delicate mind.' However, I never pressed him for information either. Perhaps it was both our faults."

Catherine turned and took a few steps to admire the peaceful view of the Kentucky River. Stephen and Jane's two oxen and three cattle grazed near the riverbank contentedly devouring thick grass. Birds warbled, chirped, and sang from nearly every tree or flew over the river searching for insects floating on the smooth green water. The melodious notes of a mockingbird's medley rose above all the other birds.

Jane walked up behind her and handed her a pewter cup filled with coffee. The brew sent steam into the air before them as they gazed at the river. They both inhaled the fragrant aroma as they waited for the coffee to cool.

"If I may be frank, your former husband sounds like he was a narrow-minded pompous bloke," Jane said. "If my husband ever said something like that to me, I would show him how 'delicate' parts of the male anatomy are."

Catherine laughed, picturing Jane's knee slamming into her husband. Perhaps she should have stood up to him, as Jane would have. Then she let out a deep breath, knowing that regrets were pointless. "When I marry again, it will be to a man who loves me and will want to share his dreams with me and care about my dreams too. That's what a marriage should be—two people bound together by love—not alliances arranged to mutually benefit each family."

"You're right about the importance of love, but some men don't have grand dreams. Some men are just who they are now and nothing more. And some men have the grandest of dreams and won't become who they really are until they can chase those dreams. I've learned that when you marry that kind of man, you marry his dreams too."

"Maybe it takes the love of the right woman to help a man see his dreams. You and Stephen share a dream of owning enough land to raise fine cattle."

"Yes, that's true. But on our journey, I forgot that for a while. And in that time, I lost Stephen too. I vowed never to lose sight of our dream again. Because, Stephen will never leave the path that dream will make him follow. It's his destiny."

Destiny. The same word the Captain had used. With the decision she made during the night, she would change her destiny forever. This choice would likely affect her future more than any other decision she would ever make. A part of her still wondered if Sam would ever take notice of her. "Jane, why does Sam carry that enormous blade and why is he so serious all the time?"

"I asked Stephen about the knife once. He told me that ever since Sam came home from the war, he never parts with the knife, even when he occasionally attends church. Before Sam left his family to join the Continental Army, he had just been Stephen's big brother, strong and huge, but still his carefree and cheerful hunting companion. But, when the Captain returned from the war, his former cheerful robust companion did not come back. In his place, a haggard, far too thin, seasoned soldier returned—a serious warrior whose weapon was now as much a part of him as his arm or his leg. Over time, Sam did recover physically, regaining his weight and strength, but his now serious, solemn demeanor—and the knife—never left him. Now, I can't even conceive of Sam ever parting with that blade."

Neither could Catherine.

Kelly marched up behind them and stood next to her. "Good morning pretty ladies."

Catherine gave the young woman an affectionate hug. "Sweet Kelly."

Kelly smiled and gave her a warm hug too.

The young woman's complexion glowed in the morning light as she said, "Jane, when we make breakfast, will you show me how to make those heavenly biscuits? They're the best I've ever tasted." Although still slim, since she had started eating healthy portions of Jane's good food, especially her biscuits, Kelly no longer looked rawboned skinny.

"I'd be pleased to, but the secret is in the feel of the dough. You know by touch when it feels just right. That comes with practice," Jane explained. "I'll show you later when I work the dough. And you have to have the right pans for cooking over a fire, like this Dutch oven cast iron pot."

As Jane talked with Kelly about baking, Catherine fell deep into her own thoughts—troubled about how to tell two women she had grown very fond of over the last few weeks that she was leaving.

With much difficulty, she decided that she had to return to Boston. After driving her wagon through Boonesborough yesterday, she realized that living alone in this rough and uncivilized town would be impossible. As much as she enjoyed the company of the Wyllies, she couldn't stay with them forever. They would each be building their own homes and she would not impose on their hospitality or take advantage of their kindness by doing so.

And if the taciturn Captain was going to remain a cold fish, that left no reason to stay.

"Catherine, you seem to be struggling with something. May we help?" Jane asked.

"I'm not staying in Boonesborough. Or in Kentucky. I'm going back to Boston. I gave myself time to resolve what I should do, and now that we're here, I know I must return home." She could not hide the regret she heard in her voice.

"Why?" Jane asked, aghast. "I thought you decided to stay with us."

"I just don't think I should," she said, not wanting to explain. "I'll find a family that will be traveling the Ohio River route back to the East coast to escort me. I won't have the benefit of my wagon, but that route will be faster. At least on the riverboat I'll have a smooth ride."

"Why go back when a whole new beautiful frontier awaits us? The opportunities aren't just for men. They're for women too," Jane said.

"I have no one here. What good will opportunities do me if I have no one with whom to share them? And my father would expect me to return. It isn't proper for me to stay. I'll send him word that I'm on my way home because of my husband's murder. The Captain encouraged me to decide my own future. Well I've decided. There's no rational reason for me to stay."

"Sometimes we must do irrational things to do what's right for us," Jane said.

"Going back is right for me," Catherine said adamantly.

"We all want you to stay, especially Bear. I've never seen him this way. He's acting like a boy in love for the first time. And in my opinion, you will never find a finer man, except Stephen of course, and I've already claimed him," Jane said, smiling.

Stunned, her brows collided with confusion. "Bear?"

With a sly grin Kelly said, "Jane, it's not Bear."

"What do mean?" Catherine asked tersely.

"Bear isn't the one who catches your eye, it's the Captain," Kelly said.

"Kelly, you're as wrong as you can be," Jane said, her voice mocking the idea. "Sam will never marry. If ever there was a man intent on being a bachelor, it's the Captain. I've known Sam half my life and he's the type of man that sees marriage as something for others. A person could sooner tame a wild deer than Sam. Catherine knows that. Don't you?"

Flabbergasted, she glanced back and forth between Jane and Kelly, turned abruptly and marched away, her fists clenched at her sides.

Shock ripped through her. She couldn't believe Kelly figured it out. How did the young woman know when she didn't even understand what she felt herself? What business was it of Kelly's or Jane's anyway? She didn't want to think about this and they were forcing her to do just that. Her decision was made and she wasn't going to change her mind.

Then her heart beat faster as thoughts of Sam sprung into her head, wrapping around her like a warm blanket on a cold day. She pictured his rare smile and heard his deep kind voice in her head. She had no idea a voice could even be sensuous. But his definitely was. Resonant and rich, the sound of it stirred something within her the very first time she heard it. Perhaps it was the quiet strength she perceived in the tone of it. His voice was both gentle and strong at once. Much like he was.

Why was she so strangely drawn to the man? She shared nothing in common with him. If Jane is right, she could never hope to marry a man like the Captain Wyllie. She had promised herself that she would only marry for love. And Sam showed no indication that she even appealed to him. He'd only been cold and standoffish.

Maybe he sensed something from her and it scared him away. Perhaps he's just incapable of love for some reason. Jane's right, he'll never want a wife.

She kept walking toward the river, debating with herself.

Maybe he didn't even find her appealing. Did he think her a pampered gentlewoman—too genteel, too much a lady? Well, she was learning more each day about how to take care of herself in the wilderness. It wasn't her fault she'd grown up coddled and indulged. She was who she was and proud of it. If he wasn't willing to look beneath the superficial part of her, then that was his loss.

Besides, it's too soon to even be thinking about another man or marrying again. But she was. She couldn't help it. She just couldn't. She did feel something for Sam, but was it enough to risk staying here? "Oh Lord, what do you want me to do?" she asked, looking skyward.

She listened to the gurgle and rush of the river. Her emotions seemed to be rushing through her as swiftly as the river's current. At least the river knew which way to flow. She didn't know whether to go forward in Kentucky or backward to Boston. She peered down at the mud on the riverbank, feeling like she was stuck in it.

Kelly walked up behind her. "Catherine, please forgive me if I misspoke. I didn't mean to upset you."

"Kelly, what made you say that?"

Kelly gracefully stooped down to pick a red wildflower before she answered. "The way you look at him when he's not looking. The way he looks at you when he thinks no one else is noticing. I look at William the same way when he's not looking at me. It's a look of admiration, of wanting—a look of hope. A hope that someday I'll have the courage to look at him when he *is* looking at me. A hope that he'll look back at me, feeling the same way I do."

Dumbfounded, Catherine didn't know what to say. She had to admit everything Kelly said made sense. "You're very wise for such a young lady."

"And you're very foolish for such a smart woman."

She had to laugh. "Why do you say that?"

"Because I think two men may be in love with you."

Catherine felt her eyes widen, shocked by Kelly's presumptuous and brash statement. "In love? Two? Oh good heavens, you can't mean it."

"Bear looks at you almost the same way."

"What do you mean 'almost'?"

"Bear, who is a fine man I'm sure, sees the outside of you—sees your considerable beauty and your charm. You have captured Bear's mind. However, the Captain's heart sees the inside of you. He admires who you are—your spirit—and the strength he senses beneath your beauty."

Had she been wrong about Sam seeing only the superficial part of her?

Her head bowed, Kelly paused, thinking for a moment. Finally she said, "The Captain's heart wants you but his mind is still fighting it for some reason."

"What reason?"

"I don't know—something hidden deep within him. Whatever it is, it's important."

Everything Kelly told her rang true to Catherine. "Kelly, you are remarkable. How did someone your age gain such insight into people, especially since you lived in the woods, alone for the most part?"

"My Ma was the same way. Ever since I was little, we'd talk for hours and hours about different characters in books and the stories in the Bible and about her relatives and people she had known. Ma taught me how to observe people by studying our animals. She showed me how little things they do will tell you a lot about how they're feeling. Like when a horse pins back his ears, you know it's time to watch out. He's mad and likely to kick. She said observing and figuring out people is the same—a gift—the gift of understanding what people are going to do and why. For some reason, she wanted me to be able to do that too. So even after she died, I kept on observing my animals and sometimes my Pa. I could almost always tell when he was going to beat me. When that looked likely, I'd take a long walk in the woods."

Her heart ached for what the young woman must have endured. "Kelly, you amaze me. You've led such a difficult life, yet you are so astute and clever."

"There is one thing I can't figure."

"What's that?"

"Why you wouldn't sell me that handsome gelding that

belonged to your late husband. I can give you a partial payment now and more later after I find a job in town."

"That horse was my engagement gift to my late husband. He also gave me my horse as a wedding gift. Even though I didn't love him, I readily admit that, I did care for him. He was more like a friend. He tried to be a good husband. He just didn't know how. I don't have much left of our time together, other than our horses. But now that I've decided to leave, I'm ready to part with it."

"I suspect you will change your mind about leaving. We'd best get back before Jane starts those biscuits and I miss out on my lesson."

"Yes, I think I need that lesson too. I've never made biscuits myself. We employed cooks in Boston. But before we go back, for some time Jane and I have both wanted to tell you something. And I think now may be the right time."

Kelly looked at her in surprise.

She took a quick intake of breath and hoped she would find the right words. "William and Stephen killed those two men because they were murderers and because they caught them in the act of raping you. What you experienced with that evil man is nothing at all like what happens between a husband and his wife. A man that respects you will be gentle and a man that loves you will make it something you want—even look forward to. What that man did was violent and hurtful. You must remember that it will be completely different when you marry and to not be afraid of your husband. My mother taught me that the act of coupling between two people in love is always gentle, never violent. Jane could explain this even better than I because Stephen worships her."

She thought about her own experiences as a married woman. It was all she could do to tolerate having her husband in her bed. Although he was gentle, their coupling left a lot to be desired. In fact, there was no desire. No passion. No love. It was quick, predictably bland, often uncomfortable, and always unsatisfying. Her husband tried, sometimes, but cold and aloof by nature, he had no idea how to spark her fire or how to please her. Never again.

Catherine watched as Kelly studied the red wildflower nestled in her palm. "I still dream about them. I feel them attacking me over and over. I feel their hands touching my breasts. It was the first time any man ever touched me. In my dream, I keep trying to scream. But no sound comes out and so no one comes to help me," Kelly said, her eyes glistening.

"But someone did come. William and Stephen stopped them."

"I know. Yet, in my mind, the ghosts of those men are still there. They won't ever go away. They will always be in my head, haunting me. Hurting me."

"They will go away. You can make them."

"No they won't," Kelly nearly shouted, her repressed anger and stored up tears both clearly surfacing. "I tried to make them go away, but they won't. They won't," she wailed.

"Let God have them," Catherine said. "His peace can take them away forever."

"He can't take away what they did to me," Kelly cried. "William thinks the same thing. He'll hardly look at me."

"William is trying to let you heal. Our bodies heal a lot faster than our minds. William knows you just need to be left alone awhile. He's a smart man. He will know when you have left this behind you. What happened to you was indeed horrible, but you must put it in your past, not your present. You're strong. You can overcome this."

"No man will ever want me after I've been deflowered. I'm ruined."

"Oh, you are *so* wrong. No good and decent man would ever blame you for what happened. Young men will be standing in line for a chance to even hold your hand."

"Truly?"

She saw desperation in Kelly's eyes. The girl wanted to believe what she was telling her.

"Moreover, you are one of the brightest and loveliest young women I have ever known." She genuinely believed Kelly was. The girl's perfectly straight flaxen hair hung to her slim waist. Her large bright blue eyes lit up a sweet face. Catherine knew Kelly would mature into a beautiful woman someday. "You'd look like a rose among weeds compared to most of those young socialites in Boston."

Kelly's anger seemed to be subsiding. "Really?"

"Indeed. And believe me, William has noticed. He's just being smart, biding his time until you are ready. Wait till I get you in some fashionable pretty attire and we use a few other tricks you don't even know about yet."

"Like what?" Kelly sniffled, but the tears had stopped.

"You'll see," she said mysteriously and then gave Kelly a hug around the waist as they started back. She had the means to help Kelly and decided it would give her great pleasure to do so. She vowed to herself to buy the young woman proper undergarments, including stays, and a few gowns in colors that would flatter her. Then she would teach the young lady how to style her hair and few other secrets.

"I'll remember everything you said," Kelly said, looking at the flower in her hand again. "I'll keep this in my Bible to help me remember."

And, to help her forget, Catherine hoped.

She studied her young companion. Did Kelly really have her mother's 'gift'? Was what the young woman said about Sam true? She felt her heart swell with hope. There was no use denying it any longer. She could love Sam, if he would let her. He was a man she could respect. Staying would mean risking her reputation in Boston society and her father's wrath. But Sam was worth the gamble. She would stay, she decided, for now.

And, for now, a chance for love would be her dream.

She would wait until Sam saw that chance too.

CHAPTER 7

The next morning, against the darkest grey of early dawn, John handed Bear a steaming cup. "Here, I made it strong enough to wake a hibernating bear."

Bear chuckled, taking the cup. "Good. I know I've been accused of soundin' much like one, with my snorin'. Much obliged John. I'll be needin' more than a wee bit of that coffee. I feel like I slept with a wet blanket there's so much dew this morn."

"Your snoring woke me up a time or two, or three, or…"

"No need to keep countin'. Once ye get yourself a house built, ye'll be sleeping better. Ye've been risin' earlier than normal. Tell me what's botherin' ye. Ye do na seem your normal self."

Their voices immediately woke Sam, but he couldn't make himself sit up. He closed his eyes trying to grab a few more minutes sleep after being on guard duty a good part of the night, but the smell of the coffee called to him. Then he heard John continue.

"The day we reached Boonesborough was Diana's birthday. I still miss her. Leaving her behind has only made me miss her even more, not less. I can't help but think that I've deserted her. I know it's not logical, since she's been dead these few years. Even so, it still causes me grief and most of all guilt. I went to see her grave just before we left. I keep hearing what I said to her over and over in my head."

"Aye, Diana was a lovely woman and we all miss her. But life goes on John. She would want ye to find a new life. I know she would want ye and your wee son to be happy."

"But I still love her. And as long as I do, I could never remarry. I realize now, I don't want a new life. I want my old one back."

"We do na honor the dead by lettin' them make us miserable," Bear said.

His mind seizing Bear's astute comment, Sam instantly came back to wakefulness. "But sometimes we let them," he said, getting up from his bedroll and joining them.

He could empathize with John's feelings. He felt much the same. He raked his fingers through his hair and, after pouring some coffee, studied the dancing flames, already turning some of the dry wood to glowing embers. What would it take to warm his own heart again?

The three men stood quietly for a few moments sipping from their pewter cups.

John and Bear were probably wondering who it was he had just referred to, but they knew better than to ask. If he wanted them to know, he would tell them. Parts of his life were off limits, even to his brothers.

Bear cleared his throat and then said in a low voice, "I need to tell you some news. I did na want to say anything about it last night in front of the women and wee ones. Sam, while ye and Stephen were huntin' yesterday, I met a trapper who wandered by. He said somethin' has stirred the Cherokee up again. They attacked a flatboat loaded with settlers on the Cumberland River. The same flatboat we used to cross into Kentucky on our way here. They murdered all but 'one, even the women and wee ones. They kept one man to torture—the poor soul. Burned him alive."

John gasped and his face paled in horror.

Sam remained unruffled, having seen similar scenes himself, but his warrior instinct kicked in. He quickly surveyed the area around them. Stephen was on guard duty now and was still circling the campsite.

"They tortured the man to see if he would show signs of weakness—beg for mercy or scream in fear," Bear explained for John's benefit. "His body was still smolderin' when they found him."

John shuddered at the gruesome description.

"The Kentucky and Ohio militia are pursuin' the Cherokee to the south," Bear explained.

Keeping his voice low, Sam said, "I'm surprised it was the Cherokee. Maybe the hunter had it wrong. The Shawnee are the most hostile tribe in the region. Most of the violent destruction of Kentucky settlements has been their work."

"Are there any Shawnee near here?" John asked Sam.

"They live to the north, but Kentucky is their favorite hunting ground."

"We best be prepared," Bear said.

"Agreed. We'll double our watch at night and keep the women and children close. We must be certain we're not in a position to be ambushed," Sam told them, "by natives *or* malicious white men."

Bear turned to John. "Aye, the Shawnee are vicious. They mutilate their captives to ensure they will na come back in the next life as warriors. They'll smash teeth in, cut off fingers, break leg bones, gouge out eyes…"

"Enough," John nearly yelled. "I've heard enough."

"Keep your voice down," Sam admonished, "you'll wake the others. Bear just wants you to realize what we're dealing with John. You need to know what we might be up against, if not now, then maybe later. Hostile tribes can only be punished for poor behavior, not bribed or reasoned with."

"We're up against ignorant savages, that's what," Bear said. "They do na think the white man was created by their 'Master of Life—the Great Creator.' They think of us as less than human—like some sort of animal."

"Sounds much like what you said about native Indians a few campfires back," John pointed out.

"That's different," Bear said, sounding annoyed.

"How so?" John asked, his eyes and his voice challenging Bear.

Bear pulled back his massive shoulders. "How can you defend these savages, man? If ye'd seen that flatboat and what they did to those poor wee ones, ye'd be wantin' to use your powder on every bloody savage hiding in these woods. D'ye realize how close we came to that being us?"

"I'm not defending them. I'm just trying to understand them," John protested.

Bear snorted. "I do na need to 'understand' them. Nay, I want them to leave us the bloody hell alone."

"But if you understand them, you can reason with them," John said.

Sam blew out his breath in frustration. It was too early for this conversation and he was losing his patience. "This is the wilderness, not a university," he told John. "I know that is hard for an educated man like you to accept, but reason is a weak defense. If you're being attacked, it's a poor time to try to 'understand' them."

Bear nodded vigorously in agreement. "Aye, a scalp comes off an educated man as quick as it does a dumb bastard."

"If white men used more reason than powder, they'd be able...." John started to argue.

Sam cut him off, tired of being caught in the crossfire. "What you *both* need to realize is that every tribe is different. You can't throw them all in the same sack. Some are savage animals, so brutal it's hard for white men to even imagine what they are capable of. Other tribes are peaceful hunters, fisherman and traders—far more peaceful than many white men I've known. Don't make the mistake of thinking of them all the same way. On one side of a mountain, you might find friendly, even helpful, natives. But on the other side, they can be hostile beyond belief. And by offering bounties for settler's scalps, the bloody Red Coats induced some of these natives to become our enemies, while other natives continue to fight *with* us against the British. My advice is to keep your eyes and your ears open, respect and be cautious of all men, and leave these debates to preachers and politicians."

"Maybe that's just what I should do here in Boonesborough," John said, squaring his big shoulders. The pain and fire had gone out of his voice.

"A politician?" Bear asked, looking incredulous.

"No, you big obstinate giant. A preacher, not a politician." John poured himself more coffee and continued excitedly. "I can build the town a church. Maybe I can help those who have suffered a loss, as I have. I can teach them how to read the Bible if they're not literate. Maybe, I'll even be able to help some of these natives."

Sam hoped that were true. However, he doubted that the populace of Boonesborough or the Indians would receive John's benevolent gestures as he intended. Trying to bring compassion to the wilderness might earn applause from heaven. But here it would more likely bring scorn and ridicule. Maybe worse.

Nevertheless, John just gave himself a reason to continue on here in Kentucky. And reason to go on without Diana. Sam hoped it was reason enough.

༄

As Sam and Bear put away their sleeping pallets and the others started to stir, Sam said, "I feel like a horse locked in a corral too damn long. I'll be glad when we get those land grants settled and get moving again. This doing nothing is almost more than I can stand. I feel like swearing till the leaves shake off the trees."

The men had been waiting several days for the land office to open on the first day of the month and the tedious delay was beginning to cause serious wear on Sam's already frayed nerves. The thought of another day of just wasting time put him on edge.

"Have a smoke and walk with me, while they get breakfast underway, it'll calm ye down some. Ye're wound up tighter than the sinew strung on an Indian's bow."

He hated to admit it, but Bear was right. Was it just the waiting that had him so worked up? Maybe it was their heated conversation with John. Or was he worried about the recent attack on the settlers?

"Sam, what do ye think of Catherine?" Bear asked, after they walked some distance away and both relieved themselves.

Hell fire. Maybe that was the reason he was so on edge, because the question caused Sam's nerves to tighten even more. With a clenched jaw, he reached for his pipe and tobacco as he struggled for an answer. "She's amiable and cultured. Seems to be a strong woman and well mannered," he finally said, hoping his true feelings didn't show.

"Is that all ye have noticed? Her culture and her fine manners?"

Stalling, Sam filled and lit his pipe. "What do you mean? She's pleasant to look at if that's what you're getting at." He took a pull on the white clay stem, hoping a smoke would calm his nerves. He didn't smoke the pipe often, but when he did, he enjoyed it.

"Pleasant? Is yer vision growin' dim man? That is the most beautiful lass I've ever seen anywhere and all ye can say is that she's pleasant to look at? The Queen of England could be sitting right here and I swear ye'd say the same."

"How do you know what the Queen of England looks like? You're from Scotland. You've never even been to England. She could be as ugly as a warthog for all you know."

"The Queen of Scotland then. It's just a figure of speech you contrary mule."

"The only thing you should be figuring is how to forget her. Her husband just passed a couple of months ago. It isn't right to be talking of her in that way." Or thinking of her that way, Sam admitted to himself.

"I mean na disrespect, of course, but she does na seem to be grievin' all that much. Jane says that Catherine was na in love with her late husband, and that her father authoritatively arranged the marriage. How long before ye think it would be proper to talk to her?"

"You can talk to her now you big stubborn fool." Sam kept biting his tongue. Blood would soon be dripping from the corners of his mouth if Bear kept this up.

"Ye know my meaning. Talk to her like a man to a woman." Bear glanced over at him, winked, and grinned.

Sam glared back. "What do you know about talking to a gentlewoman, especially a lady from a fine Boston family? You'd be better off trying to talk romance with one of the bears you like to hunt."

Sam pointed towards the tall white birch and pines off to their right. A large buck and a doe froze as they heard them, then, gracefully bounded back into the safety of the forest.

"Why haven't you ever married, Sam?"

The question did not surprise him. A woman like Catherine had a way of making a man think about marriage. He really couldn't blame Bear. He took a deep breath. "I came close once. But we met at the wrong place at the worst of times. My first and only love. She's the only one I ever wanted and I lost her," he said softly, his mind now in the distant past.

"How? When? I never heard about it."

"No one has."

Sam shook his head to bring himself back from the permanently scorched memory. But for some reason, this time the recollection refused to retreat. Perhaps now that he was so far away he could face his past. Maybe if he told Bear, the memory would recede. He wanted the dark cloud hanging over his head, to move on. Like his shadow, it followed him everywhere. But unlike his shadow, it was his constant companion. Yet, he hesitated. Would speaking of it make it worse of better?

Almost as if Bear somehow knew what he was thinking, he heard Bear saying, "Ye don't have to tell me, Sam, if it brings ye too much discomfort. Nonetheless, I urge ye to do so. Runnin' from pain does nothin' to defeat it. Sometimes, ye must confront the ache in yer heart to heal it—like cleanin' a festerin' wound."

Festering wound. He could relate to that comparison. He'd seen many a wound fester and the results were never good. Perhaps Bear was exactly right. The man did have an uncanny ability to cut to the truth of a matter. Maybe it *was* time to battle the ugly demons dwelling in his head.

He took a deep breath to steel himself. "You were just a youngster, about 11 or 12, the same age as Stephen. Remember when I left to join the Continental Army?"

"Aye. Remember the day well. Yer father was so proud, but yer mother cried all night."

"We trained near Concord. The army camped just outside of town. Because I could read and possessed a good mind for numbers, they put me in charge of supplies. She worked at her father's general store. The store was an important part of the community. He sold nearly everything imaginable. We saw each other for the first time there. She was so gentle and pure and perfectly made. I'll never forget a single detail of her face. She had eyes like a young doe, big, brown, innocent—the kind, that made you want to just keep staring at her. Her smile was so warm it made me break out in a sweat and I couldn't seem to talk without my tongue getting all tied up in knots. But when we did talk, happiness filled me and I'd remember every word she said for days. I'd repeat her words over and over again in my mind.

"For a few months they sent me into town for provisions at least once a week. Soon my feelings for her deepened. When we were apart, my heart ached for her. When we were together, my heart danced with joy. I only had a chance to hold her hands, but I will never forget the feel of them and the way touching her made me feel like I was holding the hands of an angel. Maybe I was.

"Soon General Washington sent us on the move again, and I was forced to say goodbye to her—one of the hardest things I'd ever done. But I swore to her we would be together again soon. It was a promise I should never have made. It made the last thing I said to her a lie.

"Shortly after we left Concord, a damn turncoat led the Red Coats to where her father hid our provisions in a large storehouse behind the general store. This turncoat had been an army scout until he joined the enemy. They blew up the storage building and burned down the store to cut off our supply source. I heard later that when the British started to attack she hid inside the store, undoubtedly afraid to leave for fear of being raped or shot. She must have waited too long to try to get out and she got trapped…burned alive." A shiver of vivid recollection shook him and he had to look away for a moment.

Once he could continue he said, "When I learned she'd died, my whole being flooded with anguish. When I learned how she died, rage replaced anguish. I've killed that traitor a thousand times in my mind." The muscles of his face tightened with remembered anger. "And I've heard her screams ten thousand times in my head." Sam squeezed his eyes shut trying to block out the horrifying image of her death.

Bear stopped walking and turned to Sam. "Och, Sam, I know not what to say. D'ye know the whoreson's name?"

"Eli Frazier." The words nearly burned his lips as he snarled the name. He wiped his fingers across his mouth.

"At the time, ammunition was in such short supply, guns were near worthless. I took all the funds I'd managed to save, borrowed a little more from my father, and bought the biggest and best knife I could find. English armorers forged the blade of steel and just before the war started, it had shipped to New York, which is where I acquired it. I made this handle myself out of deer horn to remind me of her eyes." As he spoke, he slowly ran his fingers across the rich grooved texture of the handle, worn smooth in spots by years of use.

"I fought like the devil and searched for that damn turncoat everywhere we went. Never found him, but I found plenty of lobster-backs, including one of their highest ranking. That's what got me promoted to Captain. He was a mean ruthless bastard that repeatedly showed our men no mercy. I didn't show him any either. Every Red Coat I killed, every last unlucky soul, was more to avenge her death than for the country. I was no hero. High ideals and virtues motivate heroes. Rage and vengeance fueled me." Sam realized he sounded bitter, but he couldn't help it—he was bitter.

"Revenge is a frequent motivator for war. And in war, the line between revenge and justice has always been a fine one. Sometimes so fine it disappears for some men," Bear said. "For others, the line is always there."

Sam didn't say anything. He didn't have to.

They both knew what kind of man he was.

CHAPTER 8

An uncommonly colorful sunrise washed richly textured trees in burnt orange light and added a layer of warm tranquility to the morning. The walk with Bear did help to calm his nerves and Sam now ate his breakfast, away from the others, comfortably perched on an ancient oak's exposed root. He needed to think.

Resting comfortably was not something he did often. Acknowledged as the toughest of the five siblings, he was aware that his face suffered the effects of his many good fights. If there was a battle nearby, he made a point to be a part of it. The heat of those battles forged him into a man who longed for nothing more in life than defeating an enemy.

Until now. Was it possible that he could actually want something more for his life?

Deep in thought, the stunning sunrise went unnoticed by Sam. He drew his knife to cut his meat. The shiny blade caught the sun's rays and shades of crimson pulsed across its surface with every movement of his hand. Unable to control the willful war demons of his mind, the nearly red reflections evoked painful recollections of losing young friends and the vengeful spilling of his enemies' blood. His fellow soldiers often called him Bloody Hand—a name Sam abhorred, even as he recognized the terrible red stain of truth in it. As he and his knife seasoned, the blood they drew stained more Red Coats than he wanted to remember. More than he could forget, no matter how hard he tried, no matter how often he asked God for forgiveness after waking from his nightmares. The Revolutionary War—just like the knife—was long, brutal, and unforgiving.

His stomach soured, Sam tossed what remained of his breakfast, as those disturbing shadows of his past were quickly followed by memories of the reason he bought the knife to begin with. Sharing that memory with Bear earlier reminded him that the reason still existed. The traitor's whereabouts remained unknown to him. The blade had not yet claimed the man's life.

Until it did, he could not stop those shadows or the ache of a young heart broken long ago. He hoped coming to Kentucky would allow him to leave those haunting memories behind, but as much as he hated to admit it, they were still there—just as vivid and troubling as ever. He shrugged in resignation. There was no escaping his painful memories. He would bury them, as usual. Unfortunately, each time he did so, he seemed to bury a little bit of himself.

But he was here now and still hopeful that he could find a new beginning in Kentucky. He shook his head and tried to focus his thoughts on the scenic river instead. He needed to think about the future—not the past.

A new life on the frontier. The very thought excited him. A chance to be on the leading edge of the wilderness. He found it hard to believe a man would want to be anywhere else.

Before they left New Hampshire, he had ached for a challenge, something to test his courage—as though too much of it was building up inside of him. He enjoyed the challenge of getting here, and the journey certainly tried all of them. He and Stephen nearly lost their lives and the harsh reality of the frontier tragically took the lives of two of their family. One trial after another tested their courage and their strength.

The loss of family devastated him, and remembering, he swallowed the lump in his throat. But he had nearly relished the other difficult trials they had continuously faced. Unlike their overly cautious brother Edward, the only brother to remain behind in New Hampshire, Sam didn't hesitate to face life head on. A man shouldn't just want to live life, he should want life to truly live.

Would he need someone like Catherine to make that happen?

His heart said yes. Could he get his mind to agree?

&

"How old do ye figure that tree is?" Bear asked, walking up to Sam later that morning. "I bet even its branches are older than me self."

"Old as Methuselah I reckon. Nice of it to make me this chair," Sam said, tapping the huge root to empty the ash from his pipe. He often admired the 'furniture' of nature, finding a simple honest beauty in it more precious than the gilded and highly polished furniture of the wealthy. He also found more comfort on a carpet of pine needles and leaves than a finely woven woolen rug.

"I just saw Jane playing with the children like she was a kid again. She seems to be in much better spirits these days," Bear said.

"She is. Our journey was hard on Jane," he said. "I sure hope coming here was right for their family. I know it was right for me and for you. We were both restless back home. And we all believed leaving for Kentucky was the only way to keep Jane truly safe." He remembered how Bomazeen, a slave trader for the Algonquian tribes, nearly stole Jane and Martha. They all knew the devil would come back for her again and Stephen thought going to Kentucky was the best option for keeping her out of Bomazeen's nasty clutches. He had agreed with Stephen, but now, after all they endured getting here, he was having second thoughts. "But was coming here the right thing to do?"

Raising his thick coppery brows, Bear appeared surprised by the question.

Bear's answer surprised Sam even more.

"Maybe 'tis for God's sake. Maybe He has a purpose in their comin' here—in our comin'—only He knows. He puts these desires in our hearts. We can only try to answer them."

Sam exhaled slowly as he considered Bear's answer. As his breath faded away, so did his doubts. "You're a wise man Bear."

"Well, I do na know about that, but I do know I was na lettin' you and Stephen go trottin' off to some Kentucky paradise without me."

Sam chuckled. "Wouldn't think of it. Besides, I needed your help to keep Stephen and Jane under control. There's enough spirit in those two for fifty men and women."

"Aye, that's the truth. Remember their weddin'? The two of them danced us all into the ground. Then, just before they finally took off, ye and William tied that dead chicken to the back of their buggy and then let that skinny huntin' dog loose. He chased them for a half mile barkin' and yappin' before Stephen shot at it to scare it off," Bear chuckled.

"But instead, he shot the poor dog's tail clean off. That dog was dumb as a tick and always hungry. That's how we knew it would chase the chicken," Sam recalled, laughing. "And it had a yap so shrill it would drive a monk to swear."

"Every time I saw that dog with a wee stub for a tail, I would laugh."

"It was a month before Jane would speak to me again. When she finally forgave me, we laughed for an hour. She didn't care as much about the dog's tail, as she did that we killed the dang chicken. She was mighty fond of her chickens. She sure was glad when Kelly brought her flock along with her."

"Now and again I enjoy their wee eggs," Bear said. "But it takes a dozen or more to fill me up."

"I agree. We need some real food. Get on with hunting now. I'm guarding the camp. And for heaven's sake, try to shoot something big. I'm near starving."

"Aye, I'll be doin' just that, man. I'm sick of eatin' skinny rabbits and boney fish," Bear said, grabbing his rifle and powder horn, "and those damn wee eggs."

Sam watched Bear march away. He knew exactly what Bear had meant about talking to Catherine like a man does to a woman. He was wondering the same thing himself. He just didn't know what to do about it. And if he did figure that out, could he say anything?

He had not thought seriously about a woman for nearly twenty years. Just recently, all he could do was think about her. He woke up thinking about her and his last thoughts before going to sleep were of her. He was starting to dream about her too. Every time he reflected on her during the day, he felt guilty and foolish. And if his dreams at night got any more interesting, he'd start feeling guilty about those too.

You're acting like a besotted adolescent, he told himself as he stood to begin his morning walk around their camp. He wondered if Jane or Catherine could tell how he felt. Catherine had a way of looking at him so directly he could barely think. In fact, this morning he carefully avoided being around her at all.

As he patrolled, Sam scolded himself for his foolishness. He had no business even considering her. She's probably more interested in Bear or William anyway. They're both younger and longer on looks than he was. He was just an old soldier, nearly forty. She probably found his face frightening to even look at.

Sam resolved to put her out of his mind. But his resolution, like most resolutions, was short lived and lasted only until he reapproached their camp again—until he saw her.

CHAPTER 9

Catherine stood by the cook fire about to get herself a cup of coffee. Her long hair hung unbound. Rich shiny black waves tumbled carelessly over her shoulders and back. He had never seen her wear her hair that way. As she bent down to the pot hanging from a rod above the fire, her voluptuous cleavage revealed itself. Sam felt his eyes widen and a twitch in his loins at the beguiling sight.

She was a vision. He wanted to freeze this moment in time so he could just watch her. Mesmerized, he realized he had stopped breathing. He took a deep breath before he strode into camp, trying his best to appear nonchalant.

"Join me in a cup of coffee Captain?" she asked, giving him a luminous smile as soon as she saw him walk up. "Jane is down there at the creek with John and the children fishing for our midday meal. I would think they would have tired of fishing, and eating fish, by this time, but they still seem to be enjoying themselves. Stephen and William are nearby watching them. I just finished washing my hair. It's so thick it takes it forever to dry." She felt it for dampness. "Almost ready to braid."

Sam wished he could touch the dark shiny tresses as well. What would her hair smell like? "You shouldn't be here alone," he scolded, "especially with both Stephen and William down there."

"They are all just a stone's throw away and I've got my dagger and my rifle handy," she said. "Besides, I knew you were somewhere nearby standing watch. She ran her long fingers through her damp hair.

The motion caught Sam's eye and momentarily distracted him. He wondered how her hair would feel wrapped in his fingers. Silken. Soft. Smooth. He could almost feel it. The thought nearly unraveled his self-control. He swallowed hard to stop the alluring images filling his head.

"You seem a little on edge this morning, Captain," Catherine commented.

He stiffened at the question. "We must stay ever alert here. Danger has a way of surprising us, as you found out on the trail."

"I still can't believe William and Stephen went after those two murderers. But for my husband's sake, God rest his soul, and for Kelly's rescue, I'm glad they did."

Sam understood the reason William and Stephen had to go after the killers. He lived himself by the same code. Only for him, it wasn't so much a respect for the written law as the unwritten. Honorable men stand up for what is right and have the courage to do whatever is necessary to oppose wrong. Whatever and wherever. Good men don't shirk that responsibility no matter where they were. It was the law of their father and it would be the law of their sons.

Sam wondered if he would ever have a son. The unexpected thought surprised him.

He laid his rifle aside and she put a hot steaming cup in his hand, but she was warming more than his hands. Her nearness caused his senses to leap to life and a pleasurable heat pulsed through his body.

As she drew her own hand back, he got the faintest whiff of her fragrance. She smelled like lavender and maybe a trace of roses.

What was he doing? He'd never noticed a woman's perfume before. Good grief. What was happening to him? Sam tried to force his mind back to things that mattered. "Where did you get that dagger?"

"That's a long story." She sat down on a nearby trunk.

"I have the time. Can't do much but cool our heels here until we get those land grants."

She eyed the dagger pensively, and then looked up into a nearby Cypress tree. A Mockingbird filled the silence with a charming piece of music. She waited for the bird to finish the last note before she began. "My maternal grandmother was from a long line of nobility in England. She was quite a woman. My grandfather, also of noble birth, gave the blade to her as a wedding gift. It has her birthstone, the sapphire, on the hilt and his family crest at the top. She was so beautiful he knew other men would have difficulty resisting her. So, he gave her the dagger making her promise that she was to use it on any man who touched her with the intention of violating her honor. If she did not, he promised he would use it on her. I know that sounds harsh, but he was a harsh man. Noble and courageous, but war hardened him."

Sam could relate to the man. "Tell me more about him."

"It wasn't long before she was forced to keep her promise. She stabbed an Earl when he accosted her while my grandfather was on a hunting trip. The Earl lived but blamed her for the whole incident, saying she deliberately attacked and stabbed him in a fit of feminine rage because he would not accept *her* flirtations.

"Because of this insult, grandfather challenged the Earl to a duel. As soon as the Earl was well enough to participate, they arranged the duel. Grandfather was a master swordsman, and swiftly killed the Earl with his rapier. As you know, gentlemen consider duels an acceptable method of resolving disputes. But for grandfather, it was a matter of honor, not just a dispute.

"After that, things were never the same for them among the local nobility. There were always whispers behind my grandmother's back about what evil minds thought really happened. It made grandfather so angry. One day he told them all to go to the devil, moved his family to the colonies, and set up his law practice and a bank in Boston. So, in a way, this weapon is responsible for moving my family to the colonies.

"My grandmother gave the dagger to my mother as her wedding present, and keeping with the tradition, my mother, as a wedding gift, gave the dagger to me. And now, as you know, it saved not only my honor, but probably my life, out there in the middle of nowhere," she said, pointing toward the east where she and her husband were attacked.

Sam considered what it must have been like for her to have to kill one of the three men that murdered her husband and attempted to attack her. He was glad William and Stephen found and killed the other two, but he almost wished he could have carried out that justice himself. Not only were the men murderers, they were rapists. And he would have joined their pursuit of the outlaws if his healing broken ankle hadn't kept him from it. It had healed well, but was stiff on occasion.

"Did your mother have you make the same promise?" he asked, with a half grin tugging at his mouth.

"No. She knew me well enough to know I wouldn't hesitate to use it if I needed to. But she did insist on teaching me, as her mother taught her, how to use it. My brother and I would practice throwing our daggers for hours at a time."

Another one of those smiles spread across her lovely face. They were dangerous for a man who wanted nothing more to do with women. He could not help but be dazzled by them. They transformed her already comely countenance into something so radiant and stunning it stole his breath.

He sipped the coffee to make himself stop staring. "May I see it?"

Now her eyes smiled with a sensuous spark. "Only if you'll agree to let me see your knife," she bargained.

It was the first time any woman had ever asked to see his most cherished possession. Somehow, it didn't surprise him that she would want to examine it. "Of course," he said, carefully handing his blade to her and then taking her dagger. Her nearness assaulted his senses, making every quickening heartbeat drum inside his chest.

As he willed his heart to calm, he studied the extraordinary blade. The workmanship was exquisite. The hilt, cut from a semi-precious stone, displayed chiseled in scrolls and inlayed silver fittings. Two diminutive horse's heads pointing in opposite directions formed the hand guard. Each horse had eyes made from tiny sapphires and bridles gilded with gold. The artistic armorer decorated the silver scabbard by chiseling each side with a magnificent cross. "It's remarkable. I've never seen anything quite like it." He turned it over and the crest's sapphire winked up at him. "This stone is nearly as…blue as your eyes." He almost said as beautiful as your eyes, but stopped himself just in time. That was close.

"Thank you, Captain. Your knife looks nearly as fierce as you do," she said, appraising the weapon. "This is a fine-looking handle. Did you make it yourself?"

"Yes, but that's an even longer story. Maybe I'll tell it to you sometime," he said, looking away. This was not the time to pursue that story again. He already regretted sharing it with Bear. He should have kept it buried forever.

"Do you prefer the knife to your pistol?" she asked instead.

"Yes, in most situations. It is always accurate, doesn't require dry powder or loading. It's quiet when there's a need for stealth, and it's unaffected by water if I need to swim a river or I'm caught in a storm." The knife also served him in many other ways. He used it to skin and dress game, eat with, mend saddles and harnesses, cauterize wounds—often his own, and on one occasion to dig a grave for a fallen comrade.

"I'm sure you'll face all those situations and more in Kentucky. You're like a knight clad in buckskin Captain. Something tells me you will face them without fear."

"Not so. Even noble knights felt fear. But a brave man must choose whether fear will make him strong or weak. Armor or buckskin, a man is only as strong as the courage of his heart."

Suddenly, those words held new meaning for him. Would his heart ever again be strong enough for love? Love takes courage. He'd learned that long ago. He clenched his fists, angry with himself. He was letting fear make him weak. He was afraid of the future because of the pain of the past. He was a coward when it came to love. A damn coward. Pure and simple.

He turned his attention back to studying the dagger, not wanting her to see his face.

Of all the failings a man could have, he disliked cowards the most. He called such men parasites who freeloaded off the courage of others. He scorned cowards more than an enemy. At least an enemy fought for his beliefs or his own motives. Like clouds without rain, cowards were men with vaporous souls. During the war, men who showed even a tendency toward cowardice did not last long under his command. They got mess duty or became someone else's problem. He did not allow cowards to put the lives of brave men at peril. Warfare has rules.

But so does life. He didn't like feeling like a coward. Could he muster enough courage to love someone again?

Sam offered the dagger back to her and took his knife. He studied the blade's edge for a moment, still lost in thought. The war finally ended. His trust in the lessons of war and his big knife did not. Firearms were optional. The knife was not. It was the one thing in his life that never disappointed him. More than once, wrapped in the hands of a soldier's courage, the blade had saved his soul, even as it claimed the souls of others. For pistols held only one shot, and a hatchet, once buried deep in an enemy, took precious seconds to withdraw. But the knife was quick and, when needed, savage.

Like other tested soldiers, he discovered that when two men battle, when one must live and one must die, the victor is often the most savage. People like to think that victory goes to the most virtuous—but virtue often stands on both sides of a war. And even an enemy who holds no virtue at all can still kill you.

But Sam didn't want to think about war now. Just the opposite. He sheathed his knife and glanced up.

She was staring at him. This time, he held her gaze—keeping his eyes locked on hers. They gleamed with an entrancing inner light and seemed to nourish some remote part of his soul. He drank it in, like a fine aged wine or smooth whiskey, savoring it, letting it reach his senses and linger. Again, he longed to smell and touch her freshly washed hair. He wanted to bury his hands in her tresses as he kissed those crimson lips.

She gave him a half-grin that seemed to convey some secret knowledge.

*

"You said courage comes from the heart. But, where does that courage come from?" Catherine asked.

"Courage comes from recognizing and challenging danger. Fear comes from turning your back on threats and running from them."

Her mind raced, searching for understanding. What was going on in that enigmatic mind of his? Was he talking about Kentucky or something else? Did he sense peril now? "Are you concerned about dangers here, Captain?"

"Danger is a part of life, the part that keeps us sharp. You can't escape it. As I once told my brothers, danger has a way of finding us no matter our place or how many precautions we take. The important thing is to stay ever alert and to be prepared to respond appropriately."

"But, what if you don't?"

His eyes seemed to cloud with a hidden worry. "All life involves what ifs. What ifs can smother your life in the dust of doubt."

Again, his voice, rich and deep, stirred something within her. It was the type that compels others to listen. They also listened, she thought, because the Captain could parry with words nearly as skillfully as with his knife.

She wanted to listen to him too. But he wasn't saying what she wanted to hear. She needed him to say that he wanted her to stay in Kentucky. That he could find enough courage to see if the two of them could have a future here. What if he would never be able to? Maybe she should just give up.

No, she wouldn't let doubts smother her newfound dream. She would be patient.

Sam yanked out his knife again and slowly turned the blade, a pensive look on his face. The cutting edge glistened menacingly, evidence of its readiness. "Life is much like this knife. If it's rusty and dull, *or* if you're afraid to use it, it's nearly worthless. Sharp, in the hands of a man of courage, it can fight for life. Conquer life's enemies." Sam paused. A muscle on his jaw quivered before he said, "I, for one, do *not* intend to become useless and dull."

Without warning, Sam threw his knife. Her eyes followed the blade's path across the campsite. It slashed through the air in the flicker of a second. Yet time suspended, froze with her heart, so hard was her concentration on the blade. The knife pierced a nearby tree, ignoring the strength of the big oak.

The air vibrated with the thud of its impact. With the sound of its power.

Then, she heard only silence, except for the sound of Sam's words in her head. And, the red-hot fire changing dead wood to glowing embers.

She plucked her dagger from its sheath and threw it. It landed nearly adjacent to Sam's knife. "Neither do I," she said.

☙

Sam could not believe his eyes. He stared at her dagger and his blade imbedded in the tree side by side. Yes, danger has a way of finding us no matter our place. She was dangerous and he recognized it. That knowledge turned and twisted inside his brain. It was pointless to deny his attraction to her. He needed to respond appropriately.

If he didn't, he just might become useless and dull.

Without taking his eyes off their blades he asked, "What are your plans Catherine?"

"I hesitate to continue to impose on your family, another mouth to feed, and another female to protect. You didn't ask for that burden and I won't impose on your family's hospitality. It's just that I have no one in Kentucky and with the only inn in Boonesborough full, I see no other options for now. I should return to Boston. But, after traveling for so long, I don't want to leave just yet."

He turned to face her. "From what I've seen, you've been more of a help than a burden. As far as protecting you, you're obviously quite capable of protecting yourself. All of us depend upon one another for strength against our enemies. There's strength in numbers. You would add to that strength, not detract from it. I can speak for the others. You're welcome to stay with us as long as you need. You can write to your family and let them know what has happened. They can contact our brother Edward in New Hampshire and he can offer proof of our family's good reputation."

"What about Stephen? He may not agree that it's the right thing to do."

"Stephen will agree with me." At least Sam hoped he would.

"I'm still not sure Captain. Living in Kentucky with your husband is one thing. Staying with a group of men—four of whom are unmarried—that I have known for only a few weeks is quite another. What will people in Boston think? What about preserving my reputation?"

"Reputations are made on the frontier, not preserved. Sometimes life forces a person to live by new rules. Life can be uncivilized and unpredictable. You've learned that already as much as anybody. We have to adapt—not live by rules that fit another place and another way of life."

"It's all so bloody confusing."

"It's simple really. It comes down to this. Do you want to live in Kentucky in this virgin wilderness? Are you suited to life in the west? Or, would you be more at home among polite society in Boston. If it's the frontier, it's time to make your own rules, your own life."

"I've never thought about it quite like that. I've always followed the rules of civil society. I just did what my father and husband wanted me to do—what they expected of me. They were my guardians and made every major decision for me. I never felt any control over my own future. At least....not until...this very moment." She said the words slowly and deliberately, as if their meaning sunk in only as she spoke them aloud.

"That's what the wilderness is all about. Making your own destiny. And living it. Truly living it. That's why I wanted to come here. I needed to feel alive again. And I do here. Don't you feel it too? It's almost an awakening. Here you don't just live life, you have life to live."

"Life to live. I like the sound of that."

So did he, especially when she said it.

CHAPTER 10

Sam hiked through the woods, several miles from their campsite, searching for small game. Except for Bear, he was the best hunter among their group and could usually guarantee fresh meat for their dinners. He admired the abundant red maple, walnut, hickory, cottonwood, and oak trees that crowded between pines for their place in the dense forest, a storehouse of nature for heavy lumber. Soon these impressive trees might become homes, stores, boats, wagons, furniture, and even weapons, like the rifle he carried.

As he entered a clearing, he peered up. A bald eagle soared overhead, its immense brown wings spread wide, stroking the air with graceful glides. The eagle whistled a series of high-pitched notes. He thought the eerie call of the regal bird unlike any other in nature. He hoped the eagle would have a successful hunt today as well.

Sam returned to scanning around him, seeking signs of the slightest movement. He stopped abruptly. An overturned and abandoned kettle lay across the path. He glanced around, found a moldy and shredded woman's shawl, and then spotted a bright spot among decaying leaves. An embroidered child's bonnet. He bent over to pick it up and slowly ran his finger across the faded fabric. A family would only give up these precious items for one reason. Indians.

Sam's gut wretched as he imagined the horror the head of this family must have experienced as natives stole his wife and slaughtered his child before his eyes. Likely, the Indians then tortured the man. Now nothing remained of their existence here, except these few rotting clues. These poor folks never got the chance to be a part of the conquest of the wilderness. The wilderness conquered them.

His hands grew damp and his stomach knotted. A disturbing cold crept through him and he tried to push it back into the dark where it belonged. He tossed the bonnet back into the brush. "Not me. No, never again. Hell no. Once was enough," he whispered to no one but himself.

He should just acquire a small parcel of land, he decided as he swiftly resumed walking. Just enough for a cozy cabin tucked into the woods. He only needed a shelter. Just a place to store some of his things. He did *not* need a family.

He swallowed what felt like a pang of regret, blew out a slow breath, and continued quietly searching the forest. It smelled of both fresh and rotting wood. A medley of life and death, each fighting for a place. But life always managed to struggle to the surface.

It was time for him to let life surface in his own life.

He would find out what this new state of Kentucky looked like from top to bottom. That's what it means to truly live. Finding places you have never seen before. Here there were places no one had ever seen before. That made it all the better.

The thought of riding his horse all through Kentucky seemed appealing too. His previous mounts never managed to earn his admiration or affection. But Alex's spirit seemed an excellent match for his own temperament. Sam smiled as he noticed that the handsome buckskin's coat was the same shade as the buckskins he wore. And the horse's mane and tail were almost an exact match to Sam's dark hair. He laughed. They were nearly a matched pair!

As far as making a living, he had been thinking that there would be a great demand for fast horses in the west, where a man's horse could make the difference between life and death. In the wild, the horse was a valued intermediary between man and nature. Good trail horses needed both speed and stamina and he thought both were possible with the right breeding. The possibility of raising horses bred to be both strong and fast was an interesting proposition. He'd ponder that further in the future, he decided.

As beams of sunlight fell on the woods, the stronger trees seemed to call to Sam, wanting him to transform them into a cozy home. He could almost see the welcoming structure. The sensation shocked him. He had never considered building a home before. Back in New Hampshire, someone who had gone west abandoned an old cabin and he promptly claimed it purely because it suited his minimal needs—a place to store his things and find shelter during the harshest weather. He made no improvements to it during the infrequent times he actually resided there. He spent most of his days and nights on one trail or another anyway. But now, as he ambled through the timber, the thought of building a home settled comfortably in his mind, surprising him.

If fate had been different, he might have someone he loved to build a home for. But she left long ago for heaven and he would probably never see her again. Even though he counted himself a believer, Sam doubted whether a man like him could ever be considered a fitting resident for heaven. There must be some other place for old warriors like him.

So why did he find himself thinking about building a home? He liked nothing better than this—exploring the wilderness. He enjoyed living free—not confined to the boundaries of four walls. And he wanted to keep it that way.

He heard a faint rustle of leaves. A rabbit with large hind feet, long ears, and a short fluffy white tail scurried across the path up ahead. His knife left his hand in the same moment. The blade instantly hit the animal, penning it to the leaves beneath it. He quickly withdrew his knife and then stuffed the fat bundle of gray-brown fur into his haversack hanging across his back.

One down, four or five to go. Acquiring enough food for all eleven of their group posed a challenge. It was one reason he usually wore tall leather moccasins rather than leather boots. The softer leather allowed him to make less noise as he walked, lessening the chances of scaring game away.

But it took more than being quiet to be a good hunter. Keeping his eyes open for hidden dangers, he would regularly stop, listen, and look. Some hunters made the mistake of walking heedlessly, as if they were out for an afternoon stroll. A good hunter needed to use all his senses because animals were better than humans at remaining unseen.

He considered the task of hunting more recreation than chore, a chance to get away by himself and think. Today he found himself thinking about his own future for a change. He had committed himself to helping Stephen and the others reach these rich lands opening up in Kentucky. But now that they were here, land seemed important to him too. With his own land, a man can be free. Free to live, as he wanted, on his own place, in his own way.

Owning land was something Sam never considered before. But now he found the idea intriguing. He had to admit that he actually envied Stephen and Jane for having another child on the way. Maybe that's what he was missing. Maybe that's what was making him think about a home and land for the first time.

Sam adored his nephew and nieces. On their journey, he grew even fonder of them, especially Little John. The first Wyllie son to be born to the five brothers, Little John held a special place in his heart. Sometimes, when he thought about the boy, as he was now, he regretted not having a son of his own, a family to come home to. For most of his life, he lived the life of a soldier—wedded only to his country. But a country didn't warm your bed at night or run in to hug you in the morning. A country can respect its soldiers and honor its heroes, but it can't love them. Countries give their heroes metals, not a family, not warmth, not love.

As he walked further, he realized that only a few had dared to venture out into these woods—to set their eyes on what he saw now—a virgin forest filled with chirping songbirds sprinkled among a colorful pageant of blooming dogwoods, redbud trees, lush green ferns, meandering vines, and sweet-smelling wildflowers.

Strange, earlier, he smelt only wood. But here, the air smelled like life itself. He inhaled the fresh fragrance deeply and it seemed to settle him.

Then he began a stealth walk ahead. He needed to focus on finding food or they would all be sleeping with growling stomachs. The gobble of wild turkeys warbled up from deep in the woods.

After a couple hours, Sam turned back toward camp with his haversack full of plump rabbits and a wild turkey slung over his shoulder. He would cut the breast out of the turkey and let Jane fry it up in a pan with her special seasoning. Then he would skin the rabbits, skewer the meat on a rod, and set them to roast over the fire until they sizzled and their delicious aroma filled their camp. The thought made his mouth water.

But as he hiked, something kept itching at his mind, distracting him. He just wanted to reach in and scratch it—to stop it from irritating him further. What the heck was it?

Then he knew. It wasn't what, it was who—Catherine.

He imagined her figure, curving and regal, coming out the front door, and standing on a large porch of a home that he built. In his mind, he saw her beautiful smile as he approached from nearby timbers. Then, he pictured a little child peeking out from behind her skirts, and the boy smiled too and then started running toward him.

He had to admit, his heart warmed at the thought.

હ

That evening, Catherine didn't feel the least bit sleepy. She walked towards the creek bank, until she spotted Bear cleaning animal skins.

Sam stood nearby, grooming Alex, trying to comb knots out of the horse's long black mane.

This could be interesting. She marched straight to Bear.

"Would you be kind enough to sharpen my blade Bear?" she asked, extending her hand and the dagger.

"Of course I will, lass." Bear wiped his hands on a rag and then put his big palm under the hand that held the dagger. He slowly took the blade with his other hand, letting his hands linger longer than necessary.

As Bear touched her and met her eyes, she felt nothing, only the rough texture of his strong hands. She remembered feeling a tremble inside her when Sam made only the slightest contact with her hand when she passed her treasured blade to him.

Bear began to sharpen the blade with his whetstone. She glanced around to be certain Sam stood close enough to hear them. Good, he was.

She saw Sam take a glance back at her. His expression grew somber. Keenly aware of his scrutiny, she felt her face flush as he looked at her enigmatically. What didn't he understand? If he wasn't going to pay attention to her, then what did he expect?

"Bear, you're so skillful at handling a knife," she said, fluttering her eyelashes at Bear.

Bear smiled broadly at the compliment.

"Will you show me how to sharpen it?" She knew full well how to sharpen her dagger, but decided something might be gained by Bear's lesson. That something had little to do with a sharp blade.

"Aye. Have a seat here next to me and I'll show ye," Bear said, moving over on the fallen tree trunk that served as his bench.

She sat as close to the giant of a man as possible, tucking her skirts beneath her.

"Hold the whetstone like this," Bear said, demonstrating, and then putting the stone in her hand.

Her long braid fell over her shoulder and touched the stone.

"We canna have your lovely hair in the way now can we," Bear said, gently pushing her braid behind her back. She felt Bear's hand rest on her back for a moment.

Catherine glanced up just in time to see that Sam did not miss

Bear's gesture. It had just the effect on Sam she'd hoped. His lips pinched together and eyes narrowed, he looked like he wanted to give Bear a lesson in the use of a knife. With a black look over his shoulder toward Bear, Sam shifted to the rear of the horse, putting his back to them, and began raking the comb through the gelding's tail with a vengeance.

Enjoying this, she could not help smiling to herself. After all, the Captain deserved it. His cool, aloof manner irked her. If he'd been more attentive, she wouldn't have to play these silly games. It was his own fault. First, he suggests that she stay in Kentucky. Then, when she did, he pointedly ignored her.

She would make him travel a lot further than the thousand miles from New Hampshire to Kentucky. She'd make him journey from a cold heart to love. No matter how long it took, she'd keep trying, she decided. A man like Sam would be worth every mile of effort. Eventually, he'd have to stop running, and when he did, she suspected he'd grab love with a passion as strong as he was.

She respected Sam's strength. It wasn't just the obvious physical strength reflected in his height, broad shoulders and well-muscled arms. She admired the strength of his character. A character made rich and deep by the difficult life he'd led—the battles he fought, the enemies he'd defeated, and the challenges hurled at him by the dark side of nature. She could tell the Captain not only faced life's challenges, he actually welcomed them with a confidence born of courage.

She wondered how he would handle this new challenge.

"Aye, that's the way. Ye've got the hang of it now," Bear said. "Ye'll be able to keep a fine edge on any blade."

This playful flirtation would hopefully get Sam's attention without hurting Bear. She liked Bear well enough, thought a lot of him. She even found him more entertaining than Sam. But Bear didn't make her insides tingle as if she'd swallowed a dozen butterflies. He didn't make her think about him the minute she woke up. He didn't make her want to find ways to be near him. But Sam did that and more to her. When she tried to figure out why he affected her so, she had a hard time narrowing it down.

His observant eyes captivated her—their intensity seemed to reach all the way to her soul. His sensuous voice warmed her as no one else's ever did and gave her comfort and a sense of security. It carried a unique force and she felt safe just hearing it. And, his smile, though rare, made her happy. His keen mind made her want to talk to him for hours about anything and everything. But perhaps more than anything, in his chest beat the heart of a lion of a man. Sam exuded courage and self-assurance. That trait made him a natural leader. And she now knew she would go anywhere with him. All he had to do was ask.

This had to be what love felt like. She was sure of it. What else could seize your heart and mind with such boldness?

Nevertheless, with a man like Sam, she would have to wait until he too recognized love.

She found it difficult to concentrate on the sharpening lesson. "Perhaps you should finish it for me," she told Bear. "I know you can put a fine edge on it."

Bear took the knife back into his hands and she gazed over at Sam. She wanted to tell the Captain how much she had learned since she left Boston. There, her biggest concerns were the latest fashions and choosing what attire she should wear to the next social function. She understood how to live blissfully in highborn society, but she had known next to nothing about how to survive in the rest of the world.

But that pampered young lady no longer existed. She had changed. She was not the same weak-willed woman that left Boston. She would never be the same. She could take care of herself. She did not need to return to Boston just to let her father tell her what she should do. She could make her own plans. Determine her own future. And that meant staying here and learning even more—about life, about love. About Sam.

Now, she could answer the question that Sam asked her some time ago. Yes, she was suited for life in the west. And she hoped that life could include him. But even if it didn't, she could persevere.

Suddenly, she heard Bear's voice and wondered how long she had been thinking.

"It's sharp enough now to peel a grape without losin' a drop of nectar," Bear said, his face beaming as he held the dagger up for her inspection.

She laughed and stood. "That could come in handy. A woman never knows when she might need an edge like that. My thanks, Sir."

"It was my pleasure, sweet lass."

Catherine felt Bear's admiring eyes follow her as she strolled away. But as she glanced back, the Captain's eyes focused only on his horse.

Bloody hell.

߷

"What the blazes were you doing?" Sam demanded, as he marched up to Bear.

"Sharpening the lady's wee knife," Bear said. "Sure is a pretty thing."

Sam recognized that Bear referred to Catherine, not her dagger. His stared, trying to force Bear to be less evasive.

"I've told ye before how I feel about her. She's as bonnie a lass as there ever was."

"And I've told you before, you're acting the fool. She is too fresh a widow. Stay away from her."

"This is na the army. And ye'll na be issuin' any orders here, Captain."

"Order or not, it's how it's going to be."

"Ye're daft. Ye've gone and left your wits out there in the forest somewhere."

"This is no joke," he said, steeling his voice. He felt sweat dampening his face and his hands shook. Unable to control his growing anger, he grabbed Bear by the shirt under his neck and yanked the giant's face directly in front of him. "I don't know if I'm about to whip you, or you're about to whip me. Either way, I'm not going to like it."

That was the honest truth. He thought of Bear as a brother and hated the prospect of fighting him, but he would if Bear persisted in showing interest in Catherine.

Bear stared wide-eyed back at him. His face only inches away from Sam's, Bear raised his coppery eyebrows and his scowl turned a shade redder than his hair. "I guess you did na see the way Catherine looked at me just now? Or notice that she came to see me, not you."

"I saw more than enough," he growled, releasing Bear's shirt. "As I said, stay away from her."

"Don't ye think the lass can decide for herself?"

"She most certainly can. But she's not ready to decide. Her husband died but a few short months ago."

Bear's eyes peered into his. "It's clear ye have feelings for the lass. But maybe it's ye who is not ready."

Sam recognized truth when he heard it. And the harder he struggled to ignore the truth the more it persisted. He glanced away, in the direction she had walked. "We'll talk of this later."

"Nay, Captain. There is much of which we can talk, but I doubt we can talk of Catherine."

"Would you rather fight?" Sam snarled.

"She is a woman worth fightin' for, to be sure. But the decision is hers not ours."

"You'll not be talking to her about this," he said in a tone he hoped left no room for debate. "She's not ready to choose."

"Again, that would be the lass' decision."

It vexed him to admit it, but Bear was right.

CHAPTER 11

"The thing that bothers me is why Adams felt he could make a trip to Kentucky on his own. Was he in a hurry to leave for some reason? And why would he take a fine lady like Catherine into the wilderness with only one man to protect her?" William asked.

"Indeed," Stephen said. "That foolish decision cost him his life and nearly got her killed."

"It doesn't make sense," William said. "He must have had a compelling reason."

"She told Jane that Adams was after a prime site of land in Kentucky. That could compel a man to leave in haste," Stephen suggested. "Still it's odd that Adams and Catherine left Boston on their own, without the protection of traveling with others."

Sam stepped up closer to the two.

"Some men think with their cocks," William said, "makes them overconfident, as well as stupid."

Stephen shook his head agreeing. "Perhaps Adams was just arrogant enough to think he could protect her."

"Does it matter? The man's dead," Sam said. His tone sounded hotter than normal even to him. "Let the poor man rest in peace."

"Don't get your dander up, I just wondered what kind of man Adams was since Catherine seems to have joined with us more than temporarily," William tried to explain.

"Her late husband's plans and character are none of our concern," Sam said vehemently.

"But what about Catherine's..." William started to say.

Sam interrupted. "Now that we're here, she can make her own plans."

"You're a little testy this evening don't you think?" William asked.

Truth was that after his near fight with Bear, he was cross, and as jumpy as a drop of water on a hot skillet. But he was not about to admit to it. "Think so?" he snarled.

"Yes, I most certainly do," William said, cocking an eyebrow at him.

"What did you mean 'make her own plans'?" Stephen asked, keeping his voice low.

"Just that. She has a right to make her own decisions," Sam said, realizing that he just echoed what Bear had said earlier. Damn. He took one long look in Catherine's direction. She was saying goodnight to Jane and the girls. "She may stay or arrange to return to her family. None of it is our concern."

"But..." Stephen and William both said at once.

"It's getting late. I'm going to bed," he said, hopefully dismissing them and the topic.

Stephen and William stared at each other, and then back at him. Both of them were now smiling.

He grumbled as he strode swiftly away to retrieve his pallet.

❧

Still awake after an hour or more, Sam decided it would be a very long night.

Not because the ground seemed especially hard and damp tonight. Sam was used to sleeping on the trail. In fact, he preferred a carpet of leaves and grass to a fancy bed. The night would be long because Catherine had awakened emotions in him he assumed long dead. Now they were alive again, tormenting him.

Very alive if truth be told. And he didn't like it.

Perhaps these thoughts were just lust, something he could overcome in time. Even as he thought it, he realized it was a lie. These feelings ran deeper. They were more than a mere physical hunger and an ache in his manhood. His very soul seemed to ache as well. Just being near her made all his defenses fade away like morning fog in the face of a brilliant sun.

He rolled onto his side, remembering that long ago he decided he was a man better off single, a warrior at heart, born for life in the wild—not the tame life of a married man.

He could try to avoid her, but since they were sharing the same camp, that was impossible. Even the impenetrable shield he built around his heart seemed a weak defense. There was no way to avoid those deep penetrating blue eyes, which appeared to reflect a spirit akin to his. And those sensuous lips, the color of a crimson rose. They looked as if they were begging him to kiss them. Every time she spoke, he found himself studying her mouth, wanting to cover her lips with his.

He remembered when she had let him hold her dagger. Imagine, a woman who treasured a knife. That in itself sent bolts of desire surging through his veins. He knew then that they were cut from the same cloth.

And just holding something that she cherished seemed important to him for some reason.

Had he been waiting all this time for her? Would she even consider him? She was cordial and friendly, but she also was towards the other men. Especially Bear. He growled to himself.

No, he couldn't risk losing another woman. If Catherine didn't have feelings for him, he would lose twice. No, he would not let himself feel the agony of loss again. Once was more than enough. He already decided that, *damn it*, when he was hunting. But, as he had hiked through the forest, he had also thought about a home and pictured her there on the front porch, looking so welcoming.

And now, he was wide awake churning it up all over again.

He rolled onto his back trying to make his mind stop racing. He covered his eyes with his arm attempting to stop the images. But, his mind overflowed with conflicting emotions, like a river out of its banks, his thoughts spread where they didn't belong. He pulled his light blanket over his head as if to hide from his feelings, but they refused to release their hold on his body. He pictured her sleeping in her wagon, as he had many nights before. Did she sleep peacefully or was she was as miserable and tormented as he?

He also wondered how her bare body would feel lying next to his, his arms around her, his face buried in that silken mass of black hair, his hands on her shapely hips that tapered to long straight legs. What would those legs feel like wrapped around him? Could it possibly be as pleasant as he imagined?

Damn. It could. He was sure of it.

He rolled to his other side, finding it hard to get comfortable.

His confused mind continued its struggle through a labyrinth. Only a female could make a man's mind take so many convoluted twists and turns. How in damnation was he going to get out of this maze? He had found himself in many a difficult situation in the past and he always managed to find a way out.

Sam listened. A myriad of eerie sounds—a concert for the brave—filled the cool night air. The creatures of the night seemed as uneasy as he was. In the distance, coyotes yapped in grouped frenzy as they chased some poor doomed creature. There were probably only a half dozen, but they sounded more like sixty than six. He could never figure out exactly why. Maybe the thrill of the hunt magnified their rapid shrill yelps. Maybe the coyotes wanted their prey to give up in despair. He had no doubt that they often did, just like men.

He was running from something too. But he knew that wasn't like him. He always faced life's challenges head on, no matter how difficult. He never ran from danger and he never gave up. He welcomed a good fight.

He rubbed his gritty eyes, torn by conflicting emotions and sick of the struggle within him.

A few yards away, Bear started to snore like a real hibernating bear. He didn't want to fight Bear. The only person he really needed to fight was himself.

But it's difficult battling with yourself. Perhaps the hardest battle of all.

He started to roll over again, then decided getting any sleep was hopeless.

He stood and marched out into the night to wage war with his heart.

CHAPTER 12

The next morning, Sam, Stephen and Bear located the office of Tom Wolf. The small but neat room contained a desk, old law books, ledgers, and an assortment of maps and smelled of fresh tobacco and old pipe smoke. A rifle, powder horn, and saddlebag hung by the door, from a massive buck antler nailed to the log wall.

"I share this humble office with the surveyor, but fortunately, he's gone most of the time," Wolf said, grinning as he shook their hands. "Hope you had a chance to rest up from your long journey." He lit an oil lamp to replace the light lost to the cloudy sky.

"We did," Sam said, sitting down on the only chair other than Wolf's. Constructed of rough hickory with a deerskin seat, it felt surprisingly comfortable despite its crudeness.

"Where's that entertaining brother of yours William?" Wolf asked.

"He went over to the Fort to meet some of the local militia and the men on duty there," Sam explained.

"How can I help you gentlemen today?" Wolf asked, looking

from one to the other.

Stephen spoke first. "As you know, Sir, we traveled a fair distance for the settlement opportunities available here in Kentucky. The Land Office is still closed but we understand that it will open tomorrow. We heard you were a man who might know where good land is still available and have advice we could trust. If you are agreeable, we hoped to get your counsel before we went to the Land Office."

"My apologies," Wolf said, "for not being able to meet with you sooner. I was away visiting my son and his wife. I am now at your service, Sirs."

"We are indebted to you, Sir," Stephen said. "I'm looking for quality pasture land suitable for cattle."

"Stephen was the best breeder of cattle in the northern colonies," Bear bragged, "he just did na have enough good pasture and the harsh winters there made it hard to keep livestock alive, especially their wee calves. Wait till ye see the herd he'll raise up here with all that fine blue Kentucky grass. In no time, he'll likely be feeding beef to half the state."

Sam thought Bear was right. The new state's exploding population would need food—beef Stephen wanted to raise. Stephen planned to buy up all the cattle he could find, save every heifer born and sell off the bull calves. If he could start with ten cows, he'd have fifteen or so after the first year; more than twenty in another year; and at least thirty five by the next. With the thick grass growing here, it wouldn't take long for Stephen to build a thriving herd.

"I'll make application for a bounty grant tomorrow," Sam said.

"The Captain's a hero of the revolution," Bear told him, "that's why they made him a Captain. He's also a mapmaker and guide."

"I'm no hero," he said, turning scolding eyes on Bear.

"What about you, Sir?" Mr. Wolf asked Bear.

"Well, I'm more inclined toward huntin' and trappin' than farmin', so I'll be lookin' for land suitable for huntin'," Bear said. "John, who you met when we arrived, is guardin' our camp and the women just now. John and William both plan to live here in town. John's an accomplished architect and builder and William was our town Sheriff back home and is nearly a lawyer too. Been studyin' the law for some time."

Sam eyed Bear. He never realized how proud Bear was of his adopted family. They were all proud of him as well. He was literally and figuratively a giant among men—the kind of friend one finds only once in a lifetime. Bear hadn't changed much over the course of their journey, still the steadfast friend he always was. He wondered if Bear realized, after all they'd been through, what he had learned. That they were truly brothers. That they were family. He resolved not to let Catherine come between them again.

"This town could use an architect with all the buildings going up. Moreover, we certainly need knowledgeable men of the law; all we have now is a young constable, who lacks experience. Not sure how much it pays though. Since Colonel Boone left, things have come apart at the seams a little."

That worried Sam. Frontier towns without the benefit of strong men of the law or the military were breeding grounds for mayhem. Without the influence a man like Colonel Boone, the town could quickly deteriorate into lawless anarchy.

"Looks like between the lot of you, you'll be helping Kentucky to grow. Our new state needs more men such as yourselves. So many of our colonists lack education and resources. I'll help in any way that I can," Mr. Wolf offered graciously. "First let me describe how new settlers acquire land."

He folded his hands neatly in front of him on the slab table and cleared his throat. "The first thing you must do is secure a receipt from the State Treasurer in Frankfort, which in turn you will take to the Land Office within the county where the land you desire is located. The county will issue a warrant. The warrant will authorize you to locate and survey a certain acreage. By the way, these county warrants may be traded, sold, reassigned, in whole or in part, anytime during the process. After the warrant is completed, you must return it to the Land Office for entry in the county surveyor's book. The Land Commissioner will register the warrant and record your intention to file for a patent. These entries are not binding and may be altered or withdrawn. Next, an actual field survey must be completed describing the metes and bounds. If there are no problems, and there often are, a Governor's Grant is issued, usually within six months. This finalizes the patent process and conveys title."

"Six months!" Bear and Stephen said in unison.

"In total, more like a year," Sam said, disgusted. "How can we get homes built before winter?"

"I don't make the rules gentlemen; I'm just here to sell land. You'll have to argue with the Kentucky General Assembly and the Land Office about the merits of the system, although I admit, it does pose difficulties for those who need land quickly."

While Wolf spoke, Sam wandered over to the crude fireplace, impatient with Kentucky's bureaucracy. A shelf over the stone fireplace held several books. He noted among them the Bible, an almanac, The Pilgrim's Progress, and Shakespeare. The playwright's book seemed out of place in this wilderness town. Shakespeare was his mother's favorite writer. On winter evenings when the snows were deep, she would read passages aloud to her sons, in her nearly musical voice. Sometimes she was so animated it was more like watching the plays rather than just listening to them. He grinned at the pleasant memory and picked up the volume. As he flipped through the pages, he wondered what verses Shakespeare would have written about Kentucky, this 'Land of Tomorrow.' Undoubtedly, this remarkable land would have inspired the poet. It almost seemed as if it had. Here, men clashed with both nature and natives and definitely suffered 'the slings and arrows of outrageous fortune.' He feared that the 'Dark and Bloody Ground,' as some called Kentucky, would require their taking 'arms against a sea of troubles.' Had those troubles already begun? Would they be able to, as Shakespeare wrote, 'by opposing end them'?

"Do you enjoy Shakespeare, Captain Wyllie? Wolf asked.

"It's been an exceedingly long time since I have," Sam answered.

"Then you must borrow my book sometime," Wolf suggested.

"What do most folks do then?" Bear asked. "Sounds like yer land system will keep lawyers busy for many moons but it will na put land in the hands of folks that need it for some time."

"You may buy land that someone else received as a patent. These are simply a county responsibility and are known as a 'deed.' These are much easier to come by," Wolf explained.

"But that means buying the land, not receiving a grant," Stephen said.

"Yes, that's right. Land sells for between a dollar and two

dollars and acre this way—the better the pasture land the more it costs."

"Two dollars, that's outrageous," Stephen bellowed.

Sam stepped to the window. As the others talked, he found himself thinking about Catherine. He wondered again, what it would feel like to hold her. Sometime around midnight, when he was finally able to fall sleep, he dreamt of her. Every time she reached for him in the dream, he stepped away before she touched him. And every time he did, he grew more annoyed and disgusted with himself.

Scowling, he tried to push thoughts of her from his mind. He turned around and did his best to concentrate on the conversation going on behind him. But after just a minute or two, he decided he would leave the tedious details of the land process to Stephen. Stephen had more patience than he did. He turned back to the window.

He noted the sky clouding up even more than when they arrived. Might have a thunderstorm tonight. Then he noticed them.

The same scruffy bunch of hunters they'd encountered before were waiting across the street. Their vulgar leader seemed to be eyeing Sam's horse, tied just outside Wolf's office.

His eyes narrowed as he studied the big man. Wariness crossed his mind before he turned back toward the others.

"Time to go," he said.

CHAPTER 13

"Wait, just a moment longer Sam. Mr. Wolf, what do you recommend we do?" Stephen asked.

"Apply for your patents as soon as you can arrange. In the meantime, pool your money and buy something you can build on now. You can always sell it later, probably for a nice profit."

Sam continued to study the men across the street. The large-caliber rifles they carried and their manner of dress confirmed that the fresh skins he'd seen were their kills and that they were indeed buffalo hunters. He had little respect for hunters who massacred defenseless animals by the hundreds just for the profit their hides would bring. It was pure slaughter and a waste of the precious meat.

"Do you know of any good sites available?" Stephen asked.

"Indeed I do, Sir. Fifty acres near here just became available, half wooded and half cleared with a young orchard. The cleared land is in good fence. The title is indisputable. The previous owner, John Marshall, relocated to Louisiana. I just bought it from him. It's got a nice dwelling on it—not much more than one large room and a hearth, but it's snug and will keep your women and children warm and dry while you men add on to it or get a bigger house built."

"We appreciate your time, Sir, and we'll let you know if we want to look at that land," Stephen said. He stood and shook Mr. Wolf's hand. The rest of the men followed Stephen's lead and bid Mr. Wolf good day.

Sam stepped out of Wolf's office first. As he untied his horse, out of the corner of his eye, he looked across the street. The wide-shouldered leader of the hunters stared directly at him with cold, hard eyes.

Trouble, he decided immediately.

They mounted and turned their horses toward camp.

"Hey, new settlers," the man yelled, striding directly toward him, carrying a heavy rifle in the crook of his arm. His five other men, still looking disheveled and menacing, followed behind the man. "I want to buy that horse mister. I'm partial to buckskins, always was." The man grabbed the gelding by his bridle and turned the horse's head toward him, eyeing Alex with a sinister envy. "Buckskins are as tough as wet leather."

Alex shied away from the stranger. Sam felt his horse's muscles bristle beneath him. The gelding didn't like this man any more than he did.

"Keep your grubby paws off my horse," he warned through gritted teeth. "My horse is not for sale."

The man stepped back and blatantly appraised Sam, then said to his grungy companions, "I bet he's a good horseman. Can't wait to have him between my legs."

It was a threat couched in an insult. A disgusting insult.

Sam said nothing but he glared with disgust upon a man already his enemy.

The fellow's five companions, all wearing whiskey induced grins, came closer.

Their leader strolled around Sam's horse. "Yup, this horse will suit me just fine," the hunter said, his mouth curled in a mirthless smile. He spat a brown stream of tobacco, some of it dripping into his oily beard. "Get this man a couple of cases of whiskey. I'm about to trade for a horse," he instructed one of his men.

"Forget the damn whiskey," Sam snarled. The only thing he would trade with this snake would be punches.

"If you men are looking for a fight, we'll oblige you, but I'd advise you to move on. My brother here is slow to anger but once riled, watch out. He won't be stopped," Stephen warned, his voice smooth as silk, but his eyes full of threat.

The man gave Stephen a mocking smirk and said, "He doesn't worry me none. I have more muscles in my cock than he has in both arms." He wrapped a hand on his manhood and thrust out his hips.

Sam's lip curled at the revolting gesture.

"I want this horse and I'll have him by God," the man continued to insist.

"I doubt God has anything to do with the deals you make," Sam growled. "More likely, they are made with the Devil. I've told you once the horse is not for sale and I am not accustomed to having to repeat myself. Move on, *now.*"

He motioned for Stephen and Bear to leave too as he turned his back on the man. He tapped Alex's sides with his heels and started down the road.

"Hey coward, running off *again?* Afraid of a little brawl with real Kentucky men? Come on, let's settle this. I'll fight you for the horse," the man taunted.

Sam leaned forward and looked over at Stephen and Bear. Bear's nostrils flared with fury and Stephen's face was a mask of rage. They exchanged a long deep look with him, their eyes as angry and dark as thunderclouds.

"You three cockteasers are running off like virgin hens," the man said mockingly.

"*Boc, boc, booccc,*" the other hunters cackled and then broke out into raucous laughter.

The man's words seemed worn, used too often, by the shallow petty man and the others with him. But his contemptuous tone, the insolence in his voice, singed the tinder of Sam's anger. Sam struggled to quench the spark threatening to erupt, clenching his teeth together so hard they threatened to crack.

"Is that pretty young blonde a virgin too?" the leader drawled.

That was it. Sam's control blew apart like a volcano. His blood began to boil. His throat grew hot and inflamed. Mumbled curses spewed from his hardened mouth. He shoved his boots against the stirrups and tugged back on the reins bringing Alex to an abrupt halt. Seething, he whirled the horse around, back toward the laughing men. He pushed the big gelding right up to the man.

Alex seemed perfectly willing to trample the hunter, who took a big step back to avoid being stepped on.

His eyes blazing, Sam glared down at the man. "Apologize. Now!"

The hunter just stood there, tall and insolent, but silent.

"Good Lord, you *are* a stupid fellow," Stephen told the man, as he pulled up next to Sam.

Stephen was wrong. There was nothing stupid about this man. He was cunning and calculating. Sam could see it in the man's dark eyes. He was after something more than this horse and he was deliberately provoking this fight. Carefully controlling his hardened voice, he said, "I don't know your name Sir, but apparently you need to learn mine. My name is Captain Sam Wyllie, and these gentlemen are Stephen Wyllie and Bear McKee. And now that you know who we are, we will teach you not to insult our family again."

With a face that would make a grizzly look friendly, the leader stood in the middle of the six men.

Sam took each man's measure with battle experienced eyes.

Then he, Stephen, and Bear regarded each other, each silently recognizing what the others had to do.

They dismounted slowly and, in unison, advanced toward the six men.

Always protective of Stephen, Bear took position in front of the biggest hunter, who appeared to be the most menacing. "Don't want to take away from your fun," Bear told Stephen, "but let me take this wee one here in front."

Each heavily armed with knives, axes, and pistols, the six large grubby men continued to taunt them.

"The bugger's proud of his 'good' name," one shouted, "Let's show him what pride buys here in Kentuck'."

"A 'good' beating," said another, "that's what."

Wearing vests made of buffalo hide, the hunters gave the

appearance of a small herd of mangy buffalo themselves. But unlike buffalo, these men would not be easy prey. The whiskey the hunters had obviously been drinking would make them even more dangerous. Intoxicated men were not as quick, but the liquor would make them wilder and rasher.

They narrowly avoided fighting these men the first time. But this time they were in for a serious fight. They would each have to fight two. But neither he nor Stephen would back down now. And Bear always enjoyed being in the middle of a good fight.

"Lay down your rifles men, we wouldn't want to miss these bastards and kill one these good townspeople now would we?" the leader asked with a contemptuous half-smile.

"We'll just give 'em a good beating before we skin 'em," the biggest man replied.

"I will give you but one more opportunity to apologize for your ill manners and insults," Sam informed them. He pulled his shoulders back and waited.

"You pilgrims know there are three of you and six of us?" the big man asked haughtily.

Bear answered before Sam could. "Aye, we do. And if ye think ye'll be needin' more help, we'll be pleased to wait while ye go and get what ye think ye will need."

The leader's face turned red as he said, "You son-of-a-…"

The hunter never had a chance to finish his sentence as Sam's fist took the word out of the man's filthy mouth. Then he ducked to avoid the leader's fist before shoving a right hook upward into the fellow's bearded chin, causing the man to stumble. Spinning around easily on his moccasin-clad feet, he kicked a second hunter in the stomach, sending the man flying to the ground, gasping for air.

Bear had taken on the giant of a man he had singled out, who was nearly as large as Bear. Sam could hear the two standing there growling at each other while the hunter on the far left came at Bear. Using his left arm and fist like a giant club, Bear whacked the forehead of the man coming at him, knocking the hunter down with one blow, all the while continuing to snarl at the man swaggering menacingly in front of him.

Sam grinned to himself as he detected a Scottish burr in Bear's deep growl.

The fight was dirty from the beginning. As he expected, the hunters fought for the chance to bully, rather than the honor in it. These men were not to be trusted. He would keep one eye on Stephen and Bear. If they needed help, he would make sure they got it.

As the leader pushed himself up from his knees, Sam's fist slammed into the jaw of the man. He felt the skin of his knuckle tear open. Despite the force of his powerful blow, the hunter still stood upright. The two exchanged blow after blow, both refusing to show any sign of weakening. He tasted blood as his lip split open but he would take punches from here to eternity if he had to. He wasn't going down. He put all his weight behind his next punch and the man finally went crashing to the ground, landing on a fresh pile of Alex's dung.

"That's as close as you'll ever get to owning my horse," Sam swore.

The second man regained his breath and came at Sam, trying to knee him in the gut. He stepped aside just in time, grabbed the man's elevated foot, and twisted the ankle backwards and to the side. The hunter bellowed in pain before collapsing to the ground, unable to stand.

Swiping at the horse shit on his face and baring brown teeth, the leader came at him again. Sam charged and rammed his head into the man's ample stomach. Gasping for breath, the big fellow fell backwards onto his back.

One of the other men tried to knee Stephen in the groin. Stephen shuffled to the right just in time, turned in a tight circle, and kicked the man on his ass, which sent the hunter sprawling to the ground face down in the mud and muck.

Sam glanced at the leader, now on his knees, who was still trying to wipe manure off his face with his shirt sleeve. A corner of Sam's mouth twitched with mirth.

The hunter stood, nostrils flaring, and charged, grabbing Sam's shoulders. Sam threw his arms up between the leader's arms and grinding his teeth, grabbed the man's throat. He could feel veins pulsing and twitching on his own neck as he considered whether to strangle the fellow.

Then the man thrust a powerful blow, hot and weighty, into his stomach. It momentarily sucked his breath away. Panting for air, he shoved the leader violently and the hunter fell to the ground face down. Sam roughly turned the man over and sat on the leader's soft ample belly, using both legs to pin the man's arms. The man glared back at Sam with burning, ruthless eyes, the stench of rotten teeth and whiskey heavy on his hot breaths.

Sam was about to ask him if he was ready to end the fight when the worm spat in his face.

"Shit!" Fury almost choked Sam. As slimy spittle dripped off his jaw, he hissed, "Nobody spits on me." His mouth twisted in wrath and he began pounding the son-of-a-bitch's face with both fists.

Somehow, the man mustered the strength to use his legs to throw Sam off. The hunter turned, jumped up, and quickly scrambled away. Had the repulsive fellow given up?

Sam sprang to his feet, about to go after the leader again, when he saw Stephen gasping for breath. As his brother sucked in air, he charged Stephen's attacker, using his shoulder and elbow to knock the brute to the ground. Then Sam lifted the rascal by his shirt and bashed his fist into the man's face.

Stephen appeared to regain his breath, and then graciously said, "Thank you, my Captain," before returning to the fight.

The hunter whose ankle he had twisted was now hopping toward him on one leg. As Sam drew his right fist back to strike the man, he remembered how painful his knuckles felt when he threw the last punch. So, instead, he simply swept his foot against the man's leg, knocking him down again. "I believe, if I was you, I'd stay down," Sam said in his most threatening voice.

The remaining boorish men fought like the wild animals they were. Scanning the rest of the fight, he saw one man claw his black fingernails into Bear's face as another took a vicious bite out of Bear's ear.

Bear let out a particularly potent Gaelic curse. Then he roared deafeningly, doing a fine imitation of a real bear, and the two men suddenly seemed intimidated. The two hunters would soon regret their ungentlemanly like behavior, especially the one with Bear's blood on his mouth.

"These fellers fight like wee lassies," he heard Bear yell. Bear used sarcastic humor whenever he was truly vexed.

"Indeed, like bad-mannered little girls," he drawled with

distinct ridicule, looking at the man on the ground.

Sam quickly located the leader again, who had retrieved his rifle and was checking the powder.

"I'll show you how a little girl fights," the leader yelled, focusing his battered eyes and the heavy weapon on Stephen's gut.

Sam's horror and anger instantly flared. But he was too far away to reach the whoreson before the man could fire. He heaved out his long knife. In a heartbeat, it flew across the fight and sliced into the man's arm, making a grisly sound as it cut through bone and flesh. The knife's impact knocked the rifle out of the hunter's hand and caused the weapon to fire. The explosive sound momentarily stopped the fight.

Sam's huge knife protruded grotesquely through the other side of the man's arm as he screamed and dropped to his knees. Dark blood sputtered out both sides of the long blade and trailed down the dangling hand.

Springing toward the man, Sam swiftly retrieved his knife. Giving the leader a look of pure contempt, he pushed the hunter to his back and yanked the blade free as the man continued to yell in horrible agony. He ignored the terrible cries, which brought even more people, running from all directions, to watch the fight.

He wiped the bloody blade on the man's vest causing him to cringe, and then sheathed the weapon.

Sam heard Stephen groaning and snapped his head in his brother's direction. Two burly men were still attacking Stephen. One held his youngest brother while the other repeatedly thrust his fists into Stephen's stomach.

Despicable bastards!

Sam leapt close to the three, and grabbed the man's wrist

before he could throw the next punch. Using both hands, he twisted the hand and wrist in opposite directions, bringing the hunter instantly to his knees. The man's face would soon become unrecognizable, even to his own mother.

Stephen stomped his boot heel onto the foot of the man holding hm. His brother's wiry strength and quickness on his feet served him well. Stephen turned and began punching the hunter in the stomach, returning the belly punches he had just received.

Sam spun toward one of the men attacking Bear. At the sight of Sam hurrying toward him, fear burst into the man's eyes. The man jerked out his skinning knife. Before the hunter could use it, Sam grabbed the wrist holding the knife with both hands. He twisted with all his strength until the knife pointed away from him and toward the buffalo hunter, but the man's other hand grabbed his throat. He felt the big hand pressuring his windpipe. His throat hurt more with each breath he tried to take. He felt himself loosing strength in his arms.

The hunter's eyes blazed with ferocity as the knife came closer to Sam's face. The scent of death seemed to emanate from the man but Sam refused to breathe it in.

With renewed determination, the blade just inches from his face, he managed to pry the knife out of the man's hand. Then, grabbing a good chunk of the man's hair, he wrenched the hunter to the ground and pressed his foot against the man's back. He tossed the man's knife aside and had his own knife at the man's throat in half a second.

"Sam don't," Stephen yelled, scrambling up and darting over to him.

He gaped at Stephen, his pulse speeding and chest heaving.

"Don't!" Stephen repeated.

He hesitated long enough to calm his killing rage, but he couldn't resist slicing through the man's hair held in his hand, cutting so close to the scalp it shaved the top of the man's head. He stood and then threw the dirty hair onto the now pink sheared head. Then he rolled the man over and with a brutal stare said, "Bother us again and next time your scalp comes off too."

Bear's foe did not fare much better. Holding the hunter by the throat until the fellow's face turned blue and both eyes were bulging, Bear finally let go, dropping the limp man on top of the one with the fresh haircut. "This is for me ear," Bear said, punching the man in the face as the hunter sucked in air. Blood ran from the broken nose, now angled toward the hunter's left eye.

Bear stepped away. The two men sprawled on the ground evidently did not possess the will to fight further.

By the time the fight was over, Sam saw five buffalo hunters scattered across the road, bleeding and groaning. The sixth could only bleed. Dead, he was the unlucky recipient of his leader's gun's discharge.

Pointing the long knife, all thirteen inches, at the leader's face and then the other hunters, he said, "If you, or any of your men, ever again point a weapon at one of my brothers, I swear I'll plant this blade in that man's chest."

Breathing heavily, he sheathed his knife, and then wiped at his face and hair dampened by sweat. Taking slow steady breaths, he surveyed the people standing in front of the shops and other buildings surrounding them, and then noticed the darkening sky and thunder rolling in the distance.

Under the gloomy grey clouds, the townspeople, including

Tom Wolf, stared in stunned disbelief. Sam suspected it was the first time anyone had answered a challenge from the unruly and insolent hunters.

"Someone needs to take care of that weasel's arm. He's not far from bleeding to death," Sam declared, then spit out some of his own blood.

None of the town's people even budged to help. In fact, nearly in unison, they took a step or turned away.

Finally, one of the buffalo hunters, who could still move, crawled over to his suffering leader and tied a belt tightly around what was left of the arm.

Although obviously in tremendous pain, the man struggled to prop himself up on his good arm. The hunter's face turned white but he still managed a vicious stare.

Sam filled his eyes with menace, as he swiped the blood from his lips with the back of his hand.

Hatred oozed from the eyes that glared back at him as readily as the blood seeped from the man's hemorrhaging arm.

As Sam kept a wary eye on the five hunters, he, Stephen, and Bear remounted their waiting horses. All three horses were trained to remain standing wherever their rider dismounted, even when weapons were being fired.

Sam glowered at the hunters' leader as he settled into his saddle. "Like I said, the horse is not for sale."

CHAPTER 14

"That ill-bred man bought trouble just as soon as he called us chicken," Bear said, as they rode back to camp. "It was an unfortunate choice of words. In fact, I canna think of a worse choice."

"He should have listened to Sam," Stephen said.

Sam ignored them.

"Clearly, he should have been a bit more courteous," Stephen added.

"Aye. I bet he doesna make that mistake again," Bear said, raising his bushy eyebrows. "His biggest mistake was pointin' that rifle at you with Sam and his big knife anywhere around."

Stephen scratched his stomach. "I feel itchy. I swear those mongrels had lice or fleas."

"Aye, probably plenty of both," Bear said. "Most dogs do."

Sam heard the two trying to suppress their mirth.

Swallowing his chuckle, Stephen said, "We'll need a good bath in the river later with some of Jane's lye soap."

"D'ye think we can scrub that disagreeable look off of Sam's face?" Bear asked. "Those quarrelsome fellas did not improve his disposition any."

He did feel surly and didn't see the humor in the situation that Bear and Stephen obviously did. He stewed in silence, rubbing his sore jaw, the only noise coming from their saddle leather and the horses' movements. After several minutes he said, "That's not the end of this. It's just the beginning. Men like that don't turn the other cheek. We'll fight them again. We'd best get ready."

Something about the hunter's leader bothered Sam. It was more than the foul man's rude and drunken behavior—it was something in his eyes...

"Maybe that Mr. Marshall had the right idea moving to Louisiana," Stephen said, interrupting Sam's thoughts.

"We've been travelin' for months, we're here a few days, and already ye're ready to move on?" Bear asked.

"So far I'm not much impressed with Boonesborough," Stephen said. "Between their abundant and convoluted land laws and the kind of people living here, I'm not feeling particularly friendly towards the place."

"Kentucky is a hard place. Hard places bring out the best or the worst in men. That bunch is an example of the worst. They've been made savage by the wilderness," Sam said.

"Let's see what happens at the Land Bank. Things could look different in the morn," Bear said. "Maybe that's why they call it 'Land of Tomorrow'."

Sam glanced over at Bear, not appreciating Bear's cavalier attitude nor his humor. Normally he would, but just now, he was in no mood for levity.

They rode into camp and tied their horses as Jane, Catherine, and the others walked up.

"How did it go with the land specula...? What happened? You've had trouble," Jane said.

Kelly and the children stood behind her.

"Looks like Boonesborough is not very hospitable," John said, still carrying his rifle.

"They insulted our family," Sam said, scowling as he loosened the cinch on Alex. "I do not insult others," he said, and then glanced up, "unless they deserve it."

"This is a fine start. We're not here a week and already you're fighting. How many were there, four?" John asked.

"No, six," Bear corrected. "The same six bastards who gave us such a warm welcome on the other side of the Fort."

"It's a miracle one of you wasn't killed!" Catherine said, looking directly at Sam.

He detected true concern in her voice and saw distress in her eyes. It felt strange having a woman be concerned about him. But it was somewhat comforting too.

"One of us nearly was," Bear said. "It didn't get serious until their leader, a brute of a fellow, ugly as a hog and about as dirty as one, nearly made Stephen's first week in Boonesborough his last."

Jane gasped. "How?" she sputtered.

"When we started getting the better of them, their leader decided he needed his big buffalo rifle. But Sam made him drop it," Bear said, smiling at Sam.

"How?" Catherine asked, glancing from Bear to Sam and back

again.

"Divided the man's arm nearly in two. Sam threw his knife nearly thirty feet across the fight right into the fellow's arm, about here," Bear said, pointing to the spot on his own arm. "The flea bag dropped his rifle and it discharged. Killed his own man."

"Mercy's sake," Jane said, appalled. "It could have been Stephen."

"Nay, not with Sam within striking distance," Bear said. "And I had an eye on the wicked man too. I had me hand on this hatchet until I saw Sam releasing his blade."

"A man was killed?" William asked, looking worried.

"*We* didn't kill him," Sam said simply.

❧

Catherine wanted to weep with relief that the fight did not result in getting Sam or the others hurt or killed, but there would be time to think about that later. For now, she needed to help Jane see to their wounds. "I'll heat some water and get some bandages. Every one of them is bleeding in at least one spot or another," she said.

"Kelly get my medicine kit from the wagon," Jane ordered. "John, please help get some food warmed before this storm that's brewing puts out our fire."

"What happened to your face and your ear Bear?" Little John asked.

"A couple of those buffalo hunters did na think they could win fightin' fair, like a man, so they did what comes natural to an animal—bitin' and clawin'. But the dogs know how real men fight now," Bear said. "And I bet his nose looks a sight worse than me ear."

After Catherine and Jane got the four patched up, Sam and the others gathered around the cook fire and ate quickly, keeping an eye to the sky, while they discussed Mr. Wolf's suggestion.

"It makes sense," John said. "I don't see that we have another choice. We could build a permanent home for either William or I since both of us want to be close to town. We could make it big enough to hold all of us, until the rest of you get your land."

"Let's see what happens at the Land Office before we decide. If it still makes sense, we'll find out what Mr. Wolf wants for that place and go see it," Stephen said. "But, I'm not expecting much. He's out to make a quick profit at our expense."

"Mr. Wyllie, why are you always so suspicious of people?" Kelly asked. She sat next to William, listening to the conversation.

"I am," Stephen said, as though that was all the explanation needed.

"With four older brothers he learned to be distrustful to survive," Sam explained.

"I can vouch for that," Bear said. "Every day at least one of them, and sometimes all four, gave their youngest brother a hard time or played some prank on him. Made him ornery and wary of other's motives. Their father used to say Stephen didn't even trust the preacher."

"I didn't. Still don't," Stephen said. "They're only human too."

"Bet that's why Stephen befriended you so early on Bear," William said. "You were so big we didn't dare pick on Stephen when you were anywhere around."

"Still true," Sam said.

"Whenever Bear came into our house, he would give Mother a big hug. She always said, 'Daniel you hug like a big bear.' That's when we started calling him Bear. The name fit him perfectly," William told Kelly. "Every time Mother saw him coming we knew she was going to the flour to make a cake. As far as Mother was concerned, his surname wasn't McKee, it was Wyllie."

"I loved that good woman," Bear said.

"So did I," Sam added wistfully.

As the first drops of rain kissed Catherine's face, she saw a sad faraway look fill Sam's eyes. She suspected that he was remembering their boyhood home as well as their beloved mother. Some time ago, Jane had explained to her that a massive mountain slide of rock and mud buried the stately Wyllie home and the vast majority of the family land, along with Sam Wyllie Senior, their mother, and sister. Sam not only lost his inheritance, in one day he lost three of the most important people in his life.

No wonder he had a hard time loving.

A bolt of lightning, followed immediately by a loud clap of thunder, sent them all scurrying for cover. But as Catherine climbed into her wagon, wishing Sam would follow her inside, she looked back. Sam sat alone and still, letting the rain wash over him.

꼬

Just before sunset, the rain stopped and soon afterwards, a rider came up the muddy road to their camp. "Heard you gentlemen had some trouble today," the man said. He dismounted as they gathered around him. "I'm Constable Mitchell, currently the only law officer in Boonesborough. I must get your version of the incident."

They introduced themselves to Mitchell. A gangly young man of perhaps 20 years, he looked to Sam like his only experience at fighting might have been with his brothers and sisters. The boy was clearly nervous, but seemed determined to exercise all the authority he had and then some.

As usual, Stephen spoke first and succinctly explained the incident.

"That nearly matches their version. So, you started the fight by dismounting from your horses and advancing towards them?" Mitchell asked.

"Only after considerable provocation," Sam said.

"And, Captain Wyllie, you threw your knife into Foley's arm, causing him to drop the weapon and kill one of his own men, even though Foley had not fired his gun?" Mitchell stared wide-eyed at the knife sheathed at Sam's waist.

Sam gripped his weapon's deer horn handle. "I don't know what kind of a place this is, but back where we were raised a man didn't wait till a ball did its damage before he defended himself or his family." His hot tone reflected the ample annoyance he felt.

Mitchell tore his eyes away from the knife and turned toward Bear. "And I understand that you, Sir, nearly strangled a man and then broke his nose," Mitchell said, his voice nearly shaking.

Bear towered over the constable who had to tilt his head back and look up to see Bear's eyes.

Sam felt his mouth curl in a half grin when Bear took a step forward and the young man quickly took a step back.

"Sir, I'm rather fond of me ears and that son of a dog had some of mine for his supper. He's lucky I did na kick him where he deserved, although I doubt there's enough manhood there for it to have mattered," Bear growled.

Sam heard both William and Little John snicker.

"My apologies ladies," Bear said to the women before he continued. "Next time, I…"

"Constable Mitchell," William interrupted before Bear could finish. "I held the position of Sheriff in our home town in New Hampshire, and I assure you I understand your important responsibilities here. Speaking as a former officer of the law, I can tell you those bullies had it coming. They provoked a fight. My brothers were simply riding down the street when they grabbed Captain Wyllie's horse wanting to buy it. He told them the horse was not for sale, but they acted as though that didn't matter. They were impertinent, called my bothers cowards, and insulted our women for the second time. The first was when we arrived at the Fort. This time, their leader drew a rifle on Stephen intending to use it. Sam threw the knife defending our brother. You cannot blame him for that. We desire no further trouble with these men."

Sam's shoulders tipped back. Whether they desired it or not, trouble was coming.

Mitchell swallowed hard, and appeared to gather his courage, before he reluctantly continued. "Your former occupation Mr. Wyllie is irrelevant in this matter. As for the insult, the law does not provide justification for fighting because a man is insulted or because a horse is simply touched. Foley claims that he was just trying to buy the horse and that he picked up his weapon intending to leave the fight fearing that Stephen Wyllie was about to kill him. The man's eyes are swollen shut and from the looks of him, it does look like someone tried to kill him. The doc is amputating the man's hand, just above where the knife hit, right now."

"If I'd wanted to kill him, I would have," Sam snarled.

"Never…the…less," the constable stammered, "Mr. Foley is willing to not press charges against Mr. McKee since his ear was damaged."

Bear snorted. "Press charges?" His bushy brows drew together in an affronted frown.

"However, he wants you, Captain Wyllie, arrested for murder since your actions caused the death of his man, and I regret that I must do so."

Everyone stared at the constable in stunned disbelief.

"No!" Catherine cried. Intense astonishment paled her face.

"Mister Stephen Wyllie, you are also under arrest for assault and breach of the peace. The hunter also plans to sue for the loss of his hand. Knowing Mr. Foley, I hope you gentlemen brought a bundle of cash. I must ask you both to come to town with me."

CHAPTER 15

Murder? The charge was absurd.

The corner of his mouth twisted in annoyance, but Sam refused to give in to worry. He would figure a way out of this. But this whole mess could delay their acquiring land and getting settled in homes. That would not be good. Winter was just a few months off.

He gave Catherine a sidelong glance. Her face had gone white and her mouth still hung open. Would she think him a quarrelsome bully because of this mess? People often thought of him as an intimidating tough warrior, but in truth, he considered his nature to be temperate and kind. He just didn't tolerate bad people very well. He'd put up with them only to a point. Tolerating bad behavior just promoted more bad behavior.

"Constable Mitchell, this is beyond absurd, surely you must know what kind of men those brutes are?" William said. "Pray tell, is this the first time they've caused trouble?"

The constable ignored William. "Leave your weapons here," he told Sam and Stephen.

Stephen just laughed. "Hell no!"

Sam did not say a word or move. Keeping cool and composed, he just looked at the constable, his eyes penetrating deep into Mitchell. Annoyed with the distinct note of censure in the young man's voice, he wanted to shake the constable's unearned confidence. Then he let his annoyance show, hardening his eyes and twisting his lips.

"Lo…look Captain Wyllie, Sir, I…I'm only doing my duty here," the young man stammered, his oily face shining in the campfire's light. "This is nothing personal. The Circuit Judge, not me, will decide what actually happened between you, Foley, and his men. He should be in Boonesborough within a few days."

֍

To Catherine's surprise, Sam showed no reaction to the constable's pronouncement. In fact, he seemed unnaturally calm. Then their eyes met and she felt a wave of self-assurance come from him. The man wasn't worried. For God's sake, he'd just been charged with murder!

Catherine turned and watched the nervous constable warily study Sam.

Sam gave Mitchell a cool appraisal and then she saw his eyes narrow and his mouth twist into a threat as he widened his stance and crossed his arms.

The young man quickly glanced away, his confidence no match for the Captain's aura of sheer menace.

She could not believe this was happening. It all seemed so preposterous. How could a simple fight result in Sam and Stephen's arrest?

But a man had lost his life and another his hand. It wasn't simple any more.

Had all the suffering the Wyllie's endured been for naught? Their long journey for nothing? Would their dreams vaporize in this nonsensical twist of events? Would Stephen miss his first son's birth because he was in jail? It was inconceivable. Yet it was happening right before her disbelieving eyes.

She heard a bird singing from the trees, the bright notes a stark contrast to the palatable tension in the damp air.

She scrutinized Sam. His mouth was tight and grim and a muscle quivered on his check, but he still didn't look worried. He appeared to be weighing his options. He stood tall and straight, his massive body rigid, his bearing conveying power.

Why would fate put her and Sam together on this journey and then let this happen? He could be imprisoned—maybe even hung. The thought made her stomach lurch and her heart tighten in her chest.

She wanted to go to him. Let him hold her, calm her rising panic. Even though he had never held her, she was sure his touch would be reassuring. To have him hold her would be both comforting and sensual. Right now, despite the tense situation or maybe because of it, she longed for both.

But she held herself back. She drew a deep breath. Leave him alone. Don't underestimate him. Sam is accustomed to dealing with misfortune.

He'll figure a way out of this.

൞

Sam did not move even a fraction of an inch. He wasn't going anywhere. "Sir, I am a former decorated Captain in the Continental Army. On my honor, as a gentleman, we will not run and will await the Judge if you allow us to stay here at our camp, but I will not spend a week inside a damn cage like some trapped animal, particularly for some trumped-up crime."

As the constable took his time considering the idea, Sam felt his chest expand as he remembered receiving the prized Badge of Merit, created to reward soldiers for, "Singularly meritorious service, instances of unusual gallantry and extraordinary fidelity and faithful service." General Washington personally designed the award, the figure of a heart on purple cloth. While he had served, Sam proudly wore it, as required, on his left breast. Someday, he would have to show Catherine the medal.

When Sam returned his focus to the young man, the constable stood shifting from one mud-covered boot to the other and chewing on his bottom lip. Mitchell was probably dreading riding back to town with him and Stephen, much less keeping them a week. He was probably also dreading facing the hunter's leader without Sam and Stephen in his custody.

The constable glanced at Stephen who sent the obviously nervous young man another squinty-eyed look of cold anger. Stephen was clenching his jaw so tightly Sam thought it might crack.

Mitchell's resolve did crack. "All right, but I'll have to ask you for a bond, payable in cash right now. Should you decide to flee, Mr. Foley will receive the money and a warrant will be issued for your arrest." The constable seemed to gather his nerve and walked over to Sam. "You'll need to give me your knife as evidence until this whole matter is resolved."

"Sir, there's only one way I'd give you my knife, and trust me, you wouldn't like it," he barked.

Constable Mitchell quickly said, "Perhaps we don't need that piece of evidence after all." He took several steps away from Sam, and his knife. "But be sure to bring it to your trial."

Stephen marched over to Mitchell, faced him. "I assume you will provide a receipt?"

"Of course, Sir." The constable borrowed ink and paper and quickly wrote the receipt while Sam and Stephen got the coins to pay the bond.

"We wish you God's speed keeping those thugs at bay," William told the man as he left.

෴

After Mitchell left, John turned to face Sam. Ire burned in his brother's eyes. "Now look where we are. We will probably lose the money we brought to buy land. Your combative nature and Stephen's pride got us into this mess. Disputes do not have to be settled with violence!"

"Now hold on...," Bear started.

"And you, you probably fought for the fun of it," John said, raising his voice and pointing an accusing finger at Bear. "None of you are living as God wants you to."

"You sound like a self-righteous sanctimonious idiot," Sam yelled. "You were not there and you have no right to wrongly accuse us."

"I wasn't there, but I know what losing our land money will mean. We're in trouble and you're going to regret this fight for a long time to come," John shouted. "This is trouble we didn't need—we already had more than enough to deal with. We will be lucky to get any land, if Indians or storms don't kill us first. Or, you'll get us killed by provoking others with your belligerent behavior."

He could only glare at John. He did not want to say what he was thinking. Instead of making John a tougher and stronger man, the wilderness seemed to be taming him. And the wilderness was no place for the tame.

"You could have walked away from those men," John continued. "You can't be acting like a bunch of ruffians and louts. We must set examples for others, rely on using our heads, not the might of our muscles."

"You let others fight our battles and then stand in smug judgment?" Sam asked with grim impatience.

"I'll fight any battle that needs fighting. But this one didn't. It was pure vanity and foolish pride. Now we may lose our land before we even get it," John yelled.

"If anyone's being foolish here, it's you, John," Stephen said, keeping his voice calm. "Keep it up and you will be fighting a battle—with me."

"Another battle. That's just what we need," John said contemptuously. "This is serious. Stephen, you will wind up in jail for Lord knows how long. Sam could even be hung. This situation is out of control."

"The only thing out of control is you," Stephen swore.

"Hung?" Martha wailed. "No! No!" She started sobbing loudly, which made Polly and Little John start crying too.

Seeing the children upset tore at Sam's heart. Forgetting his annoyance with John, he quickly stooped down to comfort Martha. "Uncle John is mistaken. He just doesn't understand yet how things work here in the wilderness. No one is going to hang. I promise you that little ones."

Then he patted Little John's head, stood, and turned to John again. Keeping the tone of his voice level and calm, he said, "John, you are succumbing to panic. The worst possible thing you can do in a situation like this. The only thing you are succeeding at is frightening the children." He lowered his voice even more and shifted closer to John's face. "If you intend to persist in censoring our behavior, I suggest you go stay in town. My patience has reached its limit."

Now, Little John wailed in earnest. The children had rarely seen the adults fight and Sam realized they didn't know what to think. Even Kelly appeared on the verge of tears.

Jane, however, just got mad, her face turning nearly as red as her hair. She seldom lost her temper, but once she did, it was good and lost. "For mercy's sake stop this! All of you. You sound like a bunch of foolish schoolboys, arguing over who started the fight. You are tired—beyond tired, exhausted. You're discouraged because it looks like getting land will be far more difficult than we planned. And you experienced a vicious fight that you didn't ask for. But all this will soon be behind us. John, remember nothing is out of control that is under His control. Where is your faith? Your faith in the Almighty and your faith in your brothers? Can you really lose it that easily?"

She turned from John to the others, her green eyes blazing. "Save your anger for our enemies. We must stick together like the family we are. This Foley man can't hurt us unless we let him come between us. We agreed before we left to stick together no matter what and I will not let you forget it," Jane bellowed. "Now act like you're Wyllies, including you Bear, not one of those thugs."

No one spoke for a minute, except with their eyes. Among family, a lot can be said without uttering a word.

"Please forgive me for interfering in a family matter, but Jane's right," Catherine said, lifting her chin and stepping forward. "You haven't come all this way to let a few dirty buffalo hunters stop you from fulfilling your destinies. They may be able to bring down buffalo that can't defend themselves, but, by God, they will *not* bring down this good family."

Sam arched an eyebrow at the vehemence he heard in her voice.

"The law will protect us," William said.

Sam groaned. "To hell with the law. We've seen what the law looks like around here. We'll protect ourselves," he barked. "As John said, we'll use our heads, *and,* if necessary, brute force. Whatever it takes to keep our family safe."

He could sense the steam escaping from John as he leaned against a nearby wagon wheel. John's anger was cooling, but his brother's concern was not. Worry still filled John's downturned face and his voice. "My apologies to all of you," John said. "Especially to you children. It was wrong of me to frighten you. I'm troubled that we're off to such a bad start. I don't want to see us lose our hard earned land money to a bunch of hooligans." He picked up Little John, wiped away the boy's tears and looked into his son's eyes. "And I don't want you Little John, or Martha and Polly, dragged into some feud that threatens your safety. I just want to keep you safe."

"We didn't ask for this trouble, but we sure as hell will deal with it," Sam swore. "Those men will not harm the children or anyone else. Nor will they ever see as much as a coin of our land money. You have my word on that. Before this feud is over, we may have a battle, but we beat them once, and we can do it again."

"And tomorrow morning we'll be at the land office waiting for it to open. This will *not* stop us from doing what we came here to do, by God." Stephen said.

"Amen," John said.

"Amen!" Little John repeated, wrapping his little arm around his father's shoulders.

Lightening flashed across the now dark sky and then a clap of thunder boomed nearly overhead, as though God said "amen" as well.

The storm had returned.

CHAPTER 16

The next morning, Sam waited outside the Land Office, along with Stephen and Bear. He and Bear leaned against the log building, patiently waiting for the office to open, while Stephen impatiently paced back and forth on the building's wood plank porch.

Sam took notice of one family of about twelve in number who arrived shortly after they did and also awaited the Commissioner. As the father walked up, he carried an ax and a rifle on his shoulders. The plump wife carried the rim of a spinning wheel in one hand and a baby in the other. Several little boys and girls, each with a bundle matching their size stood clustered together beside two poor horses, heavily loaded with the family's necessities. A milk cow, with a bag of meal on her back, also waited with them. The family seemed not only patient, but cheerful, filled with the expectation of seeing happier days here in Kentucky. Sam hoped their desires would be more than fulfilled.

Finally, Commissioner Simmons arrived. Thick-necked, pot-bellied, and nearly out of breath, Simmons welcomed them warmly, apologizing for keeping them waiting. Wiping beads of sweat from his forehead with a handkerchief, he said excitedly,

"I've been listening to stories of your encounter with the buffalo hunters. The whole town is buzzing about it. You brave men are already local heroes."

Surprised, Sam glanced at Stephen and Bear, who also appeared taken aback. But none of them mentioned the pending charges against them.

"You men did Boonesborough a favor yesterday. It would be an honor to help you," he added. Addressing the large family, he said, "I'll be with you good folks as soon as I finish with these gentlemen." He unlocked his office door and motioned them inside.

The bright early morning sun lit up the maps nailed to every rough log wall in Simmons' dusty office.

Sam began studying the maps, paying particular attention to the Filson Map of Kentucky, published only a few years before. As a mapmaker himself, he appreciated the fine work of John Filson, and the effort and personal sacrifices taken to create it. The popular map clearly showed the location of rivers and creeks as well as mountains and hills.

"Much of the land we have for settlement in Kentucky was negotiated in the Hopewell and Holston treaties. Unfortunately, many of the treaty boundary lines remain unclear and are often disputed by the native tribes and fighting has continued on and off for the last seven or eight years. Let me show you what may be your best choices," Simmons said, pointing to Filson's map.

Sam moved aside to give the others room to see the intricate map too.

"The most recently developed area, with the least threat of Indian trouble, is about 75 miles west and south of here. Unless you go too far west where the Chickasaw lands begin and counties are not yet organized. Northeast is quite mountainous and the Shawnees still use it as hunting grounds. You'll certainly want to stay away from them. The southeast is best for traders and trappers because of its access to the Cumberland Gap and the Wilderness Road," he explained, "but the Cherokee still hunt the majority of the area and therefore the land is not available yet for patenting."

"We saw some lush grassland there on our way here," Stephen said. "I wondered why that land looked as if it had not yet been claimed."

"In a word—Cherokees," Simmons said.

"Indians killed a whole flatboat of families—even the poor wee bairns," Bear said, "not long after we crossed the Cumberland River."

"I heard about that unfortunate event," Simmons said. "Before we go on, I need to explain something to you Captain. Earlier you said you would be making application for a Bounty Grant. The Bounty Grants for Revolutionary service are now only for men who served from Kentucky and Virginia. You will only be entitled to a regular land patent, the same as everyone else."

Sam stared at the Commissioner for several moments, then crossed his arms. "Show me the statute, Sir," he ordered.

Simmons turned to his cluttered desk, opened a drawer, and after several moments of searching, pulled the statute. He read it aloud to Sam, stammering over a few of the words.

"Hell of a note," Sam snarled when Simmons finished. "I didn't just fight for New Hampshire. We fought for the whole country, including Virginia, of which this new state was formerly a large part."

"You did," Simmons conceded, "but the General Assembly recently recognized that Kentucky would run out of land if too many veterans from other states made their claims here."

"Fine thing to tell a man after he's made a thousand mile trip here," Sam grumbled. "None of the newspaper notices mentioned this."

"Unfortunately, Sir, the land laws are confusing, in a constant state of flux, and poorly understood. This has led to many misunderstandings and armed conflicts. We established four courts to hear land disputes at Harrodstown, Louisville, Bryant's Station, and here at Boonesborough. These courts have done much good, but the settlement of the state has been so rapid, we continue to exist in a state of chaotic confusion. Settlers have claimed and reclaimed, surveyed and resurveyed, patented and repatented scores of highly desirable tracts. Not only have numerous acrimonious disputes occurred, many are unfortunately resolved only with bloodshed. Countless are still unresolved."

"Hell," Stephen said, expressing in one word his disappointment and frustration.

Their troubles seemed to multiply with each new day, but Sam refused to succumb to apprehension.

"Might I advise you gentlemen to take a look at Nelson County? It's still quite rough, but prime land is still available there," he suggested. "You'd travel there going due west to Harrodsburg, established in '74 by James Harrod. The area is quite prosperous, with six gristmills in operation for the corn and other grains raised in the area. Harrod's men constructed Fort Harrod west of Big Spring on the hill, to be safe from flooding. The fortress offers protection for settlers until they can get their own homes built. It's one of the largest in Kentucky with more defenders and ammunition than Boonesborough or Logan's Station. Harrodsburg is located in the bluegrass region and has three warm mineral springs. Settlers seem to thrive there."

Sam began to wonder if someone paid the man to steer new settlers in that direction.

"Or you could try to get a grant south of the Green River. Until recently, no person could enter a survey within this great area except a soldier. As soon as Kentucky became a state, new legislation opened up the area south of the Green River to any persons possessed of a family and over twenty-one years of age. Such persons are entitled to not less than 100 acres and not more than 200 acres. But, you must be bona fide settlers living on the land and improving it for one year before you come into actual possession."

The Commissioner described both areas in detail, showing it to them on the map, and gave them a list of sites still available that might meet their needs and be reasonably safe from Indian attacks. "Be sure to mark your boundaries by chopping notches into witness trees, and file your papers as soon as possible," Simmons said.

They left with instructions for the patent process and a rough map to Nelson County, less than a week away, about 75 miles due west of Boonesborough on the waters of the Salt River. In addition to describing Harrodsburg, Commissioner Simmons told them about Bardstown, the town just beyond Harrodsburg. The seat of Justice for Nelson County, the well-established town was also the home of Cedar Creek Church, organized in 1781. In fact, he said at present the town boasted elegant homes, posh inns, and reputable learning institutions. Best of all, Simmons described the land around Bardstown as lush rolling verdant pastures, punctuated by stands of Oaks and Walnut trees.

As they left Simmons' office, Sam could tell Stephen was still worried and would likely remain anxious until he secured his acreage.

"Sounds like we're headed further west," Sam said, trying his best to sound optimistic.

"Sam, why were ye so disturbed about the Bounty Grant?" Bear asked. "Ye did na care about land when we started this trip."

"It's the principal of the thing. Besides, a man can change what it is he cares about," he said.

"Looks like we'll have to keep moving," Stephen said.

"As long as we do na fall out of the saddle, we'll still get there," Bear said.

"That depends on how stout a horse you're riding," Stephen countered. "And if it gets hit by lightning."

Sam shuddered at the recollection of his near encounter with death from a lightning bolt that killed his horse on their trip here. "No one said this was going to be easy. The future belongs to those willing to go after it," Sam said.

"You're right," Stephen agreed.

"Wait here for me a moment. I'm goin' in this shop to buy some tobacco and a new whetstone for Catherine," Bear said. "She needs one to sharpen her wee dagger."

Sam scowled as Bear turned and went into the general store, the Scotsman's big body taking up the entire entryway.

"Speaking of Catherine, why did you suddenly turn cold

towards her?" Stephen asked. "Every time she's anywhere around, your face clouds with uneasiness."

Sam crossed his arms and frowned, surprised by Stephen's question. He tried to manage a feeble answer, but all he could come up with was, "I don't want to discuss the matter."

"If you weren't so damn independent, you'd realize what a blind fool you're being."

"I said, I don't want to talk about it," he said, louder this time.

"You have a chance at happiness, Sam, don't miss it."

"Damn it, Stephen, mind your own business."

"This is my business," Stephen pressed.

"How the hell do you figure that?"

"Two reasons. I told her she was welcome to stay with us and you're my brother."

"She stays with us only until she can find a home of her own."

"If you don't make a move soon, Bear will," Stephen said.

Sam glowered at his brother. "If that's what she wants, so be it."

"She scares you, doesn't she?" Stephen asked. "You've fought the bloody British when you were outnumbered ten to one, you've fought swarms of natives with nothing but your knife between you and a gruesome death, and you've faced bears and mountain lions like they were dogs and house cats, but you can't face her. She scares the hell out of you and you're too stubborn to admit it." Stephen stared at him, a haughty rebuke on his face.

Scowling at his brother, he smoldered for a bit before responding. "All right, she scares me. I am not used to being scared. It's something I don't do well. You're a fine one to condemn stubbornness. You'd take on the fires of hell with no more than a water bucket."

"And you'd lead the way," Stephen retorted. "You realize she loves you? I've seen the way she looks at you."

Sam didn't say anything. His insides rolled like the clouds above them. He turned his head slowly to look at Stephen. He felt as if lightning struck him again. He could feel his throat closing up and he found it difficult to even speak. "I...thought she...," he hesitated, "I thought she wanted Bear."

"The way a woman acts is often a poor indicator of what she actually wants—sometimes it's the opposite of what appears obvious. I know it is confusing and can befuddle a man, believe me I know. Women are just not as plain to figure as men are. Like horses, you have to understand their nature to get them to work with you, not against you. In fact, women can be very much like horses. For instance, they prefer a gentle voice and a soft easy touch. There are many other similarities, but I'm getting side tracked. If Catherine paid attention to Bear, it was just to see if you would rise to the competition, but her real target is you."

A warning voice whispered in his head, arousing old fears and uncertainties. "How do you figure that?"

"Because you two are like two sides of the same coin," Stephen said. "Don't be afraid of her. You're a bigger man than that. Whatever is holding you back is not as important as she is."

Stephen was right. Could he tell that warning voice inside him to shut the hell up?

"Remember what you told all of us once, when we were trying to decide whether we should make this journey—all life involves risk. That is especially true of love. This risk is yours to take, if you have the courage," Stephen added with emphasis.

Sam remained quiet for a moment, and then as casually as he could manage said, "I'll be right back. I need to buy a new razor. I think it's time for a shave."

CHAPTER 17

Over the next couple of days, the men decided they should assume their legal problems would eventually be resolved, and Sam told them that they should restock their supplies to prepare for their journey further west, towards Nelson County.

They bought powder and ball, always in short supply, but the shop owner had just received a shipment the day before. They also bought a supply wagon and filled it with saws, augurs, braces, chisels, planes, squares, and other tools and building materials that they would need to establish homesteads once they found land. Lastly, with nearly a dozen horses to care for, they bought a good supply of oats and grain.

This morning, Sam went with Stephen to patronize several of the town's other shops. His brother bought Jane a new delicate teacup and saucer made in England, some tea, and two new high-waisted gowns that would more comfortably accommodate her rapidly expanding stomach, one practical and one just because he liked it. He said she would look gorgeous in it. For Martha and Polly, Stephen found new dolls.

Sam bought himself a new white linen shirt. The weather was really warming up and it would be cooler than the buckskin he was wearing, he rationalized.

"That shirt will make you look like a proper gentleman," Stephen teased, after Sam had made the purchase. "Never thought to see you wearing one."

Irritated by his brother's mocking tone, he scowled and wondered if Stephen thought he had bought the new shirt to impress Catherine. Well what if he did? How he dressed was his own business. His mouth twisted with exasperation as he ambled over to the store's knife display.

"I'm looking for a small boy's knife," he told the man behind the counter.

The pudgy man wearing spectacles on his long nose pointed to a knife in his display case and said, "That one there once belonged to Daniel Boone when he was a young man."

He thought the shopkeeper might be capitalizing on Boone's reputation, but Sam liked the idea enough to buy it anyway and surprised Little John with it later that morning.

The majority of the next few hours, Little John just stared at the knife and showed it to anyone who would look at it. He got Sam to show him how to use it again and again and he patiently obliged his nephew, remembering how excited he had been when his father gave him his first knife.

While Sam spent time with Little John, John went to town to find out where church services would be held on Sunday. He learned that Boonesborough had no preacher but the local congregation met occasionally in the schoolhouse whenever a circuit preacher came through town.

"No town should be without a church. It's like a man without a soul," John told Sam when he got back.

Sam had met a few soulless men over the years.

At once, John started planning a church building. It would have a tall white steeple with a bell that people would be able to hear for miles. John had no idea how he would finance the construction and hoped that someone would donate the land and perhaps the congregation could help with the building materials. John could pay for a small part, but not all of it, and would donate his services as architect and builder.

Sam thought it would be a good way for John to demonstrate his skills to the people of Boonesborough. The growing town would generate a building boom in the coming years.

After the noon meal, Sam went to town again with William to talk to as many people as they could about the buffalo hunters. However, it soon became obvious the townspeople were afraid of the evil hunters and although they were grateful to the Wyllies for giving the hunters a good thrashing, they were reluctant to talk.

Sam and William did learn that the six hunters also traded in whiskey, drank a good deal of their own supply, and supplied a constant source of trouble. They often provoked fights and people suspected their leader, Frank Foley, in at least one unsolved murder.

What surprised Sam the most was what Lucky McGintey had to say after he and William encountered the old fellow on Boonesborough's main road, pulling a pack horse loaded with fresh kills. From the looks of it, Lucky's luck as a hunter had not run out. He'd provide fresh meat for many of Boonesborough's residents that night.

"They couldn't beat you men in a real fight so now they'll try to beat you in the courtroom. Sometimes the law works against honest men, as it did with Boone. You'll need to find some way to discredit Frank Foley and I think I know just the way. About a day's ride north of here live a couple of Irish brothers named O'Reilly. One of them, Jonathan, is a friend of mine. He swears he saw Foley lead the British to his militia, resulting in the death of many of them."

"Why hasn't he turned Foley into the militia here?" Sam asked Lucky.

"He's afraid to say anything about it 'cause he thinks Foley would kill him or his brother, or have the other buffalo hunters kill them both."

"Jonathan's right, Foley would." William said.

Sam understood that the Revolutionary War confused and blurred the lines of loyalty for many men. Most colonists found the milk of mother England bitter, while others wanted to keep suckling off a familiar tit even if it was hard to swallow. But traitors were different. They chose sides for profit or gain, not loyalty. Often, men became traitors to save their own skin.

Frank Foley might be as bad as Eli Frazier, the man he had sought to kill for so many years.

William responded to Lucky, "I doubt the fellow helped the Red Coats out of loyalty to the Crown or because he predicted the British would ultimately win. Based on our experiences with Foley, I suspect the man became a traitor for the great motivator—greed."

"Men like him betray their fellow man for a few pieces of silver," Sam said.

The three agreed that getting Jonathan O'Reilly to testify would be imperative.

On the way back to camp, William asked Sam if he remembered seeing any British scouts who looked like the buffalo hunters' leader.

"Hiding behind all that hair and filth, it's hard to tell what the man actually looks like," Sam said. "And, of course, a man's appearance can change a lot in fifteen or more years." He paused as something just sprang into his mind from the distant past. "I do remember that several men taken prisoners by the enemy became scouts for the British. Damn turncoat traitors, every one of them should rot in hell."

"If he's one of them, maybe we can make sure this one does. What if we get all that hair off of him?" William asked.

"How can we do that? You want me to give him a shave?" Sam yanked his knife out and held it up to his own black beard, still unshaven. After they left New Hampshire, he and Bear had both let their beards grow, while Stephen, John and William had done their best to remain clean-shaven. He had bought a razor a couple of days ago, but had not yet used it. Something made him hesitate. If he did shave, he wondered if Catherine would notice.

"No, you might shave the bastard a bit too close and 'hurt his feelings.' I'll ask the Judge to order the man shaved."

"Would he?" Sam asked, incredulous.

"If it meant identifying a turncoat, the judge should be willing."

"Even if I could identify him, it would still be his word against mine."

"Not if we get that settler Lucky told us about to come back and testify too."

"Do we have enough time to get O'Reilly to Boonesborough? Do you think he would come? Lucky said he was afraid to testify."

"We could get the Judge to talk to the witness privately. And, yes, I think we have just enough time to go get him if we hurry. Bear or John could go get him. You and Stephen can't leave, and I have to stay in case the trial starts, since you both want me to defend you. I still think you should get a lawyer."

"We can't trust a stranger. Besides, you might as well be a lawyer as well as you know the law."

"Knowing the law and practicing the law in a courtroom are two different things. Like knowing how to shoot a gun and being able to hit something with one. Nevertheless, I promised you I would do it and I will. Just pray my aim is true."

Sam and William told the others of their plan. After considerable debate, they decided that John should be the one to fetch the settler. John argued that he wanted to do his part to help. And all of them, including John, wanted Bear to be the one to guard the women and children while Sam, Stephen, and William were in town at the trial. Other than Sam, Bear was the most competent fighter among them and if some of the hunters tried to attack the women while the trial of going on, they would be safer with Bear there.

Jane maintained that she and the other women were quite capable of guarding their camp without a man to protect them. "We're close to town and besides we are not helpless women who must be guarded constantly," she said. "I can guard the camp, especially with Catherine and Kelly's help. Catherine has already proven she can take care of herself and Kelly knows how to shoot. She had to hunt her own meat out there where she lived. And we've taught Martha how to load and fire a weapon if she had to."

"You are as far from helpless as the east is from the west. I know you can shoot as well as the rest of us, except maybe Sam, nobody can beat him, but these despicable men have no honor and do not fight fair, even with men. No telling what they might do to you women just to spite us. I'll not take that chance," Stephen said. "Bear stays here."

"But it's late in the day, he should at least wait until morning," Jane said.

"I agree, leaving now is far from ideal," William said, "but we need that witness to get here as soon as possible. He can't wait. He has to go now."

John quickly gathered up his weapons and some cold biscuits and dried meat. He got the detailed instructions supplied by Lucky to the O'Reilly farm and prepared to leave. He embraced Little John and then mounted his horse.

Sam silently prayed it would not be the last time his brother would hug his child.

It was a somber camp after John left. They all realized the importance of his success, and the risk he was taking. No trip into the wilderness was without risk, and traveling alone made the risk even higher.

John was barely gone five minutes before Sam started having second thoughts about their plan. However, they had decided this as a group. He needed to abide by that decision, even if he thought it wrong. He let out a pent-up breath as Stephen walked up, his misgivings increasing by the minute.

"We've made a mistake," Sam said, "and John may be the one who pays for it."

"Give him a chance to prove himself. He might surprise you," Stephen said.

"It's what might surprise him that has me worried."

※

Without saying a word to anyone, after John left, Bear immediately saddled his horse Camel and went to town. Something in his gut told him they had just made a terrible decision—John should never have gone alone. He tried to convince them that he needed to go with John. But they wouldn't listen. John was not his brother and he did not feel he could tell Stephen, Sam, and William they were all making a mistake, even if they were. And John seemed so determined to do this on his own. Understandably, the man wanted to prove himself to his brothers—prove that he had the same courage they did.

Sometimes the brothers' courage outran their judgment. It seemed to him this was one of those times. Bear had stood by, helpless, unable to stop John or persuade Sam and the others that John needed his help. Even though he usually felt like family, today he did not. He just had to leave for a while.

As he rode into town, he thought about Catherine. His conversation with her that morning had not gone as he had hoped, and that was also making him feel dejected. After buying the whetstone, he had presented it to her wrapped in a beautiful white handkerchief, tied with a blue bow. He told her he had bought the blue ribbon to match her eyes, and that he had grown quite fond of her. Although she did her best to soften the blow, saying he was a fine man and any woman would be lucky to have him, she made it clear she only felt as a sister to him. Well, if he had to lose the bonnie lass to another man, he was glad it would be Sam. Although she never mentioned Sam, he could tell where her heart was leading her.

He sighed, and gave a resigned shrug. As soon as he arrived, he went into the tavern hoping an ale or two would calm his nerves and improve his disposition. Maybe he'd even have a wee droppy of whiskey.

Lucky sat alone at a table, carving his powder horn. Lucky's horn served as a journal of sorts, where he carved symbols of his adventures and expeditions through the years. The horn not only kept Lucky's powder dry, but Bear thought it a skillfully decorated piece of art.

He joined Lucky and ordered an ale and a whiskey.

Lucky continued to carve and said nothing.

Bear swallowed nearly half the ale in one gulp, and then wiped his mustache and beard with the back of his hand.

"That's the reddest and thickest head of hair I believe I've ever seen," Lucky said, pointing to Bear's head with the knife in his hand. "Indians would sure like to get ahold of you. I'm told some of them fancy red scalps—think it gives them strong spirits."

"Aye, red hair does seem to give a person strong spirits, but it has to be attached to the body it came with," Bear said.

Lucky grinned and then, turning serious, put up his carving knife. "You look troubled."

"John is on his way to fetch your friend O'Reilly. Alone," Bear said, finishing the ale.

"Alone? I thought you would be going too."

"Nay, 'twas decided differently. Stephen wanted me to guard the women and wee children when he and the Captain and William all had to be in town at the trial. John left a little while ago. Sam was reluctant to let him go alone, but John insisted, saying there had been no recent Indian problems near Boonesborough."

"He's right, but going north at night and alone is not a good idea. His life won't be worth spit if he encounters natives or thieves."

"That's what's got me worryin' so. He knows less about Indians and the wild than any of us."

"The trip there is only about a night's ride on the road that leads due north. But I had no idea one of you would be going alone and at night no less." Lucky shook his head. "How good a fighter is he?"

"He can hold his own, but he'd be the first to admit he's the worst fighter among us. He's more inclined to try to reason with people rather than fight them."

"Yes, we spoke the other day while he was buying supplies. He seems a man of strong faith. He told me he would like to preach someday and maybe build a church here in town. Lord knows, we sure could use one. Although some will think differently. Bear, you'd best go after him—and do it quick like or it's likely he'll never get that church built and we'll never get a chance to fall asleep during a sermon. You most likely will get back before the trial starts anyway and John's going to be a lot more vulnerable where he's travelin' than the women and children will ever be this close to Boonesborough."

"Stephen is worried more about the buffalo hunters bothering the women than he is Indians," Bear said, "because Sam thinks the bunch of cutthroats might try something during the trial."

"Those varmints will be nursing their wounds for a week and if

John doesn't get O'Reilly to talk to the Judge, those hunters will be causing Stephen more than worry. Eventually, they will come after you folks. The only way to stop them is to be sure Frank Foley finally gets what is coming to him. I'll go after John. He might be needin' some of my McGintey luck."

"Nay, thank ye just the same. We can take care of our own. And John's me brother," he said emphatically. He drank the whiskey in one gulp, stood up and tossed a coin on the table. "Will ye do me a favor, man? Ride out to our camp and tell them I have gone to join John. I do na want to waste any more time."

Lucky pushed back his chair and grabbed his rifle. "I'll do it. And Bear, keep that scalp of yours on your head."

CHAPTER 18

Sam listened to the rhythmic sound his blade made scraping against the whetstone held firmly in his hand. The sharpening took the edge off his restless mind as much as it put an edge on the blade. When forced to sit for any length of time, it had become his habit to hone the weapon until it was so keen it might cut a man who just looked at it too closely.

He thought about Bear sharpening Catherine's knife. Was she, as Stephen had suggested, just trying to make him jealous? If so, he had fallen for it, like a lovesick schoolboy. He wouldn't make that mistake again.

William sat near him, his blonde head bowed over a makeshift writing desk, making careful notes. His brother wanted to record everything the townspeople told him about Frank Foley and the other hunters and outline a defense strategy with Sam.

From what Sam had heard, the Judge was fair but impatient, and they both knew William would need to be both accurate and concise.

While William scribbled his notes, Sam worried about John. Like a sore tooth, his apprehension kept niggling at him. "I think

I should go after John," he finally told William. "We were beyond foolish to send him out on his own." He sheathed his knife and stood, then grabbed his rifle and powder, preparing to leave.

"You can't leave. You gave that constable your word," William said adamantly. "Neither can Stephen. The trial will start as soon as the judge arrives, which could be anytime. You'd both better be there or you will be presumed guilty, and you'll forfeit the bond money we gave the constable."

Sam sat down reluctantly. "Then Bear should go. Where the hell is he anyway?"

"I wouldn't be surprised if he was already on John's tail. I saw him leave earlier."

"I hope you're right. What were we thinking sending John on that errand alone?" Sam stood again and paced.

"He wanted to do his part, remember? He will be fine. He's not as green as you think."

He wanted to disagree with William about that, but it would serve no purpose. They needed to concentrate on preparing for the trial. He sat down once more.

What concerned him the most was what William had learned from reading the statutes in the constable's office. Kentucky law allowed liberal financial compensation to those unjustly injured in a fight. Lawmakers designed the new law to discourage the frequent fights commonplace among frontiersmen. There just were not enough lawmen or judges to discourage fighting, and many situations here fostered intense disagreements. So, they wrote the law to make a man think twice before he seriously injured someone.

He and William had visited with the constable several times, trying to get the young man to tell them everything he knew about Frank Foley and his companions. Mitchell was not much help. In fact, he seemed to be protecting the man for some reason. Sam felt sure Foley had blackmailed the constable or threatened him in some way. And William suspected that Foley and his followers deliberately picked a fight with them, intending to fake some serious injury, and then file a lawsuit to claim compensation for the damages. When William had asked the constable if this had happened before, the young man had clammed up, refusing to say any more.

The rest of the townspeople also seemed more than a little afraid of Foley. They acted as though they all knew something, but they would not give voice to it.

"I can't believe we have to defend against these beastly men," William said. "It's absurd enough to be laughable."

The sound of steel scraping against stone stopped as he glanced over at William from his nearby seat. "Boone wrote that Kentucky is a paradise, but he also said it was a howling wilderness, the habitation of savages and wild beasts."

"Indeed."

"What are you working on?" Kelly asked as she strode up. She dried her hands, wet from washing clothes, on her apron and then tossed a log onto the waning cook fire before sitting down beside them.

Sam watched as the log sent sparks and bits of ash flying all around them. One evil man can send trouble out in many directions, he mused. How many lives had Foley hurt and how many more would he hurt if they could not find a way to stop the loathsome man?

"Preparing for the trial," William answered. "Do you have any ideas?"

"Perhaps. Have you ever been somebody's lawyer?"

"No, technically not. However, I studied the law of the colonies for several years and would have started to apprentice with a law firm in Durham next year if we had not left New Hampshire. However, I have sat in on more trials than I can remember."

"Are you worried?"

"Maybe somewhat. I want to be competent enough to ensure my brothers receive a fair hearing and, of course, a dismissal of all these trumped up allegations."

"Once the Judge hears the facts he'll see how preposterous these charges are," Sam said, trying to sound more confident that he felt.

"Here's what I think. I bet those buffalo hunters made that constable come out here. He didn't seem to want to be here and he didn't act as if he believed what he was saying. He was just following somebody's orders is all," Kelly offered.

"I've been thinking something similar," Sam said. "You're quite shrewd for your age."

"I'm not so young." She got up and started pacing around the revived cook fire.

Sam noticed William watching the way Kelly moved, looking nearly spellbound. The young woman's long tresses draped against her slender body as she stepped with a natural gracefulness.

"Jane and Catherine and I were talking. One thing that worries the three of us is even if you are able to get the charges dismissed, what will keep those men from coming after us again? They will be boiling mad if the Judge does not find the Captain and Stephen guilty and they'll be apt to find their own justice. We've made them our enemies."

Sam could hear the fear in her voice. "They were already our enemies," he replied. "That sort is the enemy of all decent people. We were bound to tangle with them sooner or later. It's probably a good thing it was sooner. Somebody must stop them from hurting more people. It needed to be us."

"Why?" Kelly asked.

Sam chewed on the thought before answering. "Some men were made to defend the weak or the wronged. The Almighty made us strong men of principle and honor. He did that for a reason. This is one of those reasons."

"Like when William and Stephen helped me?" She stared at Sam. Her violet eyes sparkled with moisture in the firelight, but she didn't let the tears come.

William peered up at her and answered. "Yes," he said softly.

She did not say anything, but Sam could see her struggling to regain control of her emotions. He admired how brave she was trying to be.

"I'm glad we were able to help you Kelly. I'm glad God sent us there that day," William said.

"If you hadn't come, then...," Kelly started to say.

William finished the sentence for her. "I would have never met you."

Kelly smiled sweetly. A smile directed purely at William.

Sam decided he should go check on his horse.

"I need to get back to washing," she said.

"I need to get to work as well," William said, looking back at his notes.

Kelly suddenly seemed reluctant to leave. She started pacing around the fire again. "Is there any chance they'll give this up? After all, you men beat them in the fight."

"They did take a beating, but that won't stop them," Sam said. "They're not intelligent men ruled by logic and morality. Wielding power over others and insatiable greed control them. They prey on the weak to get that power."

"Then why did they challenge the group of you?" Kelly asked. "Heaven knows, you sure don't look weak."

William answered this time. "Men like Foley spend their lives climbing the ladder of evil. Every time they get comfortable with one crime, they try another even worse, especially if no one ever challenges them. Evil feeds on evil. It makes them cocky. Makes them think they are bigger and stronger than they really are. I think their leader has done enough bad things to enough people to make him think he could get away with even more."

"And they had numbers in their favor," Sam added, "six to three."

"What will they do to us next?" Kelly asked, sounding worried.

"They're cunning. They will try to catch us off guard. Maybe an ambush," Sam said. "But don't worry. We're not prone to be caught unawares. In fact, Stephen is on guard right now. And William is skilled at dealing with villains of this sort. You're safe with us."

"What do you think of Boonesborough?" William asked, changing the subject.

Sam understood how the bustling town would be a stark contrast to her old remote cabin in the woods. He wondered if she would be able to adjust.

Kelly appeared surprised by William's question. "I think it's noisier than chickens worrying about a fox and more crowded than a bee hive, but at the same time it's exciting. People starting new lives in a new place—just like me. I suppose I ought to try to find work here soon, but I haven't the vaguest notion of where to begin looking." She twirled her long blonde hair between her slender fingers.

"Perhaps that Mr. Wolf could introduce you to some folks around town. I'll speak to him about it if you like," William offered.

"That would be very kind of you." Kelly stared directly at William's eyes.

Sam rubbed his beard with his fingers and looked away. It was definitely time to check on his horse, he decided.

And later, after the evening meal, maybe he would give himself a shave and a haircut too, followed by a long swim in the river.

☙

Catherine gaped in stunned disbelief as her fingers touched her parted lips.

She glanced over at Jane who had stopped mid-stride with a stack of just washed plates in her hands. Her face frozen in an incredulous dazed look, Jane slowly sat the plates away.

She felt Kelly gripping her arm, as the young woman said, "Oh my."

Looking back, she took a deep breath, trying to slow her

galloping heartbeat.

Jane came over to the two of them and grabbed her other arm. "Do you see what I see?" she whispered. "Or are my eyes deceiving me?"

Catherine felt a sudden fluttering in her stomach. "And I thought he was handsome before." Her tentative smile was quickly followed by a little giggle, as she realized what she had said aloud.

Then Jane let out a bark of laughter and asked, "Is that *our* Sam?"

"Hush you two, or he'll hear you," Kelly said quietly.

Catherine spread her fingers out in a fan against her chest, as if to hold in the sudden tingling she felt through her breasts.

Sam stood on the other side of camp, talking to William.

Her gaze locked on his profile. His full beard was gone and his shorter shining wet hair hung just above his shoulders. His face, bronzed by wind and sun, appeared completely different. His jawline was even stronger, and as he stood there, she could see the smooth skin under his high cheekbones for the first time. His lips, now revealed completely, were full and sensual. A sudden longing to kiss them surprised her.

He also wore what appeared to be a new shirt. The crisp linen stretched across his broad shoulders, revealing his muscles far more than the fringed buckskin had allowed. The shirt had an open V-neck with laces on either side, which he had left hanging loose. She could see a few dark curly hairs poking out and she yearned to run her fingers over his muscled chest.

She sensed an awakening within her.

Her eyes roamed over his entire tall form—now he was even

more innately captivating and boldly handsome. As always, he exuded an air of authority, but now, you could more clearly see the power coiled within him.

Then, all of a sudden, he turned and smiled at…was it her….or all three of them?

He gave her a subtle look of amusement and she looked back at him for a long moment. For an instant, his eyes sharpened and then he turned his attention back to William.

"Did you see that smile?" Kelly asked.

"Yes," she breathed. She still felt its affects, all the way to her toes. Unable to stop herself, she stared with longing at this positively mesmerizing man.

"You know he did that for you don't you," Kelly said.

"Did what? Smile?" she asked.

Kelly grinned. "No silly, the shave and haircut. And the new shirt."

Jane's big green eyes grew even bigger. "I think you may be right, Kelly," Jane said. "I have never seen him in a shirt like that."

Catherine made herself stop staring and tried to throttle the dizzying desire racing through her. Her dormant body had come to life.

With a ripple of excitement, she took the other two by the arm, and turned them all around, before walking them swiftly away. "Come with me ladies. Jane grab some of your rose soap. There's just enough daylight left for us to go to the river and bathe and then you can help me into one of my special gowns," she said, unable to hide her high spirits from her voice, or to stop the butterflies from flittering through her insides.

NEW FRONTIER OF LOVE

❧

Just before sunset, anxious to try the new fresh tobacco he purchased in town, Sam found a quiet place by the river's edge to smoke his pipe. He studied the untamed splendor before him. The spectacular sandstone cliffs on the opposite bank awed him. He admired their natural stone formations and the lush shoreline, covered with tall hardwoods. The shelter provided by the high banks and the river's winding course, ensured that the wind had little impact on the water's surface.

On his side of the river, the ancient trees cast dark shadows on the blue-green water, so smooth it looked like glass. On the opposite side, the water's surface reflected a perfect upside-down image of the timber lining that bank. The images festooned the river's edge like garlands of ribbons and lace. He decided this would be his favorite spot while they remained in Boonesborough.

Would Catherine remain in Boonesborough or would she continue on? He hoped she would not decide to return to Boston. He had to admit, he didn't want her to leave.

As he filled the bowl with the tender fragrant leaves, he thought about what Stephen had told him in town. Could his brother be right? Could it be that Catherine loved him? The thought made his heart pound faster in his chest. But whether it raced because he wanted her to love him, or because he didn't, was still unclear to him.

Before he could light the pipe, he heard a sound behind him. Instantly, he stood, unsheathing his knife, gripping it tightly in his hand.

"It's just me Captain," Catherine said.

Sam took a slow deep breath and sheathed his blade, then

looked up. At the sight of her, he lost his breath again. His gaze roved as he appraised her, traveling first to her face and then to the creamy expanse of her neck and chest.

He cleared his throat, pretending not to be affected by her. "Please, join me," he said. He motioned to the large log that served as his perch.

"Goodness Captain, you have quite a view," she said, looking around them after she sat down.

Her slender hands unconsciously twisted together. Was she nervous?

"Yes, I do," he said, his eyes never leaving her. He did not want to tear his attention away from her for even a moment. Her beauty was exquisite, almost ethereal in the dimming light.

She wore an exceedingly becoming gown that he had never seen her wear. The burgundy satin nearly glowed in the evening light and the gown's low neckline revealed the soft mounds of firm breasts. Her long black hair hung loose and curling around her shoulders and framed the flawless pale skin of her face and chest.

As usual, her beautiful dagger hung from the sash tied about her small waist, yet she looked every inch a lady.

"Don't you think it's time you called me Sam?"

"Well, Sam, if you insist, it would be my pleasure." She smiled at him with lips that were full and rounded over even white teeth, and if he wasn't mistaken, he smelled fresh mint on her breath.

"You're looking particularly lovely this evening in that fetching gown." She was slender, but the gown accentuated every enticing curve.

"Thank you. It's my favorite gown," she said, stroking the rich fabric with her long fingers. "Frankly, I had had enough of feeling ugly and ill-kempt. For this one evening at least, I wanted to feel like a gentlewoman again for some reason. And there's nothing like wearing a fine dress to lift a lady's spirits."

"You could never look ugly, even in dirty rags. As for being a gentlewoman, you will always be one, no matter your circumstances. Although I admit, the genteel are few and far between here on the frontier."

"Indeed. But that doesn't mean we have to give up good manners and fashionable clothing. Sometimes, I miss feeling—well, like a lady."

"I'm sorry, if we haven't…"

"No," she interrupted, "it's not any of you. You've been most kind and gracious."

"Then?" He found his eyes trained on the distinct bow of her upper lip. It was perfect, and tempting. So tempting. His mouth nearly watered with an overwhelming urge to kiss her.

They seemed to share an undeniable physical awareness of each other, as an intense, nearly palatable, attraction built between them.

Pensively, she looked out into the near darkness. "I want to feel…," she hesitated, "I want…"

She turned her head back to him and gazed up and into his eyes with such need, he could only yield to it. He grabbed her waist, circled it with his arm, and tugged her against him. He could feel her soft breasts pressing against his chest and, within him, his heart, long cold and dormant, warmed and came fully alive.

She opened her lips to his. Then he lowered his mouth to hers, drinking her in, tasting the sweet wine of her lips and mouth. His kiss was urgent and exploratory. So this is what it felt like. A delicious, intoxicating sensation. He had wondered hundreds of times, far more than he wanted to admit, how it would feel to kiss her. And now he wanted to kiss her a hundred times more.

She quivered and he felt her body soften, yielding to the hunger growing between them. She gave herself freely to the passion in his kiss, demanding more with her own forceful domination of his lips.

As he roused her desire, his own grew stronger. But he controlled his demanding lips, making them caress hers, become slow and gentle. Touching her like a whisper, his tongue traced the fullness of her lips, moist and warm.

She returned a tantalizing feather-touch kiss. He nearly shook with the sweet tenderness of it.

When he began to feel his head spinning and heat flaming in his loins, he released her, while he could still put the fire out.

Raising his mouth from her lips, he gazed into her sparkling eyes.

Catherine, breathless, stared back at him with a searching earnestness. A soft pink flush, like sunrise on snow, rose on her cheekbones. As she caught her breath, she studied his eyes and he was lost in hers. They were speaking to him, eloquently, compellingly. He was beginning to believe Stephen was right. He saw love in those beautiful sapphire pools.

No, it's only the same smoldering desire that filled him.

"Sam, I..."

"Do you feel like a lady now?' he interrupted on purpose, tracing a fingertip lightly across her moist bottom lip.

"Sam, I never realized a kiss could feel like that. I...."

"Neither did I," he confessed, shocked at his own response. His lips still burned with a nearly uncontrollable urge to kiss her again.

He ran the same fingertip down her neck and then slowly across her chest. His hand nearly shook with the desire to touch her breast.

He could so easily become besotted with this woman.

But, he needed to end this now, before he took another step toward the abyss gleaming in her eyes. He was already smitten, it wouldn't take much more to make him fall in and drown. The first time he touched her, her pull was a delicate but tantalizing thread. Now it was stronger, and even more compelling.

"Shall we return to camp? It's getting quite late," he suggested before he said or did anything else.

He could almost see Catherine swallow her disappointment.

"Yes, of course." She turned away, no doubt weary of his reticence. Gathering her skirts, she abruptly started back to camp, her dark hair swinging about her proud shoulders as she walked.

He followed, closely behind, wanting to reach out and stop her with every step he took.

But he didn't.

CHAPTER 19

John kept his horse at an easy trot. Although harder on the rider, a trot allowed a horse to cover a long distance without wearing out. His horse should be able to get him there sometime tomorrow. The trail that led toward the O'Reilly brothers' farm was not difficult to follow. In fact, John found it quite scenic and, after traveling with such a large group for so long, the solitude seemed refreshing. He realized he needed some peace and quiet—time with only the good Lord as a companion.

Dusk began to descend but John decided he would not make camp until late tonight. The full moon would make staying on the trail easy enough and he wanted to get as far along as he could. He would press on until his horse started to give out.

He hoped he would be able to convince this O'Reilly fellow to come back to Boonesborough with him. Lucky McGintey had said O'Reilly was a reasonable man and had no wife or children and had only a brother who lived with him so he should be willing and able to leave quickly. Nevertheless, John also knew that anyone with a Scots or Irish name could be stubborn, sometimes for no apparent reason at all. He hoped this would not be one of those times.

When the moon hung nearly overhead, John finally stopped to let his horse rest. He decided against a campfire, afraid it might alert thieves or natives, so he settled for cold dried beef and biscuits. By then, he was so hungry they tasted delightful. He threw his blanket beside the saddle and leaned up against it, both his pistol and his Kentucky rifle next to him. He took in a deep breath, smelling the musky scent of the deep woods. The timber smelled differently here than it did back home.

Home. He closed his eyes and thought of Diana. What would she think of Kentucky?

He fell sound asleep within a few moments, the fatigue of being in the saddle at a hard pace all day catching up to him.

ತಿ

"If ye snored any louder, you'd waken the dead," Bear said, kicking the bottom of John's boot.

John tried to clear his head of the dream but part of it still lingered. He had slept hard and dreamt of Diana. A dream so real he could still feel her presence here with him. Maybe he *had* woken the dead. What did she say? In the dream, she seemed worried about something. She kept trying to speak to him, but no matter how hard he tried, he just could not make out what she said. The words were there but weren't there at the same time, as though they could reach his ears but not his brain.

John rubbed his eyes and rose up on one elbow. "What are you doing here?"

"Thought ye might be lonesome out here all by ye self."

"Bear, why are you here?"

"Something in me gut just told me I should join ye. Na other reason. Had an ale with Lucky just before I left Boonesborough and he said the same."

"You mean you came all the way out here to take care of me?"

Bear grinned broadly. "Like a mother would her babe."

John resented Bear's protectiveness. "You should have stayed at camp. That is what we all decided. I can take care of myself."

"Aye. Nonetheless, gettin' this witness is important to all of us. If ye do na mind, I'd like to help you get the man back to the Judge."

"All right, now that you're here. But in the future, let me take care of my responsibilities." John realized he should gladly welcome Bear's presence, but his pride stood in the way.

"I meant na disrespect, so do na take any," Bear said, pulling Camel's saddle off.

John stood to stretch and fixed his eyes on the heavens. The crisp air and the clear night magnified the brilliance of the full moon and stars decorating the black velvet sky.

He never felt closer to God than when he looked upon the night sky. Why? Maybe the sheer magnitude of the heavens made an individual man feel trifling and in need of protection. Or maybe it was just easier to see spiritually at night. Perhaps the unseen world was more visible with less light—or even no light. Maybe a person can see that which is spiritual more clearly without the distractions of light and color.

Bear interrupted John's theological ponderings. "I sometimes wonder if there's one of those wee stars for each of us."

"Maybe so," John said, his eyes still fixed above.

"Do ye believe that old Indian legend about a fallin' star?" Bear asked.

"You mean the one about when you see a falling star it means someone you know is going to die?"

"Aye. That's the one. It makes me na want to look up at those stars."

"I don't know," John said. "Nothing in scripture says that, although natives are a spiritual people. Maybe they've been given their own kind of wisdom."

"Their beliefs are pagan."

"Even so, could there be truth in it? What if their religion is just as holy as our faith?" John asked. "The earth is populated with many different peoples, of many different faiths."

"There's only one source for the Lord's word—the good Book. Everythin' else, written or spoken, painted or carved, man created, although they may have received the inspiration or talent from God, I would na call it 'holy.' The actions of those Indians we killed on our trip to Kentucky do na reflect the truths of the Lord's word. Unprovoked, they attacked us—nearly killed Stephen with that arrow—and not just the men, but Jane too. And they'd have killed or kidnapped the wee children if they'd had half a chance."

Bear carefully scanned the woods around them before he continued.

"And do ye know what they would have done to us if they'd captured us, man? I'll tell ye, because I've seen what was left after they've done it. First, they mutilate ye. Then they emasculate ye. Then they burn ye alive. I've beheld those blackened remains of what used to be a man. Spiritual beings could na do such a horrible thing."

John shuddered. "It is barbaric, but we're moving into their lands, their hunting grounds. They're protecting what's theirs."

"What makes it theirs? Just because it's their huntin' range? How can they be so greedy as to claim this entire vast wilderness as theirs? Besides, they do na have firm claim to most of their land. Tribal rivalries cause the boundaries between tribes to shift all the time. There's na difference between fightin' another tribe and fightin' us for land. D'ye know what they did a few years back to General St. Clair's army? They killed six hundred of his men and then stuffed every one of their mouths with dirt. Every one. It supposedly symbolized satisfyin' in death their lust for Indian lands."

"I believe they will eventually come to know Christianity as we do."

"Nay. My prediction is that 100, even 200, years from now, they'll still worship pagan gods. They will never willingly leave their culture or completely become a part of our country. But, that's their right I suppose."

A howling wolf broke the silence of the night and the eerie sound sent a chill skidding down John's spine.

Bear's hunter eyes methodically searched the surrounding area until he was satisfied there was no threat.

John glanced down at the tomahawk in his belt. He had reluctantly taken it when Sam said there was no such thing as having too many weapons in the wilderness. His older brother had said the west was welcoming to all types of men. You just had to be tough enough and smart enough to survive. He thought he was smart enough. But was he tough enough? He was beginning to have his doubts.

John's gaze turned back up to the heavens. He caught his breath as he watched a star fall from the sky.

Almost in response, wolves howled again in the distance, playing their long haunting notes.

"I'm worn out. Thought I'd never catch up to ye."

"Get some sleep. I'll stay awake," John said.

"I could use a wee nap, but stay very alert," Bear warned. He threw his pallet down near Camel. Bear's snoring, echoing through the forest, soon replaced John's.

John carefully scanned the darkness around them before getting comfortable again. The woods seemed to shudder as wind gusts made the branches of nearby trees quiver. The full moon sent whispery white beams through every tree bough, making the darkness seem full of menacing ghosts. The dream must still have him on edge.

He hated to admit it, but Bear's presence was comforting. Normally Bear was a gentle giant, but when danger confronted, the giant could handle most any danger fearlessly and ferociously.

John placed his rifle across his lap. The sounds of insects chirping, owls hooting, and bats flapping crowded the night air. He listened to them for some time, fighting sleep. Then he heard coyotes yap. They were close.

Both horses whinnied nervously.

John listened intently as seconds passed slowly. Now, a chill black silence surrounded them, the forest quiet. Except for Bear's rhythmic snoring, there were no other sounds.

Clenching his hand until his nails entered his palm, he peered over at Bear—thought about waking him. Decided against it. Bear needed rest. Probably just some animal making the horses nervous. He decided to relax and quit being so jumpy. He needed to be brave, like Sam.

Then his scant bravery turned to absolute terror.

Their locks feathered and their half-naked bodies and faces streaked with bright paint, two Shawnee came from nowhere.

He managed to fire his rifle, but the shot only hit a nearby tree.

One Indian grabbed him by the hair and arms while the other howled like a coyote.

His heart beat wildly as the howling brave grabbed his legs too. He struggled against a blurred sea of arms and hands, gripping, pulling and twisting him, forcing him to the ground. The raw musky scent of them was overpowering, so strong he could almost taste their smell. He screamed, as much to let out the vulgar taste in his mouth as his extreme fear.

ತಿ

Bear awoke abruptly to the sound of rifle fire. John? Instinctively and instantly, he rolled to his side, while grabbing his knife and hatchet. A tomahawk slammed into the ground where he had been.

Indians surrounded him, but he scrambled to his feet before they got a good grip on him. He put his hunting knife through the belly of the closest brave.

The Indian's eyes grew huge and glazed. He shoved the dying brave toward the others, causing them to fall back as they watched their companion's horrible death. The dying Indian held his stomach, trying to hold himself together before collapsing on his side at their moccasined feet.

Bear slammed the knife back into its sheath while pulling his pistol to defend against the other braves. Accustomed to fighting with both arms equally well, he shot one in the face, and then used the hatchet to slash another, nearly cutting through the man's arm.

He whirled to stare at another brave lunging at him. He sidestepped just in time, spun, and swung the hatchet in an arc, slamming it into the backside the Indian's skull.

He withdrew the ax and, as he raised it, another Shawnee wielding a knife came at him. The brave's blade ripped through his hunting shirt and etched a path across the skin of his chest. Blood spurted down his torso in a nearly perfect horizontal line. If he had not been so tall, the wound would have been across his neck. But the surface wound only vexed him. He stood taller, thrust his wounded chest out to his two remaining attackers and, teeth bared, growled at them.

They stepped back, prancing around him in a circle, one holding the knife dripping with Bear's blood, the other a hatchet. He was so much taller, they could not get anywhere near his head. Then the two braves positioned themselves on either side of him.

Bear took a firm grip on his own weapons as Gaelic curses spewed from his mouth.

ಹ

John fought with all his might but could not fend off his two attackers. Drowning in a flood of increasing fear and shock, before long he would be unable to breathe. One Indian sat on his legs and made it impossible for him to dislodge the brave kneeling across his stomach.

He repeatedly flailed his limbs and thrashed about, but the

braves quickly tied his hands and feet with rawhide. One of them straddled his stomach and snatched John's knife out of his belt.

Horrified, he suddenly realized what was coming and with all his strength writhed from side to side, trying to get away. But the brave only rode him like a wild horse. When John's strength gave out, the Indian smirked, seeming amused. Then the brave moved the knife closer to his face. He tried to bite the hand that held the knife.

Quick anger rose in the brave's eyes before the Indian slapped him hard.

He gasped, panting for air, his heart jumping in his chest.

The smack unnerved John and sheer black panic swept through him. He choked back a cry.

Frantic, he wildly sought out Bear. Where was he? He peered, wide-eyed, over his shoulder behind him. Bear was engaged in his own vicious battle. They were hopelessly outnumbered.

Overwhelming dread filled John as he realized they were both going to die.

God, he prayed, *take care of Little John*. Grief and despair stabbed at his heart.

The Indian seemed to enjoy watching his utter terror.

He could stand it no longer. He closed his eyes and prepared to meet his maker. Then he screamed as the blade slowly began to lift his scalp.

CHAPTER 20

Catherine glanced nervously at Sam as he rode beside her. This morning he had agreed to escort her to town so that she could see a lawyer or the Judge to go over her late husband's will and papers. Sam said he would get his horse shod while she was taking care of her business in town.

She liked riding beside him, but she found his nearness both exciting and disturbing. He was so ruggedly handsome, especially now that he was clean-shaven. And everything about him radiated strength. She would feel safe anywhere with him beside her.

What made her nervous was that her thoughts kept returning to the night before when he had held her in his arms and kissed her as no man had kissed her before. Not that she had that much experience with kissing, but Sam's kiss was in a league of its own. It stirred such desire in her that she wanted nothing more than to have him kiss her again. And then again, and again.

But he didn't and abruptly suggested that they should return to camp. It had taken all of her will to turn and leave, letting him follow behind her in silence the short distance back to camp. With every step, she had experienced a gamut of perplexing emotions.

All her loneliness and confusion rushed through her, chased by an overwhelming yearning for love and an intense desire. With him following so closely behind her, she had to silence the screams of frustration at the back of her throat.

What else could she do to get Sam to take a chance on loving her?

When they had reached their camp, he had simply taken out his pallet and laid down without saying another word. With everyone else either already asleep or getting ready for bed, she had no choice but to climb in her wagon, remove her special gown, and try to do the same.

She had worn one of her finest gowns that evening and taken extra care with her hair. And although he took notice and complimented her appearance, he seemed content with a brief conversation and one kiss. Because his kiss sizzled with passion, his abrupt change in mood puzzled her.

She had hoped for so much more. She wanted to tell him she loved him. But the opportunity was lost.

As she rode, her mind fought through the cobwebs of a night of little sleep. Tormented by chaotic thoughts about Sam and her future she was unable to fall asleep for hours. As she tossed and turned, she forced herself to plan her tasks ahead. She finally decided she needed professional advice about what her husband's papers revealed and would talk to a lawyer the very next day.

If only she could get expert advice about that astounding kiss. Even more so, about why Sam had not kissed her again. Instead, he had quickly put a shield between them and that baffled her.

Now, as they rode to town, Sam boldly met her gaze. What, for heaven's sake, did that look in those captivating eyes of his mean?

Did he suspect what she was thinking? She pulled her horse to an abrupt stop, tired of this emotional limbo.

As she did, Sam tugged on Alex's reins, stopped, and turned his mount toward her. "Is something wrong?" he asked.

The confident set of his broad shoulders, his commanding manner and obvious inherent strength were almost more than she could handle. Her pulse quickened with desire.

"Yes. I mean no. What I intended to say was…what I intended to ask was…," she tried. "Oh for pity's sake. Just forget it." She felt her face flush and her lips purse with anger. Or was it frustration?

"If you're thinking about last night—about that kiss—I wouldn't blame you. I should beg you to forgive me for being so brash, but I won't apologize for it." There was a slight hesitation in his eagle-like eyes, then he said, "It was perhaps the most pleasant thing I have experienced in many years."

Her anger instantaneously cooled.

"But, it was just a kiss Catherine."

Her anger immediately flared again.

She sat back in the saddle, affronted. Just a kiss! For heaven's sake. It was not just a kiss. It was more than that and he knew it. Why was he acting so distant? She had had just about enough of his acting standoffish. "You're right, of course, Sir. It was just a kiss. It meant nothing. Shall we proceed?" She nudged her horse to a swift trot and took off, leaving Sam behind to follow her.

She kept her mount well ahead of Sam. She damn sure wasn't going to let him ride next to her and let him see the angry tears that kept threatening to fall from her eyes.

A few minutes later, they reached Boonesborough, and she

wiped the back of her glove against a tear that had escaped.

Sam stopped at the office of the Land Speculator to have Mr. Wolf direct them to the office of an attorney.

Catherine waited outside, mounted on her horse, and still fuming. But as Sam came back outside, she took a deep breath and tried her best to appear unruffled and to stifle her ire.

"Mr. Wolf tells me Walker Daniels, a lawyer from Louisville, is in town. His office is next to Henderson & Co. trading post, just down the street," he said.

He remounted and they located the office. After verifying that Mr. Daniels was in his office, Sam helped her dismount and then said, "I'll leave you here to discuss your affairs with Mr. Daniels. As soon as I finish my business with the blacksmith, I'll come back and see if you've finished."

"Thank you *Captain Wyllie*," she said, deliberately not calling him by his given name. If he wanted to keep things formal, she was happy to oblige him.

"Catherine, don't take my actions as indifference," Sam said. "I have the highest regard for you and your friendship holds the greatest value to me."

His eyes and voice displayed concern, but she saw no evidence of anything more.

A jumble of confused thoughts beset her, fusing together in a surge of indignation. "I don't know how to interpret your 'actions' Captain." *Or what 'highest regard' means*! "But this is not the time or the place to discuss this," she said. Striving to conceal her inner turmoil, she looked away. A war of emotions raged within her. She wanted to punish him and make him want her at the same time.

Crossing his arms and widening his stance, he said, "You're

right, of course. If you finish before I do, please wait for me inside the attorney's office. I don't want you exposed unescorted to some of the men of Boonesborough."

Who did he think he was? He had no right to tell her where to wait. With a disbelieving shake of her head, she turned abruptly, picked up her skirt, and opened the door to Mr. Daniels' office before nearly slamming it behind her.

ॐ

Torn by conflicting emotions, Sam stared at the banging door, feeling his eyebrows squish together. Baffled, he shook his head. Stephen was right. The actions of a woman can definitely befuddle a man. As he walked Alex toward the blacksmith's, he puzzled over their conversation that morning.

Clearly, the kiss had meant more to her than he assumed. He had not intended to kiss her, but he had been helpless to resist her beauty and those inviting lips. What did she expect looking like that? She was dazzling.

In truth, the taste of her had shocked him to his core. He grinned, just remembering the feel of her lips as she returned the kiss with far more fervor than he expected. His instinctive response to her eagerness was powerful and he had not anticipated one kiss to inflame him that quickly or as intensely.

He had forced himself to cut it off after that. If he hadn't then he might have taken them where they definitely did not need to go. She wanted love and marriage—he wanted neither.

But he enjoyed being with her. He liked talking to her. He fancied looking at her. He admitted to some affection for her and he couldn't deny the strong attraction. But that was all his heart would permit. No more. Not yet.

≈

After Catherine finished with the lawyer, she went next door to Henderson & Co. William, who seemed to have learned everything there was to know about Boonesborough, had told her that Daniel Breedhead, an enterprising businessman, owned the store and he suggested she might enjoy visiting the shop while she was in town. William explained that Breedhead made purchases of merchandise in Philadelphia, which he then transported across the mountains in freight wagons to Pittsburgh, and thence by boats to Louisville, the site of his first store, and lastly, again by wagon to Boonesborough. His stores were the first in Kentucky that sold foreign goods.

As soon as she opened the door, she sensed a pleasing mixture of fragrances—cinnamon, coffee, honey, rum, pepper and leather. The shelves of the well-stocked store brimmed with an enticing array of commodities. Her eyes widened at all the wonderful choices. What to buy? The inevitable dilemma faced by women shopping in stores everywhere. Finding something pretty to purchase was never her problem. Narrowing her selections down often proved difficult and she frequently solved that conundrum by just buying them all. Her bedroom in Boston overflowed with hat boxes, gloves, hair combs, shawls, slippers, boots, and other items, crammed into every nook and corner.

If she stayed in Boonesborough, and that remained to be determined, she would arrange to have all her pretty things shipped to her. What she didn't need she could share with Kelly and Jane.

Catherine began to stroll around, picking up items now and then to inspect them. A pair of tin wall sconces caught her eye. No point buying them though until she had a home to put them in.

She wondered how long that might take.

"Good morning to you Madame," a kind male voice said.

She glanced up to see a tall, slim, well-dressed man addressing her. His carefully groomed hair was as black as hers. And his green eyes seemed to widen as he scrutinized her.

"Good day," she responded.

He gave her a cloying smile and then said, "Is there something specific I can help you locate?"

She suspected that this was Daniel Breedhead. "No, I am just familiarizing myself with what your fine store offers."

"We offer the best of everything that I am able to acquire and transport. Every year, our inventory grows larger. In fact, next year I plan to double the size of this store. And I'm sending more and more goods back from here—tobacco, salt, corn, furs, and other commodities needed in the states."

"Henderson & Co. Where does that name come from?" she asked.

"It was the late Judge Richard Henderson that chose Daniel Boone in 1775 to lead a party of axe men to clear a path through the Cumberland Gap. The store is named in honor of him," he answered. "Please let me know if I may be of any assistance to you in any way," he said, before turning back toward his paperwork.

"Have you any new books?" she asked.

"Indeed. They are over here," he said, leading her to a long wooden shelf in the center of the crowded store.

Catherine heard the store's door open and looked behind her. Sam ducked his head and entered. She turned back and pretended not to notice.

"I have a fine assortment," the man said, pointing to the full shelf. "Perhaps you might enjoy 'Poems Chiefly in the Scottish Dialect' by Robert Burns, or 'The Age of Reason' by Thomas Paine. And if you enjoy cooking, I have a copy of 'The Accomplished Gentlewoman's Companion Cookbook.' It contains an excellent recipe for Apple Tansey that will make your mouth water."

"What's this?" she asked, picking up 'A Vindication of the Rights of Woman.'

"I thought I would find you here," Sam said, coming up behind her. He pointed to the book in her hand. "That book was written by Mary Wollstonecraft about five years ago. A thought-provoking book, she argues that instead of viewing women as society's ornaments or property to be traded in marriage, women ought to have the same fundamental rights as men, including an education."

"So you are familiar with this work, Sir?" Breedhead asked.

"Indeed," Sam answered. "I've read it."

Catherine could only stare at Sam, his profile strong and confident. So this book was the source of his enlightened views.

"Daniel Breedhead," the man said, extending his hand.

"A pleasure to make your acquaintance, Sir. I'm Captain Sam Wyllie, recently relocated here from New Hampshire."

"It is a delight to meet a well-read man. Here in Boonesborough, I fear that occasion is rather rare. Yes, the book was surprisingly well-received and recommended to me by a publisher in Philadelphia. I have not yet read it myself, but my understanding is that the author claims that women are essential to the nation because they educate its children."

"More than that, she also believes that with an education of their own they can contribute to society and be more interesting companions to their husbands," Sam added.

"Rather than mere wives?" Breedhead asked.

"A woman is never 'mere' regardless of their education," Sam answered.

"I will take all four books," she said, still stunned by Sam's familiarity with the book. So, he reads books too. This unpredictable enigmatic man surprised her yet again. What else could he do?

"And I'll require enough candy to keep three children happy for a while," Sam said.

The man wrapped up a nice assortment of candy and they paid for their purchases.

As they turned to leave, she stopped and asked Sam, "Why did you read Wollstonecraft's book?"

"I make it a point to read as many books as I can get my hands on. Jane enjoys reading as well and she passes books on to me, including that book. After reading it, I decided the book was one reason Jane exhibits such a strong spirit." He regarded her with amusement, before adding, "Perhaps Stephen needs to read it as well."

She looked up at him with wonder. It amazed her that this hardened soldier should have such enlightened views of women— so unlike her departed husband, who thought women incapable of making decisions on their own, except perhaps those regarding fashion or food. Even in those areas of her life, the man often felt compelled to supply her with his patronizing opinions. After her husband's murder, when she was confused about what her proper course of action should be, Sam had encouraged her to decide her own destiny.

He was a complex man, an ever-changing mystery. After all this time, she was still learning new things about him. She was also still annoyed with him, but despite herself, she just could not stay angry with him.

"You are a puzzling man Captain," she said. "Here. I bought this one for you." She handed him the book of Burns' poetry. Perhaps the book by Scotland's romantic bard would inspire Sam to look more favorably on love.

CHAPTER 21

Bear's torn shirt flapped open. He felt his blood running through the fur on his chest. Then he heard John begin to scream. The ghastly shrill sound released a deep animal rage within him. He needed to end this now and get to John.

He lifted his arms and roared a horrendous growl.

Both braves jumped back and stared wide-eyed at him.

Bear's face, burned with anger. He thrust out his jaw and clenched teeth. He used his eyes to challenge them, hoping they would retreat into the forest. When a second or two ticked by and they hadn't moved, he acted. As fast as a streak of lightening, his knife flew into the Indian coming from behind him, and like the crack of thunder that follows, his hatchet slammed into the remaining Shawnee.

Then, over where John was, he heard a shot and the sickening sound of a man's head splitting open. The noise momentarily covered John's screaming. The lead ball exploded through the skull of the Shawnee who had just started to scalp John, throwing part of the left side of the native's head to the breeze. Dead, but still holding a knife, the Indian fell on top of John, solidly planting the blade into the ground next to John's head.

"Damn, that was too close," Bear swore. He bent to retrieve his knife and hatchet.

As he marched toward John, the remaining Indian fled into the darkness of the forest.

ଔ

Even more than the Indian laying on top of him, John felt the blade, covered with his own warm blood, pressing against the side of his head.

He was too stunned to move. He could only lay there, amazed that he was still alive.

Bear ran up, heaved the dead native off him, and tossed the body aside as if it were made of straw. Bear pulled the blade next to John's head and used it to cut the rawhide from his wrists and feet.

He tried to open his eyes and look up at Bear, but blood dripped into his eyelids. With shaking hands, he did his best to wipe the blood from his face.

"I told ye these natives are beasts," Bear bellowed. While reloading his weapons, the angry giant swore a long string of curses, undoubtedly releasing some of his anger. "Are ye more inclined to believe me now?"

John could see Bear's wild eyes searching the woods around them for any further signs of their attackers. He prayed there would be no more.

He could barely move. His arms and legs felt like lead weights. He had never come so close to death. His head spinning with shock and pain, John rolled over on his right side and emptied his stomach. Every upchuck made his head hurt even worse, but he heaved until there was nothing left but a bitter taste in his mouth. He stayed down, unable to sit up, blood dripping from the slice on his forehead.

Still breathing heavily, Bear came over, helped him to sit up, and then wiped the blood running into John's eyes with his own shirt sleeve. "Hold still if ye can bear it—I've got to move about two inches of your hair back where it belongs."

He took a deep breath to steady himself, peered up at Bear, and nodded. As Bear started to reposition his scalp above his forehead, he struggled not to scream and gritted his teeth against the pain.

"Thank you," he said, feeling lightheaded, but better, when Bear finished. "Where'd that shot come from?"

Bear pointed as Lucky calmly strode up, finishing reloading his rifle.

"Glad to see ye," Bear told Lucky. "John did need a wee bit of your luck after all."

"In truth, luck had nothin' to do with it," Lucky said. "The good Lord provided enough moonlight to take reasonable aim and made that pert wind die down a bit. It was also this good ol' rifle—she's a real fine weapon, likes a challenge. Can make a shot like that even in this breeze."

"A blessing for me," John said, his voice shaking, "another few ticks and I'd be balding at an early age. I am in your debt Sir. And yours Bear. If you hadn't been here..." His words trailed off, too weak to continue speaking.

"I think we scared 'em off for a while," Lucky said calmly,

"especially big Bear here. Did you hear that roar John?"

"Surely the whole forest heard it," John said.

"They probably thought he was a wendigo, that's the native word for a half-man, half-beast demon creature," Lucky said.

"Maybe they're right," John murmured, looking around at the carnage. He had never seen the results of a man fighting as savagely as Bear just had. Mutilated Indian bodies surrounded them. They looked like fallen human trees, cut down by some sort of axe-wielding madman. "My God, Bear."

"We'd best be heading on to O'Reilly's place before that one survivor of Bear's onslaught brings more of his comrades," Lucky suggested. "But if that brave convinces them Bear was a wendigo, we'll not see them again."

Bear helped John sit up again.

"Before this happened, I thought of them as children of the wilderness," John said sadly. He inhaled deeply and tried to stand, testing his legs. Although still shaky, he stooped to pick up his blanket. Blood dripped as he bent over and his head wound screamed as he stood back up. He closed his eyes to the dizzying pain. He gingerly touched his hairline, wincing. He felt sweat break out on his upper lip and forehead.

Bear reached into his saddlebag. "I've learned from experience it pays to carry bandages whenever ye're away from home. Here. Sit back down for a wee spell. Press this cloth to yer wound now and try to keep pressure on it while we ride. I know it will cause you even more pain, but it will stop the bleedin'. Do na worry, head wounds always bleed profusely but heal very quickly."

John gritted his teeth against the throbbing wound and accepted the cloth, glad that Bear had the foresight to carry them.

"I'll reload your rifle and saddle your horse," Bear said. "When we get to the next creek, we'll stop and ye can wash away all that blood."

☙

Jonathan O'Reilly and his brother Justin, wielding on ax and a sledge hammer as they worked on a split rail fence, looked up when John, Bear, and Lucky rode up early the next morning.

John's head wound still throbbed and burned like fire, but aside from making him break out in a clammy sweat, he was feeling reasonable.

Their shirts already soaked with perspiration from their labors and the humid air, the O'Reillys welcomed them, their musical Irish inflections adding warmth and merriment to their cheerful greetings.

The three dismounted and shook the brothers' hands. Bear towered over the two handsome brothers, both only about five-feet tall. Bear enthusiastically introduced himself to Jonathan and warmly slapped the little man on his shoulder as he greeted him. Unfortunately, Bear's strength surprised them both and Jonathan went sprawling to the ground landing on his side.

"Dear heavens!" John exclaimed, dismayed.

"Oh my, my apologies, Sir," Bear said, picking Jonathan up with one arm. "Sometimes I forget my own strength." Clearly embarrassed, Bear's ruddy complexion colored fiercely.

Jonathan straightened and brushed off his clothing, a wide grin spreading across his face. "I haven't received a slap like that since I was a wee lad gettin' disciplined by me mum."

"Again, I beg yer forgiveness. I just meant to be friendly," Bear said.

"Em, I'd hate to see you when you were unfriendly," Justin said, raising his blonde brows.

"I've seen him unfriendly, and trust me, you don't want to see it," Lucky said.

"It's not the first time Bear has accidentally knocked someone to the ground with just a friendly cuff, and I doubt it will be the last. But my head is burning like the dickens. If you don't mind, Sirs, we need to get on with the reason we're here," John said.

Lucky quickly explained why they had come.

"I'm na surprised that bastard has caused more problems," Jonathan said after listening to Lucky. "He's a damn traitor. That is God's truth. I would swear that to anyone. But I do na want Foley's brother and those other dirty buffalo hunters comin' after Justin seeking revenge if I say anythin'."

"My brother William said he would arrange for you to see the Judge privately," John said. "If he can't, we'll not put you or your brother in jeopardy. We'll find another way."

"Does Foley know you've come out here to our place then?" Justin asked, clearly worried.

"Nay," Bear said. "Lucky and I both left town separately and caught up to John on the trail leading up to your place. Only one Indian knows we're here."

"Judging from John's head, it looks like you ran into some of those forest demons," Jonathan said.

"Aye, but all but one are dead," Bear said. "He ran off."

"No doubt to describe the wendigo that killed all the others," Lucky said. Then he explained what a wendigo was and why they might think Bear was one.

"Our thanks. They might have headed here. Most of the natives are peaceful, and once they even exchanged some food with us, but occasionally small petty bands give us trouble. We've shot a few off their horses and so they usually leave us alone. John, do you need to lie down lad?" Justin asked.

"The bleeding stopped and I'm able to tolerate the pain, but I would like to sit for a short while. I could sure use some hot coffee too. We've been riding most of the night."

"Coffee it is then. I'd offer you whiskey for the pain, but we're out. Let's get some food in your bellies and then we'll head to your camp," Jonathan said, turning toward their small log home. "My brother and I need to pick up supplies in Boonesborough anyway. An Irishman out of whiskey for too long can be unpleasant to be around."

"I'll be arguing with you about that," Justin said, catching up to his brother.

"I know you won't be arguing about the whiskey, is it about going in to see the Judge then?" Jonathan asked.

"Use your head brother. It is far too dangerous. We'll wind up getting' one of us killed if you do this thing," Justin objected.

"Then killed we'll have to be. It is past time I told what I know about that evil man. A man who hides the truth also hides his honor."

CHAPTER 22

The circuit Judge pounded his gavel as he called his courtroom to order at exactly eight o'clock in the morning. The sound echoed against the room's wooden walls and floor. The fifteen-star flag of the Union hung in the corner, giving the plain room a semblance of officiousness. The Judge shuffled some papers, dipped his quill in an ink pot, and began to write, evidently creating a record of the proceedings.

Those involved and those just curious stuffed the room beyond its capacity. Bud Foley, Frank Foley's brother, and the other buffalo hunters elbowed their way to the front, forcing others to move aside. The hunters took up a good part of the available spectator space. At once, the room began to reek of their disagreeable stench—a putrid mixture of dried blood seasoned with copious amounts of dirt and sweat.

Foley's surly countenance also soured the atmosphere as he slumped in his chair next to the young constable.

The constable, his hair slicked back with grease, appeared to Sam to be far more anxious than Foley did. The young man sat in his chair as if it was a church pew on Sunday morning.

If he were honest, he was anxious himself—eager for this charade to be over with.

Catherine sat directly behind the small table where Sam, along with Stephen and William, were seated. He turned to look at her, but her eyes were focused on the Judge. She looked lovely in a new blue gown, her raven hair shimmering as the morning sun poured on her through the only window. But worry dimmed the normal brightness of her face and he noticed that her hand rested on her dagger attached to the gown's belt. He realized she was still irritated with him and wouldn't look at him. For that, he was almost grateful. He needed to be able to focus on what the Judge was saying.

Reluctantly, he forced himself to turn back around, but he couldn't force his mind to stop thinking about her. That morning, she insisted on going to the courtroom and no amount of arguing was going to stop her. It annoyed him a great deal because he did not want her anywhere near these buffalo hunters. However, as the trial began, he was actually pleased she was there. But why? He remembered their kiss—the most memorable of his life, and he had stolen quite a few as a spry young man. But never had a kiss stirred his soul as that one had. He could make himself feel drunk with pleasure just thinking about it.

But a kiss was just a kiss. It wasn't love. He didn't love her. He couldn't love her. He told her it was just a kiss. He'd been honest with her. He crossed his arms in front of him. It would remain a pleasant memory he would store up for lonely nights. Nothing more.

After he had finally given up arguing with her about attending the trial, Catherine had generously given a surprised Jane enough money to treat herself, Kelly and the children to something new.

She said it was a thank you for all the hospitality and protection their family had provided her. They all needed new clothing, and Sam and Stephen didn't want them to remain alone at camp. A shopping excursion to the general store and some of the town's assorted shops seemed a perfect solution. Jane was exceedingly worried about the trial, but her daughters needed looking after and a trip to town was just the distraction they all needed. Catherine had made Jane promise to spend every penny of the money that very day.

Sam decided to try to turn his mind to the buffalo hunters. His jaw clenched as he memorized their faces, still bruised and swollen from the fight. As he studied each one, his fists tightened, pulling his skin taut over his own cracked and swollen knuckles. His eyes locked on the one they called Big Ben. The man had a foot-long skinning knife in a scabbard under his left shoulder. The hunter's wild and cocky amber eyes glowered back at him. With a sense of foreboding, he knew instinctively that he would again tangle with the man no matter the outcome of the trial. Sudden anger clawed at him for no apparent reason, like a primitive warning.

As Sam scrutinized Big Ben, he saw uncertainty creep into the hunter's expression. Good, he wanted to rattle the arrogant bastard.

Then, a sudden chill filled him as he heard the Judge's gavel vigorously pound again.

He didn't know how any of this was going to end.

❧

"Mr. Foley, I'm not surprised in the least to see you in my courtroom based upon your history and reputation. I *am* surprised that you are not the defendant. Since you appear to be here without representation, state your complaint," Judge Webb ordered, glowering at Foley.

"I don't need no money-taking, slick-talking, lying lawyer to tell you what these dirty pilgrims did. I can speak for myself. Those men attacked my men and me. Just because they're some highfalutin' family from back east doesn't give them the right to attack honest Kentucky citizens. They killed a good man and nearly killed me. I lost this hand to the big one over there. Take a look at his knife Judge. It's unlike anything I've ever seen. A knife like that is only meant for one thing—killing."

The Judge motioned for Sam to show him the knife.

Sam stood, freed the knife from its sheath, and held the glistening blade up for the Judge to see.

"Very impressive, Captain," Judge Webb said before turning his attention back to Foley.

"He threw that knife at me like I was some kind of wild animal. I was just picking up my rifle to leave." Foley pointed a long dirty finger at Stephen. "And that man nearly beat me to death. I want them punished for what they done. They murdered one of my men and brutally beat the rest. And I've suffered more in the past week than you can imagine. The pain has been unbearable."

No more than you deserve, Sam thought to himself.

"I want them to pay me for the loss of this hand. I made an honest living hunting buffalo. I was one of the best killers of that wild beast in the state. I'll never be able to balance a heavy gun or skin a buff again. They robbed me of my living, which brought me considerable profit in the past. Kentucky law says I should get paid for my injury. They surely brought money with them to buy land. I'll take that as payment for my hand."

"I'm sure you would, but I'll decide what you get. And you sure as hell don't need to tell me what Kentucky law says," Judge Webb growled. "I asked you to state your complaint. Have you done so, or is there more?"

"Ain't this enough?" Foley answered sarcastically, holding up his arm without a hand.

"Mr. William Wyllie, I understand you represent your brothers Stephen and Sam Wyllie."

William stood. "That is correct your Honour."

"Would you please tell me what the hell happened?"

"Indeed, your Honour. My brothers and I are newcomers to Kentucky. Like many of this new state's citizens, we came here in search of the good land, so plentiful on the frontier, and so scarce in our home state of New Hampshire. Captain Sam Wyllie, Stephen Wyllie, and our adopted brother Bear McKee, had just left the office of Mr. Wolf, to whom the three men had gone to discuss land availability. When they started back to our camp, Mr. Foley grabbed Captain Wyllie's horse. Foley insisted on buying the horse, although Captain Wyllie made it abundantly clear the horse was not for sale. Foley told his man to get two cases of whiskey to trade for the horse. When my brothers then tried to move on, Foley proceeded to behave in a manner not befitting a gentleman, and referred to them as cowards. And on this and one other instance, he also insulted the females in our party. Since there are ladies present, I will not repeat his vulgar words. That insult is not something any man of character, especially my brothers, are prone to overlook. They dismounted and defended their honor, your Honour."

"So, this fight started because they were insulted?" Judge Webb asked.

"Well," William hesitated, knowing he was trapped, "yes, your Honour."

"And, did I understand correctly, Captain Wyllie threw the first punch?"

"He did, Sir, but…" William stammered.

"There are no buts, Mr. Wyllie. Either he did or he didn't. Do you have anything else to say in your brothers' defense? Do you have any witnesses?" Judge Webb asked. The Judge shifted in his chair as though he were already uncomfortable.

The prickly Judge was not the only one ill at ease. Sam could see William growing more exasperated by the second. He watched as William loosened the perfectly tied cravat around his neck, and then took a deep breath now that he could breathe a little easier.

"Indeed, your Honour, I have a good deal more to say. A ball from Mr. Foley's own weapon killed his man. An unfortunate accident that would never have happened had Foley not pointed his weapon at my brother Stephen. Captain Wyllie merely responded to that serious threat, believing our brother Stephen was about to be fatally shot. In fact, my brother exercised restraint. If you knew the Captain's ample skill with his knife, you would know that he could easily have aimed to kill Mr. Foley. Instead, he only sought to get the man to drop his weapon by aiming for his arm.

"Also, your Honour, some of what I have to say may shock the court. I have determined that Mr. Foley has, at the very least, intimidated and harassed numerous townspeople causing considerable grief. He and his men behave in an unruly manner, but most importantly…."

"Mr. Wyllie," Judge Webb interrupted, "half the men in

Kentucky behave in an unruly manner, and the other half will undoubtedly do so soon. May I remind you, Mr. Foley is not on trial here, your two brothers are. Your facts should pertain only to this case. Otherwise they are as worthless as farts in a whirlwind."

William's face turned red at the Judge's terse and imaginative reprimand.

Was his brother going to lose this case before their defense even begun? What would they do if he did? He knew one thing for sure. He wasn't going to jail. He turned to look at Stephen, but his eyes caught Catherine instead. Her head bent and hands folded respectfully, he could tell she was praying. Did she care for them so much that she would pray on their behalf?

The sight seemed to strengthen him. He could feel her concern in his heart. In that moment, he wanted nothing more than to take her in his arms and reassure her that everything would be all right. They would not lose. Somehow, William would make the Judge understand.

Despite being humiliated, William straightened, and seemed to gather his wits. "Your Honour, I am trying to establish this man's character, or more accurately the lack of it, to this court. If Mr. Foley's account is to be believed in this incident, he must be a man of honor. His actions toward others are an indication of his lack thereof."

"The purpose of this court is not to determine the virtue of a man. I'll leave that to *the* judge," Judge Webb retorted, pointing heavenward with his gavel, "and I will remind you, Mr. Wyllie, but once more. Mr. Foley is not on trial here."

CHAPTER 23

"If your Honour will permit me a few more moments of the court's time," William said deferentially.

And patience, Sam thought.

"All right Mr. Wyllie, proceed, but get to your defense quickly." Judge Webb squirmed in his chair again. "And be damn sure your facts are relevant."

"Your Honour, Captain Wyllie and Stephen Wyllie did not strike Mr. Foley and his men until provoked beyond what men of principle could be reasonably expected to withstand. And, Captain Wyllie did not throw his knife until after Mr. Foley picked up and aimed his powerful weapon with the intention of mortally harming Stephen Wyllie. I call Mr. Tom Wolf to the stand to testify to these facts. Mr. Wolf witnessed the entire fight. He is the only one, of at least a dozen men who can offer similar testimonies to these unfortunate events, who has the courage and fortitude to testify. All of the others are so afraid of retribution by these ruffians they will not take the stand. However, Mr. Wolf, as you are no doubt already aware Judge, is a man of honor and a leading citizen in this community and believes it his duty to testify. He understands that men like these ruffians must be held accountable, or his children will grow up in a place without law and order."

Foley and the other buffalo hunters glared and jeered at Wolf as he came forward.

Wolf glanced sharply back at them, his eyes blazing, and then stood before the judge.

Sam still couldn't believe Mr. Wolf had agreed to testify. He suspected Wolf had heard the same story about Foley being a traitor and saw this as an opportunity to rid Boonesborough once and for all of these troublemakers. Men like Foley's bunch were bad for business.

Wolf quickly described the incident to the Judge who clearly continued to grow impatient. The witness stressed the part of the fight where Sam could easily have killed one of Foley's men, but instead exercised restraint and mercy by only cutting the man's long hair, not his throat.

Sam swallowed. He had Stephen to thank for his supposed restraint.

"Thank you Mr. Wolf, you may leave." The Judge waved the witness away.

Foley jumped up. "That's not at all what happened. He only has one witness. I have four sitting right here. They'll all tell you that Stephen fellow there attacked me first and I never pulled a weapon on nobody. I want my brother to testify first."

"Let's save the court some time, shall we?" Judge Webb glared at the group of buffalo hunters. "Do you all agree with the version of the incident told by your leader?"

The four men all vigorously shook their heads.

"I thought so. Please continue Mr. Wyllie."

"If Mr. Foley can use his brother and companions as witnesses, than so could I. Instead, as you just heard, I have provided the court with a very credible third party, not involved in the altercation.

"Judge Webb, the most important information for the court to consider is that Mr. Foley's testimony cannot be trusted because he is a man wholly without principle. We have reason to believe that he is in this new state of Kentucky to escape probable punishment in the colonies for treason. We believe he served as a scout for the British during our war for independence."

Sam saw outrage flash across the faces of those in the courtroom, including the stunned Judge. Webb's angry gaze swung over to Foley. Treason was the most despicable of crimes.

One man in the courtroom yelled out, "You lousy red-coat hell spawn."

"You served the locusts of the nation," another shouted.

"The dogs would have enslaved us," bellowed another, "and ravished our daughters."

Sam wasn't surprised that the emotions that fueled the Revolution still ran high. But he now knew honorable men had fought for the British too. The bitterness of war, though, was a hard fire to put out.

After the shouts died down, William cleared his throat and continued. "Kentucky, like all places on the edge of civilization, harbors men running from their past as well as men running toward their future. Before you today stand both kinds of men."

Sam's brows collided, his thoughts racing. With a start, he realized that he and Stephen also represented both those kinds of men. Without a doubt, he had come to Kentucky to run away from his past. He turned his head and considered Stephen, who sat up a little straighter at William's remark. Stephen came here looking toward the future. But, despite the distance Sam had traveled, he was still stuck in his past. That explained why he couldn't let his feelings for Catherine surface. The realization stunned him. Filled with self-reproach, he swallowed his disappointment in himself.

Outbursts from Foley and the hunters, and others in the courtroom, made Judge Webb pound his gavel like an energetic woodpecker, causing him to make numerous dents in the soft pine table.

"You're a damn liar," Foley shouted, pointing a dirty finger at William, "a filthy liar."

That's the pot calling the kettle black, Sam thought.

"This is a very serious charge Mr. Wyllie. What proof do you have?" Judge Webb asked.

William answered with surprising calmness. "We are bringing in a witness to the court that will state he saw Mr. Foley working for the British as a scout. However, your Honour, we ask that you meet with this witness privately, for he too is in fear of retribution by these ruffians and does not want them to know his identity. This is why he has not brought charges against Mr. Foley heretofore."

"Are there any other witnesses to this charge of working for the lousy lobster-backs?"

The Judge seemed to perk up, indignation replacing impatience.

"You may not yet be aware that Captain Wyllie is a hero of the Revolution and received a decoration for valor from George Washington himself." William paused to look around at the people in the courtroom, giving them time to absorb what he'd just said.

Mummers of approval spread from one man to another. Sam felt his face warming as numerous eyes turned in his direction. He wished William had not used the term hero. It made him feel uncomfortable and unworthy. Many others made greater sacrifices and showed more valor than he had.

William continued, "Captain Wyllie believes he may have also seen this man with the British, but is unable to positively determine if it's him because of the man's considerable beard and hair."

"When will your first witness be here?" Judge Webb asked.

"We hope today. Tomorrow at the latest."

"Very well. Constable Mitchell, place Mr. Foley in your custody."

"What kind of court is this?" Foley demanded, as he shoved the young constable away from him. "I'm not on trial here, they are."

The Judge placed his pistol on top of his desk and glared a silent threat, shutting the man up.

Sam wondered if Foley had heard the stories about Webb gaining control of an unruly defendant or two by just shooting them. Reportedly, he never mortally wounded defendants, but he wasn't beyond causing them to limp from his courtroom.

Mitchell rapidly placed a manacle around the man's only wrist, before he realized Foley didn't have another one to lock on to. For several awkward moments, the constable didn't know what to do. Looking confused, he glanced over at the Judge for help.

"Constable, put shackles around the man's ankles. Then place him in your jail, pending the testimony of these witnesses. Have

Mr. Foley shaved and his hair cut before tomorrow morning. No one—or even one merely under suspicion—who has helped the Red Coats will ever leave my courtroom a free man."

Judge Webb picked up his pistol, gesturing toward the other buffalo hunters. "If any of you so much as go near a member of the Wyllie family or Mr. Wolf, I will personally see to it that this gun will need reloading. First, I'll shoot you where it will hurt the most, then I'll hang you. Furthermore, I advise you leave town immediately and proceed out of this state. I suggest you head north to the territories, there's plenty of buffalo up there. Do it now!"

The buffalo hunters jumped up and stampeded from the courtroom. The smell of the room instantly improved.

Sam could not help a slight half-smile. Judge Webb was a man he could respect.

Grabbing Frank Foley's good arm, the constable and two members of the local militia hauled the grumbling and cursing man off to the Fort's jail.

After they left, Judge Webb cleared the rest of the courtroom of all but the Wyllies. As Catherine turned to leave, Sam asked the Judge if she could stay. He didn't want her out on the street alone, especially if those buffalo hunters were still around.

"By all means," Judge Webb answered graciously, smiling at Catherine. "The lovely lady definitely brightens up this drab place."

"Thank you, Sir. You are most kind," Catherine said in a silky voice and then she gave Judge Webb a big smile.

Sam could tell Catherine was doing her part to impact the trial's outcome.

Webb's face split into a wide grin.

He couldn't blame the Judge. Her smile would warm a marble statue.

He then instructed William to keep the witness out of town at their camp. "I'll make sure that flea bag gets a shave, if I have to do it myself. Captain Wyllie, as soon as your witness arrives, come notify me. I have a small cabin on the east side of the Fort that I use for an office. Then we'll walk across the enclosure to the jail and you can take a look at a clean-shaven Foley before we ride out to your camp to talk to your witness."

Sam nodded his agreement, hoping their witness would indeed arrive. If not, they were going to have one vexed Judge to deal with as well as the charges still pending against them.

~

John, Bear, Lucky, and the O'Reilly brothers rode their weary horses into camp late that evening. They were all hungry and John, Bear, and Lucky appeared drained from lack of sleep, but their spirits rallied when they heard the results of the legal proceedings so far.

Jane wanted John to go into town to see the doctor about his head wound, but he refused, saying that it was late and he was just too tired and she could tend to it just fine. After giving John a cup of whiskey, she took great care to thoroughly clean the raw cut causing him to nearly pass out between his gulps of the strong drink.

Little John started crying when he saw his father's pained face. Martha and Polly tried to take him aside so he wouldn't have to see his father in pain, but Little John would have none of it. He stood by John, his little hand holding onto his father's big hand. It made Sam even more proud of the boy.

"Here, bite down on this," Little John suggested, pulling a short piece of rope from a pocket.

Seeing the small coil of rope surprised Sam. It must have been there ever since he and Stephen had given it to the boy to bite down on when Little John was badly hurt on their journey here. The rope helped to tether his nephew's pain at a time when they had nothing else to ease his suffering. The boy's injury was just the start of many tribulations he and Stephen had faced that day. Sam grimaced remembering.

"Thanks son, that will help," John forced a smile despite his pain.

John had nearly chewed through the rope by the time Jane finished putting a mixture of honey and herbs on the wound and stitching his brother's forehead. It had pained Sam to watch, especially since there was nothing he could do but lend moral support. When she finished, she put another type of ointment on the wound so it wouldn't scar too badly, but they were all more concerned about the wound festering than scarring. A wound like that could easily worsen, especially since it had gone untended for a day. She insisted John see the doctor in town as soon as he could.

"I'll be sure he does," Sam promised.

While Catherine and Kelly warmed food, Bear filled them all in on their narrow escape from the Indians, praising Lucky for his timely help. "John will have a scar that will make him want to wear a hat more often," Bear said. "I'll make him a grand coonskin cap."

"Will you make me one too?" Little John asked hopefully.

"Aye. I'll make you a bonnie cap," Bear promised.

"Now you'll have scars like Uncle Sam," Little John told his father.

"Bear, once again you've proven your loyalty to our family. Thank you for having the good sense that we didn't and going after John," Sam said. "You saved his life."

"Aye. You four are a mite lackin' in good sense sometimes."

Enjoying Bear's good-natured ribbing, they all laughed, except John, who could only manage a slight smile.

Bear eyed the four brothers and with emotion rising in his voice, he said, "I was reluctant, because he's yer brother not mine, to tell all of ye that I believed ye were makin' a terrible mistake sendin' John off by himself. Then I realized he really was me brother after all. Ye all are."

"Your name may not be Wyllie, but it might as well be," Stephen said.

"Bear, next time we're in town, I'll buy you a new hunting shirt to replace that torn one if we can find someone to make one big enough. And Lucky, maybe someday I can return the favor," Sam offered. "If you ever need an extra man, I'm him."

Lucky nodded at Sam. "It weren't nothin' special, Captain. We all have to look out for one another out here. This place is still a bit wild. But we'll get it tamed one of these days. Then it will be time for men like me to move on."

Sam nodded, anxious to move on himself. Would Catherine agree to come with them? He vowed to give that more thought. A lot more thought.

Tomorrow morning, the Judge would hear O'Reilly's testimony. Then, hopefully, the Judge would convict Foley and this whole absurd mess would be behind them.

The sky a blaze of color-splashed clouds, he turned to look at the sun setting in the west. Its beauty buoyed his spirits like a lighthouse calling a captain lost at sea.

CHAPTER 24

Sam's heart hammered as he ducked his head and took a step inside the dark jail. Would this be the son-of-a bitch? After all these years of searching, would the man be right here in Boonesborough?

As his eyes adjusted to the shadowy light, he could smell a chamber pot that needed emptying. A leaking barrel of water sat in one corner with a dipper hanging from it. The drips made a small pool of mud in the packed down dirt floor. The jail had three cells, each with a small window, providing more glare than light to the interior. The first two cells sat empty, but a man occupied the third at the far end of the room.

Wordlessly, Judge Webb led him to Foley.

Sam stared nearly transfixed by the man's cruel eyes. War memories stirred. Sorrow gripped his heart. Fury filled him.

He glared at Foley long and hard before he dared to speak, his thoughts deep, cold, and bitter.

He stiffened and shook his head decisively.

He turned and looked over his shoulder at the Judge. "As

much as I detest this man, my honor will not allow me to falsely accuse him."

"Captain Wyllie, give him one more look to be sure he's not the guy. Remember, we need two witnesses," Judge Webb emphasized.

Sam did not miss the Judge's implication. He swung his head around. "It's not him."

A sense of bitter disappointment filled him. This man was evil. Was probably also a traitor, but this wasn't the traitor he knew. "The man I seek went by the name Eli Frazer. Many soldiers knew him well because he worked as a scout for several regiments of the Continental Army, including mine at one point, before he became a traitor."

Foley glared at Sam as he spoke. The contemptible man seemed to be gloating.

He returned Foley's stare with squinted eyes. He let his mind bore into the man's heart, trying to find a soul. But Foley's heart held no honor, no integrity, and no honesty. Nothing but false pride and coldhearted malevolence flowed through this man's veins. And his soul held only poison. The only antidote for venomous men like Foley was justice. He gripped his knife, wishing the man before him had been Eli Frazier. But he wasn't.

"We'll need another witness," Sam said finally. "I will not bear false witness."

"I understand, and I respect your integrity, Sir," the Judge said.

Foley tilted his chin up. "You going to let me loose, Judge?" He gave Sam a look full of loathing.

"We'll see what the other witness has to say. Let's go Captain

Wyllie."

As they passed in front of him, Foley spat on Sam's shoulder.

Like a spark thrown on an explosive, the spittle caused Sam's already unstable mood to instantaneously blaze. In a split second, he reached in and slammed Foley's face against the rusty jail bars. The whole room shook with the force of his exploding anger. He whipped his blade instantly to the side of the man's throat.

Surprisingly, the Judge made no move to stop him.

Foley tried to pull away, but Sam's grip held the man's face close. So close, they were nearly eyeball to eyeball.

"I guess you haven't had enough of the taste of this knife," Sam taunted, pressing his blade's keen edge well into the skin on Foley's neck.

"You're lucky I didn't piss on you," Foley sneered.

Drops of red sprang up along the knife's shiny edge before the Judge grabbed the neck of Foley's shirt and lugged him back, away from the bars and Sam's blade.

But Webb couldn't pull Sam back from his rage. Until released, Sam could control his anger. But once unleashed, it was near impossible to still. His hands shook with his effort to sheath the knife and bridle his wrath.

"That's the second time you've spit on a Wyllie. There will be no third time without you dying," he swore.

❧

"You going to hang him Judge?" Constable Mitchell asked on the way out.

"I can't without two witnesses. Watch him well while I'm gone constable. He'd better be here waiting for me when I get back or I'll sure as hell be looking for someone else to send to a firing squad."

The wide-eyed constable nodded his head vigorously to let the Judge know he understood. Sam could tell no idle threats came from this Judge.

Sam and the Judge left the jail, located in the western corner of the Fort. Alex stood tied just outside. While the Judge retrieved his own mount from the Fort's stalls, Sam noted with amusement that Alex had left several mounds of droppings below Foley's jail cell window. He suspected the horse might have deposited the pungent piles intentionally.

"Let's go see your witness," the Judge said, after mounting his horse.

"First we have to get John. He's at the doc's," Sam said. On the way to the doctor's office, he explained how John received the scalp wound.

"Getting that witness was indeed costly," Webb said, "let's hope we can make it worth John's while."

Sam and the Judge caught up to John just as he was leaving. "Dr. McDowell said I was already healing well. He wants to meet Jane and compliment her work on my scalp."

"I'm not surprised she did so well," Sam said.

"Sorry to learn of your injury John. But you've just seen one of the best. Doc McDowell is recently returned from Edinburgh. He said it's a mecca for medical students from all over the world. He practices medicine in Danville, but comes to Boonesborough once a month," Webb explained as he mounted. "Watch our backs, Sam. Be sure we're not followed."

The Judge couldn't know that he always watched his back.

※

After Sam arrived with the Judge and they dismounted, Stephen strode up and shook Webb's hand. "Before we get started Judge, we must first thank you for being willing to come out to our camp." Stephen turned to Jonathan. "I also want you to know Mr. O'Reilly how much Sam and I, all of us, appreciate your willingness to testify."

"I do na deserve thanks. I should have told the Judge about Foley before now. I regret that I didn't. But, I'm here to correct me mistake," Jonathan said, twisting his hat in his hand.

"Others are coming forth now too," Judge Webb responded. "After you men confronted that weasel in court, several citizens have come forward. One man claims that both Frank Foley and his brother Bud raped his wife while Foley's other men beat him senseless. He wants to keep the rape between us to protect his wife's reputation, but he swore with tears in his eyes that Frank and Bud did it. Another man strongly believes that this group of men murdered his brother. Foley could probably hang a dozen times and still deserve further punishment."

"I know Sam would be happy to oblige," William said looking in Sam's direction, "and so would I."

It took only a few minutes for O'Reilly to tell the Judge where and how he had remembered Foley. "I know it's him. Saw him in town with that bunch of vermin. As soon as I caught sight of those deep-set evil eyes and that huge nose, I recognized him. At the Battle of Germantown, the British captured 400 of our men, including that bastard. Within the same hour, he turned turncoat. Many of those captured saw him defect. Two tried to stop him and the Red Coats shot them both right on the spot. They say he laughed, went up to the bodies, and spit on them. It was such a despicable act, tales of his treason spread quickly and far. It wasn't long before the whole Continental Army and the militias had heard of it and were all looking for him." Jonathan swallowed hard and took a deep breath before he continued.

"After Germantown, he worked for the British as a scout. He caused the death of many good men." Jonathan nearly choked on the words. "The army filed charges of treason against him, but he was never apprehended."

"I thank you for your testimony Mr. O'Reilly," Judge Webb said. "Now we just have to find a second witness."

"What?" William asked. "I thought Sam was the second. Didn't you recognize him Sam?"

"It wasn't him. No one is more disappointed than I am. The man I seek is another son of Satan turncoat." Sam wavered, trying to decide whether to tell the whole story. Then it all seemed to spill out of him in a foul torrent. "This traitor I've searched for all these years led the lobster-backs to our stash of war supplies at Concord. We saw their column coming. They marched five across and their lines went on further than we could see. We were just a small unit, so we hid behind a nearby cottage. The turncoat was at the head of their column, pointing to the storehouse. At that moment, his treacherous face burned into my memory. The British outnumbered us fifty-to-one, so my Captain ordered us to leave. I nearly disobeyed him, and if I'd know what was about to happen, I would have.

"As we retreated, we started hearing explosions breaking out everywhere. It took us months to stock up those provisions and in one afternoon they destroyed all of it. The grenadiers threw one hundred barrels of flour into a millpond and took five hundred pounds of lead and powder. Gun carriages were set afire. But that wasn't all they destroyed."

A sudden thin chill filled his heart. Sam hesitated, then despite his best efforts not to continue, more came pouring from him, like a swollen river surging out of its banks, rushing where it was forced to go, but didn't belong. "Weeks later, I learned that during their attack they also burned the general store down, and a beautiful young woman got caught in it. No one could reach her—there were just too many flames and explosions. Her father, the store owner, tried hard but he could not save her. The poor man died trying to get to her as she burned alive right before his eyes."

Sam stared down at the ground, shaking his head, trying to regain control of the slight quiver in his voice. "I've often imagined her horrible screams."

Opening his eyes, he came back to reality. The group stood in silence, the haunting echoes of a young woman's terrible death cries nearly audible in the heavy air between them.

Old pains clawed their way up within Sam. When they reached his heart, it clenched with his effort to keep them at bay. His whole body tightened, like a bow with its string drawn tight, ready to fire a lethal shot, as he remembered kneeling before a grieving mother. He had grasped the woman's hands, moist with the tears she'd just wiped away, as she mourned both her husband and child, and swore an oath to her. "I promised her mother that I would search for the traitor that led the British to their store and that I would never forget her daughter. I've kept both promises."

Why couldn't Foley have been Frazier? It would have ended it all. It would have been so simple. But it wasn't simple any more. He wanted to scream with the suppressed anger amassing at the back of his throat. His hand squeezed the deer horn handle of his blade.

He glanced at Bear, who understood the meaningfulness of his death grip on his knife. Bear's expression twisted in fiery outrage and he started toward him, but Sam shook his head. He didn't want Bear's sympathy. He just wanted to kill.

But the man he needed to kill wasn't Foley. It was Frazier.

"As much as I wanted Foley to be Frazier, he wasn't. And I won't bear false witness," Sam hissed. "Foley is a vile human being that doesn't deserve another breath, but he is not the man I sought all these years."

Bear stood there, tall and incensed, and they exchanged a long deep look. Bear understood.

"Don't worry Sam. I won't let the son-of-a-bitch go," the Judge pronounced. "Tomorrow, Constable Mitchell and I will escort Foley to Logan's Fort. Colonel John Byrd has militia from all over Kentucky, including Fort Boonesborough's, mustered there right now. A good number of those men served in the Continental Army. Hopefully there will be someone there who will recognize him and serve as our second witness. With luck, he'll soon face hanging or a firing squad—both too good for the likes of him for damn sure. I wish I could give him the kind of punishment he deserves—being burned alive like that poor young woman."

"I imagine God has in mind that exact type of punishment," Catherine spat, her eyes blazing and face flushed.

The Judge and several others shook their heads in agreement.

Foley wasn't the one Sam sought, but he was a traitor. A damn traitor, just like Frazier. They were two of a kind.

Sam couldn't speak as he struggled for control. His breaths came faster. He turned and slowly stepped away from the others.

He needed to be alone with his struggle. With the heartache that had sprung back to life despite his efforts to bury it.

He checked the sharpness of his knife and replaced the pain with anger.

It was easier to feel anger.

CHAPTER 25

Sam thrust his knife back into its sheath, picked up his rifle and powder horn and marched towards his horse. If the law couldn't do something about traitors, he could. He wouldn't leave justice to luck as the Judge had suggested. If no one at Logan's Fort recognized Foley as a traitor, the man would go free. Free to wander Kentucky murdering and raping.

There was no way was he would let that happen.

As the other men said their goodbyes, he tightened Alex's cinch and untied the reins.

Catherine put a hand on Sam's back. "Sam, hold up. What's wrong?" she asked quietly.

Sam stopped but didn't turn around.

"Sam, you knew her, didn't you? The young woman burned alive. You knew her well."

He turned quickly and faced her, fixing his eyes on hers with a hard stare. "I didn't just know her, I loved her. She was the only woman I ever loved...until," unsure of his true feelings, he stopped himself. He turned aside. "But she was stolen from me. I never had even one chance to hold her in my arms, but I've carried her around inside of me all these many years. I never stopped feeling the anguish of losing her—maybe because of how horrifically she died, or perhaps because I never had a chance to tell her that I wanted to marry her and that I loved her. And I never stopped loving that sweet girl. So instead of using my savings to buy her an engagement ring and to start a home, I used it to buy this knife. I've been looking for that traitor ever since, most of my life. Looking for retribution. I made a promise to myself never to forget her and never to love again until that man was dead."

"That promise explains a lot," Catherine said.

"Now, I'm wondering if I can keep that promise." Guilt rippled up his spine until it reached the back of his head and surged through his mind. He was not a man to break a promise, especially one he made to himself.

"If I can't kill Frazier, then Foley will just have to do. They're two of a kind anyway." Even as he said it, Sam doubted that he could kill Foley in cold blood. Foley would have to give him reason to.

"Sam, the past is the one thing even you can't fight. You cannot change the beginning of your life, but you can change the ending. The only way to stop the hurt is to love again. You've tortured yourself with that ill-gotten promise long enough. She's gone. You can't go on living with only that deep hatred and the past in your heart. As you said, you need to truly live."

"If I stop, I'd be turning my back on her and disavowing the promise I made to myself."

"If you don't stop, I promise *you* something—you'll never really live again, much less love."

Unnerved, Sam crossed his arms and pointedly looked away.

"You're afraid to love again, because the last time you did, it brought you only terrible unending pain."

Her accusing tone stabbed the air between them. "I'm not afraid of anything."

"You thought you had to be the bravest man every place you went because you were protecting your heart. You were terrified that your heart would be wounded again."

"I'm not afraid of anything," he repeated. It was a lie.

He knew no fear, except the fear of her love.

"Prove it."

Her passionate challenge went too far. He stared at her for a moment. "No. I don't have to prove anything. What I have to do is end these feelings I have for you. I'm sorry." He felt himself receding into a past only he understood, unable to part with it. He gripped the saddle horn with his left hand, but then he hesitated for just a moment. He did want his life back—to rid himself of a past that held him hostage. That was why he came to Kentucky to begin with.

Catherine quickly stepped between the stirrup and Sam. "I won't let you end those feelings," she said, forcefully. She looked up at him with love on her face and resolve in her fiery eyes.

She wrapped her arms around his waist and leaned her head gently against his chest.

Sam's heart thundered within his breast, and he felt her heart reach out to calm his.

She placed a gentle kiss on his chest. The intimate gesture nearly overwhelmed him.

She gazed up into his eyes and whispered, "I love you."

Sam's hand left the saddle horn. Had he heard her right? Slowly, tentatively, he put his hands on her. Something he had done only once before, and then it had scared him as nothing else had before.

Now, as he physically touched her, felt the reality of her, it seemed possible that she really could love him. And he could love her back. He ran his hands slowly down her back. He wanted her to fill the terrible emptiness in him, push the pain away, smother the embers of old anger. Next to her, he could almost physically feel the healing beginning.

But then his stubborn mind threw up a familiar wall of doubt.

"You can't possibly love an old warrior like me." He wanted desperately to confirm this miracle, to let her affection feed his hungry soul.

But he couldn't.

"I do love you Sam. I promise I will make you happy. And I trust you. Please trust me."

Sam jerked his hands away from her body and tightly gripped the reins instead. "I trust you. I just can't love you. Not yet."

"Yes, yes," she whispered. "Yes, you can. I can show you how to love again." She ran her fingers over the dark stubble on his cheek.

As he studied her face, Sam felt near tears for the first time in many years. His eyes begged her for the truth while his mind denied what she just said. He simply could not believe a gentlewoman like Catherine, so refined, could want him. "You don't know what it's like on the frontier. It's a long way from the easy life you knew in Boston, and I don't mean in miles. You have no business here. A woman as fine as you should go back to that way of life. Marry someone with wealth and prestige." Even as he said it, he wished he hadn't.

"I've learned what it's like on the frontier and I know it won't be easy. But every day I'm learning more and more about how to cope with it. If I go back, I won't be allowed to marry for love. My father will force me to marry someone to further his own fortune. And that husband will expect me to be the dutiful wife and the perfect society woman. Do you want that for me Sam?"

"No." Marrying another man was the last thing he wanted her to do.

"Neither do I. That's not me and never will be. We both lost our old lives Sam. But we're young, on a new frontier. So let's leave those lives behind us. Put aside old wrongs and your old love. I haven't fallen for an old warrior. I'm in love with you—a man with a brave strong heart."

"But I *am* a warrior Catherine. That's me and it always will be."

And, he realized, the hardest battle he would ever fight might be this one—the one with his own heart.

"Sam, it's time for you to lay your armor down. Let yourself be vulnerable for once in your life. Open yourself up to love."

He tried to resurrect the anger her words suppressed. He was far more comfortable being angry than talking about love. But for the moment, the tenderness in her words and her gaze snuffed the flames of his rage like rain on fire.

"Everyone needs love Sam, just as surely as we need to breathe. A life without love is just as suffocating as lungs without air. We both know that." She stepped closer to him.

"My life is suitable for only one thing—the one thing I'm good at—fighting."

"Then fight for a new life—for both of us. Fight for a chance to live Sam. Please give us a chance."

He studied the blazing determination in her eyes for a long time. He did see love there. How he yearned to lay his armor down—to not feel the unceasing weight of it on his shoulders. And on his heart. Perhaps she was right. Her courage inspired him. Maybe there was a chance her love could make him whole again. Something deep inside flared, then spread, blazing through the fortress around his heart.

He clenched his jaw to stop the sob in his throat. "In the 'Land of Tomorrow'?" he asked, his breath ragged, as he struggled for both air and love.

"No, in the land of today, starting *now*." She spoke with quiet firmness and the sense of conviction that was part of her strong character. She stared with longing at him. The implication sent a wave of excitement surging through him.

The fire rising in his loins did make him want her *now*.

His gaze dropped from her eyes to her long neck to her breasts. His jaw was near cracking with the effort to control his growing desire. When he looked up, a rush of pink stained her lovely face. Her closeness was euphoric, drawing him in, until he was helpless to resist. She smelled like falls fresh water and he drank in the scent like a man dying of thirst. And like water rushing over a falls, his blood surged from his head to his toes and places between.

He quickly gave her the reins to his horse and started saddling hers. When he finished, he took both reins and led the horses behind them while they walked a short distance from camp. Then he stopped abruptly and pulled her against his chest.

Clutching the reins against her back, he kissed her, roughly and hard, like the man he was. Then he kissed her again, softly and tenderly, like the man he wanted to be.

In an instant, her embrace changed something within him as a spark of hope kindled his heart.

He felt her tremble in his arms and her heart race wildly against his own heart.

He struggled to pull himself away from her luscious full lips. He wanted to cover her in kisses, head to toe, and back again. He wanted to love again. He wanted to love her.

He realized his life was floundering. He came to Kentucky looking for a new beginning. But maybe that new beginning wasn't just a place. Maybe it was this woman. When he arrived here, he attributed his new sense of hope to the place—to the tranquil river, the verdant meadows, and rolling hills. But it wasn't Kentucky that had reached his soul.

It was Catherine.

He handed her the reins to her horse. "Mount up. Let's go somewhere where we can talk in private," he said huskily and then helped her into her saddle.

Maybe I *can* fight for love, he decided. He stepped into the stirrup and threw his leg over Alex's big back.

In that glorious moment, the moment between the past and the future, Sam felt braver than he ever had before.

CHAPTER 26

"I'll not try another friendly pat on the back, but I'd be honored to shake yer hand," Bear told Jonathan as the man prepared to leave.

"And me knees are thankin' you for that," Jonathan replied with a broad smile.

After Bear and the others thanked Jonathan, Judge Webb told the Irishman that he was free to leave and thanked him for his testimony. He assured the two brothers that Foley would never know who the witness was and that he would promptly turn the traitor over to the military for further investigation and hopefully prosecution as well.

"Wait," Stephen called after the O'Reilly brothers as they turned their mounts toward town. He grabbed a jug of whiskey and hurried back to the two waiting on their horses. "A small token of our gratitude."

"A jug of whiskey is never a small thing. May the Lord bless ye and may the roads ye travel all lead to happiness," a smiling Jonathan said and then he waved goodbye.

"I'll wait here for a short while if you don't mind, I don't want anyone to see me with the O'Reillys," Judge Webb said.

Stephen handed the Judge a cup of coffee. "What's your decision?" Stephen asked, wasting no time getting to the point.

Judge Webb inhaled the fragrant aroma, took a sip, and then explained why it was imperative to get not only O'Reilly's testimony, but another witness as well. "Treason under the constitution consists of either levying war against the United States or siding with her enemies. It requires two witnesses to the act of treason for conviction. I will personally deliver O'Reilly's affirmation of Foley's identity to the military at Logan's Fort. Foley is clearly a traitor and probably a murderer and rapist as well. I just need more proof of his crimes. Consider the charges against you and Sam dismissed, of course. By the way, where is the Captain?"

"He left a few minutes ago," Bear said without further explanation. He realized Sam was suffering. The Captain was not a man easily hurt, but Bear had just seen angry waves of remembered heartache roll across Sam's rugged face before he had turned away from the others. He was pleased when he saw Catherine follow Sam.

He had already accepted that she belonged with Sam, not him. The two needed each other. Bear hoped Catherine could ease the Captain's old heartache. Only a woman could cure that kind of wound. He just didn't know if Sam would let her. A pain that deep was slow to ebb away. The Captain's hurt had turned to scars that were long, deep, and ugly. And maybe permanent. He hoped Catherine could see past the scars. He had a good feeling that she would.

Bear refilled the Judge's coffee and then poured himself a cup, shaking his head in empathy for Sam.

"I'll take some of that too," William said holding out his cup, "although I could use something stronger. We do have reason to celebrate. I've won my first case."

"I do na feel much like celebratin'," Bear said sharply.

They all looked puzzled as Bear sipped the lukewarm brew. Suddenly, the coffee tasted bitter and he threw the rest into the fire. "I'll explain on the way to town," he said, his voice matching the angry hissing of his coffee hitting the hot rocks circling the cook fire.

They left, and took their time getting to town, passing stands of loblolly and Virginia pines so thick it would be difficult to ride a horse through. The humid air seemed even heavier with the thick scent of pine. Bear kept one eye on the gloomy woods as they rode their horses side by side. He explained that the young woman who died so tragically in the supply store fire had been Sam's first and only love, and that Sam had never stopped loving her.

He also made clear the significance of the big knife and its handsome deer horn handle. He told them that he had just seen Sam about to leave looking mad enough to kill, but somehow Catherine managed to stop him.

"I can understand how all this has dredged up the past for Sam. And that traitor in the jail deserves to die every bit as much as the one Sam hunted," Stephen hissed, "even if he wasn't the same man."

"Don't worry, my guess is the turncoat doesn't have much time left on this earth," Judge Webb assured him.

"If Sam gets anywhere near the man, he'll have even less time," Stephen said heatedly. "I'm amazed Catherine was able to stop him."

Bear wasn't surprised, but didn't say so. He realized how much Sam meant to Catherine, and how much she could mean to him if the Captain would just let her release his broken heart.

"What little time Foley has should be spent facing his crimes," William said. "We owe that to all the innocent people Foley has harmed or killed. Justice requires that. Only the law can rightly take a man's life from him in punishment."

"True enough," Judge Webb agreed, "but sometimes, especially on the frontier, the Almighty uses men to dispense His own form of justice. Justice is not limited to the confines of a courtroom."

Bear agreed wholeheartedly with the Judge.

As they reached the edge of town, Constable Mitchell ran up to them, his pimpled complexion covered in sweat. The look of panic on his face told them everything they needed to know before the nervous constable blurted it out. "He's gone. He's gone. Bud took my pistol. Said he'd shoot me through the gut and skin me like a buffalo if I didn't let his brother loose."

The Judge spat. "I should have known better than to leave that Satan's bastard with one as green as you."

Bear saw Mitchell bite his lip and look down at the splatter in the dust and suspected the young man felt about that low. He sympathized with the young man. Constable Mitchell was lucky he was na killed. The Judge should be disgusted as much with himself as the constable. Handlin' a prisoner like Foley was beyond this boy's ability.

"How long ago?" William asked the constable.

"Thirty minutes, maybe longer. I've been looking for you

Judge, to find out what to do."

"Which direction did they ride?" the Judge asked impatiently.

Mitchell quickly pointed northwest, in the direction of the river.

The men turned their horses, back toward the campsite, leaving a thick cloud of dust behind them to settle on the constable.

"If Foley has harmed a member of my family, I will kill him," Stephen shouted to the Judge as they rode. "I don't give a damn what justice requires."

"If he has, you have my permission," Judge Webb yelled back, "if I don't shoot Foley first myself."

CHAPTER 27

Catherine couldn't believe the passion and then tenderness she had felt in Sam's kisses. She expected that he would be stunningly virile, and awaken her as a woman, but the startling sensations he created within her were even more powerful than she had ever imagined. Now she understood for a certainty that an essential part had been missing from her first marriage.

A strange inner elation filled her. Her heart had leapt at his touch. His embrace, filled with longing and possessiveness, left her glowing inside with joy and desire. She recalled the ecstasy she felt as he held her tightly against his hard body. She wanted to feel more of that. Much more.

As she rode, her fingers ached to reach over and touch him. She guessed she was not the only one with that particular longing as she became aware of his unabashed assessment of her body. His broad shoulders and chest were almost heaving as he appraised her.

With a giddy sense of amusement, she let her happiness show. She wanted him to find her desirable. As desirable as she found him.

Just as they left, his keen, probing eyes had searched hers, looking for love. Looking for hope. At long last, she had succeeded in steering him away from his desire for vengeance, to a desire for her. At least for the moment. She had no illusions. His anger still simmered, just below the surface. He carefully controlled his wrath for now. But for how long? A man like the Captain didn't just forget and walk away. And she couldn't blame him. Traitors were murderers.

How many men, women, and children fell to the British because of traitors like Frazier and Foley? She wanted to run a blade from heart to groin through Foley herself. The despicable man deserved nothing less.

And she couldn't expect Sam to love her until he could leave his old love behind. And she now understood that doing so was plainly linked to him finding justice for the young woman's death.

But the price of exacting vengeance would be high. Sam could not kill Foley without becoming a murderer himself. He might even lose his own life. The other buffalo hunters would come after Sam. Dread filled her heart.

The thought of losing him in a battle with those buffalo hunters suddenly turned her hot blood icy. Her pulse quickened at the terrifying thought and she tried to suppress the knot hardening in her belly. She looked over at Sam to reassure herself. He was a magnificent warrior. He had fought many battles and survived them all. He had more courage than any man she had ever known. There was no water in his blood.

And he was smart and shrewd. He wouldn't do anything foolish. And his brothers and Bear would all stand by him.

That loathsome man and his cohorts didn't stand a chance.

She studied Sam's tanned rugged features, as he looked ahead now. It felt good riding beside him in the summer sun, miles and miles of waving grass ahead of them. Yet, a silent sadness lingered on his face. No, he definitely had not abandoned the idea of revenge. She saw it there again, warring with the feelings she was trying to help him feel. She could almost see the skirmish in his mind as his jaw muscles quivered and his lips tightened on his face.

He could face any foe, but could he face love?

She also sensed his vulnerability. He wanted to believe her, but he needed to trust her first. Only then could he set his heart free.

He was so close. She could see it in the way he looked at her.

More importantly, she saw how hard he was looking at himself. Sam had come out here hoping a new place would heal him, make him forget his tortuous memories. But instead, the wilderness was a mirror, forcing him to look inside himself, at the most unflattering parts.

෴

At first, he was reluctant to leave with Catherine, but he realized he needed to calm his rage. He'd always considered himself a smart man, and smart men didn't allow their anger to cause them to make mistakes.

If a second witness could not be found, he might have to go after Foley himself, but he would form a plan first.

For now, he had to come to terms with how he truly felt about Catherine. About the love she offered.

He wasn't entirely sure he was doing the right thing. In fact, he was quite certain he wasn't. He was taking them both into dangerous territory. Once he started kissing her again, there would be no going back. He had held his emotions and his body at bay far too long. He could almost feel love fighting its way out of his gristly heart.

He found it hard to believe, but she wanted him. His mind burned with the hot memory of their kiss, a tantalizing taste of the passion that could erupt between them. But it came with a price tag—marriage. He wasn't going to take advantage of her. He was a man of honor and she was a lady. He would not disrespect her by yielding to their mutual lust. If he took her now, it would be for life. He had to stay in control.

He studied Catherine as they rode. She held her gelding with confidence and appeared remarkably elegant even on the back of a horse. Her dagger added to her striking appearance, giving her a look of quiet courage and strong mettle. She also looked extraordinarily sensuous. Her stays, which kept her back perfectly straight, had the added benefit of pushing her full bosom up to display soft mounds at the top of her gown. Her waist seemed impossibly small and her legs nearly as long as his. And her lovely face held a smile so dazzling it competed with the afternoon sun. He admired the perfection of her striking high cheekbones and strong jawline, but it was the strength of her character that impressed him most of all.

"You're staring Sam," Catherine said.

He nodded, managing a smile, but not trusting himself to speak. He turned his eyes to the path ahead.

How could she possibly love him? She was too fine, too beautiful, and too perfect. And he was anything but those things. He was rough, worn, and far from perfect. He had spent most of his life out in the open and it showed. Although his parents raised him to be a gentleman, he never looked the part. Nor did he want to. That just wasn't him.

But, she said she loved him.

Since the Revolution, his entire life had been a denial of love. It had been about deep-seated hatred and revenge. Could he let his feelings for her float to the top?

"What are you thinking?" she asked, inclining her head and peering over at him.

Sam hesitated, not wanting to reveal his thoughts just yet. He was still sorting them out.

"You think this is too big a risk don't you? You're not convinced that I really could love you." There was a gentle and compassionate tone in her voice.

"That's part of it," he admitted.

"What's the rest of it?"

He remained silent.

"Sam, tell me. Don't you find me desirable?" Catherine asked, sounding close to tears now.

Sam could have laughed, but didn't. He had been fighting to keep his desire from showing since they'd left camp. His lips longed for hers as he had never longed for anything else. He wanted to savor the taste of her mouth and let her essence swirl through him.

A large majestic oak stood proudly in the center of the meadow. He motioned Catherine to follow and loped over to it, then dismounted and quickly tied Alex to a heavy branch that drooped nearly to the ground. Each of the tree's four old branches pointed in different directions. It was an Indian Trail tree. Natives tied the branches with stakes forcing them to grow in each of the four directions as an aide in finding their way in the wilderness when darkness or clouds obscured the sun. Maybe the sacred tree would point his life in the right direction.

As he helped Catherine down from her horse, her waist felt firm and stiff under her stays, and it flamed his growing desire even more. He felt as if his insides were on fire and his head was going to blow off his shoulders. How could he think clearly feeling like this? Heaven help him, he couldn't.

After tying her horse to another one of the oak's branches, he took her face in his hands and lowered his lips to hers. Her kiss, hot as his blood, caused a shockwave that made his entire body shudder. It went far beyond the impact of their first kiss. Now, not only did his body experience it—his soul did as well—as though she kissed more than just his mouth. Her passion seemed to touch every part of him.

He gathered her against his trembling body.

He had never felt these overwhelming sensations before. He marveled at the intensity of feelings that could make the rest of the world disappear, as if nothing else mattered.

The few times in his life that he had coupled with a woman had been quick and lukewarm at best, with little kissing and no affection. The empty experiences left him feeling only regrets and guilt. And a hope that someday making love with a woman would be just that—making *love*.

Just from kissing her, he could tell that making love with her would be utterly different. Her lips and mouth seemed made for his, as they joined with his to form a perfect union. And the thought of joining with her made his imagination go wild. He only knew he was lost—lost to the swirling fiery chaos happening within his body.

He wanted to go on kissing her forever to keep feeling as he did now, but his hands thought otherwise. They took over his will and began to move over her body. First, down her back and the curves of her bottom, to the top of her legs. Just touching her made his blood hot. He drew her close, feeling the softness of her breasts press up against his chest. Oh, how he longed to feel their warmth in his hands. He rubbed a single finger against the bare skin of her neck and shoulder.

"Catherine, do you have any idea what you do to me?" he breathed.

"Probably the same thing you do to me."

She ran her fingertips and nails across the opening at the top of his shirt. The sensations she drew from him with just that simple touch surprised him. It made him want to tear the new shirt off his back.

"I've never felt like this." His voice broke with uneven huskiness.

"Neither have I," she whispered into his neck. "Kiss me Sam, and never, ever stop."

He kissed her until she groaned from deep in her throat. When he deepened the kiss, her lips and body asked for more. And he wanted to comply. They were both trembling with desire.

Then she nearly pleaded, "Sam, I want you, all of you," her voice fierce, yet sensual.

"I need to find us a safe shelter." If he was going to make love to her, he would take his time—savor every moment exploring her exquisite body. "We can't. Not here, not now, out here in the middle of an open pas....ture." His breath caught as she started untying his leather breeches.

"Indeed we can," she said, her voice sensuous and insistent as she rubbed her soft fingers across his abdomen. "The grass is tall, and soft."

"I wish we were a thousand miles from anywhere."

The tight muscles of his stomach tightened even further. In fact, his whole body was growing rigid with desire. He could not believe this well-bred lady was willing to love him out here in the middle of a pasture. But her feelings had nothing to do with reason. She was entirely caught up in her own desire.

He couldn't deny the excitement at the prospect of loving her right here, but his warrior instincts kept springing to life. "It isn't...safe, we're out in the open," he struggled to say.

Could he let down his guard long enough to enjoy their coupling? Could he stop thinking for once long enough to just *feel?*

Then she touched him again, lower, and he decided he could. He definitely could let down his guard. Right here. Right now.

His hand enveloped the back of her head and he brought her lips to his. This time his kiss was deep, exploring, and even more fervent. If it was possible for a kiss to be claim someone, this one did. He wanted to make her his, so he could go on kissing her like this for the rest of his life.

Then, a dark corner of his mind leapt up, warning him to stop.

If he didn't stop now, he was committed. Committed to her for life. Would she grow tired of the wilderness and want to return to all that Boston offered? Worse, what if something happened to her too? His heart did a back flip.

He quickly stepped away, trying to get the blood flowing into his head again. He needed to think. Looking down, he ran the fingers of both hands through his hair.

"What?" Catherine asked. "Please, I want you to go on. I know it wouldn't be proper. But I don't care anymore. You said we have to make our own rules here in the west. What's important is that I love you Sam. That's my destiny. If you stop now, it will kill me, I'm sure."

"That's what has me worried," he confessed, his voice cracking. "Something or someone killing you." Unable to stand the look of anguished disappointment on her face, he turned his back to her. He took a few steps away. "I've had too many people I loved taken away. I couldn't stand it if you were too."

Then she took a step toward him. "Sam, even if we have only one day on this earth together, I will love you forever."

He spun around, suddenly sure he wanted her back in his arms. "There's something important I want to say. Catherine, I...."

Before he could finish, he stared in stunned disbelief. Then in horror, as she collapsed to the ground.

CHAPTER 28

Stephen's big stallion was the first to thunder into their camp. He quickly glanced around but the only sounds of commotion came from the children playing, and William, Bear, and the Judge riding in behind him.

"What's going on?" John yelled to him.

"Is everything all right?" Jane asked, concerned.

"Frank Foley has escaped. His brother broke him out of jail," Stephen said. "They came this direction. We thought he came here."

"They must have skirted around our camp so they could make a clean getaway," William suggested.

"We saw no sign of them," John said, loading his pistol. His rifle carelessly leaned against a nearby wagon wheel.

"We're all fine, but Catherine and Sam are still gone," Jane said, sounding worried.

"John, stand guard while we circle the area," Stephen ordered. "And load that rifle too."

The horseback men split into two groups, Bear with Stephen, and William with Judge Webb. They rode in opposite directions searching the area about a hundred yards out from the perimeter of the camp.

Stephen found the three children playing hide-and-go-seek with Kelly in a tiny clearing on the other side of camp. He heard Kelly call out, "Ollie, Ollie oxen free," signaling that she had caught one of the children and the others were all free to come out. He remembered playing the game with his brothers as a youngster, but was too worried to enjoy the memory. He rode up and instructed her to hurry them over to the center of their camp and put the children in Jane's wagon.

By the time he and Bear returned, William and the Judge were waiting for them. None of the men spotted anything of concern. Now they just had to locate Catherine and Sam.

"I'll find them," Stephen told the other men. "Sam needs to know Foley's out there somewhere. The rest of you stay here with the women and children. Frank and Bud probably went to meet up with their men and then they may come back here."

As the others dismounted, including the Judge, Stephen checked his weapons and got an extra pistol and ball pouch. Then Bear helped him locate the nearby tracks of Sam and Catherine's horses. Stephen took off following the tracks that led away from the main road heading west.

"Watch yer back," Bear yelled after him. "That rake is the type to shoot you in the back."

The tracks led to a narrow trail that ran parallel to the river. It was clear the two were just leisurely walking their horses. Stephen wanted to catch up to them before Foley did. If given half a chance, Sam would kill the traitor even if it meant sacrificing his own life to do it.

Stephen rode through grass that reached his stirrup, keeping a careful watch for anyone who might be hiding in the dense brush and trees that followed the path of the river. A thick copse of pines made long dark afternoon shadows in the field. Stephen scanned the area carefully for signs of either Sam or Foley.

About a half-mile away, the tracks led back to the main road. There he noticed another set of fresh tracks. Frank and Bud's? Almost immediately, he heard a shot. The report came from the middle of a nearby pasture.

He turned George in the direction of the sound and gave the horse his head. At a fast gallop, it was only a minute or two before he caught sight of Sam.

He sat in the deep grass, slumped over.

Stephen urged George on and raced up to Sam. His brother cradled Catherine's head in his lap.

Stephen's insides tightened as he dismounted. "My God, what's happened?"

*

"We shouldna shot her. Now that big fellow will be a coming after us," Bud complained, as he towed Sam's horse behind his own mount. "I thought we skirted around their camp on our way out of town to avoid tangling with them again. I told the men to wait for us near the creek like you said."

"My plan changed when I saw him out here with just that woman with him. I figure that rider we heard coming in a hurry was one of them. He'll go back and get the others. I doubt the Captain is foolish enough to come alone after five men. Then they'll follow our trail to where our men are waiting. We'll set ourselves up further down the road and ambush all of them. Just like shooting dumb buffalo. Hell, we might even skin them when we're through."

Bud snickered. "You always was a smart one." His brother turned to look at the buckskin. "You sure got yourself a fine-looking horse here."

"That horse is just the beginning. These are rich folks. After we kill them, we'll double back tonight and get the rest of their horses, must be at least a dozen of them we can sell up in the Ohio Territory or in New Orleans. We'll also get their money and take our pleasure in their women. We left a prize back there dying with her man, too bad I didn't get a chance to taste her," Foley said.

He found it difficult to hurry. His left arm still hurt enough that he could only ride at a slow lope. Trotting pained him even more. His jaw clenched in fury at what the Captain had done to him. He could still feel the fingers of his missing hand. He kept looking down where his hand ought to be. The sensation was driving him crazy.

But he'd paid the Captain back now. He wouldn't be kissing that black-haired beauty anymore. A person shot with a large-caliber gun, if they didn't bleed to death, would soon die of the wound.

His only regret was that someone had interrupted his plan. He had intended to take the Captain's woman right then and there as part of his repayment to the arrogant son-of-a-bitch. He would have made sure that the Captain was still alive enough to hear him do it and hear her screams. That would have been all the better.

As soon as they'd heard a rider coming though, he'd told Bud to grab the buckskin while he took a quick shot at her. Then they had left in a hurry.

But he had a new plan now and he would keep the buckskin. He liked this horse. He'd wanted one like it all his life. Buckskins had more stamina, harder feet, and stronger legs than other horses. The Captain should have traded him for the whiskey as he'd offered. If he had, his woman would still be alive.

He remembered those days scouting for the Red Coats. They had paid him handsomely. He was just doing a job like everyone else. That didn't make him a traitor. If the lobster-backs had won, he'd have been rewarded for his service to the Crown, not considered a traitor. He'd have been a hero. Well, I get my own rewards now. He peered back at the fine horse Bud towed. That horse was one of those rewards, and he had waited long enough to ride him.

"Hold up," Foley bellowed to his brother. He pulled a small jug out of his saddlebag and took a long drink of whiskey. Then he stepped off his mount, dragged the rein over the horse's head, and handed it to his brother. Since he only had one hand to hold the reins, Bud had tied a knot in them to hold them together.

He took the buckskin from Bud, and tried to put his boot in the stirrup.

The horse sidestepped and his foot fell out. "You stupid son of a...," he cursed. He yanked down hard on the bit, deliberately hurting the gelding's mouth.

The buckskin set back, dragging Foley along. It was all he could do with one hand, even though he was a big man, to hold onto the stout horse. The gelding's eyes bulged with equine fury as it tried to rear up. When the horse strained against him, he yanked hard enough on the bit to tear the mount's mouth.

Serves him right.

Foley grabbed the braided handle of the horsewhip he kept on a loop around his wrist. He grunted, bristling with indignation. Holding both the rein and the whip's handle tightly in his hand, he viciously slapped the horse across the muzzle. As blood streaked the buckskin's nose red, he smirked, glad he had let the rebellious animal know who was in control.

But the horse reared, whinnying. With ears pinned back like arrowheads nearly flat against his head, the gelding strained against him, pulling his head up. Then the buckskin jerked his head down and crow hopped, yanking the rein out of Frank's hand and causing him to lose his balance. He tumbled to the ground.

Neighing in a loud prolonged cry, the gelding reared and pawed the air.

Screaming, he rolled just in time, feeling the horse's deadly hoofs pound the ground right next to him.

Despite no longer being controlled by the reins, the rebellious beast seemed to want to continue to fight him. The horse's nostrils flared with heavy breathing and the damn animal turned to kick him, throwing both back legs high up into the air.

He quickly rolled away, narrowly escaping the buckskin's left rear hoof.

Seething with anger, he cursed, as the horse took off at a full gallop. "Bastard!" he shrieked after the animal.

"Frank, let's get. That rider we heard could be coming after us," Bud complained. "You can get that horse later."

Foley snatched his own horse's reins from Bud, then spit. "I'll get them all."

CHAPTER 29

Sam stared up at Stephen, anguish suffocating his soul as he held Catherine, limp and bleeding, in his arms. The ache in his heart became nauseating and his throat tightened as he tried to speak. "Foley...he shot her. They ambushed us. I should have heard them."

Stephen quickly dismounted and knelt beside them both. As his brother checked Catherine's pulse, Sam continued to press his hand against the wound, trying his best to stop the pouring blood.

He fought to keep his emotions in check, but he was failing, miserably. His whole body quavered with heart-crushing foreboding. "She'll die, and she'll never have a chance to be happy. She said she loved me. And, oh God, I turned my back on her. I literally turned it, Stephen. That's when Foley shot her. If I hadn't turned and stepped away, I would have been the one shot." A sharp stab of guilt buried itself in his chest.

Stephen drew his knife and cut a large section off of Catherine's petticoat. "Allow me to have her," Stephen said, as he folded the cloth into a square. "I'll check her wound and tend to it. She's still alive. We just have to stop the bleeding."

He reluctantly laid her shoulders down on the ground and stood up. He gazed at her through glistening eyes. It was sickeningly familiar. And just as senseless. Catherine, possibly also lost too soon.

He remembered kissing her. Kisses that freed passion held too long at bay. Kisses filled with the promise of love. Kisses that offered a new chance at life.

Now, that murdering thief had stolen all that and more.

He wanted to scream. He clenched his fists at his sides. How could he have let this happen? He should have gone after Foley immediately. He'd known the man was a killer. Why hadn't he? He knew the answer. Because he wanted to love her more than he wanted revenge.

He loved her.

He loved her! He was certain of that now. He had never been more certain of anything.

Then desperation gripped him. Was she slipping away? He shuddered and glared down, nearly senseless with worry, barely able to breathe. He tried to focus on what Stephen was doing.

"God, don't let her die," he begged.

"The blood flow is slowing," Stephen said.

He sucked that small offer of hope into his lungs and knelt next to Stephen. They began examining the wound carefully. The lead had passed across the very top of the muscle between her neck and shoulder, just above the collarbone. Whenever Stephen lifted the cloth, blood seeped down both sides of her left shoulder.

"The ball hit the very top of her shoulder muscle," Stephen said, "not bone or lung. Fortunately, the path of the wound is rather small. No more than a half inch. With that high caliber weapon, another inch further down might have killed her. The good news is that since it was so powerful, it passed cleanly through her. We must keep pressure to the wound or she will lose even more blood. This cloth is soaked through. Use your knife and cut up the rest of her petticoat. Do it now Sam."

Stephen's tone seemed to bring Sam out of his shock. He hastily cut off a good size piece of petticoat and then, after Stephen removed the saturated cloth, gently applied pressure to the wound himself. He hoped they could stop the bleeding entirely.

"Are you sure she won't die?"

"I'm sure of it. She's strong and she has a very good reason to live," Stephen said looking at him.

He prayed his brother was right—on both counts. The ball had not hit anything vitally important, but she had lost a lot of blood as well as all color in her face. And there was always the risk that the wound could fester and poison her.

"Foley and his brother rode up to us right after they shot her. I was on the ground holding her, afraid she was dying, trying to stop the blood pouring out of her. Unfortunately, my rifle was still on my horse. They heard you coming, grabbed Alex, and took off in a hurry. I started to throw my knife or use my pistol but I didn't want to release the pressure on her wound. My hands were so slippery with her blood, I probably would have missed anyway."

"He just had to have that gelding, one way or another," Stephen said.

Sam took a quick peek at Catherine's wound. "The blood flow has slowed considerably. Cut another bandage and then take over for me," he said, his anger heating as shock yielded quickly to fury.

After Stephen finished folding the new piece of cloth and one more for later, he exchanged it for the soaked one.

Sam stood and looked down at his hands. Catherine's blood covered them and saturated the edges of his shirt sleeves. The sight made his own blood boil inside him. "I'm going after them," he hissed.

"Sam there are two of them and Foley's three other men will not be far off. Don't go. Wait till I and the others can help you," Stephen pleaded.

His rage mounted with each beat of his thundering heart. "This isn't about all of you. Or all of his men. It's about that traitor and me. Stephen, promise me you'll take care of her, now, and later if need be."

"I promise, Sam. If you must leave, take George. He'll take good care of you. My rifle is loaded."

"William and the others would have heard that shot and will be on their way." He turned to leave and grabbed the reins of the big stallion. "Get her a doctor."

"Sam, please don't do this," Stephen nearly begged.

"He has to," Catherine said in a hoarse whisper. "He needs to end this."

At the sound of her voice, he turned back abruptly. He bent down and took hold of her hand. As he pressed her fingers against his cheek, he locked his eyes on hers, hoping he could convey all the love he had failed to show before. He swallowed the lump in his throat, knowing he might never have a chance to look into those beautiful eyes again, and placed a gentle kiss on her palm. Then he leaned forward and pressed his lips to hers. Her kiss reassured him. She would live for him. But she wanted to give him even more.

"Sam...take this," she said.

He took the finely made dagger in its silver sheath from her hand and attached it to his belt. He also took the love he saw in her eyes.

"Bring it back," she said, her voice weak and little more than a whisper.

"I will," he said and then gently kissed her again. "I will love you forever."

He forced himself to stand, then turned, and jumped on George, urging the big horse into a thunderous run.

The horse seemed to sense Sam's urgency and flew through the pasture. The pounding rhythm of the big stallion galloping at full speed filled his head and calmed him. She was going to be all right. He saw it in her eyes. He felt it in her kiss. All he had to do now was kill the whoreson.

As they galloped, the horse's strength seemed to pass through to him. He understood now why Stephen thought so much of the impressive stallion.

George would easily catch up to Foley. He had no doubt about what he had to do. He would not hesitate. He just had to catch up to them.

The big stallion raced up a hill, seeming to be unaffected by the steep incline even at a full gallop.

As they reached the top of the rise, Sam saw his own horse running riderless towards him. He was not surprised. Horses can sense a bad character ten times faster than a man can. He noticed blood streaked across Alex's muzzle. The bastard's despicable deeds had no end. His anger flared higher still.

Beyond Alex, more than a hundred yards off, he spotted them.

He tugged George to a stop. It would be the second time he used the Kentucky rifle to shoot a man from a fair distance. The first time was when Indians and that evil slave trader, Bomazeen, abducted Jane.

Lord, make me your instrument of justice, he prayed as he quickly grabbed Stephen's rifle. He dismounted, bent to one knee, took a breath, held it, carefully lined up the sights down the long barrel, and fired.

As Sam released a pent-up breath, one rider fell to the right side of the mount he rode, his body smacking the ground. The other man turned and gaped back at him.

It was Foley.

He jumped on George, afraid to take the time to reload. He could not let Foley disappear into the woods or catch up to his other men.

Before they covered a quarter mile, George overtook the swine's smaller mount.

He felt hot sweat dampening the stallion's coat as he reached down for Stephen's whip. He whirled the whip above his head and as it cracked, the tip wrapped itself around Foley's neck. He had never been fond of whips, having personally felt the bite of lashes across his bare back at the hand of a particularly vicious Red Coat. But for now, the whip served his purpose well.

He hauled George to a stop, jerking back on the whip, while sliding off the stallion. Breathing hard and fast, the horse's nostrils flared repeatedly and foamy sweat outlined George's bridle.

Foley hit the ground, nearly choking. He tumbled several times before finally stopping and then clawed frantically at the whip encircling his throat.

Sam marched toward Foley keeping the whip taut. When he saw the man's face start to turn blue, he released the tension and tossed the whip on the ground next to George.

Foley scrambled to his feet, sucking in air while reaching for a pistol tucked in a large leather belt.

Before the hunter got a good grip on the pistol, Sam's right fist whacked the man's jaw like a blacksmith's hammer.

He heard the sound of teeth shaking loose, but the big man still stood. He grabbed the hunter's pistol, but could not get a good grip on the weapon. They struggled for control and he was finally able to wrench the pistol away. Then he tossed the pistol as far as he could throw it and turned on Foley.

"Stop, I only got one hand. You can't kill me—it ain't fair," Foley whined.

The pathetic man's outcry unleashed something within him. With cold contempt, he said, "Fair? You managed to shoot an unarmed woman with what's left of that arm. But I guess you're not as steady as you used to be. You only clipped her shoulder, and as disappointing as it must be to you, she'll live."

"You took my hand you bloody bugger. Shooting her was payback for that hand," Foley roared defiantly. "I would have beat you within an inch of your life and taken her while you watched if your little brother hadn't shown up. That's his horse ain't it?"

His anger turned white-hot. "You stole mine you insolent cur. You lost that hand because you were about to blow my brother in half. One hand, or two, you're still the same despicable man. Your only use for the hand you lost was to hurt people. How many women have you raped with that hand? How many murders did you commit? How many lives were lost because of your treachery? How 'fair' was that? Seems to me you haven't known what fair is for a very long time. It's time you learned."

He could just shoot this worm of a man. Or send his knife deep into the man's chest. But a quick death was too good for Frank Foley. He wanted Foley to endure pain, just as Catherine suffered now. Most of all—he wanted to see justice done—to see this traitor hang.

Like a bolt of lightning, he brought his heel up and kicked Foley in the stomach with so much force it felt like his foot had hit the man's backbone. "That's for shooting Catherine."

The hunter gasped for air as he dropped to his knees, groaning and holding his stomach.

Sam circled around behind the breathless man. He wanted to kick Foley all the way to hell. He settled for kicking him in the back, between his shoulder blades, sending the hunter face down and tasting dirt. "That's for horse stealing."

Sam stood over him and reached down to turn the devil over.

Foley yanked out a skinning knife hidden in his boot.

He pulled away, but not fast enough or far enough.

The man rolled over and thrust the knife at Sam's leg.

He gasped as the cold steel penetrated his thigh. The shock of it was worse than the pain. It only fed his fury. Hungry for revenge at last, he stopped just long enough to pull the knife out of his leg and hurl it. He saw drops of his own blood follow the knife's path through the air.

He limped toward George, feeling warm blood run down his leg and begin to fill his moccasin boot. He bent to pick up the whip, but his head spun and his stomach lurched with nausea. Just for a second, he squeezed his eyes closed. It was a mistake.

Too late to stop the man, Foley jumped him from behind. He blocked Foley's hand with his forearm, but he felt a hard object connect with his skull. At least he had managed to soften the blow. As intense pain shot through his head, he saw a rock drop next to him. He shook his head as he fought to keep darkness from overtaking him. He could not let this bastard win this battle.

As Sam turned toward him, blinking through the blinding stars before his eyes, Foley reached toward him, grabbing one of his two pistols. The hunter took a few steps back.

Ominously, Sam heard the weapon cock. It seemed like the loudest noise he had ever heard, as the distinctive sound reverberated in his pounding head.

Suddenly, George charged towards Foley, nearly running the man over and forcing the buffalo hunter to fall backwards to the ground.

The sneaky traitor has only one shot, he realized through the painful cloud in his head. Would the hunter shoot the horse or him? Knowing what the stallion meant to Stephen, he almost wished it would be him. He reached for his other pistol and made himself stand up, but he swayed on his feet.

Protectively, George reared up, aiming his front hooves at the man now the horse's enemy too. Like enormous black hammers, the stallion's powerful legs plummeted down.

Foley hastily rolled away, but George turned, lowered his head, and quickly headed toward the hunter.

Sam could finally focus his eyes in the time George had given him. He aimed his pistol at the hunter. "Drop that weapon," he ordered.

Still scurrying across the ground on his knees, Foley looked terrified as George came at him.

"George, whoa boy," Sam tried. "Whoa." The stallion refused to slow. Sam aimed his pistol to fire at Foley, but the horse stood in the way of his shot.

The hunter turned toward George and fired the pistol.

The ball slammed into George's broad muscled chest. The big stallion squealed in pain and panic.

Sam ran to the horse and saw red blood quickly spread across the black hair under the animal's neck. Helplessly he watched George's front knees drop to the ground and his own legs nearly buckled beneath him. He stared in disbelief as the stallion collapsed completely to one side.

Then he turned his eyes, bulging and burning with fresh rage, to glower down at the man who caused so much pain. So much evil.

Ignoring his own injury, he took several steps, grabbed the whip off the ground, and then barreled forward toward Foley, the venom of his wrath escalating with each step. He reached down and yanked the man's vest off to sling it aside.

The abominable man scrambled up and tried to run away but only got a few feet.

The whip uncoiled like a snake strike across Foley's back, causing the man to stumble and fall to his knees, just as George had. Then the lash struck the hunter's legs, ripping flesh away, as he tried to make the worm's punishment match his own terrible anger. He was tempted to whip the man to death.

He wouldn't kill him. But he *would* make sure Foley felt considerable pain before he stopped.

The buffalo hunter crawled on his stomach, but had difficulty moving. Blood dripped from both sides of the man's back, leaving trails of red dirt for Sam to step between as he slowly followed.

Sam's own blood flowed freely from his leg, joining Foley's on the ground. He jerked his pistol out of this monster's hand and stuck it back in his belt. Growling at the man, he could not believe he had let the whoreson use his own weapon against Stephen's beloved horse. He yanked the whip back again. With difficulty, he kept his hand from releasing it.

Foley crawled again, barely able to drag himself a few feet before collapsing.

Sam swayed, unsteady on his leg. It was time to finish this while he still could. This vile man had much more to answer for than shooting George. He tossed the whip aside and grabbed his loaded pistol from his belt.

"This is for being a damn bloody traitor. For causing so many good men to die because of you. You bastard son of Satan."

He yanked the pistol's hammer back. "Now you die."

"You won't shoot a one-handed unarmed man. You're too much of a *Christian*," Foley sneered with an equal mix of scorn and ridicule. The man drew his head back in a gesture of defiance, looking down his bulbous nose at Sam.

Sam glowered at the man, his heart stone cold, his blood seething hot. He gripped the weapon tightly, so hard he thought his knuckles might crack. It would take every bit of his will not to shoot. But he was a Christian. Would it be wrong to kill this evil man? Would it be murder or justice?

His knife burned against his waist, nearly screaming at him, begging to be unsheathed. It wanted to penetrate Foley's cold black heart. It was why his knife existed—forged for revenge—for justice that had gone unquenched for so many years. And it was time for retribution, payback, vengeance, an eye for an eye—all meant for...*another man.*

With a snarl-like smile, Foley chuckled arrogantly when Sam slowly eased the hammer back down and stuck the pistol back in his belt.

It was not a question of mercy. Like throwing pearls before swine, he would not waste mercy on a dark soul like this.

It also wasn't a question of whether he could use the knife. He could. He would do it for Catherine. He would eagerly do it for all those victims this evil man had wronged. He could finish this.

He dragged his blade slowly out of its sheath. The sound of the knife's release always sent a satisfying tremor through his heart. The steel glimmered at him invitingly, tempting him to use it.

His face hardened as he pointed the weapon's tip at Foley. "You deserved to die long ago for causing so many of our men to die!"

"It was war," Foley yelled.

"You're right it was. And it still is," Sam swore.

"The war's over," Foley screeched.

"There's one more traitor that needs to die. You. And dying will only be the start of your punishment," he taunted. "The flesh will burn off your bones for *all eternity.*"

At the sight of the long blade, or maybe the prospect of hell, stark fear flashed across the man's loathsome countenance for the first time. Foley's face turned ashen and glistening bands of sweat appeared across his upper lip and forehead.

All of a sudden, Foley's face blurred. Sam blinked trying to clear his eyes. In his mind, William moved between the hunter and him. He shook his head, trying to clear the blurred image. It must be the loss of blood.

No, it was more than that.

William, a man of the law, would want justice. And justice was more than just settling a score. Justice demanded that a man face his crimes before God and man *before* he paid the penalty. That was the difference between revenge and justice.

And Catherine would want him to choose justice over revenge. And to choose love over hate.

He had only one option.

He understood what he had to do, not what he wanted to do, what he had to do. He snarled savagely and swallowed the bitter taste in his mouth. His jaw clenched, as he concentrated on the feel of the deer horn handle in his hand rather than the alluring gleam of the blade. Suddenly, his mind, heated with the fever of anger, filled with an image of Catherine's beautiful eyes, shining with inner beauty and life.

Summoning up the image of Catherine's gleaming eyes, he forced the knife back into its sheath.

"Stand up, you slimy bastard, you're going back to hang, and then you'll be going on to Hell."

CHAPTER 30

Sam heard George wheezing, as the big horse struggled to breathe. He wondered if the beautiful stallion was waiting to die until he knew Sam was safe.

"I told you to stand up," he commanded Foley again, as he limped over to George. "Or do you want to taste that whip again?"

Scowling, Foley followed Sam's order and unsteadily stood up.

The stallion suddenly squealed in pain. At once, Sam dropped down on one knee, placing his hand on George's muzzle to soothe the injured horse.

In the same instant, he felt something split the air above his head.

The ball smacked into Foley's stomach, blowing the buffalo hunter's big soft gut in two. The ghastly sound turned Sam's stomach. The man's body punched the ground as it fell heavily backwards.

Sam instantaneously hunkered low, behind George's saddle, tasting dirt on his lips. He had come close to tasting death instead. He was in the open with no cover and nothing but his pistols, only one still loaded.

In the distance, he heard horses thundering toward him. He peered over the saddle. The three remaining buffalo hunters were heading his direction at full speed. At least they had not stopped to shoot again and were still a fair ways off.

Despite his throbbing head, Sam's mind raced. He could use George for a shield, but he would not do that. Stephen loved George too much to have him riddled with lead balls. He couldn't do that to his brother or to George. "You saved my life old boy," he whispered hoarsely. But the horse was about to lose his. He saw the life go out of the magnificent stallion his brother had loved for so long.

Sorrow seared Sam's heart, and his throat grew raw with unuttered protests and screams of anger. But he needed to reload. He needed a plan. He pulled the rifle off the saddle. With his heart pounding, he quickly reloaded it and the pistol that Frank had used to shoot George. He looked for cover, and started for it, but forced to drag his injured leg, the knife wound permitted only a ragged hop and the trees were a good fifty yards away. He gritted his teeth at the throbbing pain. He needed to hurry. He would soon have three powerful guns aimed at him. He could kill one with his rifle as soon as he had a good shot. The other two he could kill with his pistols, if he didn't miss. And, he would have to shoot both of them before one shot him. The odds were not good.

He was just moments away from a battle for his life. He might never get to hold Catherine again. Everything they might have experienced together might end right here. Too soon. But Foley is dead, even if it wasn't by Sam's own hand. The Satan's bastard could not hurt Catherine or anyone else ever again.

If he had to die, at least he had experienced love once more.

He thanked God for that.

Suddenly, Sam sensed that his life was not supposed to end this way. He wouldn't let it. He had someone he must live for. His heart swelled. His love for Catherine so strong, he had to defy death.

He had denied death before, numerous times.

He would not die today either. He had to get back to her, to go on loving her for the rest of his days. He spotted a large shrub and hurried toward it, forcing the sharp pain in his leg to retreat deep inside of him. Instead, he filled his mind with images of Catherine, and his heart filled with hope. He limped toward the bush, dragging his throbbing leg behind him.

"Big Ben, you dumb ass, you shot Frank!" Sam heard one of the buffalo hunters yell to the other, as they yanked their horses to a stop around Foley's corpse.

He saw the three hunters look down at the pathetic remains of what used to be their leader. Big Ben spit at Foley's feet and said, "Looks like there wasn't much left of him anyway."

Sam shook his head in disgust, sure the callous hunters felt neither grief nor regret. Killing and death had been so much a part of their lives for so long they almost certainly could not even feel the loss of one of their own.

"Pick up that whip. I'll use it to kill that big fellow. I'll teach him to whip one of us," Big Ben shouted.

One of the three dismounted, picked up the whip, and handed it up to Big Ben.

The hunters took off heading in Sam's direction, their horses' hooves kicking big clumps of dirt onto their leader's body as they lunged to a full gallop.

NEW FRONTIER OF LOVE

Sam hoped it would be the only burial Foley would get.

Hidden by the large bush that just covered his big body, Sam took aim with his rifle and fired, hitting the one closest to him in the center of the man's chest. As the hunter fell from his horse and crashed to the ground, Sam noticed the man's shorn scalp. When he'd cut that hair off, he had warned the fellow not to bother them again. The man should have listened.

The other two hunters wrenched their mounts to a stop and struggled to control their now skittish horses twisting in circles.

Sam hastily resumed hopping toward better cover, reloading the rifle as he went. He glanced back at the two and didn't notice the rotting log hidden by grass. He tripped, and fell on his wounded leg. Pain blasted through his thigh as the slash ripped further open and the gash on the back of his head shot searing heat through his skull. He clutched his leg trying to hold the wound together and gritted his teeth at the severe ache in his head. Blood began to seep from his leg again.

That was it. He could go no further.

He saw the two hunters heading toward him again. He plucked both pistols from his belt. He would have to make a stand right here in the open. Well, by God, he would give them a fight.

Sam fired, but unsteady on his wounded leg and feeling lightheaded from the loss of blood, only grazed the side of one man's arm. He fired the second pistol. He stared disbelieving through the powder's smoke. He had missed twice, and he never missed.

Until now. Why now, Lord?

As the two men continued to bear down on him, he glanced at the pistols in his hands. His hands and the weapons shook. His wounds were taking their toll on his body.

He stuck the weapons in his belt and pulled his knife. The grip felt good in his hands. Power seemed to flow into him from the blade, giving him courage and renewed strength.

The two remaining buffalo hunters dragged their horses to a stop in front of him, both wearing mocking grins and smelling of death. Big Ben held the whip.

He could see their malevolent intentions in their evil darkened eyes.

They would torture him.

Sam defiantly stepped forward. He brandished the big knife, and teeth bared, he glared viciously from one to the other. He would give these two only one chance. "You both need to surrender yourselves to the law," he warned. "If you don't, you'll surely die today."

Both men guffawed, and then Big Ben declared, "You're the one who is going to die today. I'm going to enjoy whipping you to death. Drop that knife, or Lucas here will shoot you in the other leg."

Sam wanted to throw the knife at Big Ben, but realized as soon as he did the other man, evidently named Lucas, would shoot him. "No, I'm rather fond of this knife. I think I'll keep it."

Big Ben put the whip over his saddle horn and lifted his long heavy gun into the crook of his arm for support. However, his horse and the other man's horse would not settle, making it impossible for either one to aim accurately.

The other man drew his pistol and fired at Sam anyway.

The ball flew past Sam's head, narrowly missing his ear.

He gave the shooter a withering stare and brandished his knife at both of them. With every blade stroke slicing through the air, it felt like he formed a barrier between himself and the buffalo hunters, as though the blade held the ability to hold back evil. He had always believed his knife held special powers. Now he knew it.

Both buffalo hunters obviously recognized the huge knife. Sam could almost see them recalling the image of a screaming Foley with the blade protruding from their leader's arm. Their faces reflected hesitation and then alarm as they both stared, nearly transfixed, at the lethal weapon.

Then curses rolled out of Big Ben's mouth as he tried again to aim his rifle, pointing it more at the knife than at Sam.

Sam stared up into the darkness of the huge weapon's barrel. He had to stay out of its path or he would die. He quickly shifted left, then right, then shuffled back, staying one step ahead of Big Ben's aim, waiting for a chance to launch his knife. The blade had to hit Big Ben with perfect timing to prevent the man from pulling the trigger and shooting him.

Off to the side, astride his horse, Lucas waited for Big Ben to make the kill.

Suddenly, the massive hunter's focus shifted away. Something had caught the man's eye.

As Big Ben's horse saw it too, the mount jerked and lurched, making aiming the weapon impossible. The nervous mount raised his head and whinnied.

Lucas quickly started to reload his pistol.

Sam followed Big Ben's gaze and then he saw them too. Their horses raced wide open across the same meadow through which he had just chased Foley.

Awestruck at the sight of the threesome, Sam's mouth hung

open, and hope filled him.

Like a huge angry beast a horse, Bear's long arm stuck straight up, holding his Kentucky rifle like a spear. His hairy-face fierce, Bear yelled a Scottish war cry, a part of his heritage learned from his grandfather. The vicious roar could make the blood of even the stoutest enemy run cold, but it gave Scottish warriors courage.

And it gave Sam hope. The battle cry fortified his heart as nothing else could have.

William, who rode beside Bear, looked like a horseback god of justice. His blonde hair had come loose, the wind blowing it behind him like the mane of his horse. His countenance held the cold determination of a noble marble statue as he thundered toward Sam.

John rode out in front, slightly ahead of William and Bear, his pistol drawn and aimed at the two hunters. Surprisingly, John's face showed the will to kill and confident courage. It made Sam proud of John in a way he had never felt before. John's weapon pointed directly at Big Ben.

William drew his pistol and pointed it in the direction of the other man, but neither John nor William were quite within pistol range.

Sam watched Bear maneuver just west of John and William's path, no doubt to fire his rifle without the two being in his line of sight. Firing a rifle on a running horse was tricky to say the least.

He glanced back at the two hunters. Big Ben had dismounted and now held his rifle against his shoulder. The man raised the weapon's muzzle to the approaching men, taking aim.

"No!" Sam screamed. He prepared to throw his knife at Big Ben, but the other hunter and his horse were in the way, nearly on top of him. He sidestepped to avoid being trampled. He tried to hobble around the horse, but the man turned his mount, this time deliberately trying to trample him.

He didn't want to use his knife on this man; he needed it for the one pointing the rifle. He limped to the side of Lucas' horse trying to get around the animal. But the hunter turned the horse toward him, blocking his view of Big Ben.

Frantic, he glared back toward John. *Fire John, fire*, his mind pleaded, knowing it would be a wasted shot. John was still out of range.

Then he saw Bear taking aim. "Shoot Bear, for mercy's sake, shoot!" Sam screamed.

Lucas shifted and Sam could now see Big Ben. He instantly raised his blade.

The terrible sound of Big Ben's rifle firing next to him burst through Sam's ears in a horrifying flash of realization.

In the next split second, Sam's eyes shifted to John. His brother flew backwards off his horse.

Bear fired and Sam released his knife, but with perfect timing, Big Ben bent his knees and hunched over. The ball sailed by the hunter's side followed by the knife slicing the air just above the stooped man.

Still crouched low, Big Ben wrenched his horse around hard, mounted and took off. The other man quickly followed as William, finally within range, fired his pistol. The shot blew Lucas' hat off his head.

William flew off his still stopping horse and knelt next to John.

Stunned, Sam forced himself to take first one and then another step toward John, knowing that Big Ben had blown his brother's heart apart.

He did not die today.

But John had.

CHAPTER 31

Bear and William crouched next to John's body as Sam limped up.

All three could tell that John's wound was mortal. Their brother's eyes now stared at something only he could see.

Sam's throat constricted with misery. His heart, that had so recently found life again, seemed to be dying of sorrow.

When he felt a single tear drip down his face, his fists balled with the urge to kill. He swiped the tear away with a knuckle. "Get me John's horse," he ordered, choking back the angry screams welling up in his chest. "And pick up my knife."

Bear remounted his own horse and went to retrieve John's mount and the blade.

Sam tried to kneel next to John, but could not bend his leg. Instead, he stood by John, fighting back hot tears as he gazed at the blood pouring from the heinous wound in his brother's chest.

"My God John, what are you doing here?" he asked, half-expecting John to answer.

William, who cradled their brother's lifeless head in his hands, answered for John. "He thought you were in trouble. He wanted to do his part."

As Bear rode off, he screamed the same war cry they'd heard only moments ago. This time though, the cry held an edge of anguish, and instead of giving Sam hope, it prepared him for battle.

Bear returned quickly, pulling John's horse. "Are ye sure you can ride?" Bear questioned, looking at Sam's leg.

Sam glanced up. Big tears moistened Bear's disheartened face.

"Help me up," Sam said, his voice cracking.

William stood and held the horse's bridle and bit to keep it still, while Bear reached down and hauled Sam onto the mount.

"You're in no condition to ride. Let me go," William tried.

"What needs doing is not a job for a man of the law," Sam avowed.

"At least let me wrap that leg," William offered.

"All right, but hurry, damn it," he grumbled through clenched teeth.

William took off his coat, gently laid it over John's head, and then pulled off his linen shirt, while Sam reloaded his pistols and Kentucky rifle. Bear was doing the same.

Sam tied the reins of John's horse together, knowing he might soon have to fight with both hands.

"What happened?" William asked Sam. "Stephen wouldn't explain. He just waved us on toward you and told us to hurry."

As William tied the shirt over the wound on his leg, Sam explained, "Foley shot Catherine, but she'll make it, thank God.

He and his brother ambushed us and stole Alex. Stephen showed up and I borrowed George to pursue. I shot Foley's brother and then went after Foley. During our battle, Foley stabbed me and killed George." He heard Bear gasp. "The other buffalo hunters shot Foley when they were aiming for me," he said, gathering the reins in his hand. "William, you and Stephen get Catherine to the doctor. Better yet, bring him to our camp. You'll need the supply wagon to fetch her and...John." He swallowed hard, trying to squelch the bitter bile rising from his stomach. "Be sure she's well cared for."

"I'll take care of them," William said, choking back emotions as he finished tying his linen shirt tightly around Sam's thigh, tucking the shirt's sleeves in near the wound.

"We'll get them John," Sam promised, looking down at his dead brother before he kicked the horse.

੭

Sam and Bear rode side by side, their horses in a nearly matching rhythm, running at a full gallop. Sam knew their minds were also in perfect rhythm. They had to find the two buffalo hunters and kill them. They would show no mercy—these men were past that now. Their ration of mercy spent on John's death.

"Are ye all right?" Bear yelled, slowing his horse and looking at Sam. "Ye've lost a lot of blood."

Sam nodded woodenly, but he was far more concerned about his state of mind. His heart, fractured in his chest, was near bursting with grief. His mind, consumed by an overwhelming need for vengeance, struggled to think clearly. He needed to regain control—to think like a warrior and prepare his mind and body for battle.

Bear resumed looking for the tracks of the two horses. The recent rain made it easier for Bear's experienced eye to quickly find the tracks again and they took off for a second time.

Soon they were only minutes behind the two buffalo hunters. Sam could smell their lingering sour scent in the air.

Bear seemed to catch the scent too, spurring his mount to an even faster run.

Sam's mind twisted with strange impressions, as if he was in a bizarre dream. If he could just get to the killers, he could save John. But for some reason, it seemed too late to save his brother. But his mind wouldn't stop trying. Again, he fought to make himself think clearly.

"They'll start slowin' soon," Bear shouted, "or they'll kill their horses."

"Doubt they'd care," he yelled back.

Sam prepared himself to kill. He would not yield until the enemy knew defeat. Catherine was right. It was time to end this.

He had no doubt that they were about to engage in a vicious battle, but it would be a war with no victory—John was already dead. No matter how hard his mind tried to deny it, his brother was gone.

"Look," Bear yelled, as they crested a hill.

Sam saw the two buffalo hunters pull into a copse thick with brush and pines. He had only seconds to make a decision. Should he and Bear find cover now or barrel towards the two men without slowing?

Suddenly sure what he needed to do, he used the reins to push John's horse to an even faster run.

Bear urged Camel to keep up and the two horses stormed towards the buffalo hunters, the pounding hoof beats reverberating against tree trunks as they wove their way through the thick trees, both riding faster than was safe.

"The one who killed John is mine," he swore loud enough for Bear to hear.

As they came closer, the atmosphere in the woods, filled with heavy late afternoon air, became darker and smelled of musk and mold.

This was a mistake. They could be riding into an ambush. Even so, there would be no stopping.

It would take God Himself to make him stop now.

☙

William spotted Stephen. Catherine's horse and Alex stood nearby grazing in the tall grass. He hurried toward his brother, wrenched his mount to a stop, and flung himself off the horse.

Stephen sat on the ground next to Catherine.

William's voice asked the question with only her name. "Catherine?"

"She's wounded, but not gravely. She spoke once when she made Sam take her dagger with him, but then she passed out again. She's been asleep ever since."

His mind elsewhere, William had not noticed the dagger on Sam.

"She's lost considerable blood," Stephen explained, "but the bleeding has finally stopped."

William bent down next to both of them. "Whoresons!" he

swore, looking at Catherine and dreading what he was about to tell Stephen.

"Where's your coat and shirt?" Stephen asked.

William peered into Stephen's face, his eyes burning with unshed tears. "Stephen, John is dead." William found the words strange—like he spoke the words in a bad dream. He wanted to spit out the bitter taste they left in his mouth. He fought to restrain his grief, but it grabbed ahold of his face, contorting it with his useless struggle to control his emotions.

He watched as Stephen's eyes darkened and his brother's face registered his sorrow and shock. "Dead, oh my God, no!" Stephen howled as he stood, fists clenched at his sides. "No, not him. Not him. No!"

William stood and put a hand on Stephen's shaking shoulder.

"How?" Stephen asked, his voice cracking.

"Two of the hunters were just about to kill Sam. John was riding hard to Sam's rescue, and got ahead of Bear and me. One of them shot John, in the heart, and then they took off."

"Bloody hell, damn them," Stephen swore. "I'll kill them."

"What about Sam? Is he...?" Catherine asked weakly.

William glanced down and realized she had come awake. He knelt down beside her. "Sam has a leg wound, but is otherwise alright. There are only two hunters left. Sam and Bear have gone after them. Don't worry, they'll get them." Moreover, he suspected they would show no mercy.

Catherine closed her eyes again and pressed a fist to her lips. William could tell she was in a great deal of pain.

Stephen threw his hat to the ground in fury.

William watched helplessly as his brother vented his growing rage, repeatedly kicking at the ground.

"I can't believe he's dead," William said, "even though I saw it happen." He rubbed his eyes, trying to banish the horrible image of John flying off the back of his horse. He swallowed the sob that rose in his throat.

"Let's get her back to camp," Stephen finally said through gritted teeth. "Will you get the supply wagon while I stay with Catherine?"

"Yes, and I'll need to tell Little John, before we have to bring his father's body back."

"Send the Judge to get the doc," Stephen suggested.

"Catherine, just rest. I'll be back as soon as I can," William said, remounting. He decided against telling Stephen about George. His brother had enough to deal with for now and perhaps it would be better if Sam told him since he was there when it happened.

"Hurry," Stephen urged in a choked voice.

As William rode away from one brother, he cried for the loss of another.

&

William rode into camp with a strong sense of dread—he would have to tell Little John and the others. How? What would he say?

The Judge strode over as William dismounted. "What's happened son? I see it on your face."

"Foley's dead, but Big Ben killed John." Again, William felt like he might choke on the abhorrent words.

"Damn," the Judge said simply.

"Foley and his brother waylaid Catherine and Sam. She's wounded, but not gravely. I'll use the supply wagon to bring John and Catherine back. Will you get the doctor? Bring him back here as quick as you can?"

"Of course. I'll go now. Are Sam and Bear going after the killers?" he asked, taking long strides toward his horse.

"They are," William said. His mind seemed disoriented, as if he was in some confusing dream moving in slow motion. He dreaded the terrible parts still ahead of him. "Where are the others?"

"The children are in the wagons and the women are armed and situated between. I thought that would be their best protection. May the good Lord be with you as you tell the boy."

As the Judge rode off, Jane and Kelly hurried toward William. His stomach clenched. Little John followed right behind them.

"William, is Stephen all right?" Jane asked right away.

"Yes…but," he could not make himself finish.

"But what?" Jane demanded.

His eyes told her to wait. He bent down and picked up Little John.

"What about Pa?" Little John asked. "And Uncle Sam?"

William swallowed hard as he faced the hardest thing he had ever done. This is when a man truly needs courage. His own heart was breaking and he was about to crush this little one's. Better to tell him now, than for Little John to learn when he brought the boy's father back laid out in the wagon. But his lips could not form the words. For a moment, they could only quiver.

"William?" Kelly asked gently, placing her hand on his shoulder.

Her touch seemed to strengthen him. He sat down on the ground, cross-legged, pulling Little John into his lap.

William glanced up at Jane who pressed her shaking hand to her mouth. Then he looked at Kelly, who now shook her head in understanding.

"Little John, your father died today saving his brothers from some evil men," William said as gently as he could.

He heard Jane and Kelly both gasp, realization sinking in.

"My Daddy is dead?" Little John asked slowly. "Like my mother?"

William nodded and then enveloped Little John in his arms, pulling the boy against his chest. He couldn't help John, but perhaps he could help his nephew now.

"And Sam and Catherine?" Jane asked gently.

"Stephen is waiting with Catherine. She has a gunshot wound, but she will live. The Judge just went after the doctor. I have to get the wagon and go back for her and…John. Sam and Bear have gone after John's killers."

"God, please protect them," Jane whispered.

"I'm so sorry Little John," William said, still hugging the boy.

"Was my Pa a hero?" Little John asked, his chin quivering and tears beginning to stream down his face.

William lifted Little John's chin and peered directly into the boy's glistening eyes. "Most definitely. He absolutely was. He was a great hero today," he assured the boy.

295

But heroes often die, William realized, tears threatening to spill from his own eyes.

For several seconds, no one spoke, as both uncle and nephew struggled with their shared pain.

William wanted to stay and comfort the boy, but he needed to hurry. He stood and gently handed Little John over to Jane.

Little John had not cried hard until Jane held him. In her arms, he began to sob miserably.

William swallowed and tried to pull himself together. "Kelly, help me hitch Catherine's team to the supply wagon. I need to hurry."

They worked quickly, first unloading the supplies stored in the wagon and then attaching the leathers to the team. As they worked, he saw tears slip silently down Kelly's cheeks. His own eyes burned as he struggled to control his emotions in front of her.

The two finished within minutes and William urged the two stout horses to a canter as he drove off for his brother. Then he would get Catherine and Stephen.

He prayed John would be the only brother the wagon would have to carry this awful day.

CHAPTER 32

A high caliber ball shattered the trunk of the large oak next to Sam.

Bark and splinters flew everywhere hitting him and the horse. Unaccustomed to the sound of gunfire, John's horse shied and Sam's heart stopped for a beat or two as the frightened animal side-stepped severely, almost jumping out from under him. He barely managed to stay in the saddle.

"Whoa now," he soothed, bringing the horse under control.

Sam took a tighter grip on the reins and quickly pressed the nervous mount toward the two men. He tried to use the dense trees to his advantage. He didn't think either of the hunters had a good shot. Every time he thought he might be in their sights, he swiftly wove John's gelding around another tree as Bear followed.

Riding hard, as he thundered through heavy timber, he heard small branches cracking and felt some ripping and slapping at his arms and back. Behind him, he heard Gaelic curses and "Ouch!" several times.

Fortunately, the buffalo hunters had no luck with the two shots they took at Bear either, one a near miss and the other completely missing even the large target Bear and his horse Camel made.

The two men had to be reloading, but he and Bear were just seconds away. They would be on the hunters before they could reload their weapons. If they wouldn't surrender and face the judge, it was time to kill.

Sam and then Bear slowed their horses. "Throw down your weapons, and we won't kill you," Sam hollered. If he were honest, he hoped they wouldn't lay down their arms. But honor required that he give them the chance.

"Go to hell," Big Ben shouted back.

"Piss on you!" the other man yelled.

These men would have to die. The men who had killed John. The men who had blown a good man's heart to shreds, killing him like an animal, with a gun meant for buffalo. In that instant, the line between revenge and justice completely disappeared. Revenge became its own wild justice. There could be no other way. This had gone too far.

This man took too much.

A verse from Exodus burst through his head, as though the Almighty also demanded this contemptible man's life. *'But if there is any further injury, then you shall appoint as a penalty life for life.'* A penalty. For John's life. For a now fatherless Little John, he would become God's own warrior.

He dropped the reins on the horse's neck and, for a moment, used his knees and legs to control the gelding while he unsheathed both his big knife and Catherine's dagger. The blades sparkled, one in each hand, even in the dim light under the canopy of thick pines. He caught the fleeting glint of the dagger's sapphire. Blue, like her eyes. He had seen love in those eyes and he desperately wanted to see it again.

But first, he had to kill these men.

Out of the corner of his eye, he saw Bear reach for his own hatchet. If his plan worked, Bear would not have to use it.

God, let me be your warrior.

He barreled forward and drove the big gelding between the hunters causing them to stagger. He leapt off the still moving horse on his uninjured left leg, landing precisely between the two as they attempted to regain their balance. Moving with the speed and skill gained from years on the battlefield, with one swift slash of the dagger he slit the throat of the man on his left and then with his right hand instantly shoved his own knife into Big Ben's chest, lacerating the man's heart.

"A heart for a heart," Sam hissed on a ragged breath.

Their souls trapped in that fleeting moment between life and death, the eyes of both men, just inches from his own, grew large with horror, then dimmed completely as hell claimed them.

Both men crumpled nearly simultaneously on either side of him.

Hot blood had splattered from the men's wounds onto Sam's own face and chest. Tasting their bitter blood on his lips, he sputtered and spit, trying to purge the coppery taste from his mouth. He staggered as he wiped his face repeatedly with his shirtsleeves, attempting to clear the blood from of his mouth. He looked down at his shirt, now red with both Catherine's blood and the blood of these two scoundrels. It made his skin crawl. He ripped the shirt off his body, wiped the dagger still in his left hand, and flung the garment onto Big Ben's body.

His face still contorted for battle, he turned toward Bear.

Clenching and unclenching his hands, he struggled for sanity. It was slow in coming.

Bear must have sensed his volatile state of mind and said soothingly, "Sam, ye've already killed the bad blokes, aye?" Bear lifted a bushy red eyebrow questioningly.

His legs spread wide in an unmoving stance, Sam could only give his head a curt nod.

They eyed each other silently for several long moments, both gasping for breath.

In a disbelieving voice, Bear said, "My Lord, Sam, I've never seen men die faster."

Finally able to move, he turned around and saw his knife protruding from Big Ben's shredded heart. He stared at it until his own heart slowed. He hated killing. But he hated killers more.

Sam reached for the blade. It had claimed the life of a murderer and, as it had many times before, saved his life. He cleaned the knife as best he could with grass and leaves, his stomach still a taut ball of tension.

He retrieved Stephen's whip from one of the hunter's mounts, and then he and Bear turned to find their own horses. Eyeing the whip in his hand, he realized that he had come close to being beaten to death with it.

Then he stared down at his own knife again. With a sense of liberation, he let out a slow breath. He would forget seeking revenge. It was over.

He and the knife had a new purpose in life.

Feeling at peace, he drew himself straighter, and relaxed his shoulders. Now he would use the blade to help him build a new life with Catherine.

It would be a new beginning. At last. John would have wanted that for him. As he thought about his brother, he swallowed the despair in his throat.

It was time to grieve for John.

As they mounted up, Sam looked back at the two bodies, now lying in black shadows under the trees.

"Let's take their horses, but we'll leave these two snakes for the wolves."

Bear sighed heavily. "Aye, Sam."

CHAPTER 33

Burying John took a hard toll on all of them. During the entire funeral, Sam held Little John in his arms, the child's pitiful grief adding to his own deep anguish.

John's death had hit him like a kick in the gut. He felt responsible somehow. He was the big brother. He was supposed to keep them all safe.

After crying against his shoulder most of the morning, an exhausted Little John fell asleep. While the boy slept, Sam spent the rest of that morning just sitting at his favorite spot on the riverbank. He needed the quiet peaceful setting to mourn.

The loss of a brother was like losing a part of oneself. He didn't know why, maybe because you came from the same womb, but it felt like part of him was suddenly missing. Part of his past was gone, a piece of his childhood, the portion of his life held only by John. Severed for the rest of this life on earth.

Stephen had told them all that John's pain had finally ended. Their brother's heart, broken and destroyed in life, was whole again in death. John was now with his beloved Diana.

Sam had watched his other brothers suffer with the same sense of extreme loss.

Stephen keenly missed his stallion too. He told Stephen about George's courageous stance against Foley, saving Sam's life. Stephen said that saving Sam was George's finest feat. But what consoled Stephen the most was the fact that George had covered Jane's mare recently and the mare was now in foal. With luck, there would be a George, Jr. born early next year. A colt born in a pasture Stephen had yet to find. About the same time, Stephen's son should be born.

Sam thought again about the only words he spoke at John's funeral, quoting Proverbs 17. *'A friend is a loving companion at all times, and a brother is born to share troubles.'*

Sam hung his head, hoping and praying that the future would hold no more losses as great as this.

&

The next morning the sun suddenly broke through the clouds and angled rays illuminated the trunks of hundreds of trees on the river's southern shore. Had heaven just lit a thousand torches to point Sam's way? Was there a home out there somewhere for him? A home that could include Catherine by his side?

The doctor had checked on both of them yesterday afternoon and said she was recovering well and would soon have full use of the shoulder and arm. Within the week, she would be feeling more like herself again.

That good news was all he was waiting for.

William returned about noon just as Jane served up the midday meal. He had ridden into town to give the Judge the large amount of money he had found on Foley's body and horse.

"The Judge decided to give a portion of it back to a farmer

that was robbed and beaten while Foley and his brother raped the man's wife. He plans to use the rest of the funds to begin work on a church named in John's honor. He also wants to establish an endowment for widows and orphans. Unfortunately, Boonesborough already has a plenitude of both," William explained. "He wants Sam to keep the hunters' six horses as compensation for going after the killers and being falsely accused of murder. They're stalled at the Fort's stables for now."

Sam suspected the horses had better breeding than their malicious owners.

The savory smell of Jane's stew filled the somber camp. It normally made Sam's mouth water, but not today.

"I hoped I'd make it back in time for your stew Jane. That's not something a rational man would miss," William said, trying his best to sound cheerful. "The doctor sent these books and supplies out for you." He sat them on her nearby trunk.

"Thank you William," Jane said, handing him a brimming plate. "Kelly give him one of those hot biscuits you made too."

Leaning back against his saddle, with his own full plate, a sense of relief flooded through Sam. Now, Catherine and the rest of his family would be safe, at least from the buffalo hunters. In fact, many people would be safer now. Much safer.

However, their safety came at great cost to all of them. They had lost a brother who found his courage when his family needed him. A man who had been there at the moment when Sam needed him. He swallowed the lump in his throat, refusing to give in to the sadness that threatened to engulf him. It was time to move forward, to leave his troubled past behind, and find his own new destiny with the person who gave meaning to the word life.

Sam peered up at William, who wore the new shirt, cravat and frockcoat he had bought to replace his old ones. The new attire made William look quite dashing, but he was glad to be back in his buckskin hunting shirt himself.

"How's your leg faring Sam?" William asked before sitting down to eat.

"Not much more than a bad scratch," he lied. "Worst part was when Jane poured hot whiskey on it. I think she actually enjoyed it."

"I did," Jane said, with a chuckle. "Quit your complaining and eat. You need to recover your strength."

"I'll heal quickly. I always do. Stephen gave me some of Edward's fine 'medicine' and that took the edge off." The doctor thought his wound a lucky one, since the blade had entered his leg at an angle; it did not sever a major muscle or vein and would eventually heal completely. He just had to keep it clean and apply a healing ointment daily. Like Catherine, he suffered from a considerable loss of blood and it would take some time to regain his full strength.

"As soon as we can, I suggest we all leave for Nelson County," Sam announced. He wanted to start fresh, as quickly as possible, somewhere away from the awful problems they had faced here. Stephen would have left that very hour if it had not been for their injuries. He glanced at Catherine who was laying nearby on a pallet recovering. Her lips parted in what seemed like surprise. He couldn't tell what she was thinking. Did she agree with leaving? Did she realize that she was included when he said 'all'?

"I'm staying," William announced.

Everyone gawked at William, pausing in their consumption of

Jane's delicious stew.

"The Judge offered me the job of Sheriff this morning. He said Constable Mitchell was too young and inexperienced for the job, but the young man wants to be my assistant. The Judge also wants me to apprentice under him to become a lawyer. Maybe even a judge eventually. Apparently, he was actually impressed with my performance in the courtroom. He said I just needed to study Kentucky law."

"Aye, ye're a top notch performer. I can vouch for that," Bear said, setting his plate down, foregoing his usual second helping. Normally, one plate could never hold enough food to fill Bear, but like Sam, he probably wasn't hungry. Bear had lost a brother too.

"Are you sure this is what you want to do?" Stephen asked William.

"For the first time in my life, I know where my future is," William said. He glanced at Kelly. "Kelly, I stopped by Mr. Wolf's office. He says if you are interested, he has a job for you as a governess and tutor for his children. His wife died last year and his mother, who lives with him, has been helping out, but she is getting on in years and is not able to keep up with the four children. You can live in his home for as long as you need to."

Kelly ran to William and gave him a hug, seemingly unable to stop herself. Then, no doubt realizing how forward she appeared, she stood aside, her face flushing.

He chuckled as he watched William, who was uncharacteristically flustered and smiling awkwardly. Interesting, Sam mused. Maybe William's future really was here in Boonesborough. Perhaps his brother could help Kelly overcome her fears and her emotional wounds.

Both Martha and Polly, who had spent much of the day crying, now giggled and clapped their hands together at the sight of William and Kelly standing next to each other. Jane tried half-heartedly to hush them, but it pleased him to see cheerful smiles on his nieces' faces. Sam suspected that the girls hoped, for some time, that their Uncle Will would start courting their friend Kelly. Sam hoped he would too.

William seemed thankful when Catherine spoke up.

"Kelly, you'll need a horse in Boonesborough. I'd be pleased if you would take my extra horse as my gift," Catherine said.

Tears of gratitude filled Kelly's eyes. "Thank you."

The young woman bent down and gently hugged Catherine's uninjured side.

Sam could tell that it pleased Catherine, as much as it did him, that Kelly might at last have a chance at real happiness. Tears of fresh joy and lingering sorrow fell from both women's eyes as they embraced.

"Mr. Wyllie, you've traveled so far. Why don't you and Jane stay here with us?" Kelly asked, wiping her eyes and looking at Stephen.

"I'm not stopping until I know for a certainty I've found where we're supposed to be," Stephen said, looking over at Jane. "I don't know that yet."

"Well then, I'll be comin' along to watch yer back," Bear said.

Stephen and Jane both appeared pleased.

"What about me?" Little John asked, his pensive eyes searching Sam's face.

Like his father, and Sam, Little John would be very tall, already at least a head taller than other boys his age. He had his mother's strawberry blonde hair and it hung as straight as a ruler on a loveable face. But an undisguised hurt and longing replaced his normal sweet expression.

The bereft boy sat on the ground next to him. The child had stayed there all afternoon, his little hands wiping away the big tears that regularly sprang up. With his head bowed and his body slumped, Little John also toyed with the small knife Sam had given him. It broke Sam's heart when Little John had said he missed his father and then clung to him, weeping.

He gently patted his nephew's leg before he answered. "Little John, I want you to be my son. I'll never be as good a man as your father, but I'll try to be as good a father," Sam promised.

Little John looked at him with wide glistening eyes. "And I'll be a good son." The boy stood, flung out his arms, and hugged Sam around his neck.

He had to admit, it felt good. He hauled Little John against his chest, embracing the boy who was now his son. He choked back his rising emotions, hoping he could provide a good home for the boy. It was time he took the first step.

He winked at Little John, smiled conspiratorially, and then edged the two of them closer to Catherine. Little John grinned back at him as though the boy suspected what Sam was about to do. This was one smart boy.

She gave Sam a weak smile and blinked with bafflement. Then she looked away, her face a mask of uncertainty.

Catherine didn't know how much he had changed. He was no longer just a protective brother chasing a secret revenge. Now he would be looking for his own land, his own home, and his own future. A future he wanted to share with Little John and hopefully Catherine. She had given him back his heart. Now he could not only live, he could love.

If she would still have him.

His stomach rolled at the possibility that she would not. But he could understand why she might not.

He had foolishly turned away from her, just before Foley shot her, and before he could tell her he loved her. Did he reject her love one too many times? What a fool he'd been.

He also got himself embroiled in a deadly feud that resulted in her nearly losing her life. Was she rethinking her choice to stay? Would she still have the courage to remain in Kentucky? With him?

Catherine learned, as they all had, that securing good land in Kentucky was likely going to be problematic and a lengthy process. Would she be willing to wait months, even years, for a new home?

She also now knew that he had used her dagger to slice a man's throat. Without saying a word, she had gulped back tears when he returned the dagger to her. Did she consider him a brutal killer? It was a brutal act, but, by God, the man deserved it.

They were all reasons she might reconsider staying. Couple any one of them with the fact that her affluent family would expect her to return and Sam realized there was a very good possibility that she would want to leave Kentucky. It would kill him if she wanted to return to Boston. Now, he couldn't imagine his life without her.

Moreover, would she accept him now that he was responsible for his brother's son? She would have to take Little John too. He would never abandon the boy.

She had to *want* both of them.

He wished he could steal her away—somewhere private and picturesque—because what he had to say was important and personal. But with their injuries and his concern for Little John, he would have to make do. He would not leave the boy now, even for an hour. Little John needed him. This would just have to do.

He took a deep steadying breath and reached for her hand. Then he smiled at her, perhaps the first genuinely happy smile he had ever given her.

Her face lit up, her grin broader this time, and it gave him the courage he needed.

"Catherine, you're the only one who has ever looked at me and seen the man I was meant to be. The man I am with you is the man I want to be. And that man is in love with you."

Happiness spread across her pale beautiful face and a cry of joy broke from her lips.

"Will you consent to be my bride, now and forever, and will you accept Little John as our child?"

Catherine's eyes, full of life and warmth, stared back at him. Then she slowly studied everyone else, including Little John. She seemed to be asking for their blessing before she answered. It was a big decision. Not only would she become a wife, she would become a mother.

He held his breath, waiting for her answer.

Then her blue eyes turned to him, sparkling with joy, as she said, "I will Sam." Turning to Little John, she said, "I will Little John."

Her answer thrilled him to his bones. He managed to lean

down enough to kiss her, feeling Little John's hands patting his back enthusiastically, while the others exploded in cheers and clapping. With difficulty, he made himself stop kissing her and look up at Stephen. "The three of us will be going along with you too, but first Catherine and I will see that circuit preacher when she's well enough, so we can be a real family."

He bent his lips to hers again. Pulling away was even more difficult this time.

He turned to his new son. "And Little John, I want you to be my best man."

"A fine choice," Stephen said, "on both counts."

"What's a best man?' Little John asked.

"A best man is a lot of things," he said, "it's someone you are very close to, someone you respect and admire, someone you can trust, but most of all, he is a man who will always stand at your side, no matter the challenges you both face."

"I can do that," Little John said, grinning.

"I know, that's why I asked you," Sam said, deliberately keeping his face serious.

"Congratulations to ye both," Bear said vigorously shaking Sam's hand. "And as soon as Catherine's healed up some, I'll be giving her a congratulatory kiss too." Bear winked at Catherine.

"As long as it's only a brotherly peck on the cheek," Sam threatened, with a half-smile.

"When you're both healed up, I'll play my fiddle and we can have a real dance," William said. Laughing, he tugged Kelly into his arms and danced playfully with her as he hummed loudly to the music in his head. Bear picked up Martha and Polly, one in each arm, and did the same. Then Jane grabbed Little John and whirled him around while he giggled the entire time.

When they all finally stopped, Kelly, Jane, and the girls knelt down and surrounded Catherine.

With delight, he watched the women and girls, also appearing lighthearted and jaunty, talking excitedly. A wedding had to be about the most exciting occasion the women and girls could imagine, and after a day like yesterday, it was nice for all of them to think about a joyful event.

He felt a grin spread across his face, his mood unexpectedly buoyant, his soul fully alive. But what made him smile the most was his own happy heart. He was in love! And he was going to be married. He had trouble believing it.

"Well now, Catherine, from now on we'll both be watching Sam's back," Bear said. "And the lad's too."

Catherine turned to face Bear and Sam again. "Agreed," she said, her face radiant with joy. "We'll all take good care of Little John." She squeezed the boy's hand affectionately.

"May I call you mother?" Little John asked sweetly.

Catherine laughed merrily. "Of course you can. May I call you John? I think a boy who is going to be a best man is too big to be called 'Little' anymore."

"Yes, Mother."

Catherine's face lit up like a perfect sunny day.

Surprising himself, Sam actually wanted to dance too, and he would have if his leg wasn't injured. It had been far too long since he had known this kind of unbridled joy. Actually, he had never known this much happiness.

He was happy for Catherine too. When she smiled at him, he saw love flowing from her eyes. It made them look like priceless sparkling sapphires. What a treasure she was.

And how rich their future together would be. Catherine had made the long journey from Boston to the Kentucky wilderness and found his heart at the end of it and a son she could love—her own destiny—a new life in a new world.

CHAPTER 34

Sam never minded being alone. He even relished solitude. Until now. Now, he could barely stand to part from Catherine for even a few minutes, and all he wanted to do was relish every inch of her. At the moment, his whole being seemed consumed with an overwhelming need to be close to her. He was tired of waiting for this moment to arrive.

They had both spent a couple weeks healing before their wedding day. Catherine had kept her arm in a sling for a week and then gradually started using it again. She recovered quickly and now had only a slight soreness and some stiffness in the shoulder muscle. She spent most of her recuperation time designing her own wedding dress and the gowns for the other women and girls to wear to the ceremony. Then she spent another week and half with the town seamstress having the woman and her helpers execute her designs. The millenary recently received a shipment of fine fabrics and Catherine seemed pleased with their selection, especially considering their remote location.

Catherine also insisted on having the tailor prepare a new set of buckskins for Sam, and a matching set for Little John, with room to grow. Relieved that she didn't expect him to wear traditional clothing, Sam had gladly complied, although someday soon he would buy another white linen shirt just to see that look on her face again when he'd worn one the first time.

He had whooped with delight when he helped Little John—no John, he reminded himself—into the boy's new buckskins and attached his little knife to the belt. John looked like a miniature version of himself.

It wouldn't be long now. He hadn't seen her since the noon meal, after which the women and girls had made some pastries and then left to bathe in the river. After the giggling bunch returned, all but Jane disappeared into Catherine's wagon. Before she joined the rest of the women, Jane sent all the men and Little John to the river to bathe with some of her strong lye soap. She told them to dress on the other side of camp and to stay away, or she would be sure their next meal was scorched black as tar. No one doubted she would do it and that it would taste like tar as well.

Sam had heard that some women thought it unlucky for the groom to see his bride before the wedding. He guessed Jane wasn't taking any chances.

At last, much to Sam's relief, the circuit preacher arrived and it was time for the wedding. As he shook the reverend's hand, there was a distinct tingling in the pit of his stomach and he felt ripples of excitement race through him. Several of the townspeople joined them for the happy event, including Judge Webb, Lucky McGintey, Doc McDowell, Tom Wolf, and the owner of the Bear Trap Tavern, Charles O'Hara, already a close friend of William's.

Along with the other men, all gussied up, he waited with the preacher in a shady spot by the river, his heart as thunderous as a summer storm.

The women finally appeared. First Polly, then Martha,

followed by Kelly and Jane. They all looked lovely, but he strained to see past them to catch a glimpse of his bride. When he did, he thought he might be the luckiest man in the world. No, the most blessed man in the world. No, both.

She glowed with a nearly surreal beauty. Like a princess from some romantic tale, she was both noble and exquisitely beautiful. Her ivory satin gown shimmered in the early afternoon sun and her shiny black hair was pinned on top of her head, with ringlets draping down her long neck. Sam chuckled to himself as he noticed that, as usual, she wore the dagger. They really were a matched pair. Soon, they would be a wedded pair. He couldn't wait.

Undoubtedly, she was the most beautiful bride ever seen in Boonesborough, or Kentucky for that matter. For as long as he lived, he would never forget how she looked now as she walked slowly toward him.

When she was close enough, he reached for her hand and brought it to his lips. She smelled like a meadow of wildflowers. Her eyes held a glint of wonder. When he mouthed, "I love you," they misted and filled with glimmering stars.

The ceremony seemed to take no time at all, but the celebration lasted well into the afternoon and early evening. William played all their favorite tunes on his fiddle, including Sam's favorite, 'Soldier's Joy,' and Catherine's pick, 'Fisher's Hornpipe.' Sam's recovering leg permitted dancing only to the slow songs, but with the help of his brothers, Catherine danced to nearly every song.

Finally, she said she'd danced enough. "My feet are going to fall off," she said, laughing, "and I might never be able to breathe right again."

Holding up a goblet of fine wine, from one of the bottles their brother Edward had given them when they left New Hampshire, Bear offered a toast in his booming voice. "May you each be able to provide what the other needs—comfort in times of sorrow, a glad heart on occasions of happiness, a clear vision through darkness, and strength in moments of weakness. Be a mighty sword and unbreakable shield against the other's enemies. But let grace and peace fill your home always. May you each be a warm sun, full moon and shining star for the other. And, after your love of the Almighty, may your shared love be the foremost part of all your days."

Sam thought it was the most inspiring toast he had ever heard and a fitting moment to say their goodbyes.

Before the wedding, he had packed a small bag. He quickly retrieved it and the considerably larger bag Catherine had packed. With dusk approaching, he started saddling their horses. He couldn't wait to get her to himself. They could ride at least a couple of hours before they would find a place to spend the night. The thought made him work at an even faster pace.

"Off so soon?" Stephen asked, walking up behind him.

"What would you do in my boots?"

"I'd already be gone," Stephen replied.

Sam chuckled. "All right then, finish saddling Catherine's horse while I get this pack horse loaded with our supplies."

It wasn't long before they headed, side by side, toward a crimson sunset.

✥

"Sam, wasn't that the most wonderful wedding?" Catherine grinned as she stepped out of the saddle. In fact, her jaw was beginning to hurt from either laughing or smiling all day. She glanced around. Sam had selected a lovely spot near a brisk creek for the evening's campsite. Their first night together. Imagining what would happen later, her pulse leapt with anticipation.

"I admit our nuptials greatly exceeded my expectations. I actually found the entire affair quite enjoyable, especially every time I gawked at you in that stunning gown. Which, I admit was nearly every second. I couldn't take my eyes off you. You looked positively ravishing. I was completely entranced." He tossed their bags down and reached for her hands.

"And there was never a more handsome groom than you. I was completely charmed."

Sam laughed out loud. "Married only a few hours and you're already lying to me?"

"It wasn't a lie. You were charming." She couldn't believe this good-looking, virile man was her husband. "And you are *now*, my Sam."

"For that flattery, I will be forced to kiss you. Keep it up and your punishment will grow even more severe."

He grabbed her around the waist and kissed her until her head spun and her knees went weak. When she finally pulled away to catch a much needed breath, her lips throbbed, branded with the imprint of his passion.

"Your punishment is too lenient," she said smiling, "I fear I deserve further chastisement."

He pressed his lips to hers again, this time caressing her mouth more than merely kissing it. She felt her heart swell another notch. As a flower blooms in the warmth of the sun, she felt their love grow with each of his kisses.

While Sam took care of the horses and then gathered firewood, Catherine set up camp. The moon was a few days away from being full and it gave her plenty of light to work by. She had, with Jane's help, changed out of her wedding gown and delicate slippers before they left. Now she wore her leather boots and a dark green riding habit more suitable for traveling horseback. Nevertheless, she thought her getup stylish and flattering, and she still wore her new delicate lacy undergarments underneath. She hoped Sam would like them—and enjoy taking them off her later.

As she worked, she stole secretive glances at her new husband. She could see that, as ever, he was alert to his surroundings. He carried his shoulders with latent energy, ever ready to be a warrior. Just his presence made her feel safe, protected, even here miles from anywhere. He moved with such strength and self-assurance. His well-muscled arms removed the heavy saddles and supplies from the horse's backs as if they weighed nothing. As he wiped down the three steeds and gave them water and grain, she perceived a gentleness and a quiet calmness. He will make a kind-hearted father to Little John. Yet she believed he would also set high expectations. She blinked back tears and swallowed hard, trying not to let her emotions gain the upper hand. How she wished she could give him a child. But she managed a half smile as thoughts of Little John, now just John, entered her head. He had called her Mother. She couldn't wait to show the boy a mother's love.

Sam sat an armload of firewood and kindling down, dusted his hands and arms off, and reached for her. She inhaled his scent deeply, letting it reach all the way to her heart. He smelled of wood, spice, and the leather of his new buckskins.

She reached up and grabbed his arms in her hands as he kissed her again. The feel of his strong muscles beneath her fingertips sent tingles to her toes and back again. This would be an evening she would remember forever. Her prolonged anticipation of this night during the weeks before their wedding was almost unbearable. And tonight, her heart teemed with excitement.

When Sam finally pulled away, he said, "I better stop before I get carried away. I need to get this fire made. It will keep wild animals away and let me see every charming inch of you this evening." He bent down to start his task.

Catherine could feel the hot blush on her cheeks, and was glad he probably couldn't see it in the moonlight. Even though she'd been married before, and wasn't some frightened virgin, the thought of Sam seeing her unclothed caused her entire body to flush with heat.

"Do you want some coffee and warm corncakes?" she managed to ask.

"Coffee would be nice. But you're the only cake I want."

"But Sam, you need to keep your strength up. You might need it later."

"Later? Now, why would I need it later?" he teased.

Later, he did need his strength and she did too.

It had started slowly, a gentle kiss, a soft caress down her back. But within seconds, Sam's desire flamed to a roaring firestorm of passion. They had both waited too long for this. Their need for each other had been delayed, put off, held back, pent-up, until, once released, there was no slowing it.

He quickly discarded his clothing while she slid her riding jacket off her shoulders and stepped out of her long skirt. When she glanced up, her lashes flew open and she felt her mouth drop. She stood there, amazed, trying to breathe.

Unclothed, he appeared even more powerful. She ached to touch him to see if the muscles defining his broad shoulders were as hard as they looked. Dark hair sprinkled across his massive chest and down the center of his rippled abdomen.

Her eyes, more daring than perhaps they should be, could not resist roaming over the rest of him. The irresistible and impressive sight made her heart tremble and her head spin.

Deliberately taking her time when she reached her stays, stockings, and lacy undergarments, his bold stare assessed her unhurriedly and seductively.

After his head-to-toe caressing gaze, he eased her down on the blankets she'd brought, the light from the fire illuminating their already hot skin.

Sam stared at her with a greedy possessiveness. His eyes grew darker, revealing the urgency of his need. He shifted his body above hers and she heard herself moan with pleasure at just the feel of his marvelous body against hers. His shoulder muscles were as hard as they looked.

She buried her hands in his hair and wrapped one leg around him, drawing him even closer while his hand lightly explored her waist and hip. The gentleness of his touch made her feel protected and valued, as though she had just entered a haven of love. She wanted to weep with joy.

He slid his hand beneath her and gripped her bottom. Her desire surged at the intimacy of his touch. Her head lolled back as his warm lips trailed a path of kisses down her throat, across the top of her shoulder, and descended her chest to her burning breasts. If she weren't already laying down, she would have swooned with sheer amazement. Her eyes bulged and she gasped, at the wondrous sensations Sam made her feel for the first time in her life.

He nuzzled her neck as she held him as tightly as she could. He was all muscle, head to toe, and his sheer masculinity made her heart beat even faster. Every place she touched made her ache for him, for the love she waited her entire life for.

Even more astounding, he was her husband. "Husband," she breathed, her heart full.

"Wife," he whispered the word reverently.

Then he recaptured her lips and her world changed forever.

It was heavenly ecstasy.

Only God could design love this powerful, this exquisite, this meaningful. In his arms, she felt valued and cherished by his soul. She had never known such happiness. Such love. Such tenderness. It was exactly what her life had been missing.

He was her champion, her knight in buckskins, and he saved her from a loveless life. Yet, as powerful as he was, he never tried to control or dominate her, but rather supported her strengths with his own.

And, at last, love shattered the hard wall that he had built so carefully around his heart. Now they could share their destinies in a future together. She could tell that he had stored up a lifetime of love for her. And she sensed the strength of that soul-reaching love in every kiss, every tender caress, and every urgent breath she had to take as explosive bolts surged through her.

As their passion raged, the bolts became lightning, flashing through every vein, and she surrendered completely to the thunderous joy.

She wanted to match his ardor with her own, to take him to a place he had never been. A place where no pain existed. No doubts and no fears.

Only pleasure. And love.

She ran her fingers slowly across his chest. The golden glitter of sweat made his muscles and dark hair shine in the fire light. Her fingers prickled with the heat radiating from his skin. She savored the feel of him, as her hands and lips continued their hungry exploration of his magnificent body. Then her lips traced a sensuous path to pleasure. The intensity of his response to her seduction stunned her.

His heartbeat pounded against her ear as his hard body covered hers and they met flesh against flesh. Heart against heart.

And soon they experienced the unbridled glory of love's fulfillment.

CHAPTER 35

A few days before the wedding, Lucky McGintey had quietly suggested a place to Sam to take his new bride for a honeymoon. Lucky said it was one of the prettiest spots in Kentucky and that it was relatively safe. Sam quickly decided to take Catherine there so they could more privately get to know one another. And they both needed some time to recover fully from their wounds and the ordeal they had just experienced. It would also be a chance to see more of Kentucky.

The couple would meet up with the rest of their group at Fort Harrod in two weeks.

Lucky recommended a place called Cumberland Falls on the Cumberland River, south of Boonesborough in southern Kentucky. Lucky thought that the presence of the Fort at Harrodsburg made the area reasonably safe from Indian attacks. Organized attacks in the area had ended with the Battle of Blue Licks, fifteen years ago, in 1782.

It took them nearly three days to get there, but Sam decided it was well worth it. Cumberland Falls was one of the most scenic places he had ever seen. The 125-foot wide curtain of water, framed by verdant woods on both sides, was a dramatic backdrop both day and night for their campsite near the river's edge. The constant sound of the water, rushing over the nearly seventy-foot high sandstone bed, provided an appealing and soothing backdrop for lovemaking and for healing.

Every evening they basked, with upturned faces, in the soft beams of the moon—its silvery rays caressing their souls like a healing balm. And last night, the now full moon had played an extraordinary and dramatic role in their romantic surroundings. As the moon glowed against the clear sky, they witnessed a spectacular lunar rainbow.

According to Lucky, local settlers called it a Moonbow. After he realized Sam and Catherine would arrive at Cumberland Falls shortly before the full moon, Lucky had excitedly described the rare phenomenon to Sam. Sometimes elusive, the lunar rainbow failed to show itself to everyone who tried to view the amazing sight. Some believed it only showed itself to those who possessed a good heart. When it did choose to reveal itself, Lucky explained, the Moonbow formed when moonlight glowed through the mist emanating from the waterfall.

Sam had hoped they would be lucky enough to see the lunar rainbow and, without telling her why, positioned them that evening so that they sat in a perfect viewing spot on a soft fur rug he had brought.

"My wedding gift," he had told her when the Moonbow appeared out of the blue, as if by magic. The magnificent arch of light started at the base of the falls and continued downstream.

Spellbound, Catherine looked as if she might faint at the stunning sight. He would never forget the wide-eyed look of awe on her moon-gilded face if he lived to be a hundred. And he would never forget, no matter where they finally lived, the blessing the bow from above bestowed on their love that night.

As he made love to her under the glowing arch of the Moonbow, it seemed to carry them to some mystical other world. This hard world could never be this special—this remarkable and wonderful. Yet it was. He had held her in his arms and felt her tender affection pour into him, cover him as completely as the moonlight.

He still couldn't believe, even after nearly a week together, what the sight of her bare body did to him. Feelings he thought long dead now sizzled within him, and they were there more often than not. In truth, he wanted to hold her constantly. His need for her touch seemed insatiable. He was glad they would have a lifetime of being able to love and hold each other. And no matter what the passage of time did—whether it greyed her beautiful black hair or thickened her slim waist—he would still love her as much as he did now.

This morning, the air felt fresh and crisp and the rising sun gilded the limestone cliffs and hills around them with gold light. The water rushing over the falls looked like silver sheets of glassy ice in places and sparkling snow in others.

As the water struck the river below, it sounded like the pounding hooves of a hundred running horses. And further down the river, the water loped and cantered over rocks and trotted through mats of cane and vegetation along the shoreline. The lush woods behind them teemed with birds soaring, fluttering, and hopping about in the cool breeze.

"A beautiful place for a beautiful bride," he said to himself, as he contentedly gathered more dry wood for the cook fire. For some reason, he took pleasure in building their camp fires here as though the ancient forest offered up the wood he gathered as a sacrifice, and the burning of it joined him to this particular place.

Catherine never woke easily and still slept but soon started to stir when the coffee began to brew. She stretched, sprawled out on her pallet, and he admired for the hundredth time her shapely figure showing beneath her sheer nightdress. Even after a night of loving her, he found his body gleefully responding to the pleasant sight and tried his best to suppress the feelings for now.

"Sam, I was dreaming of you," she said, yawning. "And you'll never guess what you were doing in my dream."

"Oh, I can guess, my love," he said, amused. "Are you hungry?"

"Ravenous. I can't remember ever being this hungry in my entire life."

"That's because we didn't eat last night, remember. We were preoccupied."

"The Moonbow and what we did afterwards was well worth the loss of a meal," Catherine said. "But I think it's more than skipping our dinner. You made my body feel things it has never felt before. I feel so alive. Sam, will it always be like this?"

"I pray that it will, if a person is allowed to pray for such a thing."

"It does seem a miracle. I mean not just that we love each other and that the loving part of it is so remarkable, but that we were put together at the right moment in time for both of us."

"Some call that a divine appointment," he said.

As the flames of the fire grew, he marveled at his good fortune. They could so easily have missed each other on the Wilderness

Trail. But God literally put her right in his path. He had been a fool to have taken so long to realize what the good Lord had sent him.

"I put some yams in the coals earlier to bake. Give me a few minute to clean the fish on the line and fry them up and then we'll take care of your hunger."

"What if I'm hungry for more than food," she teased.

Her comment sent a tingling vibration up and down his spine. "No worries there either."

"Sam, are you sure we're perfectly safe here?"

He didn't want to say that no place was perfectly safe. He checked to be sure that both rifles and his pistols were nearby. They were. "I'm told the natives are north of the Kentucky River for the most part and are not often seen here near the Cumberland. If we do happen upon any, I'm usually able to settle things with a trade or two, using sign language. If not, I have both our rifles nearby and loaded."

"I didn't know you knew sign language," she said, sounding amazed.

He showed her a sample.

"What does that mean?"

"May the Great Spirit make a sunrise in your heart." As He has in mine, he thought.

"Sam, you continue to astonish me. That was beautiful."

"Sign language is the one common means of communication between all tribes. Surprisingly effective and eloquent."

He extracted the plump fish from the river and held them up

for her to see, their scales glistening in the morning light. "One or two?" he asked.

"One. That big fat one. He looks like a tasty fellow."

He unhooked two for him and the big one for Catherine. He had caught the fish the evening before and kept them fresh in the running cool water.

"Do you think it was a mistake not to take Little John with us?" she asked.

"We've discussed this. We agreed that we could hardly take a boy on a honeymoon. He understood."

"I hope you're right, but I know he's missing his father and needs us. Sam, I think we should leave soon and go back to the others. Little John needs us to be his parents *now*—not later. And a couple of weeks can seem like a couple of years to a child."

It amazed Sam how quickly the maternal instinct had captured Catherine's heart. In truth, he felt conflicted about it himself. Part of him yearned to stay here forever. Another part of him wanted to be with Little John and the others. He guessed he would never outgrow trying to be the protective oldest brother. And now he was a father too. Becoming the child's guardian had been the natural thing to do for both of them.

Catherine was right. By the time they got back, they would have been away two weeks. That would just have to be long enough.

"You're right, of course, but leaving this amazing place and the privacy we have here will be one of the hardest things I have ever done," he nearly moaned. "I've never known such happiness Catherine. It's almost more than my heart can bear."

"I know. I never knew what it felt like to feel loved. More than loved, I feel treasured."

"You *are* my treasure," he responded, hearing a catch in his own voice.

"And you're all I ever dreamed of husband. Good heavens, it brings me pleasure to be able to call you that."

"And you're my wife—the bride of Cumberland Falls. As long as I live, I'll treasure every moment of the time we've spent here." He wrapped his arms around her waist and drew her closer to him. "I wish we could remain, making more memories, but we can't."

Unexpectedly, she put her hands on his chest and slowly pushed back, releasing a pent-up breath. "Sam, I've been trying to find the right moment to tell you something. Somehow, it never comes. So, I'm going to force myself to do it now. Oh Sam, this is so hard." She chewed on her quivering bottom lip and then stepped away, putting her back to him.

His brows furrowed and he slowed his breathing, worried about what might be coming. "What is it? Tell me." What would she find so difficult to tell him?

She turned back toward him and he saw a shadow of trepidation pass over her face. "I...about a year...after I was married, I learned I was with child."

Did she have a child back in Boston? Why hadn't she mentioned it before?

"After about four months, I lost the baby," she said, her words soft and her lips quivering. She swallowed hard and bent her head before she could continue. "It was a little boy. It was the worst thing that ever happened to me—maybe the worst thing that will ever happen to me. I cried for weeks. Not only did I lose my son, the doctor said I might not be able to have another baby." She looked up, her eyes glistening.

The admission, dredged from a place of deep pain and hurt, lay naked in her eyes. Sam wanted to reach out and hug her, but he could tell she wasn't finished.

"I know I should have told you before we were married. But I was afraid it would cause you to harden your heart towards me again. I know it's important to a man to have a son. I can see it on Stephen's face every time he looks with such hope at Jane's growing belly. I was so afraid of losing you over this that I decided to keep it from you." In a tear-smothered voice, she continued, "That was wrong of me. I'm sorry now. Forgive me, I wish I had told you sooner."

"Catherine, I...," he started, but she interrupted him.

"If you want to annul the marriage, I'll understand, or at least I'll try to." She was crying now. Her tears flowing in earnest. It was the first time he had seen her weep and it broke his heart. He would do his best to be sure he never gave her reason to cry.

He reached for her hands and squeezed them. "My love. Have you forgotten that God has given us a son? Not just any orphan—he's a Wyllie—and he's ours. If we are meant to have more children, then we will. If we are not, then the three of us will be family enough. Never again worry about this or anything else from your past. You can tell me anything and I will only love you more because I will know and understand you all the better. As husband and wife, we need to share everything. The good, the bad, and everything in between."

Catherine threw herself into his arms.

As his lips covered her wet face with kisses, he tasted the salt of her tears. The taste of it touched his very soul. She had shed those tears because she did not want to deny him a son. Because she was afraid he would end their marriage. He gazed directly into her moist eyes. "Catherine, know this, nothing, nothing, will ever make me stop loving you."

"Or, I you," she said, sniffling and smiling now. She hugged his chest again before she stepped away and took a deep settling breath.

She stood on the shoreline with her back to him for a few minutes, her bare feet in the clear water. She seemed to be deep in thought.

He regarded her with somber curiosity. There was something else on her mind. "Do you have anything else you need to tell me before I satisfy that hunger of yours?"

"Well, what hunger are you talking about?" she teased. "Food, or…?"

"Either one. Your wish is my command, my lady."

"Well, my knight in buckskins, there is one thing." She turned back to face him.

"Is it a big thing or a small thing?"

"You might consider this a big thing," she said, nervously chewing on her bottom lip.

It made him want to nibble on her lips too, but he made himself focus on her eyes. He searched her face anxiously for the meaning behind her words.

"A *very* big thing," she added, gripping her hands together.

CHAPTER 36

Sam felt his pulse quicken. Now what? He hoped it would not be something else that caused her pain. The silence lengthened, and she seemed reluctant to speak. He raised his brows in question.

"I haven't told you much about my life in Boston or my late husband Mr. Adams. He was a relative of John Quincy Adams and his friends were among our country's most well-known patriots and influential men. And, he was wealthy. Do you remember what I told you? That, before he was murdered, my husband was going after a prime parcel of land here in Kentucky. He purchased it several months before we ever left Boston. He was well acquainted with Isaac Shelby, Kentucky's first Governor. The Governor ordered the Land Office to set aside a first-rate piece of land for my husband and to expedite the processing of his claim. He was in a hurry to see it. I wanted him to wait until we could travel with others, but he was so haughty and self-important, he foolishly thought he could take care of us himself. Well, as it turned out, he could not. He told me that the land would be mine if something happened to him on this trip. He showed me where he hid the deed in our wagon, along with his will naming me as the beneficiary of his estate. He also hid a rather large quantity of gold and currency. It's also still hidden in the same place."

Catherine paused to catch her breath, and then added, "Remember when I went to see the lawyer? I showed him the papers and he confirmed that they were all in perfect order and that I have an undisputable claim to the land."

"How large a parcel of land?" he asked.

"Ten thousand acres."

Taken aback, he nearly swallowed his tongue. "You own ten thousand acres?"

"*We* own it."

Sam felt his mouth drop. "No, I can't..." he started to protest, shaking his head.

"You just said as husband and wife we share everything. Do you believe that or not?" she asked with a defiant lift of her chin.

"I believe it, but..."

"No buts, my Captain. We share it. Period. I'm not giving it to you, I'm giving it to *us*."

Still unable to believe his ears and speechless, he started to pace, trying to take it in. Was he man enough to accept all this from a woman? Yes, of course he was. He dismissed the idiotic thought as quickly as it had arrived. He would expect her to accept it from him if the circumstances were reversed. What difference did it make where it came from? It was all a gift from the Almighty anyway.

He couldn't believe he and Catherine were landowners, and ten thousand acres to boot. He stopped abruptly and gawked at her. "Do you realize what this means?"

Her extraordinary eyes blazed with excitement. "Yes, I believe I do. It means you, Stephen, Bear, and even William if you can get him to leave Boonesborough, will all have the land you need. It means we can begin building homes for all of us now. For *our* family Sam. They're my family now too and I want to help them. If you're willing."

"Willing? Of course, I am. I'm still stunned, but I'm also elated. We can help them build a future in Kentucky. A future for all of us."

"When do you think we should leave?" Catherine asked, as she hurriedly braided her hair.

He could hear the eagerness in her voice, and realized she was anxious to share her good news with the others. As was he. Stephen would be beside himself. At least Sam hoped he would be. Stephen was a proud man. He was sure his brother would want to pay a fair price for the land, or trade horses and cattle for it once he built up a herd. But at least now, he wouldn't have to worry about all those complicated steps and potential conflicts involved in securing a parcel of land. Yes, Stephen would be happy. And so would Jane. If they all hurried, they could get a home built for Stephen's family before the baby came. And before winter. And in the spring, he would get a home built for Catherine and Little John, and if the Almighty blessed, maybe more. But for now, three of them seemed perfect. Absolutely, completely, perfect.

"Sam, I think we should be on our way soon, don't you?" she asked again, tossing the long braid behind her back.

"Sorry, my mind is racing. I'm still trying to come to grips with what this means to all of us. As for leaving, it will be hard to beat a morning like this and we're about to have a good meal. If it's what you want, we could leave after we have eaten."

"Oh Sam, I could stay here *forever*, but I want to get back to the others—to our family."

Our family. He liked the sound of that. Wait. She had never told him where the land was. "Catherine, where is the acreage?"

Her eyes twinkling, Catherine starting giggling. Then she was laughing. Then she was clapping her hands and twirling in a circle. What had gotten into her? She seemed about to burst with glee. Finally, she stopped laughing long enough to say, "Cumberland Falls on the Cumberland River, south of Fort Harrod."

The shock of her revelation hit him full force. "Here?" he asked, incredulous. "Right here?"

"Yes, yes, Sam, right here. The deed described the land and location. I asked Lucky to suggest this location to you for our honeymoon. He knew right where it was and enjoyed sharing my little secret. He'd been here to see the falls. He told me it was beautiful, but I had no idea it was this stunning."

Little secret. Ha! The secret was about as big as they got. He still couldn't believe it. He loved this special place. Even before she had revealed the location of the land, he had felt at home here and dreaded having to leave. And she was telling him it was theirs. He stared wordlessly at her, his heart pounding.

"I'm speechless," was all he could think to say.

"I have another confession," she said almost timidly, as she sat down next to the fire, tucking her legs under her. "Promise you won't be mad?"

Sam nodded. This was getting out of hand. Wondering what was coming, he just sat down next to her and studied her twinkling eyes, waiting. What could she possibly have left to tell him?

"I told you before, when we talked about my dagger's crest that my family was from the nobility. Well...I have my own inheritance of land and a sizable estate and fortune back in England. My grandfather left his colonial properties, including a Virginia tobacco plantation, to his daughter, my mother. My brother will inherit the plantation from her. But my grandfather left his English estate, Brympton, to me. It's considered one of the finest country estates in England. After the Revolution, I went there several times with him. It's managed by a family that has been with my relations for generations."

"Where is it?" Sam asked.

"A few hours from London. It's very beautiful. And it's quite productive, producing a handsome income each year."

She almost seemed embarrassed saying it. She stared at him expectantly, waiting for him to say something.

This time Sam could only laugh. It started bubbling in his belly and spread to his chest. Most of all, his heart laughed. Clutching his stomach muscles, he was soon laying on his back, his eyes crying from chuckling so hard. It felt marvelous. It had been far too long since he'd experienced such unrestrained joy. Soon, he managed to stifle his laughter and just snicker, and occasionally snort, as he continued to shake his head in wonder. "If you have any more confessions, please keep them to yourself. I can't handle any more good news this day."

"No, that's all there is." She smiled almost coquettishly. "For now."

"For now?"

She just smiled mysteriously.

"Do the others know any of this?" he asked as he sat up.

"No, I wanted to be sure the man I married was marrying me for love, so I told no one. I married once, per my father's directive, for money and position in society, not love. I was never going to let that happen again. And, as you helped me realize, *I* wanted to determine my destiny—not let my wealth or my status determine it for me. I'm sorry all this comes as such a shock to you."

"I believe I can force myself to become accustomed to it eventually," he said, grinning, but wanting to laugh again. "As long as you don't expect me to dress or behave like a dandy."

"If I'd wanted a fop, I would have gone back to Boston. There are plenty of peacocks there. Sam, you're the perfect man for me. I don't want any of this to change you even a little bit. I married you because of your good heart and your strength. I knew I could trust you with sharing my fortune. I just hope it will make your life easier from now on—provide you and the others with opportunities you wouldn't have had otherwise and fewer struggles."

"Your trust means everything to me," Sam said.

"Do we need to discuss any of this further?" she asked.

"For now, I just need to get breakfast finished so we can be on our very merry way." He started to laugh again, but managed to stop himself. It was all so much to take in. When he woke that morning, he didn't think he could be any happier, but Catherine's revelations had done just that. Now their future was secure. He no longer had to worry that he would not be able to provide a comfortable life for her. The kind of life she deserved. And, although, life in Kentucky would undoubtedly force the two of them to face tremendous challenges, it was a relief to know poverty would not be among them. And, they could now also ensure a bright future for Little John and could help Stephen and Jane do so for their girls. And, if Catherine agreed, he wanted to help Kelly too. Maybe send the precocious young woman to a good school. She deserved a better start in life than she had received so far.

Catherine stood, but for the moment seemed in no hurry to dress on this warm morning. Perhaps she found leaving as difficult as he did. She peeled off her sheer nightdress and walked knee deep into the river, shivering as the water hit her bare skin.

"You're making it difficult to concentrate on cleaning these fish," he called to her, admiring the perfect shape of her backside.

Laughing, she said, "I'll take care of that." She slid down into the water until she was submerged.

When her head came back up, he asked, "Are you sure you should be swimming with your shoulder so recently healed?"

"It will help work out the stiffness," she yelled back. "And give me a chance to bathe."

He watched as she swam gracefully to the middle of the river before stopping and turning to glide on her back. Her flat stomach and long legs floated to the water's surface. The soft mounds of her breasts revealed themselves as she titled her head and hair back into the water. She looked like a mystical ghost, all white, her skin shimmering on the river's sun kissed sparkling surface. The ghost bride of Cumberland Falls. Sam grinned. A rich ghost.

He had no idea she was such an excellent swimmer. Satisfied that she was not going to drown, he forced himself to turn his eyes away and take the fish to the frying pan. She said she was starving so he tried to concentrate on the task of preparing their food, adding more wood to the fire and starting coffee to brew. He dipped the fish in the salted cornmeal and added the filets to the pan, now sizzling with melted fat. Within a few moments, the savory aroma of the fried trout made his stomach growl.

They had brought an extra horse loaded with enough supplies for a few weeks. He wished that they could stay longer, but Catherine was right. Little John needed them. Besides, he couldn't wait for them to be together as a family.

He poured himself some coffee, savoring the rich fragrance and warmth in his hands. Catherine would need the hot fresh brew too after being in the cool water. He poured her a cup and strode back to the river's edge.

Sam scanned the surface of the river, not finding her. She was gone.

CHAPTER 37

He held his breath, waiting for her to surface. When she didn't, his inner alarm sounded and dread quickly rose in his chest. The normally pleasant sounds of the gushing waterfall battered against his mind as he tried to think. He tried to calm himself and slow his thundering heart. Perhaps she was just relieving herself in the woods.

But what if she wasn't?

A cold knot formed in his stomach and a wave of apprehension swept through him. "Catherine, where are you?" he shouted as loud as he could. He heard nothing in response and tried again. Then again. And again. "If this is a prank, I'm not amused," he tried.

He hurried back to the cook fire, threw the coffee down, yanked the fish pan off the fire, and grabbed his rifle. He quickly scanned the hills around them but spotted nothing unusual. He tried to listen for strange noises, but the falls covered any sounds he might have heard.

Then his mind raced. She could be in the water, below the surface, her legs cramping or trapped by something. Why hadn't he thought of that before now? Why hadn't he watched her more carefully?

Sam tossed his rifle to the riverbank, tore off his boots and hunting shirt, and dove into the water. The swift moving stream was nearly clear to his wide opened eyes. He swam under the surface for as long as his breath allowed, finding nothing. His chest near bursting, he came up for air about midway across the river. As he gasped for air, he quickly surveyed the area again, spitting water. Nothing.

He dove down again and swam deeper, closer to the bottom, searching, seeking some sign of her, his heart racing wildly. Soon his lungs begged him to stop. He had to get air. Just a gulp or two and then he'd come back down.

His head sprung above the water's surface, his chest heaving. As he took a couple of quick breaths, a terrifying realization hit him. Indians. Maybe she was taken. He'd find her, no matter how long it took. But what if she was still under water? Torn between continuing his search under water or starting to hunt for her in the forest, he shouted her name once more.

"Catherine!"

He had to find her! He turned around to check the opposite shore once more.

Uninhibited, she stood naked, watching him from the opposite riverbank. "Enjoying your swim?" she yelled out.

"For mercy's sake! You gave me a terrible fright. Where the bloody hell were you?" he demanded, treading water.

"Swimming underwater. I'm sorry if I scared you. I didn't realize how long I was under."

"Damn it. Are you some kind of mermaid?" Or ghost, he

thought again.

"My brother and I used to have contests back in Boston's Bay to see who could stay under the longest. I always won."

He swam across the river to her and came out of the water scowling. He stomped forward, stopping in front of her. "Do you realize you just scared the hell out of me—and I didn't like it. Not one bit." He stood next to her, hands on his hips, water as well as aggravation dripping from him.

Catherine just smiled at him, her eyes asking forgiveness, as she untied her braid and ran her fingers through the long waves, black as a starless night. "I'm sorry I scared you Sam. Perhaps you should find a way to punish me," she teased.

He folded his arms across his chest. "Your punishment will be far more severe this time."

She giggled and then sat down on a nearby boulder and leisurely stretched out her long pale legs.

The sight was more than Sam could tolerate. He laid his knife nearby, slid off his buckskin breeches and laid them beneath her bottom. Then he removed his leggings, wrung them out, folded them into a miniature pillow, and placed it under her head.

He silently thanked God that she was all right, and quickly forgot his irritation with her.

"Do you realize what a beauty you are?" he asked, sitting down beside her.

He thought his own body must look unpleasant to her, despite his lean muscular build, because he bore a multitude of ugly battle scars.

"You're the fine-looking one. Soon after we arrived in

Boonesborough, I said you reminded me of a knight clad in buckskins. I thought you looked powerful, proud, and fiercely handsome. Now you're *my* handsome knight."

"How you can find anything pleasing to your eye, my lady, among all my scars I'll never know." He lowered himself next to her and rested his head on one elbow.

She reached up to gently rub her fingers across a scar on his left shoulder.

The gentleness of her tender touch filled him with a sense of calm peace. He reveled in the feeling—absent in his life for so long.

She found another scar across his abdomen. "They're beautiful in way—a silent testimony to your courage."

He exhaled a long sigh. "Sometimes I'm not courageous at all. Do you know how much it frightened me when he shot you? I thought you were dying. When your blood was flowing out into my hands, it felt like my blood was flowing out too. That's when I *knew* I loved you."

Her eyes, suddenly troubled, caught and held his. "But just before I was shot, you turned and took a step away from me."

"My mind and heart were still at war with each other. A small, but very vocal, part of my mind kept denying that you really could love me. Another part feared that I would lose you too. But my heart and body wanted you more than anything." He brushed the tip of his finger slowly across her lips. "Oh Catherine, how close I came to losing you."

"But you didn't lose me. I'm here…and so are you," she said gently. "And I will love you Sam, forever, and ever, and ever."

A golden wave seemed to spread over them like a warm

mantle, wrapping them together into one soul.

"And I will love you endlessly and always." He cradled her head in his hand and kissed her forehead gently and then her mouth. The pleasure of kissing her was pure and powerful. He feathered his lips slowly across her face. Closing his eyes, he savored the soft freshness of her skin. His lips seemed to move on their own, down her neck before kissing the cold skin along the middle of her voluptuous chest.

Slowly, he relished the feel and taste of her wet body until she could barely stay still in his arms. But he would make her wait a few moments longer. She tasted sweet on his lips, like a delectable cake.

Their water-cooled bodies only seemed to magnify the warmth of their passion. Soon, the morning sun felt like high noon on his wet back. The warmth of the rock beneath them sent even more heat down his legs. He felt a firestorm building within him as he stoked the flames of her desire.

༶

It was time to put out the fire raging within them, but seeing him so alive made it almost too extraordinary to quench. His fervor nearly made sparks fly from his muscled body.

Catherine knew he would keep kissing her, embracing her, fondling her, until he could no longer hold himself back.

He kissed the inside of one of her palms, before nibbling on the sensitive skin inside her elbow. Then his tongue traced a trail across her shoulder and down to the pinnacle of her moist breast. She was nearly exploding with desire.

She arched into the curve of his body. He pulled her against him with tantalizing possessiveness.

His strong hands caressed the planes of her back and hips. Then he lightened his touch to just his fingertips. She quivered under his gentle stroking, every inch of her skin tingling with pleasure from his whispered touch. She closed her eyes and let her head fall back, reveling in the sensation of his hands wandering lovingly over her.

The scent of his fresh water washed body made her senses swirl. Like the rush of the nearby waterfall pounding into the river, a spurt of hungry desire for him cascaded through her.

She raised up and pushed him to his back before she climbed on top of him, straddling his hips. It was an instinctive act of possession. She was all his and he was all hers.

Using her fingers, she slowly massaged his shoulders. She observed him through lowered lashes as her fingers slid over his smooth skin. He was so handsome, so magnificent, so hers! She smiled, joyful at the thought, and used her thumbs to knead the muscles of his broad chest. Then with two fingertips, she drew a perfect heart around his heart.

He reached up and did the same to her.

He loved her!

In that moment, she felt a sunrise in her heart.

༄

He opened his eyes to gaze at this strikingly beautiful woman who was his wife. He still could not believe his great fortune. It had nothing to do with her fortune. *She* was his treasure.

Her long dark hair fell in wet strands across her breasts, nearly reaching to her trim waist. Sam reached up and pushed her hair behind her back, revealing the exquisite mounds completely. She was a glowing image of beauty, desire, and love. The sheer wonder of the sight of her and the growing intensity of the passion within him filled his heart with awe.

Every time he joined with her, she filled empty places in his soul and made more old pains ebb away—banished forever—to be replaced with new memories. And these memories would linger long after their moments of heated passion, surrounding them in the comforting certainty of their love.

"I love you beyond any measure," she whispered as her head fell down and she buried her face against his neck.

Then, as he held her close, he said, "And I love you my treasure. To paraphrase that fine Scots poet, Robert Burns, 'Of all the directions the wind can blow, I dearly like the west, for there the bonnie lassie lives, the lassie I love best.'"

"Aye!" she said.

As their souls collided, he decided the wilderness really was the land of tomorrow.

About the Author

Called a "deft new writer of intelligent romantic fiction," award-winning historical romance author Dorothy Wiley enjoys writing big, action-packed romantic adventures set in the American wilderness when it was still a frontier. In her exciting American Wilderness Series Romances, Wiley breaches the walls of time, bringing readers to a young America, where romance and danger are as powerful as the wilderness.

Readers describe Wiley's writing as fresh, unblinkingly gritty, and highly enjoyable with well-portrayed characters. Like her compelling heroes, who from the outset make it clear they will not fail despite the adversities they face, this author is likewise destined for success. In 2014, her first romance novel, *Wilderness Trail of Love*, was a Central Florida Romance Writers of America Touch of Magic Finalist and her second book, *New Frontier of Love*, was selected as an Amazon Breakthrough Novel Quarterfinalist.

Wiley grew up in southern California and found her own romantic hero in Austin, Texas, where she received a Bachelor of Journalism degree, with Honors, from The University of Texas. After a distinguished 35-year corporate career in marketing and public relations, she is living her dream—writing historical romances—and residing in central Texas with her husband (the same wonderful guy) on their beautiful cattle ranch. Yes, dreams really can come true!

She would enjoy connecting with you:

Website: http://www.dorothywiley.com

Facebook: https://www.facebook.com/DoraMayWiley

Twitter: https://twitter.com/WileyDorothy

LinkedIn: https://www.linkedin.com

Goodreads: https://www.goodreads.com

Pinterest: http://www.pinterest.com/dorothymwiley

We hope you enjoyed reading
Book Two of the American Wilderness Series Romances
NEW FRONTIER OF LOVE
the story of Sam and Catherine
CONTINUE

Dorothy Wiley's
American Wilderness Series Romances with

Book Three

WHISPERING HILLS OF LOVE
the story of William and Kelly

For release date for *Whispering Hills of Love*, please visit
www.dorothywiley.com

Book One in the series is
WILDERNESS TRAIL OF LOVE
the story of Stephen and Jane

Each book in the series can be read independently.
All books available from Amazon.com and other online stores.

One Last Thing…

If you enjoyed reading this book, I would be honored if you would share your thoughts with your friends. Regardless of whether you are reading print or electronic versions, if you particularly liked the experience of reading Sam and Catherine's story, I'd be extremely grateful if you posted a review on http://www.Amazon.com. Just enter *New Frontier of Love* in Amazon's search box and it will take you to the correct page. Thanks for your support.

All the best,

Dorothy

Acknowledgments

As I did in *Book One* of the series, *Wilderness Trail of Love*, I would like to thank the daring and brave first-wave pioneers of early America. Their hard fought struggles for a place in the vast wilderness gave us the majestic country we enjoy today. Their stories must be remembered. Although this is a completely fictionalized and romanticized story, it still reflects some of the many challenges our ancestors faced. My husband's brave ancestors, who actually did travel through the frontier and eventually became some of Texas' earliest settlers, inspired this series of novels. There are many stories I would like to write about those amazing journeys and their life on America's frontier.

Secondly, I would like to thank my husband (also my muse) and my wonderful sister for their help in polishing this manuscript. Thanks for your continued faith in me. And my thanks to my fellow author and friend Deborah Gafford, a wonderful writer, for her suggestions and support.

Third, my thanks to my cover designer Erin Dameron-Hill whose creative talent transformed my vision for the books' covers into a beautiful reality.

Now, on to *Book Three* in the American Wilderness Series Romances, *Whispering Hills of Love*. I can hardly wait to write about the adventures and love of William and Kelly...

Listen to the wind. It speaks.

Listen to your heart. It knows.

Made in the USA
San Bernardino, CA
02 August 2015